Copyri

MW00958400

All rights reserved

The characters and events portrayed in this book are fictitious. Any similarity to real persons, living or dead, is coincidental and not intended by the author.

No part of this book may be reproduced, or stored in a retrieval system, or transmitted in any form or by any means, electronic, mechanical, photocopying, recording, or otherwise, without express written permission of the publisher.

ISBN- 9798870060255
Independently published

Cover design by - The Little Book Designer

For anyone who's had to fight the darkness for the one they love.
This one's for you.

CONTENTS

WARNING

Come Back To Me is a work of fiction. This is strictly an adult only book. No one under the age of 18 should be holding a copy.

PLEASE BE AWARE TRIGGER WARNINGS FOR THIS BOOK INCLUDE:

Open door sexual content
Drug use
Male mental health content, including PTSD and anxiety
Organ trafficking
Organised crime
Violence including death, murder and manipulation
Death of an animal

COME BACK TO ME

By
Emily Catlow

GLOSSARY

Biker cut: A biker's vest, usually leather, displaying the club's unique patch and colours
Bottom rocker: Contains the member's charter location and is stitched on the back of the cut at the bottom
Centre patch: The large patch stitched on the back of the vest between the top and bottom rockers
Charter: A local or regional division of the club
Church: An official club meeting
Clubhouse: A meeting place for club members and associates
Club secretary: The person responsible for keeping all of the club records, written reports and correspondence between outside organisations
Flash: Small patch of material sewn onto the front of the cut
Hangaround: A potential prospect who is hanging around the club
MC: Motorcycle Club
Old Lady: A member's female companion
OMC/OMG: Outlaw Motorcycle Club/Outlaw Motorcycle Gang
One Percenter flash: A small patch sewn onto the leather depicting that 99% of motorcycle riders are law abiding citizens, and only 1% are outlaw
President: Leader of the club
Prospect: A member in training
Road Captain: A road captain plans all club runs
Sergeant at Arms: A club officer responsible for security, weaponry and discipline
Top rocker: Contains the club's name and is stitched on the back

of the cut at the top

Vice President: Second-in-command

PROLOGUE

ROCCO

Preston, 1989

My insides are twisting, my stomach aching from the pull towards her door. Each step I make, I think about stopping and going back. She won't want to see me again; I've left her too many times like this. This time though, I'm not flying back to the other side of the world. No, this time I'm staying here. Granted, we'll be closer than ever, but this will be the last time she sees me.

I wish it wasn't, but it has to be. Jainey Fletcher is getting married.

Michael Reed's a nice guy; always was. Top of the class at school, head boy, captain of the tennis club, the man never put a foot wrong. I heard he and Jainey stayed in touch after high school, even went to Ibiza together before Jainey started her nursing. If she deserved to be with any guy in the world, *he* would be the best person for her. *He* could give Jainey the life I know I would never be able to give her. The one where she wouldn't have to hide or hate in order to survive.

But there's one problem; I know she doesn't love him.

I step closer to her house, her favourite red roses hidden behind my back. When I first left her, Jainey cried into my shoulder, and being only sixteen at the time, I had no fucking clue what to say, or what to do to make her feel better. I snatched the biggest rose I could see from a nearby flowerbed lining the pavilion we were sat at. Bastard thing cut my hand, but she accepted it; promised to always think of me whenever she looked at one.

The organ in my chest had thumped so loudly in my ears when she said those words that from that moment, I knew how I'd make sure she never forgot me. I sent roses every birthday and made sure to leave one on her doorstep whenever I flew back.

My heart starts thumping in an all too familiar way as I push open the iron gate at the end of her drive. I don't manage more than five steps before the front door to Jainey's house slips open and she's stood on the doorstep, looking at me.

The same moment passes between us like it did when I saw her last month at the Emberley High School reunion. Her eyes lock onto mine; fire and ice colliding in a vortex of heat mixed with pain.

I step closer, lifting my feet steadily, one after the other.

"What are you doing here?" I hear her whisper from the door.

I plant my final step and go to lift the roses towards her, but her face changes; her eyes drop and fill with glistening liquid in the corners. "Jainey?"

"You can't be here, Rocco."

I sigh. "I know, I won't be here long, I just—"

"—you need to leave."

Looking up, I catch a tear leave her eye, and she moves quickly to wipe it away.

"Jainey, I—"

"—it's okay," she says, cutting me off again. "I need you to go, please… just go away."

Something's up. "What's wrong?" I ask, stepping closer to

her. Needing to touch her.

She moves towards me as if she needs me close to her too, and the smell of her perfume has me shutting my eyes, wishing I could lose myself in her again.

"Rocco, please—"

"—Jane, who's there?" I hear her father call from the kitchen in the back.

She looks at me, wiping another tear off her face. "Postman, Dad."

Her reply makes me smile.

She pulls the door to behind her, and I don't move as she steps forwards, her body close to mine now. "Rocco… I need you to leave, and," her bottom lip shakes, "and don't come back."

I know I came here to say goodbye for good this time, but the scared look in her eyes makes me wonder whether something else is causing her to be upset. My hands instinctively move to stroke the sides of her arms.

Jainey sees the roses and her eyes don't shift from them. Her lips wobble again, and I lower my hands from her arms, holding the roses in front of her. "Delivery," I say stretching a smile.

"Rocco," she whispers, taking them from me.

I pull her into my arms, and we share a still silence before she speaks.

"You need to leave." Her words come out like she doesn't mean them, cutting me like glass even though I know she's right.

I lift her chin to look at me. "I heard you're getting married to Michael."

She sniffs. "Yes, I am." Regret lines her words.

"Is that what you want?" I question, my heart rate rushing.

She stills in my arms.

"Does he make you happy?" I can't help how stern I sound.

"Yes," she snaps, as though she's annoyed that I asked. "He makes me happy, but… look please, I need you to go. And no more roses. You can't leave those things on my doorstep anymore." Jainey pushes me away from her.

But that's what I do. "Why?" It's a stupid fucking question. I know why; Jainey loves me, and although I love her, I've never given her enough of me.

"Because it's not fair on Michael. He's going to be there for me, for our family, Rocco. He deserves to not have to always wonder if and when you're going to randomly show up again—"

"—family?" Jainey's eyes widen and her face goes slack. "Jainey?"

"Rocco, I…"

"Jane, come in now," her father shouts again.

Fuck. My fucking heart is skipping beats left, right and centre. Jainey's pregnant? "Jainey," I harshly whisper so that her father can't hear me. My gruff voice forces her to look at me. "What do you mean, family?" I could cut the tension between us with my knife.

"I'm pregnant."

It's as if time freezes around me. I came here to say goodbye, to let Jainey finally go and live a life of happiness without me haphazardly dipping in and out of it. But hearing she's having a baby makes a jealous heat wash over me. It should make my goodbye easier, but more than anything, I'm just fucking sad that she's not having a baby with me.

"Rocco," she says.

I lift my eyes to look at her. Everything I've ever wanted is looking back at me, telling me she needs me to leave. She's marrying another man and having his baby. I have no right to feel the way I do. All I have ever done is steal moments of this woman's love for me, then leave her for the life I chose.

Straightening my spine, I summon the guts I came here with and push down the unusual emotions I rarely feel. "I'm sorry. I'll go." Placing my hands either side of her face, I lift her chin to mine and kiss her soft lips. A fuzzy heat prickles every fibre of my body. I want to consume her, to lift her up and take her away. But my lifestyle, the club… it won't allow it. Pulling my mouth away, I rest my forehead against hers.

I hear Jainey take in the biggest breath, and her soft lips part. "It's yours," she says.

My eyes pop open. I move my head back to look at her properly.

"Michael and I, we haven't slept together yet. You're the only person I've been with."

Her words are coming at me thick and fast.

Fuck. That's why she's getting married. No doubt her father is making her settle down. Michael's a nice guy; he's stable, he's got money... legal money, anyway. I could bet Jainey's lied to make sure her father doesn't hate her. Better to say it's the nice guy's baby, as opposed to the criminal's.

"Say something," she tells me.

My eyes flit between hers. "The reunion?"

She nods her head.

We slept together in the back of her car after everyone had left the school hall. Years of wanting each other but circumstances never permitting it, we stole the first opportunity we'd been given as soon as we could.

And it was fucking perfect. "Michael's going to raise this baby as his," she says, pulling me from my memory of that night. "I don't want anything from you, Rocco. I know the life you live is dangerous. All I ask is that you let me go. Let me raise our baby in a safe home."

I take a deep breath. A harsh ball burns in my throat, and my lungs fill with hot air. Looking at Jainey, I see she loves me. I can see how much it's hurting her telling me this. As much as I want to scream that no fucker, however nice he may be, is raising my kid, I know what she's asking and saying, is true.

If I raise this baby, the baby I've never envisioned myself having, I will forever be looking over my shoulder. One day I'll be back here, but things are kicking up and it's only going to get more dangerous. Jainey could get hurt. *My* baby could get hurt.

I don't want that. I don't want the woman I love to be in danger. Hell, that's why I came here. That's why I'm stood on her doorstep. I came to let her go.

I'm giving up what I love so that I can protect it. And up until thirty seconds ago, the decision to leave seemed straightforward. Now, it's a thousand times harder. And it's going to hurt a thousand times more.

"Rocco, please say you'll let me go."

We stare at each other before my words come out. "Jainey," my voice cracks. I take a steadying breath before I continue. "Loving you has been the easiest thing I've ever done. Letting you go, will be the hardest." I swallow, trying to stop myself from crying. "I've never told you just how much you mean to me. I can only hope that my actions speak loud enough for you to understand. It's always been you." My heart drops as I speak. I swallow another lump now in my throat. "I'll stay away whilst you raise our child, but I will never stop loving you."

Her head drops and her tears flow freely. Jainey quickly steps forwards, dropping the roses to the ground as she takes me in her arms one final time. Her wet lips push against mine, and we share a final kiss, one I'll never allow to be etched from my memories.

As I move my foot back, the toe of my boot crunches a stem on the ground. I break our kiss, and bending down, I pick up a single rose. Like I did the first time, I hold it up for her to take. "Promise me one thing?"

She nods, slowly taking the rose between her fingers.

"Promise me if my child is a girl, you'll call her Rose?"

Jainey smiles and wipes the tears running down her cheek.

"And don't tell her about me," I add.

Jainey's eyes jump up. "Rocco—"

"—please, don't tell them who I am." I bow my head. They deserve to think Michael is their dad. "Just keep the baby safe and healthy. Live the life you deserve." I kiss her forehead before I turn quickly and walk away from her; before I change my mind and stay and shatter her life completely.

At the end of the drive, my heart has all but failed as I look back and watch her, the mother of my child, watching me. She wipes her face one last time before stepping inside and closing the door.

I'll never love another woman like I do her. From this day forward, I promise if I ever see Jainey again, it will be the last time I leave her.

CHAPTER ONE

UNKNOWN

Villainy is dangerous. A warped mind, stepping into the darkness. I've done it more times than I care to remember. Sent on this path, I know what will be waiting for me at the end.

Closure. Peace. Revenge.

Will anyone expect anything less? Will anyone think I should have been something more?

"You getting all this?" the tall one says, bringing me to the here and now. He's dressed smarter than the first time I met him.

I look up, nod, but offer nothing more.

"You'll have access to everything you've requested. Everything you'll need is in here. Contacts, phones. Passport."

The short one slides an envelope across the table.

My eyes slowly look up, passing between both of the men sat opposite me. "The contents of that envelope doesn't mean shit unless you agree to my final term," I say.

"We can't let you—"

"Then my answer's no." I cut the tall one off, standing from my chair.

He stands with me, but turns to look out the window of his office. He's thinking, weighing up his options. He has none.

I wait.

"You stop him, then you can do what you want with your man."

The two men exchange a look which I don't miss. Their silence gives me my answer. There's no questioning my end of this deal.

Nodding my head, I bend and pick up the envelope from the table. "I'll be in touch." I turn away from the short one who holds out his hand to me.

No need for pleasantries.

I have work to do.

CHAPTER TWO

DEAN

T*ick, tock, tick, tock, tick, tock.* I look up. Two minutes left until Doc calls me in her office.

Do I wish I wasn't here? Yes. Do I think this is a waste of time? Yes. Did I make a promise to a certain someone that I would come? Yes.

I pull up a message to that someone.

Me: Should I get more chocolate spread on the way home?

I know she's sat at home, no doubt holding up her phone and smiling at the screen.

Mads: Apparently we need to. You wasted good chocolate this morning!

I don't call licking chocolate spread off every inch of Mads' body a waste. Especially when I can still picture her coming all over my face and screaming my name whilst I ate her pussy this morning.

Fuck. One minute until I get called in and now my dick's hard.

Me: Not a waste. Breakfast

Mads: VP... shouldn't you be in the session by now?

Me: Doc's a very punctual lady. I have thirty seconds until she

opens the door. And you can't call me VP anymore, how many times do I have to remind you, beautiful?

Mads: So, I should just call you, P?

I smile looking down as my fingers move.

Me: You can call me Daddy

There's a slight delay before her next message comes through. I'm still smiling because I know exactly what's running through her mind. I'll always be her VP, no matter what she calls me.

Mads: Eww, no

Me: You'll be calling me Daddy soon enough

Mads: I hope you mean that in a non-sexual way?

I do, but still, it doesn't hurt to have some fun.

Me: It's Daddy now

Mads: Stop saying daddy. You have four months until anyone starts calling you that

I can't help but smile again. Through dark times, Mads is the sunshine I need.

Me: I love you

Mads: I love you x

"Mr Carter?" Here we go again.

Sighing, I stand and stow away my phone in my jeans seeing as I'm not wearing my cut to this, *charade*. I would have, but the way the doc looked at me the first day I walked into her patient's room; she practically shat a brick in front of me. I haven't worn it since.

Doc's been seeing me for four weeks now. I'm not, *not* grateful for her time, Lord knows I'm one of the lucky ones who's been able to see a mental health professional face to face, but as far as I'm concerned, this is a waste of time. This... *intervention,* might be fucking necessary, but the only intervention I *actually* need, is sat at home.

I can picture her now. She'll be in my clothes, sprawled out across the sofa, book in hand eating some fucked up combination of food that makes me retch. Lately it's pickles dipped in chocolate or mayo. Or sometimes both. I love her, but it makes me queasy just thinking about it.

I shake away the thought before I gag, and take a seat in the blue suede chair opposite the good doctor.

She rounds her desk pulling out her chair.

These sessions with her are always informal, just like the room we're in. I'm guessing it's to help patients relax and spew out their feelings. But every time I come in here, there's something that always catches my eye.

"The Lady of Shalott," Doc says making me look at her.

I can feel my forehead scrunch, embarrassed I've been caught looking at the giant painting on the wall.

"That's the Lady of Shalott," she says again.

I shake my head dismissively, pointlessly adjusting my shirt to distract myself from the woman on the wall looking at me.

"She catches your eye every time, does she not?"

"Uh, yeah. I suppose she does." My voice is non-enthusiastic, but I sure as shit want to know why I'm intrigued by a bloody picture.

"She was imprisoned," Doc says turning to look up at it. "Her situation is like that of many individuals who struggle to step out of their comfort zone to experience life to its fullest."

I look at Doc who's clearly trying to tell me something, then up at the lady wearing white. She sits in a boat on a lake. With long red hair hanging down her front, she looks like a hippie, although the date inscribed at the bottom says 1888, so she can't be. She's pale, standing out against the dark background of reeds and dark woods that surround her. She looks lost. Broken, maybe.

"Dreams come to existence through the chances you take without letting doubt and fear get in the way."

The room falls silent. *Shit.* I heard two words. Fear and doubt. "Right," I say, locking eyes with Doc in a hope that we can get this show on the road.

"Three things, Mr Carter, go."

I nod my understanding as Doc sits on the chair behind her desk. "My girlfriend, my unborn child and my club." *My* club.

Doc looks up over the rim of her glasses. "Good. And the other three things?"

Again I nod, understanding that every session starts the same way; state three things I love and three things I would change. She already knows what I'm going to say. "Me, myself and I."

As predicted, she looks up at me again, this time removing her glasses and placing them on the notebook she has with my name on it. "Mr Carter—"

"—Please, call me Dean." Not Daddy.

"Fine. Dean." Doc sits back in her chair, thinking. "Why do you think you always say me, myself and I?"

Easy. Because if I could change what I do, I would. But I can't, so… "Because it's true." I do bad shit, have done bad shit, and will continue to do bad shit until all the other shit goes away.

"You think your partner would want you to change?"

My eyes meet with the doc's. No, she wouldn't. So actually, perhaps Mads needs to be the one sat in here because clearly, she is the one with the problem; giving her love to a man who was set on destruction. Totally undeserving.

Was? Not *is?*

Progress?

"You think you're undeserving of her love?"

Fuck me. *How did she do that?* "What?" I ask caught off guard.

"You still think you don't deserve happiness? Because of what's happened in your past, and because of the things you have done."

Jesus, I'm sweating. "Doc look—"

"Please, call me Miss Monroe. Or Melissa, if you must, but not Doc. I'm your therapist, Mr Carter, not your doctor."

That's me told. "Sorry." I sit back in my chair throwing my arm over the back, and wait for her to speak.

"Moving on." Doc—Miss Monroe, or Melissa if I must, stands from behind her desk and sits opposite me in another, equally blue chair. "Dean, you started these sessions by telling me that what you do is something you couldn't change, that you had lived somewhat of a solitary life before you met your partner."

I nod and watch her mind replay seeing my leather cut for the first time, trying to work out what it *is* that I really do.

"You said that your partner had given you hope and was... what was it you said?" She flicks through her notes looking back to our first session.

"My sunshine."

She stops flicking pages and smiles. "Right." I watch her shift in her seat. "Dean, I think throughout our sessions it's been clear that you and," she looks at me for help.

"Mads," I say.

She smiles again. "It's obvious that you have overcome a huge amount of turmoil with the help and support from Mads," that's an understatement, "but what isn't clear, and I had hoped with only a few sessions remaining we might have already uncovered it, is why you still feel undeserving?"

Well with only a few sessions left, I can only guess that I'm about to be hit with Melissa if I musts' conclusions.

Truth is, I only agreed to come to these sessions for Mads.

And what Mads wants, she eventually gets. And fuck me, if I hadn't found out she's Rocco's biological daughter, I would have guessed it, because as stubborn as she has been since the day I met her, I swear a tiny bit of outlaw has come out in her since we found out.

Or maybe it's the fact she's growing a human inside her? Hormones all over the show. Either way, I already know why I feel the way that I do. I had a hard life before the club, but I chose to lock my emotions away and I buried them. Deep. I never talked about them or opened up about what happened, and whilst I thought I was managing to hide how I really felt, turns out those closest to me had me figured out.

I was drowning.

Then, *undeservedly,* Mads fell at my feet, dug up and opened the box I'd buried and I had to face that shit head on. It was fucking difficult, and in no way is it fully dealt with, but it's better —*life,* is better.

Except for losing Jack. That's the fucking worst.

But why I feel undeserving, is because somewhere inside me, I can feel a familiar heavy weight trying to swamp me again. The blackness waiting to consume me. I can't place it—can't fucking put my finger on it. All I know is that whenever there is good, there is bad. And I can't ignore the knot in my gut telling me that something dark is looming with this new deal we're going to sign off on. The new player bringing bigger guns and a fuck load of cash… it goes against every instinct I have, but it's the lesser of two evils needed to keep the peace.

Peace. There's been plenty of it; our understanding with The Sodom Saviours upheld. So, naturally, something bad is coming.

I wake up every day praying I can keep the promise I made to Mads; that I would love and protect her and our baby. But what am I protecting her from? My life? The club? Saviours? I ask myself daily; would she be safer without me in her life?

The answer is undoubtedly yes. Would she be happy though? Probably not. Would I? Fuck no.

So here we are. In love. Good and bad. Sunshine and the dark.

Balanced.

Melissa if I must looks down at her notes, gently tapping her pen against the edge of the paper before she looks up. When I don't offer up my answer, she crosses one leg over the other and leans forward slightly. "I think our trauma focused cognitive behavioural therapy sessions have helped you to understand what happened to you as a child wasn't your fault?"

Agreed, but I always knew that.

"So, tell me in your own words, if your past wasn't your fault, why do you still feel undeserving of the love that clearly is helping you come to terms with everything you've faced?"

That's the same question worded differently. So, it's the same answer. "Because if we hadn't met, I wouldn't need to worry about protecting what I love. But without the things I love, what's the point in living?"

Melissa hums, and I can only look up at the lady on the wall, my heart rate unexpectedly picking up speed. The lady on the boat's holding a chain from her incarceration. Fuck, did I trap Mads?

Don't let fear and doubt get in the way.

I look down at my hands as my phone vibrates in my pocket. I know I shouldn't, but I pull it out to see who it is, desperate for a distraction.

"Is there something else, Mr Carter?" Melissa says as if reading my fucking mind once again.

I blink long and hard before looking up at her. "It is what it is," I say shrugging. I want to get back to Mads.

"Is there something making you feel afraid?"

Her quick-fire question makes me double take, those

eyebrows of hers raising higher on her oval face. She's hit the nail on the head. I am afraid. I'm afraid I won't be a good dad. I'm afraid that Mads will want a better—*safer*—option one day. I'm afraid that after three times of asking, Mads is never going to say yes to marrying me.

My heart starts kicking wildly in my chest, the back of my neck's suddenly clammy. I look up again.

There are three candles at the front of the lady's boat, but only one lit. Two are already extinguished. Why are two snuffed out in their family of three? I look back to Melissa. "I," my voice croaks. Damn it. I was so close to riding through these sessions without my fear of being a shit dad coming out.

"Dean?"

"Thanks for your time, Doc." I push out from my chair.

"Mr Carter, wait, we still have thirty minutes left of our session."

No. Fuck that. I stride towards the door.

"Mr Carter!" Melissa shouts, as I pull open the door and leave.

A cold breeze hits my face as I walk outside.

Breathe. I almost forget my phone in my hand still vibrating. "Hello?" I answer, not even checking who it is as I swallow hard.

"Need you at the clubhouse, boss." Travis' voice is matter of fact. Welcomed. A distraction.

"Everything good?"

"Got something you need to see."

I sigh pinching the bridge of my nose. Is this it? The something bad I knew was inevitably coming for me. The end to the peace we've lived with for the past five months. "I need to go home first." I need my girl.

"Sure, brother." He knows.

I hang up, jump on my bike, and ride as fast as I can back home. Opening the door, I make Mads jump as she turns, surprised to see me back early.

There she is. My reason for living. My air.

My fucking sunshine.

CHAPTER THREE

MADISON

It shouldn't taste as good as it does, but my body's craving it. I feel mischievous as I unscrew the lid. And frown. There isn't much left in the jar. Urgh, VP. Maybe Lynn next door will have some? I look back down to the jar. There's just enough to satisfy my need, maybe. But as I shove the pickle in the chocolate, my mouth waters with need. I scrape every morsel I can grab, then sumptuously shove it past my lips as goosebumps riddle my body. Satisfaction at its finest.

Pregnancy is weird.

Weird and wonderful.

Scary, weird and bloody wonderful, actually. I don't even like pickles, yet here I am, practically French kissing the slippery condiment, licking small scrapes of sweetness from the end as if it's my last ever meal.

It tastes like heaven, and my tummy gurgles as if it thinks so too. "You like this, huh?" I ask my bump casually, looking down at the protruding bulge. I read that at twenty weeks the baby should be able to hear my voice. Talking and singing can help to create a bond, so whenever I can, I sing or talk aloud having a conversation with my bump.

My baby.

I double dip the next pickle and lift my feet to the coffee

table as I lean back against the sofa. Working a half day has never come with such satisfying perks. I'm eyes closed, halfway through my second pickle, happily slurping. Content.

I hear the key in the front door and I jump, my eyes turning to see Dean stood still, watching me.

"Jesus, babe," he purrs. His voice is raspy, but I can't tell if I'm turning him on or if he's repulsed.

Pulling the pickle from my mouth it makes a light popping noise. I quickly lick my lips like I've been caught cheating.

Dean closes the door behind him, then slowly walks towards me. He drops his keys and helmet on the coffee table.

"You're back early," I say sucking the tips of my fingers, still a little flustered. It's four in the afternoon, he doesn't usually get home until gone five after seeing his therapist.

"I realised something whilst sat with Doc." He holds out his hand for me to take.

I scrunch my eyes placing my hand in his, letting him pull me to my feet. My free hand naturally curls around my bump as I straighten in front of him. "What's that?" I ask smiling, happy to see him.

He cups my face in his hands and takes me in. Our eyes are dancing, silently reading each other. "That I'm the luckiest fucking man to walk this planet."

I smile bashfully but place my hands on his arms holding me. We're still looking directly into each other's eyes as he continues, "You, Madison Reed, are my reason for living. My purpose in amongst all the chaos."

I smile but grip his arms tighter. He's worried about something, I can tell. The signature line dons his forehead, and his eyes start moving between mine a little erratically. "Dean?" I ask, forcing his eyes to slow. "What is it?"

The corner of his lip stretches as he closes his eyes. Gently placing his lips on my lips, he then dips his forehead to touch mine. We share a still moment before he bends at the waist, leaning down to kiss my swollen belly in his hands. "VP," I whisper, watching him through my now misty eyes.

His lips are still touching my small bump. I run my hand through the back of his hair. He's worried about bringing our baby into this world. He doesn't have to say it. I can feel it. I feel it in the way he's looking at my body. He's scared he won't be able to protect us. Scared he'll somehow lose us.

Things have been quiet with the club. Yes, he's been busier, setting up a new deal with the Saviours, but nobody's been hurt. There's been no death. No threats. No drama. Just us, learning to live together. Learning to live in the not so normal world we live in. "I'm right here," I say softly.

He kisses my belly again then turns and sits on the sofa.

I stay standing in front of him, my bump now in line with his face.

He looks up at me through his lashes, then shutting his eyes, he kisses my bump one more time, keeping his lips close to me, his hands on either side of my tummy.

This man. My VP. So riddled with self-doubt. He's the strongest, bravest man I know, yet his demons never fully allow him peace.

I suggested a few months ago he seek seeing a professional. He hated the idea and told me I was the only therapy he needed. Then he threatened to leave when I made Jess fast-track a referral for him. I knew he was joking, of course, but the idea of sharing his trauma with an outsider had him in a spin.

Eventually, I convinced him that it might help. But I'm not stupid. I have no doubts that when he goes to a session, he never fully opens up. The man I love doesn't do anything he doesn't want to.

He likes complete and utter control.

Today's different though. Something's changed. "I'm not

sure what I've done to deserve you," he says to my bump. His voice is full of love and worry as he speaks. It's the kind of worry any father would have before his first child comes into this world. It's also the kind of worry that comes from living in a dangerous world and at the same time, preparing yourself to bring something so pure and innocent into it.

"Dean." I wait for him to look up. When he doesn't, I lift my hand, ever so gently cupping the side of his face with my palm. "Please look at me."

His eyes slowly lift and when they find mine, I see it. My home. My love.

"You're afraid something's going to go wrong?"

He lets loose a small huff but he smiles. "Told you I didn't need to see a therapist."

The corner of my lip raises. "I know you well enough now to know what you're thinking."

He settles into the sofa, watching me as he runs his hand through his hair. We stare at one another, and I feel my heart pick up pace. He lifts his hand, lightly stroking my bump. "Tell me what I'm thinking," he says.

Looking at his hand on my bump, I lift my hands and place them on my hips, slightly cocking my head to one side a little playfully as I look back to him. "You're thinking you're going to cook your pregnant girlfriend her favourite dinner, join her in the shower then massage her feet until she falls asleep."

He laughs, the sound melting me. "I'll do all those things, babe. But still, humour me."

My smile drops and I look at him. "Seriously?"

He nods, just watching me. I contemplate making another joke, but he wants to talk. This is good. He wouldn't have done this three months ago.

I lick my lips before I speak, remembering to be direct and compassionate. "You're worried something's going to happen; to me, the baby, the club." My voice is soft and calm as I speak. "You've never not worried, but today's different, somehow."

His hand movements slow, his eyes widening a fraction. "You think you don't deserve happiness so you're just waiting for the bad to come get us."

His lips pull into a straight line across his face, and his eyebrows pull together. His reaction proves I'm bang on the money. "Anything else?" he asks seriously but with a slight smile.

I have my suspicions that there's one more thing. It's the same thing I question, daily. But for him, he shuts down his fear—doesn't allow himself to feel any part of it.

With a slight sigh I say, "You're questioning whether you can protect us, and moreover, you're doubting your ability to be a good—"

He quickly stands to his feet, his hands guiding me to make room for him. His lips hit mine, and I know what he's doing. Distracting me. Because I'm right.

Gripping the tops of my arms he tries to deepen our kiss, and whilst I can feel myself wanting to give myself over to him, he needs to keep talking to me.

"VP," I whisper against his lips, catching my breath.

I feel him smile against me. "Mads," he says softly.

I blink, looking up to him. "Don't let your head haunt you anymore," I whisper.

The look in his eyes when he opens them is nothing but vulnerability. Vulnerability because he doesn't need to be strong all the time now that he has me.

"Don't doubt how good a father you'll be."

Taking a small step back, he looks down at me. With a sigh, he kisses my forehead before he speaks. He knows I won't let him walk away from this. When he needs me, I pick him up. When I'm falling, he catches me.

"Loving you, protecting you... giving you whatever you

need—*whatever you want*—Mads, I can do that. And I can promise to love you 'til the day I die. But you need to know…" He pauses as if he doesn't want to say what comes next. His eyes close tight as he speaks. "If ever a day should come when you want to change your mind, or escape this new life we have, I will never hold it against you. I would let you go if that's what you wanted."

Hot tears prickle my eyes, but I don't let them overflow. "Why are you saying this?" I ask.

With another sigh, he scratches his beard. "Because I have this horrible feeling that a shift is coming. And I will not risk you, or my child. We both know we can't live without the other, but if you needed to leave—*needed to protect what's ours*—I would respect any decision you made. With every fucking fibre of my body, I would respect your wishes, no matter how much it kills me."

I stare at him, fiercely. I hear what he's saying. He's saying what Rocco, my biological father, said to my mother years ago. He's giving me an out. Letting me know that I don't need to stay with him if I don't want to. Well screw him and his out. I said I would love him forever when we got back together last year, and I meant it.

"Dean, with all due respect… you can shove it."

The idiot smiles at me, and it's the most gorgeous smile that expands across his face. He takes my hands in his. "Thought you might say that."

The smallest of grins hits my face. "If you thought that's what I'd say, why say it?"

His eyes jump to mine. "Because I fucking mean it. You need to tell me if you want to change your mind."

"Well, I mean it too. You can shove your words up your arse."

His eyebrows lift and he stares at me. It's hard not to smile. He acts so put out when I challenge him, but he loves it. It's how I've always been with him. "In a minute, beautiful, I'm going to bend you over the back of the sofa and shove my cock up your arse."

I snort with laughter. It's a guttural, unattractive snort.

Dean pulls me into his arms, laughing with me.

"You're an animal," I chuckle.

He kisses my neck as I wrap my arms around his, tilting my head to one side to give him more room. "Only because you drive me wild." His next kiss is tender. "I love you," he says against my skin, his hands holding my body close to his.

"I love you." I pull my head back to look at his face. His green eyes shine bright, his love staring me down. "I'm not going to change my mind, okay?"

He smiles closing his eyes and nods his head. His head then lowers and we kiss. It's a slow kiss. Meaningful. It's not urgent or rushed, it's just, love.

"Then marry me," he says against my lips.

He's asked me three times since we got back together. On Christmas Day morning, out on a random bike ride, and when he took me back to Malham where we camped late last summer. Each time I say no. Not because I don't love him, because I absolutely do. And every day that passes, I think I love him even more, it's just… with him, I don't need the ring. I don't need the fancy wedding or the piece of paper that says we love each other. I just need him.

Plus, I've had the other stuff before and look how that panned out.

But he wants to give me all of that—wants to do it right. One day, maybe, but for now, I like what we have. That and I've said no so many times, it's becoming a bit of a running joke between us.

Warm waves of bliss blanket my body as he nips at my neck, waiting for me to speak. I spy the back of the sofa, suddenly wanting him to do as he said. "Dean," I whisper.

He hums against my skin.

"Tell me what I'm thinking."

His eyes are blazing as he pulls back to look at me, his erection against my front hard to ignore. He slowly trails one hand from where it rests on my hip and slips it past the top of my leggings, into my knickers.

The tip of his finger against my skin makes my breath hitch. I keep my eyes on his, feeling a wave of arousal flutter through me. Tipping my head back, he moves his hand, brushing through the thin strip of hair between my legs. "Dean," I whisper.

He smiles. "You're thinking," he starts, as he pushes one finger inside me gently.

My arms are still wrapped around his neck, and my mouth opens as he dips closer to me, lightly grazing his lips over mine, the tickle of his short beard making the hairs on my arms stand to attention.

"You're considering saying yes to marrying me."

I smile wide forcing him to do the same.

"But first, you want me to bend you over the sofa and fuck you." He slides another finger into my pussy, making me moan.

He's right. I want him to have his way with me. My hold on him tightens, and I can't help closing my eyes as my body clenches around him.

"You want that, babe?" he asks. He curls his fingers as his thumb starts circling my clit.

Jesus. "Yes, VP." My voice is doused in want. I'm hot and growing needier by the second.

"Tell me exactly what you want, Mads."

I whimper again. The pleasure I feel is immediate whenever he touches me like this. Now that I'm in my second trimester, if I'm not wanting to eat everything in sight, I want the man I love to worship my body.

Because he does it so well.

Another finger slides in, and I close my eyes as he stretches me, preparing me for what he's about to do next. Christ alive my mouth is dry as I enjoy the way he's waking up my body with his hand. "Yes," I pant, "I want you to love me, VP."

He smiles against my neck before he carefully spins me. Walking me forwards, my shins hit the sofa, but he doesn't stop moving. I have no choice but to lift my legs up to kneel on the cushions in front of me.

He caresses my bum before he gives it a light smack.

I smile at him.

Pulling my leggings over my bump and down to my knees, he trails his hand between my legs to the front of my knickers. He moves the material to one side, slipping one finger inside me again.

He moans, and my mouth opens as he circles deep, a buzz of pleasure warming my body from within. I'm craving what's about to come. "Dean," I beg needily.

He grips the bottom of my jumper, and I lift my arms for him to take it off. He lifts it above my head, throwing it to the floor before he unhooks my bra, freeing my rock hard nipples.

"My girl," he purrs. "I love your body. So, fucking beautiful." He cups my exposed, now larger breasts and kisses my neck.

I lift my arms up, arching my back, wrapping them around his neck behind me. I can feel his arousal pushing against me.

Moving his hands from my breasts, he undoes the fly of his jeans and slides my knickers to one side. He lines himself up, and I lean forward resting my hands on the back of the sofa, bending my body in front of him.

He moves slowly, coating the tip of his cock in my arousal before edging himself inside me. "Fuck, Mads," he hisses.

My legs twitch with the thrilling sensation of him filling me. He's not even halfway in, yet my eyes roll to the back of my head. I need him to give me release. I turn to look at him over my shoulder as he pushes in further, then withdraws all the way to the tip. God, that feels so good. My body tightens around him. I can't take my eyes off him as he continues to slowly push and withdraw.

My lips part, a long breath escaping my mouth. I need more. Pushing back onto him, I start circling my hips, encouraging him to speed up.

He watches me riding his cock for a few moments before his fingers grip my hips, and when he next drives forwards, a cry escapes me.

"Fuck, VP, just like that!"

Gritting his teeth together, I keep watching as he starts driving faster. The feeling of him working my body deep with precision, turns me on so fast, I can feel my orgasm suddenly at the surface.

"Dean, I'm coming!" I cry.

He doesn't tell me to wait or slow down. Instead, he surges and thrusts into my body, driving me to my climax.

I come with a rush, pulsating around him as he lets go as well. My breaths are laboured and exhausted. My hands scrunch the sofa cushions as the last waves of pleasure have me twitching.

"That's got to be a record," he breathes, his fingers still squeezing my hips as he eventually slows to a stop.

I smile, my face resting in my arms on the back of the sofa.

He pulls out, cleans me up, then adjusts my knickers and pulls my leggings back into place.

Pushing to stand, a sharp pain emanates in my ribs, stealing the air from my lungs. "Shit," I wince.

Dean's hands still hold me. He looks at me as he helps guide me to my feet. "What's wrong?"

"Pain. Here," I say, clutching the left side of my body, the pain easing slightly as I move to stand.

"Usual pain, or pulled a muscle?"

Every now and again I still feel a niggle where I broke a few ribs, but this feels different. "Must have pulled a muscle. Lost my core strength whilst growing a human." I stretch my back, hands on my hips as Dean smiles at me with an eyebrow raised.

"Core strength?" he questions mockingly.

"Hey, I'd give you a good run for you money," I say laughing, still rubbing the affected area. We both know I'd never win a fight, but that wouldn't stop me giving it my best shot, and he knows it.

Dean grabs my jumper from the floor, scrunching the opening for my head in his hands. He hoops it over my head, and I put in my arms, happy to leave my bra off.

Sitting on the sofa, he holds his arms open for me.

I move to sit next to him but he carefully pulls me to his lap.

"Soon, I'll be too heavy to sit on you," I say, turning my body into his.

"Babe, you could be the size of a whale and I'd still want you on my lap."

I smile, and he holds me in silence, my eyes lazily closing as he strokes the tips of his fingers up and down my spine, his other hand holding my bump. I love our moments like this. The three of us. Quiet. Happy.

"Do you think she'll love me?" Dean's question immediately makes my eyes spring open.

I push up from his chest to look at him. "What?" My eyes scrunch together confused.

"The baby. Do you think she'll love me?" It hurts my soul that he asked that question. And it breaks my heart that he thinks his child would *not* love him. What's not to love? His selflessness, his bravery, his ability to care and to protect the things that are precious to him. Yet he believes he deserves nothing in return.

He believes he is worthy of nothing.

Tears are threatening to run down my face. I want to slap

some sense into him. I contemplate it, but it won't help. "Your money's still on it being a girl?" is all I say instead.

His eyes meet mine. He looks shocked that I haven't laid into him or addressed his, in my eyes, ridiculous comment. "It's a girl," he smiles.

He's been adamant from day one that it's a girl. Never once has he changed his mind. Not even when I suddenly developed a habit for preferring savoury over sweet which, according to Eva, the new lady at work, means it's a boy. "Well, tomorrow we can find out. Unless you still want it to be a surprise?"

"What do you want?" Dean asks me.

I like the idea of a surprise, I really do. But I also really like the idea of knowing so we can be organised. I was shocked when he suggested waiting to find out to be honest. "I want you to decide. I also want you to come to the scan tomorrow knowing, that girl or boy—"

"—girl," he interjects.

I laugh and continue, "girl *or boy*, they will love you, more than anything or anyone ever has. Because you are their daddy. And you are brave and fierce." I see his eyes glaze as his thumb starts stroking my bump. "We are yours," I say, my throat suddenly burning as I place my hand on top of his, "and you will always be ours."

Dean pulls me closer to him, and we fall into silence.

CHAPTER FOUR

MADISON

An hour later, freshly showered and smelling like a god, Dean walks downstairs to me.

"Didn't think poker started until eight?" I ask, looking up at the clock.

It's almost six, yet he picks up his wallet and keys as if he's going out now. "Travis called earlier, needs me at the clubhouse before it starts." I watch his eyes flick to me as he puts his things in his pockets.

"Oh," is all I reply. There's curiosity in my voice. Dean knows that I know they've been searching for Lauren. I wonder if why Travis needs him is related to that?

It's been three months and I've had a few texts from her.

That's it.

I drove myself crazy at the start, literally driving around in my car at God knows what hour trying to find her. But as the weeks dragged on and the evenings grew darker, I concluded that if she wanted to see me, she would reach out.

After she messaged me the day of Rocco's funeral, I thought she'd be coming back. But when I asked where she was and wanted to know if she was safe, she didn't reply. She only reached out to me after that to say 'Merry Christmas', two months later.

I'd let her down. I should have done more to protect her. Part of me feels broken that she's out there somewhere with nobody, and I'm here, not helping her.

"If it's related to Lauren, I'll let you know," Dean says as if reading my thoughts.

I smile at him, even though I know he probably won't. He won't give me any false hope.

I was kept in the loop at first, but the deeper things get with the club, they're starting to leave me out of it. He and Travis don't want to stress me or the baby out. "Thank you," I say anyway.

Dean bends over me sat on the sofa and places a kiss on my head. "What are you doing tonight?" he asks.

"Oh, I have a hot date," I quip, trying not to dwell on my failings.

Dean smiles. "Who is he? Where does he live?"

I smile back, tapping the book on my lap.

"What's his name?"

"He's a billionaire book boyfriend." I laugh when he looks down trying to get a better look at the cover.

"I'll kill him," Dean jokes.

"Thank God he's fictional and you can't hurt him." My phone vibrates in my hand, making me look down. I smile seeing the name on the screen.

"If he were real, he'd be dead," he says jokingly, making me look up as he turns to retrieve his helmet.

"He has brothers," I mutter under my breath, lifting my phone up to answer.

"What?"

"Nothing. Have a good night, dear," I mock.

He smiles from the door, then turning slowly, he comes back to me, stealing one more kiss before he bends to kiss my bump. "Love you," he says.

"Love you," I mouth, and he turns and leaves me to my call. "Hello."

"Took your time."

"Sorry, Dean was on his way out. Everything okay?"

I hear Bex sigh. "If you count peeing 24/7 and not being able to bend over properly as okay, then yeah, I'm *okay.*"

"That bad, huh?" I ask. I shift on the sofa, pulling the blanket further over me.

"What am I now... thirty weeks almost? Hang on, let me show you." She switches the call to FaceTime.

"Bloody hell, Bex!" I remark shocked. "Are you sure you're not carrying twins?"

"Oh, God no. Twins! The thought of carrying two makes me feel sick. I'm barely hanging on with one in there!"

I chuckle, admiring her full tummy. Her bump is solid and round, her back arching with the weight on the front. "She's going to be big," I tell her fondly.

"Like her father."

Kyle walks past in the background giving me a wave.

I wave back. "How's he doing?" I ask, knowing full well he'll be doing everything around the house for her.

Bex smiles, looking over her shoulder at him. "I'd be lost without him."

He gives her a wink.

"Still his fault though," she says a little louder.

"You never complained when we were in the trying phase," Kyle shouts.

Letting her face do the talking, Bex looks back at her phone. "Anyway, speaking of fathers, have you heard from yours yet?"

I shake my head. "Not since I called a few weeks ago."

Bex gives me a half smile. "It'll be hard for him. Now he knows that you know the truth, he's probably reliving it."

"I know," I say with an exhale. My poor dad. He isn't my father. But he *is* my dad. Nothing would ever change that. Seeing him will be good for both of us.

Bex breaks the silence. "Right, I've shown you mine, come on, show me yours."

I throw the blanket off me, then stand trying to hold my phone so Bex can see my bump. "Oh my God, Madison, you're tiny!"

"I know!" I move back to sit down. "I'm having weird cravings now. Pickles seem to be my current thing."

"Ow yeah, dip them in something sweet."

"Yes! Thank you. Dean thinks I'm vile."

"Tsh, what does he know. They're not the ones growing people."

I laugh.

"Is he okay?"

Nodding, I lay back down, propping my phone on my bump, leaning it against my bent legs. "He's fine," I say, truthfully hoping I'm right. "I think he's nervous."

Bex smiles then mouths that Kyle is too.

"I think he'll be fine once the baby's here though."

"Same. This is new to all of us and let's be honest, it's fucking terrifying."

"Agreed."

"Have you thought about names yet?" Bex asks.

"No, not yet. Have you?"

"Yeah, I have a list as long as my arm. I'm really not sure I can only pick one though."

"Oh God, you're not going to give my God-daughter a triple barrelled name are you?"

"I might." She laughs clearly giving it away that her name choices are certainly going to be more out there than mine.

"Do I want to know?"

"You wish. I'm saving it for the baby shower. You can still make it, right?"

I nod. "Yep. Still think it would be less stressful if you were having it now and not bang on your due date though."

Again, her face says it all. "Look. The longer I leave it, the more likely I am to deliver her whilst you're down here."

"I'm not sure she'll care whether I'm there for her delivery, nor will she remember," I chuckle.

"True. But I will."

I smile. "Anyway, isn't the first child the hardest to deliver? She might want to stay in the cozy home you've given her. I might come all that way and she refuses to show herself in time."

"Maybe. But I'm willing to risk it." We laugh together.

"You're mad."

"No. I just want my best friend holding my hand. I want you there when she comes. That's all."

Tears seep and my eyes turn foggy. "Bitch, you made me cry."

"Made myself cry too." She dries her eyes with her sleeve, and we chuckle at ourselves.

"Miss you, Bex," I tell her.

"Miss you too."

"And I'll be there, okay. I wouldn't miss it. Oh, and Jess confirmed she can come."

"Perfect." Her smile is warming. They're not the same as face to face, but our weekly catch ups are something I hold dear to my heart. I miss my best friend. "Right," she starts, "short and sweet tonight. I'll call next week?"

"Sounds good to me. Speak soon, love you."

"Love you," Bex replies, blowing me a kiss and hanging up.

I can't believe she is making me wait so long until I next see her, but when I do, it'll be worth it.

CHAPTER FIVE

DEAN

I hang my helmet on the handlebar then pull out my smokes. Stopping in my tracks to light it, I take a moment to myself before I step inside the clubhouse. Mads put my mind at rest, as I knew she would, but I'm no less anxious about the news Travis is about to deliver. It could be Lauren. Saviours. Who knows what waits inside.

If I don't go in, I don't need to have my day ruined. *It might not be ruined. It might be news on Lauren.* It won't be news on Lauren. I've been looking for that little shit for months. She doesn't want to be found.

Blowing a smoke ring, I flick my cigarette to the ground after one drag. I need to quit anyway.

Walking to the bar, I pat Travis on the back.

He turns in his seat and nods his chin up to me. I feel his eyes assessing me, but he doesn't say anything. He's the only one who knows about my therapy sessions. I promised that if he ever mentioned it, I'd cut his dick off and feed it to him.

Sliding a beer across the top of the bar, I take a long swig then rub my face. I'm tired.

"Set for tonight?" Travis asks.

"Who's in?"

"All of us except Mop and The Joker."

I nod knowing The Joker, who transferred here from the Midlands, wouldn't be coming. A recent run of bad luck with gambling had him pull out. Wise man. "And Riggs?" I question.

Travis signals yes as he sips his beer, then points at our newest prospect, Legs, behind the bar for another. "Vincent called."

My stomach flips at those two simple words. I wait for Travis to elaborate but he doesn't. "*And?*" I say, urging him to continue. This must be why he wanted me here earlier.

"And... well, do you want the good or the bad news?"

Fucking hell. There *is* bad news. Sod it. "Bad news."

With a slight sigh, he takes a large mouthful of his fresh beer keeping his face forward. "No one else is privy," he whispers.

I lean in closer, noting his quiet voice.

"A threat's been made to the Saviours."

I stare at the beer in my hand. "A threat? From whom?" I ask, keeping my eyes down.

"Unsure. Mop's gone to see."

"See?"

"There was a package."

"A package?" My eyes flick up to look at him.

"Yes, a *fucking* package," he snaps, all hushed at my repeating him.

I sip my beer.

"I sent Mop to check it was credible and not some bullshit."

"Good. And the good news you had?"

"We sit down with Costa in a few weeks. Should have the first route, pick up, drop off, you name it, locked down by then," Travis replies.

I take another sip of my drink.

This new player Vincent has brought to the table, I've met him once. Irish. Bringing big money. It's money we don't want. Money we need. Business we can't let the Saviours have to themselves. "Everyone on board?" I know the money's desirable, but that doesn't mean my men will like working with the Saviours.

"Just Cap' who needs a push," he says patting me on the back. Checking his watch, Travis then pulls out his phone, placing it on the bar. "Mop should call any minute." As he says it, his phone skates across the wood. God bless Mop and his punctuality. "Yup," Travis answers.

I watch as he nods and agrees with Mop on the phone. When he hangs up, he looks at me, dipping his chin quickly. It's real.

Fuck. I see a wall go up in my peripheral vision.

"I'll go meet him, you stay here, enjoy the poker."

"No, Trav, I'll go."

He stands, glugging his beer. "No. I'm your VP now. You've got tomorrow to think about. Stay. I'll call if I need you." I open my mouth to argue as he slaps me on the back. "I said I can handle it. We don't know how bad it is yet, and I'll be back anyway, just don't let them drink the top shelf without food. Prospect's going to have one hell of a night cleaning that up if they do."

The young prospect looks up and laughs at Travis' comment.

We stare deadpan at the twat. "Don't smile," I scold. "He's fucking serious. Last time we had a full poker table, they were cleaning Chinese food off the ceilings."

That was a fun night, until Rocco had had enough of the men continuously being able to buy into our game. He flipped his lid and went on a rampage tearing up the place.

The prospect's face drops before he continues to fetch my men their drinks.

I nod at Travis as he leaves. I should be going. But he's right. Showing my face seeing as I missed church today will be better for morale. Not that morale is low, more because I missed church.

Missed church for a fucking therapy session.

I scoff and sip my near empty beer. I wonder what Rocco would make of me? I've kept things in line for three months. I hope with our new business I can keep it that way.

Come nine o'clock, Travis still isn't back. I thought he'd have at least called by now. I've checked my phone more times than I care to admit. I've had one glass of the hard stuff, but I haven't allowed myself to have anymore. I don't want to rely on it. Even though my nerves are shot, I need to be ready if Travis calls with news.

Damn, I sound like a chick.

What news that will be, I don't know. Is it a threat? A fucking threat to our rivals? I call them rivals, but we haven't had any trouble with the Saviours for months. A few niggles here and there when we ironed out the finer details, but nothing on this scale.

I wanted peace. Wanted to protect the people we love. And I got it. I'll go out of my way to keep it that way, even with new ventures on the horizon. I'll end anyone that wants to step on my toes and threaten my club or my Mrs. *She aint your Mrs.* No, she isn't. But she will be. One day.

"Dean?" Captain says.

I look up noticing his lazy eyes on me.

Poor sod. How the fuck he can see the road when riding blows my mind. Not one, but two slightly wonky eyes. I quickly look at Beats. Bollocks, I wasn't paying attention. I've missed his classic tell of rubbing his ears when he's holding a decent deck. Fuck it. "Fold," I say, slapping my cards on the table and leaning back in my chair.

Beats laughs, clearly happy I'm out. "Pussy."

"Fuck you." I flash a grin and shake my head.

"Show us your cards," Captain instructs Beats and Len.

"Eye eye, Cap'." Beats cockily and slowly places his hand of cards down.

I hear Captain call him a cunt for mocking his vision before he looks, *I think*, at Len whose lips start stretching across his face.

I start eye rolling him before he even gets the words out. I know what he's going to say.

"Read 'em and weep, fuckers."

Every. Time.

"Prick has the same fucking hand every time we play, I swear!" Beats bangs the table, angry he's just lost the fat wedge of money we played for.

"Shouldn't have been so confident," I tell him as I pick up my phone from the table.

"Suck my dick," he mumbles.

"Wanna come closer and say that to my face?" I ask him.

"Why, you deaf or something, cunt?"

I throw my head back hysterical at his little outburst. He's worse than a toddler.

My phone starts vibrating in my hand.

"One more game?" he asks as I look at the screen. No doubt he wants to win back what he just lost.

"No, I'm out. Got to take this." I wave my phone at him as I stand and leave the room. I head to the bar downstairs as I answer. "Trav?" I say, my heart rate picking up a little. "What's going on?"

"Just leaving now," he says.

I hear Mop say something in the background. "Mop alright?"

"Yeah, all good, boss." I don't think I'll ever get used to him calling me that.

I breathe out the breath I was holding. "What was it then?" I ask.

"It's definitely a threat."

My heart drops. "What did Vincent say?"

"Let me catch you up when I get back, eh?"

I want to know everything right now, but I know the stubborn mule won't budge. "Right," is all I say.

At almost ten, we're all sat around the table, boxes of takeaway food scattered across the surface. I texted Mads telling her not to wait up for me before Travis and Mop brought us up to speed on the threat; a box of toy fucking guns delivered straight to the Saviours' front door.

Shit doesn't get more obvious than that. Somebody knows about our new deal.

Anyone who passes through our turf, we've kept tabs on since we made the deal. We recruited more members; The Joker and Captain to name a few, as have other charters on both sides further north and in the south. It's a necessity to ensure things run smoothly when moving the drugs and guns.

Fucking, guns.

Why the Saviours are so set on trying to be the biggest player in firearms ceases to amaze me. We source handguns for our own supply, granted, but it's high-risk fucking stupidity trying to be anything more. I guess it's how the world fucking rotates now. He with the biggest dick, fucks the hardest.

It's how Uncle Ronnie likes to run things. Meanwhile back here, I've been trying to run things more smoothly. Trying. That is until this package arrived.

"Who is it?" Beats asks, still looking at the images on Travis' phone. "Got to be someone wanting in on the guns, surely?"

"Who else deals with guns that we know of?" Travis replies.

"No one around here," Riggs starts, leaning forward resting both arms on the table. "Think about it, Saviours are the first local MC in years to want in on guns. And now there's—"

"—us," Mop finishes Riggs' sentence, his voice barely audible.

Mine and Mop's eyes meet as a short silence falls. "You think whoever it is knows *we're* involved?" I ask, a snide snarl combing my words.

He tilts his head. "If they don't already, they probably will soon."

Fuck. My worst fucking nightmare. The thought of someone watching my family and my club.

"Vincent knows we know their routines; the days they have shipments and run our county lines. Rippers will be top of his shit list now, given he knew of our doubts going into this new deal. But at least we got a call," I say.

"Phone call or not, I'd bet my left nut-sack he thinks it's us," Beats blurts out. "You meet him face to face he'll kill you on a hunch."

I hear Travis huff and rub his big head with his palm. Vincent can't kill me on a hunch. Shit doesn't work like that.

"Or it's a trick; a ploy to set us up as the bad guys," Skitz comments subtly.

"We're all bad guys," Mop says.

He isn't wrong. "Could be a ploy. Or what's more likely, is that it's real and was made by someone neither us nor the Saviours know," Travis says.

"How can you be so sure it's real? It was a box of plastic fucking guns," Beats points out on a sarcastic laugh. "Could just be some little shits pissing about."

I spy a £20 note poking out the top of his pocket on his cut. He won back the cash he lost in poker, now he's rubbing it in Len's face.

"Vincent didn't spare us many words, but they sure as shit seem to think it's real," Travis replies.

I consider Travis' comment. "The timing and contents can't be a coincidence either."

Skitz snorts into his beer.

"You think it's fake?" Travis asks, swinging his head to him.

My eyes are dancing between the two of them.

"You're fucking right I do." Skitz's eyes widen, and he takes a quick sip of his beer. "What's to say they didn't plant it themselves, to lure us into thinking there's danger or some shit?"

"Then what?" Travis asks, turning his palms to the ceiling briefly and hunching his shoulders.

Skitz rubs the back of his neck. "Then wipe us out! Snatch the deal we're about to make for themselves, take all of our turf and run the entire north of England."

"Why now though? Why not last week, or a month ago? Don't make no sense waiting this long to then fuck us over."

"Makes perfect sense to me," Skitz fires back.

"And me," Dennis adds.

"Me three," Legs pipes up.

I look at him and frown at the long-legged bastard.

"Take the advice on your shitty t-shirt, Legs," Travis points down, "and shut the fuck up." He's getting pissed off with the tempers starting to fray in the room. The poor choice of Legs' clothing isn't helping.

I take a breath, pinching the bridge of my nose.

"Dean?" Mop says. His calm voice makes me open my eyes. My men are all looking at me, waiting for me to speak.

I look at them all in turn.

Each one of them came here when we called. It doesn't matter the hour, if the boys are told to get to the clubhouse, they drop what they're doing.

Travis, Beats and Riggs sit to my right. Travis is still shaking his head at Legs, who isn't cowering, but has settled back into his chair in between The Joker and Mop. Both of them are cool and collected; ruthless as fuck when needed though. Captain is deciding who to look at sat opposite Travis, and next to him sits Len, Dennis and Skitz, our three oldest members.

We're a sight for sore eyes, but we're family. An extension of one another. "Real or not, it means a sit down with Vincent is needed." I speak matter-of-factly, my voice calm.

"Last time you two ended up going a couple of rounds, you

sure you want that again?" Travis asks.

I quickly smirk remembering when we first fleshed out all the ways in which this understanding would work.

Prior to mine and Vincent's last sit down, he and Rocco had almost lost control with one another, the same night Vincent had ordered my kidnap and instructed Alex to bring Mads to the lock-up I was being held at. I knew the guy wanted me to pay for my sins, but when I met him face to face a few days after Rocco's funeral, the two of us beat each other to a pulp.

I was raging at everything that had happened. On a *real* slim technicality, I guess he never broke his word; his vow that only *I* would pay. Still, what Alex put Mads through, that was on him. So, I unleashed my demons and let him have both barrels.

He did the same to me.

I spent almost a week at home to recover, needing Jess to come over and stitch a nasty gash above my eye. A tiny divot now sits prominent near my brow, but the beating needed to happen. There's no love lost. We'll never be mates. The one thing in common is our love for our clubs and our men.

Which makes it possible that this *is* just a rouse to trick us. But it doesn't make sense for it to be them. Why now? And why risk everything when he's trying to rise to the top? "It won't go that far again," I say, slowly twirling my lighter between my fingers resting on the table. "We either choose to believe each other, or we're against each other. It's a shit fucking reality, but it was inevitable."

Like always.

CHAPTER SIX

MADISON

I wake up all warm and cosy, Dean's arms draped around me, my back close to his front. Turning under his hold, I nestle my head closer to his chest and breathe in his scent.

I've loved it from the moment I first smelled it. Whenever he's near, it still brings my skin out in goosebumps. Throw in my pregnancy, and my ability to smell every detail of him has increased tenfold.

There's wood as fresh as a forest after it's rained; bold hints of oak blended with pine come through thick and heavy. And the spice... its delicate blend has me closing my eyes and dreaming of late evening summer rides we took last year. How each time I'd held him close as the warm breeze kissed my skin, riding through the vast countryside we're fortunate to live in.

I take another unapologetic sniff but detect something else. What is that? Bourbon? Fresh from the barrel? He must have had a drink last night before riding home.

No, there's something else. Something, stale. No longer earthy and sweet, the old tobacco smells rotten and undesirable. I lift to my elbow and press my nostrils to his neck.

Yep. He definitely smoked. He promised he'd stop, but I have the nose of a lioness now. He can't hide it.

I feel him smile, and when I pull back to look at him, he

kisses my lips, keeping his eyes closed. "Am I in trouble?" he asks, his voice husky and low. He knows full well he's been found out.

"No," I say, still hovering above him. "Not in trouble, just..." My voice trails off as I brush a loose strand of his hair off his face.

He keeps his eyes closed, but a small hum leaves him as my fingers repeat the action, softly stroking through the overgrown tendrils.

I lean in closer to him, trying hard not to breathe in the smoky smell as I push my lips ever so gently to his. He sinks into his pillow, his strong hands cupping my back whilst he pulls my body closer to his.

I can't hold my breath any longer. Taking in a small amount of oxygen, I'm hit with the smell I don't like. My insides recoil a fraction, and I move my face away from his.

His left eye peeks open, the new scar above his eye scrunching tight towards his forehead.

"I can't kiss you," I say flatly, wrinkling my nose dramatically.

Dean lifts his arm, smelling himself, then seemingly not that bothered, rests his head back down on the pillow, eyes closed. "That's pure man, babe."

I eye roll him.

"You need to stop doing that," he says, one eye peeking at me.

Damn. "Doing what?"

"Rolling those pretty browns. It's becoming a nasty habit."

"Not as nasty as yours," I say, laying my body back down against his chest.

"You used to love watching me smoke. Couldn't watch me lighting one without getting wet."

I hit his arm, giving him a light smack at his crudeness. Secretly, I love his playful arrogance. "I still do, I just don't like the smell anymore. So pick one; smoking, or kissing me. You can't have both."

"Giving me an ultimatum?" Dean rolls his body towards me. His hand slides down my leg sending tingles up my spine. "That's an easy choice, Mads." Gliding over my inner thigh and across my tummy, his hand pushes his t-shirt that I'm wearing, up towards my breasts. I keep my eyes closed as his fingers dance over them, grazing both nipples in turn.

My back arches slightly, and his hips push forward, his erection now squashed against me. "I'm not sure what you're planning," I start, knowing exactly where this is headed, "but I am not going anywhere near your ashtray mouth."

He moves, and his teeth sink into my shoulder. The gentle nip makes me swing my hand to swat him away, but he catches my wrist, slowly raising my hand above my head.

God, he's so handsome.

His green eyes look dreamy and full of lust as he looks down at me, ready to take complete control of this moment between us. "What I've got planned doesn't involve kissing your mouth." Slipping his arm out from underneath me, he rests on his elbow.

I roll flat onto my back, gazing up at him, my breasts exposed. I lift my other arm so both are now crossed above my head.

"You don't have to kiss me, but I'm going to devour every inch of your body, beautiful." His voice still has the morning ruggedness to it.

My thighs instinctively squeeze together. I can't deny that I'm already wet.

His lips dot small kisses on my neck, forcing me to lift my chin.

"I can smell it in your hair," I say still enjoying every minute of what he's doing, but playfully pinching my nose as though repulsed. I sound like a flight attendant.

He laughs before moving his mouth to my breast. His hand

scoops up all of my now 36DD, and he sucks my pebbled nipple between his lips, his wet tongue delicately flicking the very tip.

"Oh," I moan, eyes rolling into my head, my back arching my body closer to him for more.

"Guess if I smell so bad, I should just stop?"

"No," I moan again on a hot breath. "Never stop."

He chuckles, then sucks my nipple into his mouth once more.

"Jesus, VP."

His teeth tease the solid bud at the same time his hand drags down to my hips. "You always lose to my temptation," he says, releasing my nipple, licking his lips as he looks at me.

I'm flushed. Hot. My body vibrates in anticipation of what he's going to do next.

Eyes locked, he moves to lie flat on the bed, parting my legs as he moves. He tickles his fingers along my skin, stopping at the juncture where my legs meet my pussy.

I whimper softly as my body tightens, the sensation of his touch making me close my eyes.

His thumb brushes the lace of my knickers over my clit, and I bite my bottom lip.

"My girl," he says. "You look fucking beautiful."

I smile thinking about how I must look to him. Arms behind my head, my t-shirt scrunched up to my chin, breasts out and my legs parted wide. Keeping my eyes closed I manage to reply, "What? At your mercy, letting you do as you wish with my body?"

He smiles placing a kiss on my hip. "Exactly. Surrendering to my control."

The pad of his thumb presses harder against my clit. His fingers sweep past the lace material. Soft lips then kiss my knee, making me moan a soft noise as they trail up my leg.

Dean smiles against my skin. When he pushes his fingers

inside me, he rotates them as he withdraws.

My insides tighten around him, a warming sensation pooling in my tummy. It feels like heaven.

Goosebumps scatter when he adds another finger, still pushing against my clit making heat rise within me.

My legs part wider, but I decide I want to have some fun. "The thing with control," I moan as he continues his steady rhythm, "is you've never really had it with me."

He stops kissing my leg and looks up at me. Stilling his fingers, mine thread through his hair, and I lightly curl them into my palm.

"You think you're in control here?" he asks playfully.

Easy. "I *know* I am." My right hand moves from above my head and skims over my right breast. I squeeze and tease, arching my back as I moan at the sensation of pinching my nipple.

Dean's lips part. He starts moving his fingers inside me, circling his thumb, rolling his fingers. When I push down against them—wanting them deeper, suddenly his fingers are in my mouth. He dips them past my lips, and I suck my arousal off his fingers, using my tongue to lick the taste clean as he watches me. He moans, and my hips raise needing his mouth on me.

His fingers run a wet trail over my chin, down towards my breasts. He cups his hand around mine that's still squeezing, slowly guiding it to my parted legs.

He wants to watch?

I'm happy to oblige.

Letting go of his hair, both thumbs slowly slip under the soft material, skating my knickers over my hips.

Throwing them to the floor, he licks his lips, breathing heavy, watching as I coat my fingers with my arousal before pushing them inside.

I moan closing my eyes, a trickle of tingles racing to my neck. My hold on his hair is put back in place, tightening as my other fingers plunge inside again. "VP," I breathe, steadily pleasuring myself in front of him.

I start circling my clit as he breathes a little heavier. The sensitive bud is swollen and warm. Feeling my orgasm start to build, my fingers quicken. I don't want this to be over too soon, but my fingers won't stop. *I* can't stop.

Tightening my grip in his hair, I push Dean's head down, rolling my hips, moving him where I want him, wanting him to lick every inch of me.

He groans as I cry out. "Dean, I'm coming!" I lift my hips off the bed.

Dean suddenly grabs my wrist making me stop.

My hips are still moving, my breaths still laboured. "What are you doing?" I ask rushed, the tiny pulse in my clit beating fast. My chest rises and falls as I look down to him.

He's so turned on, staring at my bare pussy before him.

Looking up at me through his lashes, he slowly drags his tongue from my entrance, right to the top of my pussy, stopping over my clit.

I throw my head back as he sucks it into his mouth, his fingers digging into my skin. "VP," I moan, angling my hips, pushing myself against him.

One more like that and I'll be in ecstasy.

"I have a better idea."

He pulls me into his arms, carefully rolling me, holding me tight. He's laid back with me on top of him, my legs parted near his mouth.

"VP," I say on a lost breath.

He smiles so sexily. "I'm always in control," he says confidently, lifting off my t-shirt then giving my bum a smack. "Now bring your needy pussy to my mouth. I want you to come on my face."

I can't help but blush on a grin. "I'll flatten you," I try to protest in vain, moving my body away from him. I don't get very far.

His hands glide over my bum before his fingers sink into my skin. "I said sit." His voice is stern.

A moan escapes me when he pulls me onto him, his tongue flicking across my opening.

Curling my hands in my hair, my eyes close, my head throws back. I start rolling myself against him.

Swirling in circles, his tongue lights up my body, causing my skin to pimple as the warm heat glides over me. I wonder if he's breathing? His hold on me hasn't faltered. I try to raise to give him air, but I can't budge.

Two of his fingers suddenly push inside me. Deep.

I sink lower, pleasure arching my spine. The circles my hips are making start getting quicker. I let out breathy moans letting him know I'm close. The lower half of my body is screaming. The feeling, euphoric.

As I allow my hands to cup and play with my breasts, we both start moving quicker. In no time at all, my back arches and stars begin dotting my vision. "VP, I'm... I'm..." I squeeze my breasts harder. With a shudder and a scream, my body convulses, twitching and shaking as Dean sends me out of this world.

I'm still catching my breath when he scoots out from underneath me. He nudges my knee wider, one hand gripping the back of my neck as the other guides his cock into me. "Fuck," he chokes. He doesn't stop until I'm completely full.

His hand around my neck pushes me down, my fingers splaying on the sheets as my body bends. Trailing his fingers down my spine, my back arches before strong fingers then hold my hips.

He starts slow, moaning deep as he fills me. Then he pounds relentlessly, rocking the bed, wet slaps resounding around us until he's close. "Fuck," he hisses, and I feel him start to stiffen.

I start pushing back against him, arching my spine, giving more of myself to him. When I look over my shoulder, our eyes connect.

He reaches forward, grabbing me by the neck, pulling me upright. He holds my head against his shoulder, his fingers curling around my throat. Then he stills, slowly letting go, his lips parted against my neck as he comes.

He's still breathing heavy, dotting kisses as his hands caress my skin, one of them stroking my bump. There's a thump from deep inside me. "Shit!" he cries, withdrawing and jumping back on the bed still on his knees.

I gasp, turning my body towards him. Both my hands cradle my bump as I look at Dean. "Did you feel that?" I ask him hopefully.

"Feel it? Bloody thing scared the shit out of me!" He comes closer, placing both hands over mine. "Was that her? Did she kick?"

"Yes! That was it!"

My voice is wobbling, completely filled with excitement and love in this moment. I've been able to feel flutters and little knocks for a few weeks now, but he has always timed it wrong. Each time I've told him to place his hands on me, the baby stops kicking.

But not now.

My heart starts doubling in size as I watch Dean. His eyes are glued to my tummy so tight, it's like he thinks if he blinks, he'll miss it. "Come on, you can kick your old man again." He looks up at me, embarrassed at how he's talking to my bump.

He shouldn't be. My heart's filling with pride and love and... and now I'm crying.

Thump.

He's smiling broadly as he shimmies his body to get more comfortable. He doesn't look at me. His eyes are scanning my bump, his fingers pressing gently as if to encourage the baby to kick again.

He then presses his ear to my skin and waits. Thump, thump. "Oh, fuck this is fucking amazing," he says.

My hand instinctively curls into his hair and I watch on.

There are no demons holding onto him in this moment. No shards of his past holding him close to the edge. This is the man I love, at peace, even if for only a moment. He's not at war with himself, not overthinking or fighting for control. Right now, right here... he's free.

And right now, watching him; seeing the man I love—the father of my child—smile in sheer happiness... I'll make sure he never loses himself again.

Dean takes my hand in his as we sit in the waiting room at the hospital. We've barely spoken; nervously excited to see our baby again, neither of us really knows what to do or say.

He ended up working this morning with Travis, finishing up a paint job they've had on for the past few weeks. He looks tired, which makes sense considering he got home late and then unexpectedly had to go out, but he's happy.

He lifts my hand and kisses the back of it.

I study him as he does. Tiny flecks of white paint dot the top of his hair and his cheeks. He looks handsome, but every part of me wants to lick the tip of my thumb and wipe them off. "You have paint here," I say, tapping my finger on my face.

He looks at me and starts wiping his skin.

"No, higher... up a bit...oh just—" I lick my thumb and impatiently swipe at his cheek.

"Hey!" he argues, shocked by my old-fashioned mum move.

I smile and start moving my thumb closer to him again when a nurse calls my name. "Madison Reed?"

"Ha!" Dean swats my hand away in mid-air. We stand together, his hand at the small of my back as I walk forwards, following the nurse into the room.

With no windows in the room, a large machine with a surprisingly small monitor sits on one side of a large bed. "Come in, pop your bag on the chair and take a seat on the bed," she tells me.

I smile, passing my bag to Dean, along with my coat.

He takes a seat in the chair on the other side as I sit and swing my legs up onto the bed. The head is slightly reclined, so I lean back, shuffling my bum to get comfier.

The nurse runs through my personal details before the sonographer walks into the room.

We say hello, and she looks at Dean, smiling over the rim of her glasses. Taking a seat, she rolls up my jumper, picks up a bottle of gel and gives it a shake. "Now this may feel a little bit cold." She squirts the gel onto my tummy then picks up a hand-held probe attached to the machine.

My heart's beating like a drum in my chest. I raise an arm behind my head, propping myself up so I can see the screen.

A black and white image appears. I can't really make out what she's looking at to start with, but as she slides the probe through the gel, our baby comes into view. "There we are," she says to the machine.

My eyes are full of water. I turn and look at Dean. His eyes are fixed at the screen, a small smile spread across his face. I see him blink, then without looking away, his hand simply drops to my free hand, giving it a squeeze. He doesn't have to say anything, I know.

The sonographer slides the slick probe over my tummy, clicking and pressing various buttons as she works. Neither me nor Dean have stopped smiling.

She talks us through how the baby's heart, lungs and brain all look healthy before she starts to take measurements. I don't know how long this part takes, but the stillness of the room starts to eat away at me, and my smile falters. Trying not to overthink why a silence has ensued, or the fact that the nurse is now watching the screen, I chance a look at Dean.

He winks at me before he mouths the words, 'it's okay' to me.

"Okay," the sonographer says, making me jump.

I turn to look at her, then the screen, then back to her. "*Is* everything okay?" I ask.

"Yes, everything is fine," I let go of the breath I held, "but," I hold it again, "the baby is measuring in a little under where we'd expect to see them at this stage."

I feel my face drop.

"Now this could be a number of things," she starts. "The baby could be a little further back in your uterus, although your bladder is nice and full so we can rule that out. Or, what's more likely, is that there's a problem with the placenta, a condition commonly known as pre-eclampsia."

My heart beats erratically. Dean's hand on mine suddenly tightens.

There's a problem?

"What does that mean?" Dean asks firmly.

"It means that there could be an insufficient blood supply to the placenta, which is restricting the growth of the foetus. Now, at this stage, the only way we can detect it for sure is to get a blood test."

"Okay," I say hesitantly.

"Lizzie," the sonographer says, turning on her stool to the nurse. "Could you pass me Miss Reed's file?" She holds out her hand as the nurse passes my file to her. Her eyes scan over my notes. "Okay, so I can see you have high blood-pressure, and protein was detected in your last urine sample. Did your GP explain what causes that to happen?"

"Yes," I answer.

My GP explained that age, weight and your first pregnancy are all common reasons why my blood pressure could be higher than usual.

"Good. Have you experienced any headaches or had difficulty breathing? Any nausea or vomiting. Issues with your vision?"

I nod my head slightly. "I have headaches, and more recently I've had a pain in my chest. I broke two ribs not too long ago, I assumed it could just be that?" I look at Dean who sits forward in the chair.

The sonographer nods her head in agreement as though she's heard what she needed to hear. She closes the file and requests I have a blood test.

The nurse leaves the room and closes the door behind her.

"And the baby? Is the baby okay?" Dean asks.

"The baby is fine; all the organs are functioning as they should be, I can assure you. With pre-eclampsia, we need to monitor the growth of the baby and ensure that the mother is well looked after." She looks at me. "I don't want you to worry." She lifts her hands up in front of her apologetically. "I know that is easy for me to say given what I do, but I can assure you, if it is in fact pre-eclampsia that is causing the baby not to grow as we'd like, then there are many ways in which you'll be looked after."

I smile, deflated, but I can't find any words.

"What about treatment?" Dean asks, standing by my side in my silence.

"Unfortunately, the only way to *treat* it, is to deliver the baby."

My eyes look to Dean.

"Obviously, we have a way to go until little one can be delivered, so in the meantime, it would mean regular blood pressure checks for any abnormal increases, regular urine samples as well as extra scans. We would also electronically check the baby's heart rate to ensure little one isn't getting distressed."

No treatment. That's what the morbid part of my brain clings on to. Not that actually my baby is healthy and that I'd be well looked after. Hot tears are prickling my eyes. I'm relieved that it's not something more serious, but I feel trepidation, because of course, something had to challenge us.

It couldn't just be simple.

"Now, there is one more matter," she says, angling the monitor towards her. "Are we wanting to know the sex of the baby today?"

I'd completely forgotten about finding out the sex.

Up until this morning, I was excited to know. Dean was happy to wait; confident he already knew it was a girl, but maybe now he'll *want* to know? Maybe now he'll feel as though he has no control over the situation? I mean, he really doesn't, but what can we do here? The only thing we can do right now, is find out if we're having a little boy, or a little girl.

Problem is, I no longer want to know. It seems irrelevant. My only thought now is making sure I do whatever I'm told to keep my baby healthy. "Um," I say hesitantly. I look up to Dean not knowing what to say.

His eyes are watching the monitor again; a still image that the sonographer had taken for her measurements, sits on the screen. "Can I see the baby again?"

With a smile, she applies more cool gel to my stomach. All three of us watch the monitor with wide open eyes. "There," she coos, pointing her index finger at the screen.

The baby wriggles and jerks in a funny little motion. I really can't help but smile. He or she looks so happy, not a care in the world just floating around inside me. A tiny arm hits out, knocking against their head. I laugh under my breath.

I watch the tiny feet kick and wiggle. I want to reach in and kiss them. I want to count each toe and hold them. Boy or girl, the love I feel in my bones won't change. It already reaches higher than the stars, pure and unfaded, not forced or faked.

Wiping the corner of my eye, I look up at Dean. He's not watching the screen. His green eyes are only watching me. Doing a double take, my tears instantly spill over.

His head drops to one side slightly, my hand that he held at the start, still firm in his grasp. "Babe."

I wipe away a tear tickling my chin, our eyes still connected to one another. A few seconds that feel like hours pass between us.

Dean looks to the sonographer. "Would you write down the sex of the baby for us?"

She smiles nodding her head, then slides her stool back to a drawer.

"You still don't want to know?" I ask, relieved it no longer matters, but anxious he might be just saying it to please me.

"I already know, babe."

I smile and rest my head back, breathing out the longest breath. My bottom lip wobbles.

Dean's lips push to mine, and I'm so grateful that he knew what I'd want.

"Here." The lady holds out a folded piece of paper.

Dean pulls away from me and takes it, thanking her. He pulls out his wallet from the back pocket of his jeans, then tucks the paper away before putting his wallet back. "I'll print you some pictures for you to keep. Take a seat in the waiting room. You'll be called for your blood test once the nurse is free."

"Thank you," I say.

She tears the strip of photos from the machine and hands it to me.

I smile and hold them tight as Dean walks to the door, holding it open.

As we wait, Dean snakes his arm around me, tucking me in close. "You, okay?" he asks.

"I will be," I say hesitantly. "Won't I?"

He lets out a small breath with a smile. "I know you will. You happen to be the toughest woman I know, remember?" His hand squeezes me tighter. "Plus, you have me."

"I know." I look down at the photos in in my hand, my thumb lightly caressing the image. When I look up, I see Dean's lips are pinched, his eyes narrow. "And you've got me."

"Mads—"

"—No. Please, don't make this all about me. Remember, I know what's going on up here." I tap my finger gently to his head.

He smiles then lightly kisses my forehead. I know he'll be worrying like I am. He knew something was coming—a change of sorts. His lips stay close to my head as he speaks. "Babe, I'll be fine. There's nothing I can do except be there when you need me. Just like always."

"I know," I whisper, completely understanding that he's helpless in this situation. "Just don't bury it. Don't tell me you're okay when secretly, you're probably standing at the edge."

When we look at one another, we both know that's exactly where he is.

Rubbing his face with his hand, he lifts his arm from around me, leaning forward to rest his elbows on his knees. He brushes his hands through his hair as he exhales.

The world sits on his shoulders, yet he's no longer alone. I can share the load where others can't. I watch him, grateful that he's about to talk about whatever he's thinking.

"When I met you," he says, "it didn't matter how close to the edge my demons dragged me." My arm curls around him, and he looks at the gesture, his lip pulling in one corner as he half smiles. "I knew you'd be my parachute. I knew that no matter how hard they pushed, or how great the fall would be, you'd be the one to save me." Turning his head, he looks back to me, his hands linked together in front of him. "Mads I…" He trails off.

"Hey," I whisper, leaning forward, pushing the palm of my hand to his chest.

He turns his body to me, and I feel his heart suddenly racing under my touch.

"We're in this together, okay?" I feel my eyes swell as our gazes lock.

"I know, I just… I want you to know that, as long as you keep loving me and accepting my life, I'll keep fighting for it." Green eyes dance between mine.

"Dean," my voice all but cracks.

He pulls me in close again. "We will get through all of this," he whispers into my hair.

I can't help but wonder if he's strictly talking about the baby or implying something more to do with the club? Just when I think he's going to say more, a nurse calls my name to go through.

Dean stands and holds out his hand for me.

He's here, and no matter what happens next, no matter where we're taken, I have to trust that we'll get through.

CHAPTER SEVEN

MADISON

Pre-eclampsia was confirmed four days later. That was two weeks ago. I've been told it affects about five percent of pregnant women, and if left untreated, can be life threatening. I've definitely had more abdominal pain, and I'm very aware that my fingers appear more swollen than normal.

The doctor explained the causes and what I can do to help, but short-term, it appears that getting enough rest and exercising regularly will help the most.

Parking my car, I hear my phone ping from my bag.

VP: Sorry I was gone early this morning, babe. Went straight to the clubhouse after my run. Not sure what time I'll be home, but I'll message you later. Text me if you need me x

It's been hard not to let my mind race with everything that could go wrong. So far, I've managed to keep a positive frame of mind because together, Dean and I have remained strong.

He checks in at least twice a day to make sure me and his 'baby girl' are okay. I love how sure he is that it's a girl, to the point I've questioned whether he's secretly checked the tiny piece of paper still in his wallet. I still don't *need* to know, but he won't let me near it. He keeps that and the pictures on him at all times.

The thought that I gave him that happiness makes me smile.

Happiness or not though, the increased calls and more frequent late nights haven't gone unnoticed, plus his comment in the hospital. I know something's happening with the club. He hasn't told me anything yet, and I won't ask because I don't want to add to his stress, but something's up. Whatever business they're getting into, it's no doubt dangerous. I just hope he keeps talking to me.

I put my phone back in my bag and climb out of the car. The pain around my ribs doesn't go unnoticed as I close the door behind me. Standing straight, I hold my bump. Deep breath.

I walk up to the offices in the school and open my email once sat at my desk.

"Tea?" Eva shouts from down the hall.

"Please," I reply with a smile.

As I take out my work things, I watch Eva go around asking who else want's a brew. It's not her job, but it's something she's done since she started a few months ago.

Twenty emails sit in my inbox since I last logged on. Trolling through the usual jargon of staffing updates and the minutes from Friday's meeting, I stop at an email with a subject field which makes my heart nearly stop.

Subject: Pupil update – Lauren Gibson
PUPIL UPDATE

Further to our last email, Under Section 444(1A) Education Act 1996, we believe an aggravated offence has been committed with relation to Lauren Gibson not attending her final year at school. At this time, due to lack of communication, the Local Authority will apply for an Education Supervision Order. A supervisor will be appointed for the child who will advise, assist, befriend, and give directions as to how the child and the parents can ensure the child is properly educated.

Please take into consideration additional measures that may need to be put in place to co-ordinate with facilitation of this.

A meeting has been scheduled for 0900 at the school. We have extended an invite to all parties involved.

You will receive an update with an action plan going forward.

Regards

What? What previous email? Heat rushes to my cheeks and my heart beats faster. I quickly scan through my inbox, not seeing an email from the same sender regarding Lauren.

Jumping from my seat, I hot-foot it to Vivian's new office that's based with all of us at the school. What's going on? I haven't heard anything for months, now all of a sudden, I'm invited to a meeting presumably with her there... *tomorrow*?

Pushing the door handle, Vivian's office is locked. I peer through the glass to check she isn't sat at her PC. She isn't.

My shoulders slump as I let go of the door and walk back to my desk.

A meeting with *all parties.* Is Lauren coming to the school? If she is, I can't deny it hurts that she hasn't messaged me prior to let me know. I mean, she isn't *my* child, but she was *my* responsibility.

Scanning the email again, I read the part about an Education Supervisor. Someone who can 'befriend her and assist her in her education'. Was that not what I already did? It may be a different title, but ultimately, that was my job. I don't like the idea of someone else doing what I should be doing.

I'd promised Dean I wouldn't bombard her, and I kept that promise once I took the hint that she didn't want to talk to me. But before I can tell myself not to worry or overthink this, I pick up my mobile and hit call.

My hand's shaking as it rings. And rings. And cuts off. Looking up at the clock on my screen, it's only just after nine.

Maybe she's still asleep?

Don't overthink.

I text Vivian asking her what time she'll be in and wait for her reply, running my eyes once again through my emails. There definitely isn't another email about Lauren.

"One cup of tea, two sugars and oat milk, not cow's milk."

I take the cup from Eva's hand without saying anything.

"Everything alright?" she asks as she stands over me.

I quickly register how rude I'm being. "Everything's fine. Sorry. Thank you for the tea."

She shrugs with a smile. "No need to thank me." She turns to walk away to her desk.

"Hey, have you seen Vivian this morning?"

Eva sits behind her desk and places her mug on the coaster. "No, not yet. She did mention Friday about maybe being in later. Something to do with a staffing restructure."

Staffing restructure?

We're all relatively new, only Alex and Vivian were the original members of our team. I look around the office wondering what needs to be changed already. There are four desks. Mine, Eva's—formerly Alex's, Greg's, and Orla's. Work used to be more sporadic. Now, we share a base. It's much more practical and actually means I've made some new friends since Alex died.

Correction, since Dean killed him.

I stare off into the distance, my mind wandering.

By lunch, Vivian still isn't here, nor has she text me back. After my meeting this morning, I had sent her another message and asked her to call me ASAP. So, when I've still had no reply, I decide to just call her.

Without looking at my phone properly, I hit the call button whilst simultaneously trying to open my pasta salad. "Vivian?" I say when she answers.

There's a short silence. "I still prefer Daddy."

I sigh with a smile when I hear Dean's voice, realising my error. "Sorry, I didn't mean to call you."

"Don't apologise, babe."

I smile. "Okay. Hi," I say relaxing, my phone wedged between my ear and shoulder as I pop off the lid to my lunchbox with two hands, suddenly ravenous.

"You, okay?" Dean asks.

"I'm fine, just on lunch. How's your day?"

"Um, yeah, normal day at the office..."

The office? I lift my fork to my mouth taking a mouthful of food, when I swear I hear an agitated rustle in the background. "Dean?"

"Yeah, babe?"

"You sure you're, okay?"

"Never better," he says. "Listen, I have to price up a job this afternoon, then we have church later on, not sure how long it will take. You okay to sort food and I'll call on my way home?"

I roll my eyes, pinching my lips together. This will be another late night. "Is this how it's going to be now? Me, your little housewife, having your dinner on the table ready for when you get home?"

There's a pause. "I don't know, will it? I'm still waiting for you to say yes."

My eyes scrunch together at my poor choice of words. "Yeah well, either way, don't get used to it." I chuckle knowing that I'd love nothing more than to have exactly that.

The pictures my imagination paints of our family together, come into view. There's a dog chasing us as we walk hand in hand, Dean carrying our little girl in his other arm.

I hear him laugh at my sass then my phone beeps signalling an incoming call. It's Vivian. "Look, I have to go, call me later." I hang up before he can say anything. I've been waiting for her to call me back all morning.

"Madison," she says as I click the green button.

"Vivian, hi, where are you?" I blurt out.

"I'm on my way in now. Sorry, I should have called."

"Eva mentioned a restructure?" Unable to leave it until she's here, I realise I'm putting her on the spot.

"God, shit news travels fast. Head office want us thinned out already. I've been arguing our case, but considering we're a new team, we're the easiest cohort to go."

Shit. "But being the newest, surely we're allowed more time to see what impact we're actually having on the education of the children we work with?"

She huffs sounding out of breath, or maybe she's just as pissed off as I now am? "Exactly. Look, I'm ten minutes away, get the kettle on and we can catch up before our actual meeting."

Leaving work, I'm completely caught up and equally shattered. Today's afternoon meeting was long but ultimately simple; our team might be axed, so we need to prove we're worthy of our roles. The niggle in the back of my mind telling me that I'm not, was suppressed the entire time I had to sit there and listen to the bullshit story of why Lauren hadn't attended school for the past three months.

Officially, school have been told by her 'guardian'—her worthless piece of shit uncle who used her and pawned her for his own gains—that a voluntary written agreement was made between the school's governing body and him... meaning, he will make sure she attends school.

Unofficially, I know she hasn't seen him since she went off grid. No one has, and after how she was treated, she wouldn't go back to him. I just know it.

So, he's lying. Every part of me wants to drive to her house and have it out with him because now I'm pissed off that my job could be axed, and I also feel sick where my tummy keeps somersaulting with nerves.

My colleagues' eyes burned holes through me when we discussed Lauren and this apparent meeting none of us knew about until this morning. It's shambolic if you ask me, but I do feel emotional that I could get to see her.

What would I say? Would she talk to me? Would she even come?

I unlock my car and slide onto my seat. Tipping my head back, I let my eyes close as I think. I used to drive around where she lived when she first left. If she's expected tomorrow, she could be staying somewhere local. If I know her well enough, she wouldn't go back to her uncle's place, she's more likely to be staying with friends.

Does she have friends? She could have been sleeping rough this whole time? The thought kills me. It's unlikely I'd find her by simply driving around, but it's not impossible that word wouldn't spread if I started asking about her.

Pulling out my phone, I open a message to Dean to see if he'll help me with what I've got planned. As I type, I see him already typing to me.

VP: Taking longer than expected. Don't wait up x

My eyes close again, and I let out a sigh. What is going on with him lately?

Looking at the clock on my dashboard, it's a little after five in the afternoon. He said don't wait up, which means I have time to do what I've got planned. I'll just have to do it alone. Even though I'm exhausted, I don't want to wait around. I've got to do something. I didn't protect Lauren well enough first-time around. I won't make the same mistake twice.

CHAPTER EIGHT

DEAN

"Alright, alright, you've made your point!"

"Clearly, I haven't. You haven't given me a name or a location. So, what's it going to be, cunt? Tell us who you're working with, or do I cut off the other one?"

The man I don't know hangs from a suspension cable looped over a beam above us, his left ear pouring with red. I watch as he tries his hardest not to panic, but even I can see the veins in his neck pulsing from where I sit.

He's scared.

I peer at Travis sat to my left, giving him a knowing look. This is Vincent's way of showing us what he's capable of.

"I said I don't know anything!" the man cries once more.

"Stop fucking lying!" Vincent's man shouts in the man's face, his spit flying through the air.

It's clear what's going on here.

We came for our sit down with Vincent, only to walk in on a butchering session. It doesn't bother me what they're doing. It's the fact they dragged us to a remote location for the sit down that makes the hairs on the back of my neck stand tall.

I'm not naïve though, I know he doesn't fully trust us after they received that package. I took precautions when they suggested this place. It may only be me and Travis in this run-down barn located one mile from the nearest road, but my men are close by if things turn sour.

"I don't think he knows anything," I comment. I sit back in my chair, pulling my smokes from my pocket, thoroughly bored. We've been here thirty minutes but the hanging man isn't speaking.

The butcher looks at me, pissed off with my sarcasm. "He knows something," he starts, as he turns to the table lined with various implements designed for making people talk.

I light my smoke as he picks up a Kershaw knife from the table. "Look at him and tell me he doesn't look a man who's keeping secrets."

The man's eyes dart to me, and I hold his gaze before speaking. His arms are lifted high above his head with thick rope, the colour drained from them. "Are you keeping secrets?" I ask him.

He shakes his head, causing more blood to spurt and run down his bare chest.

Lifting my smoke to my mouth, I inhale then blow out a long breath, never taking my eyes off the man.

He's sweating, trembling with fear. His eyes stay glued to mine, until they dart to the left momentarily.

I sigh. This is why Vincent chose here. It's a test.

Scratching my head, I take another inhale before I slowly stand to my feet. The butcher watches me walk to the table, seeing I've cottoned on to what they want. "I asked you a question," I say, eyeing a tool I like the look of. I pick it up to inspect it, twirling the medieval looking contraption between my fingers. He doesn't answer.

Knowing the hanging man's watching my every move, I take another inhale of my smoke, then turn, leaning back against the table. "If silence is what you like, I guess I should use this instead."

Flicking my smoke to the dirt floor, I step on it, twisting my foot. I grab my tool of choice and walk towards him.

He doesn't protest this time, but his arms wriggle, and the beam above him creaks as he writhes.

"Open wide." Grabbing his jaw, I force his mouth open and ram the contraption past his lips.

He struggles against me, but eventually I manage to pinch his tongue in between the clamps. "Shit, you made that harder than I thought," I say smirking, blowing out a breath after our minor wrestle. "Now, you've been asked a question." I don't like the idea of being tested, but this needs to be done.

He mumbles something inaudible.

I look at Travis still sat in his chair. "You get any of that?"

Travis shakes his head. "Afraid I don't speak cunt."

I look back at the man whose tongue I have stretched out of his mouth. "He doesn't speak cunt," I say mockingly.

The man mumbles again, and because I suspect Vincent's somewhere watching my every move, I decide to show him how much of a threat I can be.

Just as I'm about to slice off the man's tongue, I'm interrupted by my phone. Reaching into my pocket with my other hand, I grab it seeing the name on the screen.

"Vivian," Mads answers.

I smile. "I still prefer Daddy."

"Sorry, I didn't mean to call you."

I look at the man who's now drooling, his saliva dripping, mixing with his blood on his chest. "Don't apologise, babe," I say, realising my girl just saved him his tongue.

"Okay. Hi," she replies.

"You, okay?" I quickly flick a look to the butcher who shrugs his shoulders wondering what the fuck I'm doing.

"I'm fine, just on lunch. How's your day?"

"Um, yeah, normal day at the office..." My eyes scan the

scene before me. I realise Mads' version of a *normal* day at the office couldn't be any further away from what I'm doing right now.

My pause has the man in front of me fighting against the ropes. He moans as they undoubtedly cut into his wrists.

I tighten the clamp.

"Dean?" Mads asks.

Can she tell what I'm doing? "Yeah, babe?"

"You sure you're, okay?"

I am now, I think to myself. "Never better," I say, before lying to the one person I should never lie to. She knows my life's far from fucking rainbows and unicorns, but I won't add to her stress by letting her know what's really going on. "Listen, I have to price up a job this afternoon, then we have church later on, not sure how long it will take. You okay to sort food and I'll call on my way home?"

Mads pauses this time. She's not stupid. She knows something isn't right. "Is this how it's going to be now? Me, your little housewife, having your dinner on the table ready for when you get home?"

My eyes widen a little surprised. I've all but forgotten about the prick in front of me when she mentions being my wife. "I don't know, will it? I'm still waiting for you to say yes."

She sighs. "Yeah well, either way, don't get used to it."

I then chuckle. Maybe she's coming round to the idea?

Just as I go to say bye, her phone beeps with an incoming call. "Look, I have to go, call me later," she quickly says, before hanging up on me.

I huff, surprised she ended the call so quickly, but given the circumstances, I let it slide. "Where was I?" I say out loud.

That's right, Vincent's test. A test to see if I'll end the guy's life. If I don't, he'll assume the Rippers left the threat. If I do, it goes someway to proving we didn't. "Last chance, otherwise I'll let the butcher here cut you open with a *spoon*." I emphasise the last word with a nod in the butcher's direction. "At least my way, you'll never see it coming."

He drools some more, and because my patience with this whole situation is starting to wear thin, I twist the clamp, stretching the muscle further out from his mouth.

He squeals like a pig giving birth, then with eyes soaked from his silent tears, he nods his head, submitting.

Releasing the clamp, his limp tongue swings by his chin. "That looks painful," I say, dipping my head towards him.

I hear Travis huff under his breath.

The man grumbles, and I just catch the word 'unknown'. "What's unknown?" I ask, leaning forward as if that will enable me to hear him better.

He mumbles again, lapping his tongue in and out past his presumably numb lips. "We don't know who…"

His body sags, exhausted. "You don't know who, what?"

He sucks in spit, his head hanging low. "We're… given instructions, then… released," he says.

Released? *From where?*

When he doesn't say anymore, I let out a huff then scrunch my fingers in his hair, yanking his head back to look at me. His eyes are closed, but his throat wobbles underneath a tattoo of a clock with no hands. He's served time inside. Is that where he was released from? "Who gives you instructions?"

He lets out a sob when I let him go. "Please, don't kill…" he doesn't finish his sentence.

Fuck's sake. "Do they know Rippers are working with Sodom Saviours?" I ask it matter-of-factly, but the fact of the matter is, this guy isn't going to speak anymore.

He has an ear missing and various openings across his arms and torso, courtesy of the butcher. His head is flopped to his chest. He's already given up.

I wait but he doesn't respond. "Fine." Turning back to the table, I spot Travis shift in his seat. I don't look at him this time. It's been a while since I did this, but I know what I have to do. And so does he.

Grabbing the smallest knife, I place the clamp on the table, then turn and walk back to the man. I lift his chin with my left hand, placing my right one behind his neck.

When his eyes finally meet mine, I quickly pull my right hand towards me, nicking the carotid artery on the left side of his neck.

His body convulses before he even registers what I've done, the blood supply to his brain quickly spurting from him.

"I hope it was worth it," I whisper.

His body then slumps over a blood puddle.

I turn around and spot Vincent stood at the entrance to the barn. "Nice of you finally join us," I say, wiping the hanging man's blood from my hand onto his shirt, the sound of his blood still slapping the ground behind me.

"I was enjoying the show," he says, confirming what I knew already. He'd been watching the entire thing waiting to see how I handled it. "But you're right, now that I'm here, let's talk." He turns, directing Travis and I through the entrance.

We follow him and come to a stop by our bikes out front. "Did I pass?" I ask, lighting a smoke as I look back inside the barn seeing the butcher unhook the man I just killed.

Travis holds out his hand for my smokes.

I place them in his palm.

Vincent lets out a mocking laugh. "On this occasion, yes," he says rubbing the back of his neck. I'm guessing he's surprised I did it.

"On this occasion?" I question. He doesn't answer. "Vince, let me be really fucking clear for a minute." I pause drawing from my smoke, blowing it up in the air. "Rippers didn't send that package. You have no reason to test us."

He shrugs his shoulders as Travis perches on the seat of his bike. "Like it or not, I needed to make sure you weren't double crossing me."

I balk. "Double crossing you? We're about to go into business with you."

"Business you don't want," he quickly replies. When he sees I'm not going to respond, he slightly lowers his head as he continues. "We knew he was the one who left the threat."

I raise my eyebrows higher, silently asking him for more details.

He sighs. "Security camera picked him up leaving it out front."

"Do you have any idea who sent him?" Travis asks.

"No," he says flatly. I study his face—so does Travis, trying to gauge if he's lying. "We don't know who ordered the threat or why, but the timing before we go into business is suspicious."

Agreed.

"He said, '*we're* given instructions'. Suggests there might be more," Travis points out.

Vincent's eyes flit between us both. "We need to work out where these men will come from then, before a threat turns into the real fucking thing and someone ends up dying. We have a huge deal to lock down. We need this done." Vincent speaks so flatly, but it's true.

But if he'd actually been in the barn or cut the man up for answers himself, he would have seen the tattoo I saw and know that this man was released from prison purposely to make a threat. I go to mention it but hold back, thinking better of it.

"We'll look into it," I say instead. I see Travis' eyes look at me sharpish. I give him a nod signalling we're leaving. "Have your men look into it. See what we both come up with."

After an afternoon of work, we pull up at the clubhouse just after

8pm. Placing my helmet on the bars, I run my hand through my hair, then look down at my hands and my clothes. There's blood splattered on the toes of my boots; crimson lined under the edge of my nails.

"You alright?" Travis asks.

I look up and put my hands in my pockets.

Wiping the top of his bald head, he then puts on his hat, and we walk to the door. "Yeah, bud, I'm fine," I reply.

Travis stops in his tracks. "I'm not convinced."

I stop, my hand pausing before pushing the door open. "What makes you say that?"

He sniffs then scratches at his beard. "Switched to the old you pretty quick earlier."

That's why he huffed back at the barn? "Meaning…?"

"Meaning, I've not witnessed that old version of you for a while now."

Right. Since I've been with Mads. There's silence. "*And…*?" Fuck, is he going to make me drag his point out of him?

"And don't forget who you are now, that's all I'm saying."

I think on that for a second as I turn to look at him properly. "How do you suppose I do my job—as your leader, if I don't go back to that?"

"As my *leader,*" he starts with a lightness to his voice. He's not trying to piss me off. "You're fucking ruthless and doing a stellar job of filling them boots you've stepped into. But as my mate, I like the new version of you. The one that gives a shit whether he'll see tomorrow."

I look down, not finding any words. All I do is pat his back and offer up a smile.

Travis slaps mine, understanding that now Jack's gone, he *is* my only voice of reason besides Mads.

Pushing open the door, both of us freeze. *Holy Shit.* "What was that you were saying about not forgetting who you are?"

CHAPTER NINE

TRAVIS

"Give me your gun." I look at Dean who's frozen on the spot. I nudge him without looking at him. "Dean, your gun. Fucking give it to me, now."

Eventually, he drags his eyes off the one person who's capable of bringing out the worst in me. *Fuck's sake, I'll get it myself then.* I push my hand to where I know he's carrying it.

"What the fuck, Travis?" Dean says sharply, knocking my hand away. "Don't be a dick."

"Don't be a dick? Don't be a *dick?*" My voice keeps getting higher and louder. He must have forgotten the past. "Gun. Now," I say more sternly.

Dean's eyes raise a little surprised by my reaction.

I hold my hand out, deadly serious.

"Fuuuck," he says, suddenly grinning.

"I will shoot you too."

"And you tried lecturing me not thirty seconds ago."

"*Gun.*"

His eyes look to the person with their back to us, sat at the bar. I know it's her without having to see her fucking face. That goddamn face. "We don't shoot women," he says mocking me.

"That aint no woman. That's just an angry, pissed off living nightmare."

"And just to clarify, you're *not* angry or pissed off right now?"

I snap my hand back, clocking him on the chest with my elbow. Dick.

He grimaces, but he's still fucking smirking, like I'm not fucking serious. Fine. I'll sneak up on her. Choke her from behind.

As I turn to my prey, Dean puts his body between me and *her*. The men and women in the clubhouse are starting to notice the two of us acting weird by the entrance. If he'd just fucking move, I could shoot her and be done with this shit. Right. Fucking. Now.

"Wait," Dean says in a rush. "Stop and think for a second."

"Think about what? Eh? I told her never to come back here." I push forward again, trying to get past him.

"Hang on!" he barks trying to keep his voice low but turning a few more heads our way. I notice *she* doesn't once turn around. Bitch. "Just hear me out quick..." When I don't reply, that's his cue to hurry this the fuck along. "How it ended with you two—"

"—what, Dean?"

"Don't you think she must have a pretty good reason to actually be here?" His hands tighten on my arm. It's cute if he thinks that'll stop me. My leader or not, this woman made the wrong fucking choice walking back into this clubhouse without any warning.

I stride past him, pushing him out of my way.

"Mollie!" he shouts, getting her attention before I can murder her.

Traitorous, cunt.

My feet are hammering the ground when Mollie swings around on the stool she's sat on. Her eyes instantly lock with mine.

As if flicking the off switch, my feet fucking slow to a stop.

Even after eleven years, she still has that fucking superpower of hers.

"Dean," Mollie says, acknowledging him, but never looking away from me. Her voice trails off like a piece of silk ribbon drifting through the wind.

My dick is as traitorous as my president who's made his way to my side. I feel Dean's eyes look between the two of us.

I'm stood over her, eyes locked, my face held tight and scrunched. "My doll rears her evil head," I spit through gritted teeth.

"Leave it, Travis," Dean says.

I'm an inch away from her and the woman still hasn't flinched or moved. Until she stands, and I'm forced to step back.

That'll be the last time I move to accommodate her.

"You know I hate it when you call me that."

I smile like a sadistic prick. "That's why I love it. *Baby Doll.*"

Mollie scowls at me, and again my dick twitches. "You always were an arsehole, Travis. Time doesn't seem to have done you any favours."

"And time seems to have done you *all* the favours," I say as if suggesting it hasn't. *But* looking her body up and down, time has served her very well. Even if I hate to admit it.

Her long, tanned legs are on show. Her black, *tight*, pencil skirt sits just above her knees and she's wearing a shirt unbuttoned just enough, I can see the edge of her bra. If I didn't want to kill her, I'd think that shirt would look good on my floor, me stood behind her, my dick buried balls deep in her pussy.

No. This woman has taken up too much space in my head over the years. She ruined my life all those years ago. I won't let her do that again. "Time away from you brought me success. Something you'll never have to worry about," she says venomously.

"Ouch, Baby Doll. That meant to hurt me?"

"No, but this is." Before I know what's fucking happening, stars are floating around my head. The stupid bitch punched me.

Now she dies.

"Fucking hell, Mollie!" Dean shouts, as he grabs me *again* and pulls me back.

"Let me at her!" I yell, reaching for her.

Mollie cradles her wrist as though it hurt her hitting me. Good. I hope she fucking broke every bone in her hand.

"I'm not scared of you, Travis," she says. "Let him go, Dean. Let him *try* to hurt me."

Oh, she's not changed one iota. "Still think you can take me, Baby Doll?"

"Enough!" Dean barks, making Mollie and I stop. "Jesus, you two are giving me a fucking headache."

My chest rises and falls quickly. Admittedly, my jaw aches too.

Mollie straightens her shirt, tugging the end of her sleeve where it's ridden up after hitting me.

"Why are you here?" Dean asks her.

Her eyes narrow at me before she turns her back on us. Reaching into a black office bag, she pulls out a large file, her cheeks still puffing out in annoyance. She turns, holding it out for Dean to take.

He looks at me pointedly before letting his hold on me go.

"What?" I ask, knowing full well he's making sure I won't react.

"What is this?" Dean asks.

I move toward a stool and sit myself down. Dean steps forward, and I hold my hands up, surrendering. For now.

"The past. That's what that is." Mollie reaches back into her bag, pulling out another file. "And this," she turns, holding it out, "is your future."

I sit up straight.

Dean's eyes trace over the file.

There's a silence as we watch Dean open it. He looks at

something, then peers to Mollie, keeping his head down. "Where did this come from?"

I wonder what he's looking at as Mollie answers, "Initially, police deemed the fire at the mill on Dewsbury Road to be arson."

Shit. If Mollie knows about the fire, then this is bad.

"CCTV footage captured a black van approaching just after 9pm."

My van. Double shit.

"There were no links between the two, but three weeks ago, a local charity wanting to clean up the community offered to help start the clean-up procedure. One of them found a bullet shell, turned it in to local police the same day."

In my chest, my heart starts thumping. I can feel my skin igniting, prickling with anger. Dean doesn't look at me. If he does, I'll be knocking him out for what he did. His stupid decision to take on five Sodom Saviours left Beats and I bailing him out of that place, in a way we didn't want to do. It was sloppy. We didn't have time to clean up properly.

"And I'm guessing now they're looking into why the van was there?" Dean says.

Mollie nods in response to Dean's question. "The investigation has officially reopened." She leans forward, turning over the top piece of paper, showing Dean something else. "This image shows one person in the passenger side window," her eyes shoot to me, all condescending as shit, "even though we know more people were there."

I huff and smirk at her.

Dean interjects before we start going at each other again. "What does this mean? Why are you showing me this?" he asks.

I stand scowling at Mollie; her eyes are burning into mine. Snatching the file from Dean's hands, I look at the image so that I don't have to look at that face.

The picture's blurry. The image of my van distorted. My reg

—or the one we used that day—not visible. "Yeah, why show him?" I ask, shrugging my shoulders. "Nothing here to suggest this was us."

Mollie's eyebrows raise and she lets out a sarcastic snort, yet again, mocking me and my question. "Because he is a *criminal*," I hate the way she emphasises the word, "and has done it before."

"That was over ten years ago. I thought your dad wiped that clean?" Dean asks her.

Mollie drops her head. "Crown Prosecution Service do not care. They're pushing this. They suspect Rippers MC are involved and have proof that you like to burn shit. You need to stay out of trouble and find yourself someone to defend you if they choose to take you to court."

"On what charge?"

Dean shifts on his feet as Mollie ignorantly starts packing up her things. "Right now, they're working out why a bullet has shown up in a wreckage and trying to clear up that image. They clear it, or find any other morsel of evidence, anything that suggests a person—or people—were in that building when it went down, then you're looking at manslaughter. Or murder, even."

"A murder charge?" Dean asks questioningly. I can hear the panic in his tone, even though his face isn't showing it.

"Yes, a murder charge. They know people are missing. If there's any evidence someone died in there, you don't stand a chance." She swings on her jacket, shaking her arms and adjusting the collar. "Tell me, how many did you kill?"

Dean looks at me.

I give him a sharp look. "Does it matter?" I snap.

Mollie doesn't look at me as she speaks. "Trust you not to give a shit about other people."

I see Dean roll his eyes as he rubs his face with his hand. "So, what do I do?" he asks.

"Find someone to defend you."

Dean eyes me again. "What, like a criminal defence solicitor?" His tone is sarcastic enough to make Mollie look at me before she looks back to him.

"Yeah, one of those."

"I already have one."

As she swings her bag strap over her shoulder, Mollie says, "What you *have* is very little time before the police barge through that door and arrest you." She points to the entrance. "They're hungry, Dean. Once they have what they're looking for, their next stop is here."

Mollie walks past Dean, and I move in the same direction, stopping next to him.

"Why the heads up?" Dean shouts, making her stop and turn to us.

I swear I hear her sigh. Her eyes stay fixed on Dean, the brown holes getting deeper. It looks like she's remorseful, but I know better. "Because, although I despise the company you keep with every fibre of my being," point proven, "you and I were friends. I made a promise that night," she looks down quickly, "that if you needed my help staying out of trouble, you'd have it." My heart fucking stops dead when she mentions that night. The night everything changed for me. And her. "Consider my warning as me holding up my end."

I'm hurting, but I can't help myself. "So you're done? We don't need to see you again?"

"Travis," Dean snaps. He turns to her. "Mollie, I'm going to need you, if what you're saying is true."

She sighs for sure this time. "It is. I give you a week. And that's being hopeful." Turning, she starts walking away.

"I have a kid on the way, Mols."

I see her body coil, mirroring my own. Mollie doesn't turn around. Instead, she tightens her grip on her things and leaves.

I shift on my feet, but she's gone. As soon as that door closes, a weight is lifted, before a barrage of baggage tumbles on top of me. I'm filled with remorse. Relief. And then an incomprehensible amount of anger.

Turning to look at Dean, I'm just about ready to tear him to shreds for mentioning he's having a kid to her. He fucking knows the significance of it, yet he still threw it out there.

Stood face to face, fists clenched, he just stares at me. Still. I quickly realise I have to bury whatever it is that's about to rip out from me before I end up doing something I'll later regret.

Taking a breath, I swallow, my hand cupping the back of my neck. Fuck, this is harder than I thought. "What do you need?" I ask him, my words forced from my mouth. It's the best I've got.

He looks up, and I know the answer.

"Go. I'll call Sonny. He might still be in contact with that paralegal officer. Worth checking if what she's saying holds any weight."

Dean rubs his face. "She wouldn't have risked seeing you if it didn't."

My fists uncurl. He has a point. Like he wouldn't have risked mentioning having a kid if it didn't hold any significance.

"Call him, see what he says. I'll call Vincent, let him know we have complications our end. With any fucking luck, nothing else will come up before we sit down with Costa."

I nod my head at his instruction.

Blowing out my cheeks, I realise I need to let off some steam. When did everything get more serious? There's sweet fuck all we can do but get ready; prepare ourselves for what's to come. I need Dean on top form—need the mate who deserves to wear that fucking president patch after all the shit he's been through and done for this club.

Out the corner of my eye, I notice one of the girls who works here looking at me with hungry eyes. She'll do. "It'll be alright," I say, trying to reassure myself as much as him.

The way he looks at me and doesn't say anything, I hope I'm right.

Once Dean's gone, I go in search of Stacey. She's young, blonde, fake tits, fake hair, fake life. Fake. Which makes what I'm about to do so much easier. It's not real. There's no connection. Nothing more than on demand pussy. Not all the girls are like this, most work the bar and keep things ticking over. But she is.

She steps out of the kitchen with Red, both girls stopping at the entrance. Lifting one arm, she hangs herself off the door frame. She's confident, which I like, but not on her. "Looking for me?" she purrs, pushing herself forward and into my personal space.

My mind sees Mollie. "Get in there." I nod towards the clubhouse bedroom.

She steps forwards, trailing her hand across my front as she goes, the smile on her face one of complete satisfaction.

"You joining?" I'm going to need a bigger distraction.

"No," Red answers shyly, unlike her. Her loss. I don't dip my dick where there's drama anyway.

I turn and walk into the bedroom, locking the door behind me.

"I'm glad I caught your eye," Stacey purrs, standing with her weight on one foot, her short dress sat high on her hips. "You look stressed, baby."

She has no idea. Seeing Mollie again has wrecked my head. Walking forward, I stand directly in front of her, my size compared to hers completely dominating. Her breath hitches when I look down at her. "Are you going to help me unwind?"

Chest rising and falling quickly, Stacey bites her lip looking up at me through her lashes. "In any way you want," she says, like the greedy little whore I know she is.

I push her to the bed, dropping her to her arse.

She smiles, clearly turned on by my complete lack of fucks for her. It's messed up. But it's what I need right now.

I spin her, pushing her body down the bed, her head hanging off the edge, her hair trailing down the side. "Pull up your dress."

She does so without any hesitation, then begins slipping her thong down her hips. She's trying to be seductive, swaying her hips side to side. It's doing nothing for me.

"Open," I tell her, tapping my finger to her upside-down painted lips.

Her lips part, her cheeks hollowing as she lies waiting for me to fill her mouth. And fill it I will.

Yanking at the fly of my jeans, I free my dick, pushing it past her lips. I growl, and she gags, choking when I hit the back of her throat.

She then parts her legs, her fingers circling her clit in a frenzy. She's loving every minute of it.

Surging on, I power my hips, repeatedly thrusting myself deeper down her throat. I take her air, wrapping a hand around her neck as I watch her lipstick mix with her saliva on my dick.

That's when her fingers slip inside her cunt, fucking herself with purpose.

When her moans get louder, I withdraw, put off by her over the top efforts to turn me on. "On your knees."

Stacey wipes the spit off her chin, moving in front of me as I make sure I'm protected. I then wrap my fingers around my shaft, stroking myself a couple of times until I'm long and hard.

I rest the tip of my dick at her entrance.

"Travis," she moans, looking back at me over her shoulder.

I wrap my hand around her fake hair, making sure I'm holding on tight. I pull her head back, her chin now facing the sky where she can't look at me.

"Please, fuck me hard, baby!" She pants trying to push back against my dick.

The tip spreads her lips, and I look down, watching as her pussy sucks me in.

Grabbing the front of her dress, I yank it down, jolting her as I free her fake tits. I pinch one of her nipples between my fingers, clamping down hard. "Stop talking." I don't need her to talk or to beg me. I need to fuck her until my mind is clear. Clear and free from the one person I never thought I'd see again.

She moans when I pinch again, trying hard not to make a sound.

Releasing her nipple, I grab Stacey's hip and ram myself home, her arse now flush with my base.

Her back curls as she struggles to take all of me, but she isn't going anywhere.

Holding her steady, her hair still wrapped in my hand, I drive, pounding her until I feel my release edging closer.

Pleasure rises. The steady waves of my climax roll over me. Stacey's moans only encourage me to fuck her harder. I grab both her hips, sliding my dick in and out of her at force until my orgasm beckons me. With a grunt, I spill my load, momentarily free, holding myself deep inside.

She pulses around me, but I don't hang around to ask her how that was for her. I tug myself out, standing back as she struggles to breathe, letting me know. Rather than tell her to leave, I dispose of the condom, tossing it into the bin, then I walk out of the room without so much as a look back.

CHAPTER TEN

DEAN

I don't know what's worse. Living within the confines of my own head, fearing nothing but being alone. Or being free from some of my demons, having someone who loves me, yet fearing everything.

I'm on the precipice of having a life I never thought I deserved, yet I can't help wondering if it was just me, none of this would matter. Our enemies believing we threatened them, who'd care? Going to prison, who'd miss me?

Now? It all matters. Every damn thing comes with a consequence. Every decision I make will have a repercussion.

My ride home is steady, given the shit news from Mollie. I haven't seen her in almost eleven years. She and Travis were a thing a long time ago. Wild and crazy. When they split, it was the worst I've seen him. Judging how they picked up exactly where they left off, all tetchy and pissed off with each other, it's really fucking clear shit still runs deep between them.

I smirk at the thought of Travis having lady troubles as I round the bend onto my street.

Had I hung around for the beer he offered before I left, I would have missed the headlights on Mads' car turning off just as I straighten up. I pull up, dock my bike and kill the engine.

What the fuck? I said don't wait up assuming she'd be home

by five, like usual.

She climbs out of her car, her body wound tight. "Babe?" I say removing my helmet, hoping she'll explain why she's only just getting home.

"Hey," she says flippantly.

"*Hey?*" I question. "What's going on? Everything alright?" I can hear my voice on the edge of panic. I swear to God with each month that passes with her pregnancy, the more ridiculous I'm becoming.

"I'm fine," Mads says as if trying to reassure me, but I heard the wobble in her voice.

Walking to the door, we're both silent as I keep looking her up and down. We walk in, dropping our bags and my helmet. "Start talking."

Mads lifts her hands to her head, her shoulders slightly jumping up and down.

"Mads?" I walk straight to her and pull her into my arms. My hands hold her, one keeping her head against my chest, the other on her back as she sobs. "Babe, what happened?"

"Nothing. Nothing's happened."

I pull back, cupping her face to make her look at me. "Is it the baby?"

She shakes her head.

"Where've you been?" A lone tear drips to her cheek. I use my thumb to wipe it away.

"The baby's fine. It's Lauren," she says, her voice fractured. "She... she might be coming to the school tomorrow. I, had an email, telling me she would be there."

"Lauren?" I ask shocked.

Mads nods her head.

That is a surprise. I wonder if her uncle knows? "Okay, but how does an email make you this late getting home?"

Mads sniffs, and I let her face go. Drying her damp eyes, she looks at me, deflated.

"Tell me," I say softly.

"I," her voice unexpectedly cracks as she starts to speak.

I cup the side of her face, my fingers curling behind her ear and onto her neck. "Mads?" I encourage her to continue.

"I don't know what's the right thing to do... what if I'm a bad mum?" she blurts out, making my heart knock against my ribs.

It's clear that the notion of seeing Lauren has my girl questioning herself. But thinking she'll be a bad mum? Impossible. "Let me look at you," I say, and I brush the strands of hair stuck to her damp cheek behind her ear. "The night that Rocco died," my heart strains as Mads takes in a breath. "I watched you put your body in front of Lauren so that she didn't get hurt. I watched you shut your eyes and prepare yourself to take a bullet for a kid you owe nothing to."

She closes her eyes pushing out more tears. I can still picture Alex's hand shaking as he held up the gun and pointed it at her.

"I didn't know you were pregnant then, but when I think about it now... it tears my fucking insides apart, knowing you could have died, and I wouldn't have known you were carrying my child. Mads?"

Saying her name, I need her to look at me. But her eyes are clamped shut. When I say her name again, she sniffs back the emotion and swallows hard. Her eyes finally find mine. "Don't ever fucking question whether you'll be a good mum or not." As if needing to make sure she really hears what I'm saying, I move my hand to her neck, cupping her chin, rendering her unable to look away as I say, "Because you knew you were pregnant, and yet you were willing to sacrifice everything you've ever wanted, to ensure that a kid with her whole life ahead of her, survived."

The tears stream down her face but she keeps her eyes focused on me. "If that isn't being a good mum, or isn't someone who knows what the right thing to do is when the time comes, then the world is a far shittier, fucked up place than I thought."

My lips part as I take in air. My breath hitches. Wiping her cheek, I slide my hand behind her head and lower my mouth to hers. It's a hard kiss, one that's stealing her breath but is built on pure, overriding emotion.

Mads grabs my neck and deepens the kiss, before she pulls back, catching her breath. "I drove around trying to find her. I know I said I wouldn't do that again… but I just thought, maybe, if she is coming to school tomorrow, then maybe she would be close by. I thought I would find her."

My heart sinks at her words. They were dark days for Mads, the first few weeks after losing Rocco and more so, Lauren. Pulling her into my arms again, I hold her tighter. "I would have come with you," I whisper into her hair, then kiss the top of her head.

She sighs. "I was going to ask you to. But you were busy."

Fuck. My black heart twists and sinks. "I'm sorry," I say, because I really fucking am. She shouldn't be driving around at night, on her own, trying to right a wrong that's not even hers to right.

After a beat, something shifts between us. Mads pulls away, leaving me feeling lost. "What's going on with you?" she asks a little hesitantly.

I contemplate hitting her with it all; tell her all the grim truths. Then I look at her. My girl, carrying my child. "Nothing."

Mads smiles at me, which is weird because she should be pulling a Mollie and putting her fist through my face. "You're such a bad liar," she says, adding, "with me, anyway."

I look to the ground, then looking back up, I can't help but smile slightly.

"Is it bad?"

"Mads—" Shaking my head I go to tell her not to worry, but she cuts me off.

"—Dean."

On a sigh, I move to sit on the sofa, and she follows, doing the same. "Please tell me," she says.

How do I put this? With my brain scrambling, I reply, "Club's got a lot of business coming up. I might have to do things you won't like. But I need you to let me."

She stares at me, her face blank. "Like what?"

Mads moves closer, and I lift my arm for her to slide under. She rests her head on my chest, and I nestle down, pulling her body with mine. "Someone made a threat to the Saviours."

Mads instantly sits up, checking my expression. "Do you know who?"

I purse my lips shaking my head. "We know *who*, but he's no longer an issue. We just don't know who sent him."

The lead balloon I just dropped sucks in the four walls around us, the rawness of what I'm saying, suffocating. "Mads?"

Her body shrinks, deflating with sadness. "It's been a long time since we had a chat like this," she says flatly.

My head hits the back of the sofa. "I know." I let a moment pass. "I'm sorry."

Conversations like this with her seem few and far between now. She may love me the way I am, but she should be focusing on getting rest and growing our child, not carrying my load.

Looking up, Mads smiles, and it warms my centre. "So, who do you think it is, making threats?"

It's on the tip of my tongue to tell her about what I did, that I know whoever sent the hanging man found him in prison—the handless clock tattoo proving he'd served time inside. That and he admitted they were released to make threats. But what will make my girl happy, is the one thing I don't think I should do anymore. The darker things get, the less I should share with her. I've tried, I really have, and I would be lying if I didn't say this kills me to admit, but when push comes to shove, talking about things simply isn't going to help anyone.

Any demons I have left will devour her angels. There's not a chance on this earth I will let that happen whilst I'm breathing. My thumb strokes the side of her face. "I don't know."

Her fingers find mine on my lap. She twines them together, her grip letting me know she's aware I'm holding back. She doesn't push me though. "You'll find them."

I kiss the top of her head slowly, my lips lingering against her hair.

"Just like you'll find Lauren."

I let out a tired breath. So much is going on, I don't know where to start trying to find her. Last we knew she was staying in a youth hostel just outside of Lancashire.

My mind trails, and the thought of what Mollie said suddenly hits me like a punch to the gut. The thought of not being around for Mads, my baby, my brothers. It terrifies me. "No more driving around trying to find her. Promise me."

Mads gives a little nod. Tightening her grip on my hand, she looks up at me. Her eyes are starting to swim, but she doesn't cry. "Promise *me* something?" she says.

Moving my hand to the side of her face, my thumb lightly strokes her cheek. I dip my chin, agreeing.

"Promise me that, whatever comes next—whatever you think you have to do..." her hand moves to my chest, her palm flat against the rhythm of my heart's beat. She looks at her hand, then her eyes lock on hard to mine. "You'll come back to me when you're done."

Her breath hitches, and my throat clogs at the reality that in order to survive this together, my life may momentarily force us apart.

But I'll always come back to her.

I am nothing without her.

Sealing my lips to hers—because it's all I can do, I realise how fucking selfish I am, asking her to love me. Taking her love without giving her what she wants from me more than anything, which is to know my own fucking worth.

She pushes back against me, and before I know it, my hands are all over her, consuming her mind, her body. Her soul. I can't live my life without this woman. I'm greedy, pulling her body carefully to mine with an intensity that's loaded.

I taste her tears on my lips, and I open my eyes watching her, needing to make sure she's okay.

Mads moves her body with my hands guiding her. She's sitting over me, her legs straddling mine. Her hands cradle my cheeks, and I do the same, my fingers pulling her head to mine. "Promise me." Her voice is doused in lust, but more than anything, it's determination. Determination to hear me tell her that I won't slip back into my darkness.

Placing her hand on my heart again, she waits.

"I promise," I breathe.

After a moment she leans forward, touching her lips to mine. The soft kiss has me closing my eyes, trying to savour this. If what Mollie is saying is right and I'm soon to be a wanted man, these simple moments need to be tattooed on my brain. They need to scar me, need to cut me deep so that I never fucking forget that this woman is the woman who, when I thought my soul was sleeping somewhere, found it and brought me back to life.

Pulling her closer to me, I can't help but let my body consume her. Her hands grip me, mirroring my every move. We're losing ourselves in each other. I scramble to remove her clothes, pulling and tugging as I bare her body before me. I can't hide from what's inside and she fucking knows it.

Mads stands in a rush, undoing her jeans and pushing them to the floor.

I quickly undo mine, raising my hips just enough to push

them out of the way to free myself.

She moves her body back over mine, and I line myself up, looking at her—my eyes never leaving hers.

Her lips part, and I let out a moan when the tip of my cock pushes inside her. It steals her breath, but without stopping, she slides herself down me until she's completely full.

Neither of us move.

Allowing my eyes to close briefly, I savour the sensation of filling her. Fuck, there's no feeling like it. When I tear my eyes open, my hands worship her. From her legs to her hips, to her breasts, to her shoulders, her neck.

Mads throws her head back, and her hips involuntarily start to rock. It feels electrifying. There's no controlling my hands as they squeeze her skin, pulling her body closer to mine.

"Look at me."

She drags her head forward, her chin rolling to her chest at my command.

But those eyes. They close the second my hips raise and I push in deeper. "I need you to look at me, babe," I say, my voice husky and full of need.

When they eventually open, they lock with mine. I hate that I'm suddenly demanding she look at me, but I need to watch the moment I free her mind of any worry. Even if only for a moment, I need to know it's *me* freeing her.

Raising my hips, I push her up and it works.

Letting out a moan, she lifts her lashes to look at me, her lips parting as she takes me. Between the delicious rolls of her hips and my body lifting her higher, love catches us in this moment.

My tongue finds hers, and I hold her face as I suck and twist my way into her mouth. Her hips never stopping moving, our eyes never leaving each other's. "Mads," I finally breathe, knowing we're close but wanting this moment to last so much longer than it will if we don't stop. "Mads," I say again more urgently, gripping the tops of her arms.

With a sob, I feel her tighten around me, her body going rigid before she completely relaxes. She never stops watching me as she comes, tranquilly, her body taking what it needs from mine as she finds her release.

"I love you," I say. And I watch. Never allowing myself to miss a moment, I watch her unwind, wanting her to take more from me.

But her sobs haven't subsided. Her mind's not yet clear.

"Mads?"

She doesn't answer me. Her arms grip me tighter, her head burying into my neck as she continues to show upset. She's holding on to me like she knows. Like she fucking knows she has to.

I say her name one more time and when she still doesn't answer me, I lift my hips, raising her body, pushing her breasts in line with my face.

She whimpers when I take one of her nipples in my mouth and roll my tongue over the bud.

"VP." Her hoarse voice quivers and shakes.

I bare my teeth, looking up to her. Her head is back, and when my teeth bite down, I pull her hips towards me, driving into her at the same time. Her crying out spurs me on. I do it again.

"Jesus, VP!" she half screams, half cries.

My hands don't stop moving her, my teeth and my tongue don't stop. I make her fuck me, driving hard into her, rolling her on my cock.

She throws her head back, sinking her nails into me. "I… I'm…" She comes again, her body quivering before turning slack. Her hands on my shoulders flex as she rides out the final waves of pleasure.

My hands keep rolling her hips for her, and admittedly, I feel my own release edging closer.

Hot blows of her breath push out from her. "I love you," she breathes.

I smile, still moving her slowly. "I know."

She smiles and sits up straighter, her arms now around my neck forcing her breasts together. They're bigger. Fuller. And look impeccable before me.

Moving my hands, I begin a trail up her back, seeking and searching my way over her body. When I tickle the tips of my fingers over her shoulders, she shudders. I don't stop until I move down past her breasts, and I'm cupping her bump.

She places her hands on mine as she begins to raise her hips, readying herself to ride me to my release. "No, babe," I say, and she slowly comes to a stop.

"What is it?"

"Tonight's about you." My head hits the back of the sofa, my thumbs running light strokes on her bump. A little nudge can be felt, and we both look down. "I think I woke her up."

Mads smiles. "Let me make this about you, too." She raises her hips again, but my hands stop her.

I don't want this to be about me. "Not tonight."

Lifting her up easily, my cock still buried inside her, she holds on tight as I stand and push my lips to hers. "Let me do this?"

Scanning my face, she gives me a subtle nod, kissing me again as I walk us to our room. Once she's laid on the bed, I make her come again and again, until she's exhausted—her mind free—passed out on top of me.

The following morning, I wake at four-thirty, unable to sleep any longer. I send Vincent a quick message telling him we need to talk. Throwing on my running clothes and trainers, I then head out on my usual route.

The morning air is bitter. The coldness of it biting my lungs. The hood on my jumper is up. The only sound around is that of my feet hammering the pavement. The rhythmic thuds keep my head clear until I reach the castle at the top of the hill overlooking the city.

I stop and stretch, using the bench at the viewing spot to hold on to as I grip my ankle and pull my heel to my backside. Memories of Mum bringing me up here after picking me up from school, slowly seep into my mind.

This was our place. And now it's a safe space for me. A space where I can gain clarity.

I allow my mind to process what needs to be done, and when my phone rings, I realise I've sat down and almost forty-five minutes have passed. "Yep," I say, rubbing a cold hand over my face.

"Your message sounded ominous."

"That's because it is."

Vincent sighs. "What do you need to tell me?"

I bring him up to speed with Mollie. If I am to go away, I'll need protection inside. As much as it grinds every gear I have for it to be him, Vincent can ensure this.

He's condescending when he next speaks. "You sure have made my day at," he pauses to check the time, "half five in the morning, Dean."

"Can you make it happen or not?"

He stays quiet for a beat. I don't like asking for protection as much as he won't like giving it to me. "The Saint's currently residing in solitary, but I'll get word to him."

The Saint. Old friend of Vincent's. He runs things inside.

"Right."

"Anything else?" he asks.

I keep the fact I think the person who sent the threats came from inside to myself and hang up, putting my phone away.

Ten minutes later, I stand and feel my muscles have stiffened from the cold. I quickly stretch and decide to just run home. A depleted feeling swims through me, but I got the clarity I needed.

When I start my decent, a lone figure approaches. I slow to allow them through the gate. Their headphones are on their head, their attention clearly elsewhere. Usually, I don't see anyone out and about this early, and if I do, it's other runners. Not a kid.

Curiosity gets the better of me.

As the youngster pushes through the gate, I make an effort to say good morning. As the words slip past my lips though, they're suddenly lost.

CHAPTER ELEVEN

DEAN

Dragging the headphones off her head, she has a look of complete and utter surprise mixed with fear. Without a word, she dips her body under my now outstretched arm trying to stop her.

"Lauren!" I shout, but she's running hell for leather away from me. Her bag drops to the floor. Fuck, she's fast. I strip the hood off my head and follow her. Shouting her name again, she looks over her shoulder before picking up her pace.

I power my arms and drive my legs. When she takes a right, heading toward the trees, I know she has nowhere else to go. The tree line only circles back around. The little shit is nippy, but I can change tactics and cut her off on the other side.

Turning around, I head back up the hill, my heart motoring on. I reach the top and spot her bag that she dropped. Scooping it up as I run, I head to the gate and wait for her.

As my heart steadies and my lungs take in as much of the crisp air as possible, I feel the weight of the bag Lauren was carrying. Not noticing so much when running, I now can't ignore the pull of it in my hand. Again, my curiosity gets the better of me.

Slowly opening the relatively small but heavy backpack, I wonder if I'm stepping over a boundary? We haven't seen Lauren for so long—although we've caught glimpses of her—it's like she all but disappeared. I want to know how a fifteen-year-old survived without anyone.

I pull it open and peer inside. The smell that hits me is clearly body odour. The headiness of it makes me turn my head away for a second. When I look back, there are spare clothes in clear need of a wash, a book that's a little worn around the edges, her toothbrush, a roll-on deodorant. Has she been sleeping rough?

I suddenly hear the patter of feet getting closer as I spot a key in the bottom of her bag. I quickly grab it and shove it in my pocket, pretending to keep on examining the contents.

"Hey!" Lauren shouts. She aggressively stalks towards me, her body language screaming that she's ready to fight. "Don't go through my shit!"

"Lauren?" I question, but she barges me out of the way, ripping her belongings from my hands. I think about keeping my grip on them, but I let go.

She stuffs the contents back inside, her chest heaving up and down as she does.

I don't really know what to say, but as she tries to move past me as if she's leaving, I grab her arm and stop her. "Where are you going?"

"Get off of me!" she barks.

My grip tightens. "Not happening."

She struggles against me before she starts the theatrics. "Rape! Rape!" she cries.

I cringe before I find myself getting pissed off with her. "Stop," I tell her.

"Rape! Please, somebody help me!"

I pinch the bridge of my nose between my finger and thumb. "Lauren, stop. Not only is what you're saying totally fucking disgusting, but I hate to break it to you, no one else is around to hear you. So, you might as well call it a day."

She scans the area, noticing I'm right, but she still tugs her arm. "Urgh, let me go." She's persistent, I'll give her that.

"Why don't you talk to me?"

"I've got nothing to say to you. Where's Jay?"

Her brother? Her voice has changed. From what I remember, she was soft, gentle. Yes, she was troubled, but now it's different. It's hard around the edges. It's lined with something I recognise.

Survival. "Tell me where you've been."

"Tell me where Jay is," she demands once more.

"I don't know what you're talking about."

She jerks her arm, trying to get free. "Let me go, then I'll tell you where I've been."

I honestly think about it for a second, but the look in her eyes suggests she'll only run off again. "No can do. Talk."

"No."

Fuck's sake. We both stare, silently assessing each other. "Why'd you look scared?"

"What?" she says shocked. "I'm not scared."

"You looked it, when you realised it was me waiting by the gate."

"Don't flatter yourself. I was just... surprised, that's all."

I can't help but smirk at her fieriness. "You've toughened up in the time you've been hiding."

She scowls at me, narrowing her blue eyes. "Had no choice. Never know who's going to come after me or want me dead."

Come after her? Dead? "Why would *I* want that?"

Her eyes dance between mine. She's thinking. "Because of what I did." Her tone has flattened. Her face suddenly falls.

"You think I blame you for what happened?"

She stills. I can see the tears start to gloss her eyes.

I loosen my grip ever so slightly, but I don't let her go.

"You don't?"

"No, Lauren. I don't blame you. I am fucking surprised you decided to bolt once Travis got you back to the clubhouse, but there's no blame." At the mention of Travis' name, her eyes droop in the corners. She's working hard not to cry. "Lauren?"

"Is, is he… mad?"

Shaking my head, I reply, "No, he's not mad. Worried. Really bloody worried, but not mad. Why would you think that?"

Even though a tear escapes her eye, her face remains hardened. "Because I hurt you all."

I sigh. She blames herself for what Alex and the Saviours had her do. "If you're about to tell me you've stayed away all this time because you think we all blame you, I might actually be about to hurt a child for the first time in my life."

One corner of her mouth twitches. Is that a smile? "I had no choice."

My face remains straight. "We always have a choice, Lauren."

Reading my tone, she lets loose a breath. "I didn't," she says flatly. "I know how things work. I know I let you all down. I tried reaching out, but Jay told me we couldn't trust you. Not after everything. So, we ran. We hid. Made sure we stayed out the way of everyone."

"You could have called me—or Mads. She needed you, Lauren."

Her head drops, and her tears fully flow. Judging by her reaction, she needed Mads too. Being a hypocrite, I begin to say, "You need to talk to—"

"—I don't need anybody!" She tugs her arm free, and I ready myself to run if she bolts. Every part of me wants to shout at her, wants to grab her, pick her up and demand she tell me where the fuck she's been hiding.

"Have you eaten?" I ask instead, noticing how drawn out she looks.

"What?" she replies, looking equally confused.

"Food. You know, breakfast. Have you had any?"

Without saying a word, she simply shakes her head.

"Come on." I turn and start walking away from her. I don't hear her following. "Well, you coming?" I ask when all she does is stand there.

"Where are you going?"

I move and hold the gate open for her. "Home."

Her eyes reflect uncertainty. I can see her mentally trying to work out what the right thing to do is. "Will Mads be there?" she asks.

I nod my chin. "It'll make her day seeing you."

She smiles, although she tries to hide it. I get lucky because she moves toward me, and we set off, together.

Back at mine, I open the door slowly and move to let Lauren past.

"I can't," she whispers with a shake of her head.

She didn't talk the rest of the walk here. "You'll be fine."

She hesitates again before she slowly lifts her foot.

We move to the kitchen, and I drop my phone on the table. "Want one?" I ask, holding up the kettle, now in need of a warm drink.

Lauren nods and moves to sit down. I'm grateful she's being compliant. "Where is she?" she asks.

Checking the time on my watch, I smile to myself. "In bed. She won't wake up 'til I take her up this brew." I notice Lauren looking around, almost frantically. "Why do you look worried to see her?"

Eyes hopping, she finally settles them on me. "Because… because there's so much to say and I don't know where to begin."

I let out a sigh as the kettle starts to boil. "She mentioned you going to the school today?"

Lauren nods. "That's right."

"So, why did I see you out so early?" Grabbing the milk, I fill the mugs and wait for her to talk.

"I was heading there. Needed to stop at a friend's beforehand."

I can't help the way my eyebrow arches. She's lying. "A friend's? At five in the morning?"

"Yes, Dean. A friend's. What's the problem?"

There's the fire again. "I didn't think kids your age were even up at that time, so it makes me question, what fucking friends?" I can't help the way my tone snaps. I might be mid-thirties, but when you live a life on the outside, you know there's only one of two reasons why kids meet at that time.

They're in danger or they're dealing.

"What friends, Lauren?" Her silence is confirmation that something shady is going on.

She stands quickly, feeling backed into a corner no doubt. "I have to go."

As she moves, I drop the spoon with a bang, managing to get my body in front of hers at the doorway. Our eyes bounce around, both trying to read the other. "Friends don't meet that early." I manage to keep my voice low so as not to wake Mads.

"I'm nearly sixteen, how I decide to live my life has got nothing to do with you," she says through gritted teeth.

"It has everything to do with me if I find out you're dealing."

She scoffs, and her body tightens, her eyes narrowing menacingly. "Get. Out. The. Way."

"No," I simply say.

"Move."

"Dean?"

Mine and Lauren's heads both swing to see Mads at the bottom of the stairs. She stands, one hand on the banister, the other holding her dressing gown around her. "What's—"

I watch as Lauren and Mads see each other for the first time.

It breaks me when I see Mads' face. Sadness washes over her, but her shoulders slump with relief at the sight of the person she cares for.

"Babe." I move closer to her, needing to touch her, feeling bad that we woke her.

Cupping her face in my hands, I kiss her forehead, then step to the side, allowing her to pass me as she takes the final step off the stairs.

A million silent questions whizz through the space around us.

"Where've you been?" Mads eventually asks Lauren, who's shifting uncomfortably on her feet. Poor kid looks like she wants to embrace this, but her guard is up. Mads looks at me, then back to Lauren. "Are you okay?"

"I'm sorry," Lauren says.

"Sorry? Why are you saying sorry? You have nothing to be sorry for." Mads steps closer, wrapping her arms around Lauren's small frame. "Shh," she comforts her, stroking her hair as she cries.

Mads looks at me with a tear-stained face as Lauren quickly wraps her arms around her. Just when I think about stepping closer, Lauren unexpectedly shakes herself free from Mads, and runs. "I'm sorry," she sniffs, flying past me and flinging the door open. She doesn't look back.

Mads' feet scramble to follow, but I stop her, grabbing her arm.

She looks down at my hand, annoyed. "Dean?"

"Let her go."

Frantic, Mads shakes her arm aggressively from my hold. "Get off!" she barks.

My eyes narrow this time. "She needs some time."

"She's had nothing but time, get off me!"

She moves to the door and begins to open it, but my hand

lands flat against the wood, banging it shut. She struggles again, her face pleading with me to let her go. No way I'm letting Mads go, not in this state.

"She'll come back," I say.

"You don't know that!"

"Yes, I do. Just leave her to figure out what she's going to do."

Mads' breathing has quickened where she's fighting to open the door. She grimaces, and I move to wrap my arms around her, to comfort her.

With my arms draped over her shoulders, I dip my lips to her neck. "Please trust me," I say, my words softly spoken.

A few moments pass between us, but Mads doesn't relax. I don't feel her body give in to me like it normally does. I place a kiss behind her ear, but she turns her head away, letting out a shallow sigh.

"If she doesn't come back," Mads starts, before slowly turning to face me. Her eyes stay fixed to my chest, and she lets out a few more steadying breaths. "I won't forgive you."

My arms drop.

Mads turns and walks back upstairs, leaving me stood alone.

It fucking hurts—the thought of her not forgiving me, but she just has to trust me.

Everyone will just have to trust me.

CHAPTER TWELVE

MADISON

I got ready for work in silence, packed myself a lunch and left the house all before eight. I know what I said to Dean hurt him, but it's how I felt.

Still is.

My head's pounding. The dull drum continuously bangs in my eye socket. I push my fingers against the sore area, momentarily easing the pain. I then slide my fingers to my temples, hoping I can sooth it away. It feels nice, for a second, before it hurts even more.

Sat at my desk, I open my daily emails, not paying attention to anything due to my racing mind. Where did Lauren go? Why was she there this morning? Why didn't she stay and talk to me?

I grab my phone and check the screen. There's nothing there. I already know in my gut that she won't come to the meeting this morning. If Dean hadn't stopped me from stopping her running out, I could have brought her here myself, ensured she did this for her own sake.

Now I'm back to square one.

Reaching into my top drawer, I find the packet of painkillers and take two, sipping from my fresh cup of tea, courtesy of Eva. These headaches are getting worse. They're not helped by the stress of work and the club, but they're definitely harder to manage.

I pick up my phone and type out a message to Bex asking to FaceTime later, as a black and white fuzz starts creeping into my vision, leaving me unable to see the screen properly.

I look at the clock. There's twenty minutes until the meeting starts. Grabbing my things and my tea, I then head towards the office. Once in my seat, alone in the room, I struggle to see where I'm putting things as the fuzz-ball blocks where I'm looking. It's frustrating and confining.

The office door opens, and Vivian joins me taking a seat by my side. "All set?" she asks.

I nod but can't bring myself to smile, then grumble, giving up on trying to get myself organised.

"Tell me."

"Tell you what?" I say nonchalant not looking at her.

Vivian laughs. "Is this your hormones or are you just in a bad mood today?"

"Probably both," I reply grabbing my mug. I take a slow sip then lean back in my chair. "She's not coming."

Vivian stops setting up her things, her eyes now locked on me. "And how would you know this?"

Letting out a sigh, I say, "She showed up at the house this morning."

Vivian's eyebrows lift. "Oh," she comments, and I can already tell this won't go down well. "And why won't she show up today if she was willing enough to show up at your house?"

"It's not my house," is my stupid response, because I don't know how willing Lauren was to show up or if Dean had forced her somehow.

"No, but you moved out of your place so it might as well be."

That's true. "I went down after hearing her and Dean talking. I thought I was imagining it—hearing her voice, but she was there." And I was so happy. "She freaked out, then ran out the door."

"Why do you think she freaked out?"

"She said she was sorry."

"For what, having a crappy care provider and being manipulated?"

I shrug my shoulders.

Vivian knows most of what happened—where Lauren was concerned anyway—after I'd had a bad day and completely broke down on her. She supports me, but she agreed we should keep it between us. "I guess she meant all of it. For thinking she'd hurt me, Dean..."

"I see." Vivian moves in her seat, checking her watch. "Listen, we have five minutes before everyone starts arriving. You need to clear your head. You're damn good at your job, and I need you here."

I offer a smile this time, placing my hand on top of hers on the table. "Thank you. I think I... I need to tell her she did nothing wrong, and she needs to know we care for her. I got through to her before she left. I just want the chance to try again."

"I get that," Vivian starts. She places her hand on top of mine and leans forward in her chair, looking at me. "But you need to understand that there are children here, at this school, who need you too. If Lauren chooses not to return, I hate to say it, but she's not your concern, Madison."

I remain quiet, not prepared to even consider that notion.

Vivian sighs. "At some point, you need to realise that some people just can't be helped. I've worked in this job long enough to know that no matter how hard you try, or how much love you give, sometimes it just isn't enough."

The sting in her words pinches, and my throat tightens. Is she just referring to Lauren? My eyes start to fill.

"Maybe take some time to decompress. Step back from this whole Lauren thing and let someone else take over?"

I immediately answer, "No."

"Madison—"

"—No, please. Trust me. I can get her back on track."

"I'm not asking you to. I'm asking you to think about yourself. You've got a lot on Madison, take the time—"

"—I don't want time off," I snap.

There's a slight pause. "I'm not asking."

"You're telling?"

She smiles, wickedly. "Ah, you know me so well now."

Giving her a blatant eye roll, she winks at me as the door opens, and the people joining us file into the room. Vivian taps my hand, then turns to welcome everyone.

An hour later, Lauren's still not here. I knew she wouldn't be, but her uncle didn't show either. We proceed to talk about the structure and planning of her case, and I'm pleased when I hear that she will be allowed to sit her final exams, even though she's missed a large chunk of school.

What's not so good to hear, is because the finer details are not known to the board of men and women sat here, unfortunately I can't plead her case and prove that the reason for her not attending school is unprecedented.

Meaning she'll have to work hard if she wants to do well.

Once we've said our goodbyes and everyone leaves, Vivian sits back down, picking up right where we left off before the meeting. "Give me your calendar so I know what needs doing."

"Vivian, no, please, I can handle it."

"Oh, I know. But it is my job to make sure you are okay. I personally feel as though a week off will do you some good. Tell me, how's the headache?"

Hurting like a bitch. "It's fine." I fake a smile and shake my head.

"Right, and on that lie, I don't want to see you here 'til Monday. Got it?"

"Seriously?"

"Deadly." Her eyes never falter. Her tone, consistently dry.

"What am I supposed to do?"

Vivian stands and starts gathering her things. "You rest. You binge on shitty food. Take a walk, listen to music, bonk. Whatever it takes to destress."

Bonk. I can't help but laugh. "Vivian!" I scold.

"What? I might not be a spring chicken anymore, but you know what I'm talking about. A good lay will set you straight. Get Dean to bonk the stress out of you—"

"—Enough! We are not having this conversation," I say laughing, but instantly regret it for the pain in my head. It throbs and feels as though my brain is rattling around up there.

She walks around her chair to my side. "Jokes aside, you're not just thinking about you anymore." We stare at each other. "You need to think about what's best for the baby. The stress of Lauren, the pre-eclampsia… be selfish. That's all I ask."

Smiling, I nod knowing she's right. "Okay."

"I'll see you Monday," she says, before picking up her bag and leaving me in the room.

Thinking for a moment, I grab my phone from the table and open up my messages.

Me: Hey, you free any days this week? X

Her reply is instant, making me smile.

Jess: For you, of course. What day you thinking?

Me: I've been given the rest of the week off. Apparently, I'm stressed… so whichever you can do.

Jess: I love your boss. The world needs more people like her. Let's say Friday?

Me: I know, right? Perfect. See you then x

Jess: See you then x

I then open a message to Dean.

Me: Are you busy? We need to talk

No more than ten seconds after I hit send, my phone starts ringing. "Hello?" I answer.

"Don't ever send me a message telling me we need to talk."

I roll my eyes.

"And I heard that."

Urgh. "Heard what?"

"The eye roll."

"You can't hear an eye roll."

"You're not denying it."

Fuck. "So, I eye rolled you, listen—"

"—No, you listen."

I instinctively cross my arms holding my phone to my ear, shifting my weight onto one foot.

"I need to apologise for Lauren being at the house this morning."

I let go of some of the angst I'm holding. "What you *need* to apologise for is letting her leave, and more so, not letting me go after her."

"I'm not apologising for that."

"Why not?"

"Because you shouldn't be chasing after her. She'll come to us."

"How can you be so sure?" I ask uncertain.

"Babe, please trust me, okay?"

Truth is, I trust him with my life. But I can still be mad with him. "Where are you?"

"Clubhouse. Why? You not at work?"

"Vivian gave me the week off. Apparently, I need the stress bonking out of me."

"What?" Dean asks with a laugh.

"Never mind. I'll be there soon. Don't leave."

"Your favourite person is here, you sure you want to swing by?"

"As long as she doesn't talk to me or even look at me, I'll be fine."

I pull up outside the clubhouse half an hour later. I'd given Vivian my work calendar and sent a few emails before I left. I don't like taking the time off, but I'll savour it as best I can.

Pushing open the door, the guys are nowhere to be seen except the prospect, Legs, and a few girls behind the bar.

"Hey, Mads," Talia shouts out from where she's wiping glasses.

I smile, heading towards her.

I found it strange hanging out here at first, considering the difference in lifestyles, but now I don't mind coming here so much. It's only Red who sometimes irks me.

"What can I get you?" Talia asks.

"Tea, please. They at the table?"

She nods before walking to the small kitchen. "Yep. Been up there a while—well I say they, Prez is up there, the rest have come down in dribs and drabs, like they've all got jobs to do, you know?"

I'm not sure I do. "You think it's anything to worry about?" I ask.

"Nah. Nothing those lot can't handle. I've not been here long but they're a tight group. Not like where I came from."

I can't help but admire the way Talia speaks. She's so confident. I heard she moved here after her partner got too heavy with his hands. She's the epitome of a strong female, takes no crap from anyone.

"I like the hair, it suits you." Shaved all up the back with the long strands tied up in a bun on top. Talia looks like a rock queen in her black, ripped jeans and Harley Davidson jumper.

"I'm going for the whole, *don't fuck with me or I'll kill you* look."

I laugh. "Well, you're killing it."

She smiles appreciatively.

The kettle boils in the back, and she leaves me at the bar to make my drink. I'd happily make it myself, but that's not how things work around here. Everyone has their place, has their job —their reason for being here.

I pull my phone out of my bag and send Dean a message letting him know I'm here. Just as I put it away, the main door to the clubhouse swings open. I crane my neck and spot a tall, long legged, smartly dressed woman taking a look around.

She wears high-waisted black trousers that hug her hips and a beautiful blouse that accentuates her breasts. Her dark hair is wrapped in loose curls that hang around her face. She looks out of place, but she carries an air of confidence about her that fills the space around us.

"Hi," I start, lifting my hand with a timid wave as I jump down off the stool I was sat on.

Her heels clip the floor as she strides towards me. "Hi, is Dean here?"

"Oh," is all I say, my heart twanging as his name rolls off her tongue. "He's in a meeting—"

"Mollie?" Dean says, as he walks down the stairs towards us. He holds out his hand as he approaches, but she doesn't take it. She already looks like she wants to leave. "You came."

Dean steps closer to me, one hand places at the small of my back whilst the other runs through his hair.

"I know I said this was strictly business, but is he here?" Mollie asks, her eyes quickly looking at my bump as she waits for his response.

My hand automatically moves to cover it.

"No, he left, but we can talk upstairs. I'll be there in a

minute."

She nods and starts toward the stairs.

Dean turns to me.

He opens his mouth but I speak before he does. "She a stripper?"

He grins as his hands move to either side of my face. "Old friend."

"Old, *stripper*, friend?"

His face tightens, and his lips pinch together. Looking down at me, his voice is flat as he says, "Solicitor."

My heart drops. Solicitor? "Shit, sorry. I was only joking. Is everything okay?"

"Fine."

Of course it is.

He grins. "Just to check though, you thought at lunchtime on a Tuesday, a stripper would come to entertain me and the lads?"

My body tightens with embarrassment. "No, I—"

"I love that you got jealous," he smirks cutting me off.

"I'm not jealous." Just a little worried he has a solicitor showing up. "You go, I'll leave you to your business."

He leans forward and kisses my lips. "I'm sorry." I'm still mad about this morning but my body melts as I lean into his kiss. "Won't be long."

"Okay," is all I say, hoping he'll give me more. When he doesn't, I slowly turn to the bar, and he makes his way upstairs.

Just over an hour later, I walk out of the ladies' to find Mollie now downstairs.

She's sat at the bar looking through some sort of paperwork. I feel bad that I joked she might be a stripper. She is clearly too professional to be taking her clothes off at this hour.

"Mollie?"

She turns to look at me as I approach her. Over the rim of her glasses, she looks up at me and smiles.

"I didn't get a chance to introduce myself earlier, I'm Madison," I say, and she slides her glasses to the top of her head before she takes my hand in hers.

"Nice to meet you." She smiles.

"Everything go, okay?" I pondered why Dean might have a solicitor meeting with him whilst I was waiting. He didn't mention anything to me about needing legal advice.

"As good as it could do." She places her glasses back on her face and turns to continue with her work.

"Can I get you a drink?" I ask.

"Tequila."

I scoff at her reply but when I catch her gaze, she isn't joking. Dumfounded, I walk behind the bar and search for the bottle of white stuff. "Here." I walk to where she's sat, placing the bottle with a shot glass before her.

"Shame you can't join me." She fills the shot glass and throws it back like she really needed it. She fills it again and repeats the motion. I stand amazed, watching her with admiration for going against the norm.

"Wow," I remark.

"Don't judge me."

I hold my hands up. "No judgement here."

Mollie smiles and takes her glasses off her head before rubbing her eyes.

"Although the shots and meeting with bikers does raise a few questions." I pull out one of the chairs and sit down across from her, hoping she doesn't mind me joining her.

"I'm just here to help Dean." She looks at me like I should know what she's talking about. My face falls, and she raises a half smile, understanding that I don't.

"Are you good at your job, Mollie?"

She checks my face, obviously realising I'm serious. I don't know why she's here, but I can guess this has everything to do with Dean acting the way he is.

"Very," she replies confidently.

I nod and pick up the bottle of tequila. "Then you deserve another."

As I pour, heels hitting the wooden floor can be heard walking down the corridor from the building's rear exit. I look up and see Red.

When she sees me, she rolls her eyes and saunters right past us.

"Who's that?" Mollie asks.

"That *is* a stripper," I say, immediately regretting my emphasis on the is.

Mollie rightly so looks confused by my comment as she attempts a fake smile, but fortunately I'm saved by the sound of the wooden doors clunking open upstairs.

As he comes down, I watch Dean walk around Mollie without looking at her. He reaches me, his whole body engulfing my breathing space. Leaning down and finding my lips, his kiss takes my breath away.

"Dean," I say, trying to catch it. My palms flat against his chest pointlessly try to push him away. "I'm still mad at you."

"I know." His kiss is gentle as his fingers scrunch in my hair.

My body hums and I relax. Vivian said to let him fuck the stress out of me, or bonk as she put it. Who am I not to follow the rules and do as my boss tells me? A smile stretches in between kissing him. "Want to make it up to me?" I nod my head in the direction of the room down the hall.

"Fuck yeah, I do." He takes my hand in his. "Mollie," Dean says, dipping his chin towards her, his features all of a sudden sterner. "You have everything you need?"

I don't miss her sigh. "Yes, I think I have it all."

What are they talking about?

Dean nods again. "Thank you."

A burly cough from behind makes us all turn around. "She can leave now."

Without any acknowledgment, Mollie stands and puts on her coat. She grabs her things then places the paperwork in her bag. "It was lovely to meet you, Madison. Congratulations by the way." Her eyes flick down.

"Thank you," I say, but I can't help looking between her and Travis. It's clear they know each other, and judging by the way his eyes are shooting daggers at the back of her head, I'd say they have a history.

"I'll be in touch," Mollie says to Dean. She turns but Travis is blocking her way. The pair of them stand face to face.

Travis doesn't move to let her past; he just stands glaring. "I'm not happy about this," he says looking directly at Mollie, but I can tell he's talking to Dean.

"I'm not exactly jumping for fucking joy," Mollie replies, her tone with him completely different to how she spoke to me only moments ago. "Move."

The way Travis' smile slowly stretches across his face, makes the hairs on the back of my neck stand tall. It's frightening.

"Move, Travis," Dean says.

Travis lets out a sarcastic laugh without looking at him. "Not a fucking chance."

Mollie tuts, then steps around him. "You're a fucking child, you know that?"

As she leaves, Travis tilts his neck to the ceiling, his neck audibly cracking, but he looks like he thinks he won that little standoff between them.

There's silence between the three of us as the main doors close shut behind Mollie.

"Anyone going to tell me what's going on here?" I ask.

Dean shifts on his heels. Travis doesn't move.

I look between the two of them. "Nothing?" I question with a sarcastic laugh. My eyes flit back and forth one more time. "Fine." I let go of Dean's hand when they offer me no explanation, and storm off to the room, alone.

CHAPTER THIRTEEN

MADISON

Lying flat on the bed, a small knock comes from the door a few minutes later. I hear Dean try the door handle, but I locked it.

He sighs on the other side of the wood, then he knocks again. "Let me in, babe."

I don't move. Needing to catch my thoughts, I turn to my side, positioning myself to a more comfortable position. I think back to what Vivian said earlier, about how it's not just me I need to think about now. My hand cups my bump.

Do I really want to know what's going on? Clearly it's something. And clearly, it's important. But how important? Important enough for Dean to feel like he needs to shut me out.

"Please, babe. Let me in."

I still don't move. I get it, I really do—not wanting to stress me out—but I don't know if the lack of knowing is helping or adding to how I feel.

When he knocks again, I sit up. "We need to talk," he says, and I smile with a sigh.

My head drops to my chest before I push myself off the bed and walk slowly to the door. My fingers raise to the lock when I reach it. "You'll tell me what's going on?" I ask him.

"Some of it," he replies.

My fingers stop. I stay silent, dropping my hand to my side.

"Mads?" he questions. I can feel the emotions brimming. This is exhausting. He knows what I want. "Mads, let me in." He's getting more worked up.

I control the wobble of my bottom lip. "Tell me."

I can picture him shaking his head, the line across his brow, probably prominent. "Just let me in."

"Promise me you'll tell me first."

There's a light thud, and I know he's resting his head against the door. "I don't know if I can."

I let out a sigh. "I have questions."

There's another pause. "I'll give you five if you open the door right now, because I really want to get my hands on you."

"Five questions?"

"Yes," he breathes.

I'll take that.

Slowly, I unlock the door, opening it a fraction.

Dean waits, then when I step back, he enters the room, eyes soft and on me. I purse my lips to stop myself from crying as he closes the door behind him.

"Why do you have a solicitor here?" I burst out.

Dean lets out a slight laugh, his hands stroking up and down the sides of my arms. "Shh, not so quick with the questions," he tells me. "You don't want to waste them."

"That is my first question. Why do you have a solicitor here?"

"Technically that's now your second—"

"—Dean."

His face drops but he doesn't take his hands off my arms. "She's an old friend."

"Why's she here?"

Dean takes my hand in his, then walks me back to the bed. He sits on the edge then pulls me onto his lap, placing his hand around my protruding bump. Lowering his mouth, he kisses my tummy, then he looks to me. "She's here because I asked her to help me with something."

"Help with what? Are you in trouble?"

He shakes his head then runs his hand over his beard. "I don't know. That's why Mollie's here. To help, in case I am."

With one arm around his shoulder, the other cups his face. My thumb strokes the short layer of hairs on his chin. "What've you done?"

Dean sighs. "It's more about what *needs* to be done."

Looking into his eyes, I wonder what he means. Is he talking about a retaliation? But for what? The threat they received? "What is it you think you need to do?" I ask him.

Dean smiles, and I return a confused look to him, my eyes scrunching together. "I'm sorry, you're all out of questions."

"Don't do that."

"What? Technically I gave you a freebie," he says being smart.

"You're infuriating."

"Don't blame me. It's not my fault you wasted them."

I move to stand off his lap, but his arms hold me in place. "Nope, you're staying right here," he says.

"Dean, I need to go home. I need to try and wrap my head around why you're being like this."

"What you *need*, is to trust that I'm doing everything I can to protect the things I love."

"Protect us from what?" My voice is harsh as I snap my question at him. "Just because I'm a woman and you're an outlaw, doesn't mean I need you to always protect me."

He's silent. Staring at me. "You're not just any woman though, Mads, are you? You're mine."

I frown at him as he continues.

"Things are changing, and I need to know that when the

time comes, you won't fight me or argue the toss about what's happening, you'll just trust me and do as I say."

Slowly, my eyes move to look at him. "Do as you *say*?" I ask, checking I heard him correctly. "When have I ever just done as you *say*?"

He smiles. "I can think of a few situations." He runs his hand up my outer thigh, not stopping until he reaches behind me, his arms completely enveloping me. "But I'm serious. Whatever happens next, please trust that I know what needs to be done?"

All I can do is nod. I can't promise I won't keep trying to find out the whole truth, but I can promise to trust him.

"Now, what was it your boss said I should do?"

I smile, defeated. "Vivian reckons I'm stressed. I can't possibly imagine what gave her that impression." I eye roll him to which he frowns.

"Babe. Seriously?"

I let out a huff. "She reckons I need a good lay, that'll sort it."

"Have I ever taken you to bed and it's not been a good lay?"

I act as if I'm thinking about a bad time. But there isn't one.

"O-kay that took way too long for you to answer."

"Maybe you should just show me. Make me remember."

The grin on his face tells me he's about to do just that. Sliding his hand back down my thigh, he scoops me up into his arms, and my legs naturally wrap around his body.

My arms hold him tight around his neck.

"I'm about to show you how fucking loved you are."

He hits his lips to mine, one hand scrunching my hair as he devours me. Dean then turns, slowly lowering me, sitting me on the edge of the bed, our lips unlocking as he does.

My legs part as he stands in front of me.

"My belt. Take it off."

I cock an eyebrow, looking up to him. "I thought this was about me?"

"Don't act like you don't enjoy occasionally being my whore," he says with a smirk.

"Your whore?" I question.

Dean just stares at me. We both know how much I love it. Sex with him is always incredible.

"As long as you still know I will never call you daddy in the bedroom, then I'm happy to be your whore. My VP." I roll my name for him past my lips with so much lust in my voice, it's practically oozing out of me. When I look up to him through my lashes, I hear him take in a breath at my giving him control.

"My girl."

And there they are. Two words that make me weak.

My breathing quickens. His fingers stroke the side of my cheek, then knot into the back of my hair.

My head jolts back.

"Belt," is all he says.

Still holding my head back, my hands move to his jeans and begin to undo them. I keep my eyes on his until his cock is free.

"Open your mouth, beautiful."

I look at his cock and see the head already glistening with his arousal. It makes me smile, knowing how much he loves this.

He licks his lips, then slowly drags the tip of his cock across my bottom lip. With his thumb and his finger, he tilts my chin to look at him. "Open," he says huskily.

A small smile cracks on my face. I wonder who's actually enjoying this more. Me or him? But I do what he wants.

He pushes his cock into my mouth, not stopping until I'm arching my head to accommodate him.

I swirl my tongue along his length, making sure to lick over the tip as I pull my head back.

Dean bites his lip, and his grip on my hair tightens. "Your mouth was fucking made for me," he says with a grunt, as I suck him again, hollowing my cheeks. Dean adjusts his stance, then rocking his hips, he starts thrusting himself deep in my mouth. He lets out the deepest of groans causing me to moan, tasting more of him as I tighten my lips.

He's close. Feeling him grow more excited, I take him to the back of my throat again, and at the same time I start unbuttoning my shirt.

"I didn't say to do that," he forces himself to say.

I keep going, not listening to him. If anything, I suck harder and move my fingers quicker.

Tipping my head back, he pulls himself out, and I lick my lips.

Dean looks at me. "I will rip that shirt off you if you don't stop."

"That a threat?" I challenge, realising I'm not a very good whore.

"Madison Rose Reed."

I throw him a shocked look. "You're full naming me?"

"Jesus Christ." He takes the collar of my shirt in his hands and rips it down the middle, leaving not one button attached to it.

My breath is unexpectedly shaky with desire. "VP!"

"Well, I told you."

I guess he did. "Okay, can I take my bra off? Is that allowed?"

"No, not yet."

I let out a laugh at his bossiness.

"Up," he says, holding out a hand for me to take.

I take it and stand, my back having to arch when he doesn't give me enough space.

"Turn around."

Smirking, I let go of him and turn slowly, my bum brushing against his bared cock.

Dean dips and grips the bottom of my skirt. He rolls it in his fingers until his hands find my hips and my legs are exposed. His grip is firm. I can't help but arch my back, pushing myself against him.

A moan escapes me when one of his hands moves over my body, caressing my breasts, stopping across my throat. My head rolls into his shoulder.

Dean's thumb then dips into my mouth, and I welcome it, sucking and licking as he pushes it in deeper. His grip on my hip tightens, and I feel his arousal getting thicker.

When I moan again, still sucking his thumb, he quickly moves his other hand, tucking it into my knickers and cupping me. Two fingers push inside. "I expected nothing less," he purrs, commenting on how wet I am for him. His lips gently caress my ear, his words still vibrating against my skin causing me to break out in goosebumps.

I bite down on his thumb still in my mouth.

"Now we're talking," he whispers. Dean slips his thumb from my mouth, moving his hand to grip the back of my neck. He removes his fingers inside me, only to move them to behind me and reinsert them.

I whimper, loving the sensation as he opens me wide and pushes them in deep. "VP." My pleading encourages his fingers pumping into me to quicken. I part my legs wider, giving him better access to my body.

When he pushes my head down, forcing me to put my hands flat on the bed, my hips start rocking with his movements.

"Fucking hell, Mads."

The wet sounds of me fucking his fingers mixed with his heavy breathing spurs me on. I start rolling my hips, taking his fingers deeper. Warm tingles then start to seep up my spine. I shut my eyes, biting my lip as the pleasure starts rising within me. "VP," I whisper, suddenly needing more.

He withdraws his fingers, and I wait, my breath running slightly wild.

Looking over my shoulder, I see him, his cock in his hand, stroking himself as he looks at my body bent over before him.

"Flat on the bed. Take everything off except the skirt."

I stand up straight, letting my shirt slip off my shoulders to the floor.

He continues to stroke himself slowly as he watches me undress, taking off my bra.

I then climb on the bed, facing him, and lie on my back.

Dean steps close to me. Releasing his cock, he trails his hands up my legs until he reaches my knickers. He pulls them down slowly, chucking them over his shoulder once they're off. Then he parts my legs wide, admiring my body, his eyes devouring every inch of me.

Gripping my ankles, he pulls my body to the edge of the bed making my skirt hitch up to my waist.

I hold my bump as he pulls me, smiling and admiring him as he loves me.

His mouth is on me as soon as I'm where he wants me. He licks and sucks with expertise, his tongue stroking me delicately.

I close my eyes and bask in a weightlessness that washes over me. I feel like I'm floating, my body succumbing to him. It's bliss. Tension starts leaving my muscles.

When he inserts two fingers, I twine my fingers into his hair. "Dean," I moan.

He hums against my skin, then works me harder.

My legs part wider. My orgasm drawing closer. "Dean I'm… I'm!" Raising my hips into him, I shatter around his face, moaning like a lovesick whore.

He doesn't stop until my body stops twitching. "I will never tire of watching you come like that," he says, flattening his tongue against me one more time.

I shudder with a smile as I try to prise my eyes open.

Climbing over my body, Dean glides inside me without any

hesitation.

My lips part, and I hold him close to me.

He's still. Watching. It's like he's counting every freckle. Every single inch of my face, he takes in. "You shine brighter than the sun, you know that?" he murmurs, his hand stroking my hair.

Pulling his head to mine, I hold his face in my hands. "Because I have you."

The smile he gives me warms my heart.

His hips start to slowly move, but I don't let go of his face. I keep him close to me as he gradually increases his pace.

He builds, and I watch. I watch him lose himself in me. I watch him become unable to stop the tightening of his face as something else overrides him. It grips him, his eyes blackening, his hands trembling.

Fear?

I consider asking him, but he holds me tighter, his body stiffening as he buries his face in my neck, finding his release. His hips then slow to a steady stop. Gradually, he raises his head to look at me once again. It's on the tip of my tongue to ask him what's wrong but he speaks first. "No more questions, Mads."

Placing his lips against mine, he closes his eyes, and his palm cups my face. We stay like this; him still on top of me, our foreheads touching, his lips every now and then pushing against mine.

I stay strong even though I sense something dreadful close by.

Once I'm dressed, we make our way back to the main room of the clubhouse. Travis sits on a stool facing the bar. He lifts his empty glass to Talia, signalling he wants another.

She moves grabbing a bottle of brown liquid, then untwists the top, filling his glass. "Prez?" she asks Dean.

Travis looks up to us. I don't miss his eyes dropping down my front, noticing the state of my shirt.

"Please," Dean says taking a seat.

I pull my shirt across my front tighter, then grab my coat from the back of the chair I was sat at earlier. I tie it up, then turn to face Dean.

"Want a drink?" he asks, looking at me.

"No, I'm good. I should go home." I pick up my bag, searching for my keys.

Travis huffs as he sips his beer. "I'd make the most of it, Mads," he grumbles.

My hand stops searching, and I slowly look up. "Why?"

The look Dean gives Travis is dark and threatening.

A tingling heat fills my cheeks. My eyes scrunch together with annoyance. With my heart suddenly racing, it's on the tip of my tongue to ask what he means, but instead I ask, "Who's Mollie to you?"

Travis' arm freezes, his glass hovering close to his mouth. The silence that ensues is heavy. It crashes through the clubhouse, and I know I've made a mistake.

Slowly placing the glass on the bar, Travis stands then walks towards me.

My arms drop to my side.

"Don't ever talk to me about her again," he all but forces himself to say. He looks so angry, but his eyes are droopy. How much has he drunk in the time Dean and I were in the other room?

"Travis," Dean warns.

Travis turns, and the two of them just stare at each other. The pulse of my heart's beat bangs in my chest. Lifting his arm, Travis points at Dean. "You can go fuck yourself."

Dean stands, his body squaring toward Travis. "No, fuck you, she doesn't know."

Travis' face turns a deep shade of red. "Isn't that a fucking surprise," he spits. "I mean it, both of you can go fuck yourselves."

"I'll not tell you again," Dean says, his voice laced with malice.

"Guys, stop," I plead, not liking them being this way. "Tensions are clearly high—"

Travis laughs hysterically at my words. "And what the fuck would you know about tensions being high, huh?"

He opens his mouth to say more but Dean slams his fist into the side of his face.

Talia and I can only watch on as they crash into one another, their fists flying. "Stop!" I shout, but it's pointless.

The main doors open as Travis gets hit and falls into a table and chairs.

The clattering noise makes me cover my ears, but unlike me, Talia runs around the bar, instinctively moving her body to try and break up the fight.

Her frame is tiny compared to them. Unable to make any headway in breaking them up, Talia jumps onto Travis' back like a spider monkey. She wraps her arms around Travis' big shoulders, trying in vain to hold him back.

"Hey!" a booming voice calls out from the door.

I turn and see a few other members come charging in.

Mop and the man they call The Joker move towards Travis and Dean.

Travis manages to get Dean in a headlock, just after he takes a solid shot to the mouth. His teeth are bared as he pulls on Dean's neck, lifting his feet off the floor.

"Cut it out!" Mop shouts, his hands frantically trying to prise Travis off Dean. "We don't have time for this shit, they're coming!"

Both of them stop fighting instantaneously.

Talia lets go of Travis, and her feet hit the floor with a thump. "Who's coming?" she asks.

Before anyone can answer, the place is swarming with

police. They cover every entry, shouting instructions at us all. One officer places his hand tightly on my arm, then loosens it immediately. He's not here for me. "Need you to move," he says, proceeding to drag me out of the way of the main crowd.

Talia steps closer to me.

The officers point their tasers at Dean and Travis, holding them still where they stand. Both their chests are sucking in heavy breaths.

"On the ground," they're instructed.

Both of them bend their knees, placing their hands behind their heads.

Two officers move to Dean. They scoop him up, bringing him to his feet.

"What's happening?" I ask, my voice anxious when I notice them not doing the same to Travis. Only Dean is handcuffed, his pockets searched and his rights read. "Dean?"

My eyes move desperately, looking at anyone who will explain what's happening.

When he looks at me, the man who walked out of that room with me only minutes ago, steps back into the shadows. The way his eyes blacken, it breaks my heart in two.

This is what he knew was coming. This is what he said would happen. This is what he was scared of. What did he do? I don't want him to leave. He can't leave me.

My feet are moving before I even register what I'm doing.

"Hey!" the officer who was holding me shouts as I move away from him with speed.

I make it to Dean just before the officer puts his hands back on me. "Please come back to me." The sob that escapes my mouth is enough to make Dean sigh. "Please, you come back to me—to us."

I can't control the tears as they pour from my eyes.

"You listen to Travis whilst I'm gone." Dean looks at the man he was fighting.

My eyes follow his, delayed.

Travis stands and wipes his bloodied chin, but he nods, an understanding between them still in place.

"Whatever he says, Mads, you listen."

"But—"

"We're all out of time, babe."

"No, please…"

The officers start taking Dean away from me. They manhandle him past Travis towards the door.

"No!" I move to reach for him, just to hold or to touch him before he's taken away from us.

Travis moves into my path, his strong arm effortlessly stopping my advance.

"Get off me, Travis! Let me go!" My arms hit at his as I cry.

Dean looks back, taking one last look at me. My legs give way when our eyes lock, forcing Travis to have to catch me.

"Come back." My sobs are muffled as Travis wraps his arms around me tighter, one hand holding my head close to his chest, sheltering me.

I grip the leather of his cut so hard, my knuckles tear in agony.

My emotions destroy whatever hold I had left on this situation. A terrifying scream fractures my chest as I let it roar out of me.

He can't be gone. He has to come back.

CHAPTER FOURTEEN

TRAVIS

Hearing Mads' scream as they moved Dean outside was enough for any grown man to feel broken. Her cries pierced the air like shards of glass ripping through it. The blood inside my veins curdled as chills ran down my spine.

I can only imagine the kind of devastation ripping through my president right now. He just has to keep it together. For all of our sakes.

We argued when he sat us all down and laid out how things were going to play for the foreseeable. It had me wanting to bury him six feet under. But when I saw Mollie show up again at the clubhouse, I lost it. I mean, I fucking *lost* it.

Dean and I fought, something we've never done—not like that, anyway. Is it possible to love one of your brothers but want to kill them at the same time? Because that's exactly where my head's at right now.

A former version of himself reared its head the day Vincent asked us to go to the barn. Dean's never not been that brutal, but I spent days after wishing I'd been the one to rip the man open for answers. We both knew it had to be him though. We knew Vincent was watching how he'd handle it.

And now, when I least want to be watched and my every move nitpicked, all eyes are on *fucking* me. Four days. Four measly days after he found out about a potential charge, he was gone. Not two weeks or even one. Four. Fucking. Days.

Mop sits to my right in his usual seat at the table. I won't sit in Dean's, that aint my place.

Captain walks in disgruntled.

"What is it?" I ask him.

"You sure we're doing this? Wouldn't it just be easier to kill them all?"

Probably. "We need this," I answer.

"Is it worth it though? Getting into bed with people we don't know for the sake of holding back our enemies?" He sits in his seat then sips his beer before pulling out his smokes.

I wish I had a fucking straight answer to that. To be honest, a part of me wonders the same thing. The deal we're about to lock down, if we don't do this *with* the Saviours, they'll take it for themselves and Rippers will eventually lose all power. Yes, it would be easier to leave them to it. But our history, it runs so fucking deep. "We have to agree to this."

We all look to one another realising we're going to be much richer than we've ever been, but at what cost, I don't know.

Banging the gavel to the table, I say, "Let's get this fucking done, shall we?"

A few of them nod. Others shake their heads but still eventually agree.

"Beats, send 'em up."

He turns to the door, heading to fetch the Sodom Saviours and our new business partners who are waiting downstairs. This is so far from any fucking scenario I envisioned us having; me doing this without Dean here. But it's what he wanted.

Everyone comes to the door of our meeting room.

"Phones?" I ask.

"I've got them, Trav," Beats says, nodding his head behind them, then closing the door and taking his seat.

"Cosy in here."

I look at the guy wearing a Saviours' cut. Lauren's uncle.

"Listen, Princess, your men chose to meet here. Let's move on, we have shit to discuss."

Darkened eyes stare back at me, not enjoying my tone. "Where's my niece?" Billy asks, his eyes sharp.

I haven't got time for this shit. "No idea." But perhaps if he'd treated her better, she wouldn't have taken off the way she did.

I look around, noticing The Joker and Skitz are the most hard-faced men in the room. They don't trust the Saviours walking in one bit. Len also hasn't taken his eyes off the men in suits. Pissed off they may be, but they're still on board. If they weren't, one false move would trip a chain of events we can't handle right now. We need this fucking deal if we're to survive. Otherwise, the Saviours will take it for themselves, and we can't let that happen.

One of the men carries an air of authority. This can only be Costa. "Gentlemen," he says. He walks around Dean's seat, his finger trailing across the back as if he's contemplating sitting there. Fucking coffee loving, bald headed prick. My first impression of this foreigner isn't good. "I know you have your own business to discuss, but I'd appreciate it if we conclude ours first. I'm a busy man."

Eyes flick at each other. Faces tighten all around me. Where the fuck did this guy come from? "First off, who am I talking to here? Just so I know who's in charge." He sits at the other end of the table.

Dick move. Trying to cause tension when we need unity. I look at Vincent. He wants to say him, but this is the Rippers' clubhouse. "I guess it's me."

Costa smirks. "You guess?"

Fuck me, I want to cut him so bad. Probably because I don't tend to trust guys as pristine as him. "In here, you talk to me. But

I can assure you," I raise a hand, gesturing towards my guys, "I don't consider myself better than any of the Rippers in here."

"What about those not in here?" he asks smugly.

Jesus this guy's riling me. Bar a few hangarounds downstairs, the only men not in close proximity who wear our cut are Dean and Legs. Dean I trust with my life. And Legs, well, he may be young but he had a tough start.

Dean gave him an opportunity to sort his shit out. He's trustworthy as fuck in my eyes. Trustworthy enough to make him Mads' shadow for the foreseeable. "Like you said, we have our own business to discuss—"

"Travis," Mop warns. I look at him, and he shakes his head subtly. "This business is important, brother." He's telling me to rein it in. He can see me getting pissed off.

Costa laughs as he sits straighter, unbuttoning his suit jacket. "You're right, I digress. Let's discuss how I'm going to make you all rich."

The man stood behind Costa is dressed similarly to him. Round glasses sit on his face. He peers over the rim as he moves forward, handing over a file.

He must be fucking Starbucks.

"Shall I get straight into it?" Costa asks.

I nod as Starbucks steps back.

"As previously discussed, shipments will be once a month. Routes for transport get locked down a few days before. This ensures safety for all parties. The less routine things are, the less likely we are to get caught. With the first shipment, Sodom Saviours will offload the guns on the west coast." He points to a map, tapping his finger to the paper. "From there, Rippers MC transports through to the east coast where my men will be waiting to offload onto my boat set for Amsterdam."

That's not what Dean signed off on when he and Vincent worked this proposal out months ago. "As we agreed? I don't remember Rippers agreeing to carry all the risk?" Costa smiles as I speak. "Sodom Saviours offload the guns and transport. Rippers earn by facilitating. Not transporting."

"I can see why you'd think that…?"

This fucker's waiting for my name like he didn't just hear it. I grind my molars, swallowing every morsel of restraint I have. "Travis," I force out.

He smiles again, knowing just how much he's getting to me. "I can see why you'd think that, Travis," he says in his subtle I don't know what the fuck accent, that wicked grin still plastered across his face. "But that *is* what your boss wanted, right? No Saviour was to stop on his turf?" He holds his hands out, looking around the table.

"That's right," Vincent pipes up. "We have a deal with Scottish charters to transport our guns. Rippers have their southern charters to move their drugs. The north… it was harder to come to an understanding. Saviours can pass through, but we don't stop."

Costa's eyes look from Vincent to me. Our eyes are locked sat directly opposite each other. "Enlighten me, please," he says.

Without looking away from Vincent, I open my mouth to talk. "You wanting to go through our home turf... it shifts the balance." I hear The Joker suck his teeth and feel eyes boring into me. "Saviours don't stop within our borders, never have."

Costa laughs. "Sorry, I thought we were hardened fucking criminals?" Neither me nor Vincent speaks. Costa looks between us again. "Sounds like you're still sucking on your mother's small tits."

I look at him then. Vincent follows. "Our arrangement with the Saviours stopped families getting hurt. This new business—we want to keep the peace, but the Rippers can't carry all that risk," I tell him.

"Then you need to let us stop within your bord—"

"Here's what's going to happen," Costa says, not allowing Vincent to finish. His voice isn't as pushy as I thought it might be, but I still don't like how goddamn righteous this prick is being. "Straight through your turf is the quickest route for the pipelines I've secured. You *will* transport directly from the west coast to the east coast," he says to me. "You pick up from the given location, and you drop off at the port my boat leaves from. That way, you protect your invisible lines you seem to care so much for, and I get my fucking cargo out of this country."

The fucking balls on this guy. "And if we say no?" I ask.

Costa's eyes rise to mine. He sits so still you wouldn't even know he was breathing. "You say no, you're going to feel the full weight of that from the south to the most northern territory you own. Saviours will rule your precious land, and nobody will ever know who the fuck your little club was."

"That's a pretty big threat to make in here."

"Mark my words, *Travis*, I don't make idol threats." We stare at each other a moment longer. "Are we clear on how this is going to run?"

Vincent nods eagerly, having got the deal of his lifetime.

I look at Captain, Mop, Riggs, Len, The Joker—all of my brothers sat around the table. They in turn each give their approval. I give Costa a nod.

With that, he stands. Irate, I watch as he and his man make to leave with Beats escorting them.

At the door, Starbucks turns back to look at me.

I have to drag my eyes to his.

"We'll be in touch. Send our love to your boss." He walks away leaving the outlaws at the table.

My mind slowly catches up with what the hell just happened. Vincent has fucked all of us by bringing this business. He says Saviours further north caught wind of Costa. But this is his move to get our turf. Petty motherfucker. "Where're we at with Dean's protection?" I ask Vincent, acting like that threat to wipe our club off the map didn't just happen. If I think about it, I'll end up in the cell next to my president, Costa's head under my arm.

Silence seems to stump everyone. Some heads are down. Some faces are angry. "He still hasn't sat down with The Saint."

When I see the corner of his mouth twitch, my temper goes from five to nine, pretty fucking quick after everything that just happened. "You said you could arrange that as soon as I called you Tuesday? It's fucking Saturday!"

"Like I told him *and* you, The Saint is in solitary. There's fuck all I can do about that."

I bang the table not liking that at all, as Beats walks back in. I also don't fucking like the fact that the person who runs things inside is an old friend of Vincent's. "You better pray he sits down with Dean, or—"

"—or what?" Billy cuts me off.

The sudden confidence since Costa's departure pushes me to ten. I push out from my chair quicker than a greyhound darting out the gate. In one swift move I have this cunt by the throat, pulling him toward me.

"Enough! Fucking leave it!" Len shouts.

The Joker and Skitz look hungry for a fight. Both of them stalk closer, ready to go by my side.

"He's right," Captain bellows, physically tugging me back to sit down. "Won't achieve nothing if we act like a bunch of dickheads."

Len moves to help him.

Having my arms pulled back, I let go of Billy's throat and shrug everyone off, my eyes still making it very fucking clear I want to kill this guy. "Alright!" I shout, straightening out my clothes as they both give me some space. I begrudgingly turn and pick up my chair. "He was moved this morning. What's he meant to do for a few more days?" I ask Vincent, slamming the legs to the floor.

"I'm sure he'll figure something out."

Dropping my head, I pinch the bridge of my nose, really trying to keep my temper in check. "And if he doesn't?" I ask.

Vincent gives me the smuggest look I've ever seen grace a man's face. He rolls his hands together, then points one finger in my direction. "Guess that'll make you boss."

Taking a few steady breaths, I look at Mop quickly. No matter the situation, he's the calmest Ripper I've ever met.

He talks for me, knowing I can't find the words. "That isn't an option. Now, tell us what happened five days ago."

Dean had called Vincent to let him know the police were closing in on him. Vincent told him another threat had been made. That's what sparked all of this last-minute planning.

"It was more than just a threat; it was an invasion of privacy."

"And you have no leads as to who it was outside your guy's home?" Mop asks.

"No," Vincent says. "We still don't know where these men are coming from, or what their angle is."

Dean has some idea. He said he'd seen a tattoo on the man he'd killed in the barn, and that the man was released from prison by someone unknown. So, whilst he'd managed to talk Mollie into sticking around and defending him should he end up inside, I only accepted what he asked me to do when I was under the impression he'd have fucking protection.

Without it, he won't last five minutes.

Still my mind races trying to work it all out. Whoever has the ability to release men from prison, has power. And if he's that powerful, he most definitely knows of our connection with Costa. In which case, our new business could be the most dangerous yet.

I try to steady my thoughts as I say, "Tell me what happened exactly."

Pulling out his smokes from his pocket, Vincent holds them up to me.

I nod, agreeing to letting him light one at the table.

"I woke up to a call from my guy." He puts the smoke in his mouth then inhales as he lights it. "Said someone was on his property." He drops the lighter to the table before he continues. "Psycho was staring through the window to his bedroom. Just stood there, watching him."

"Did he say anything?"

"Didn't get a chance to say anything, the prick was gone by the time he got out there."

Creasing my face, my fingers interlock on the table in front of me. "And where were these guard dogs of his?"

Vincent leans forward in his chair, resting on his elbows. "Whoever was there had tied both of them up, got them under control."

My face wrinkles with confusion. "What's the fucking point of guard dogs if they don't guard? Surely they would be trained to attack if anyone came onto their property?" Mop sighs so loud, I turn my head to him. "What?"

He shakes his head knowingly. "Means they knew exactly what to do so the dogs *didn't* attack."

Shit. Someone really is watching closely. Which makes what I have to do when I get back to Dean's make even more sense. I take a breath, filling my lungs. "We have to assume eyes are on *all* of us. From dusk 'til dawn."

"See, this is where I have issues, because *you* are yet to have received any threats. The Rippers seem to be getting off pretty fucking lightly from where we stand."

I won't deny it, I see how it looks. "We're about to go into business together. If this shit happens to you, it impacts us. And who says tomorrow it won't be one of us?"

Vincent locks his jaw, his eyes hollowed and locked on mine. "You'd better pray something *does* happen to you, otherwise I'm going to start assuming the Rippers are taking us for fools. And well, you've seen what will happen with your own eyes."

What I saw was my president—the closest thing I have to a best mate—end a man's life where Vincent wouldn't. Just because someone hasn't come after us yet, doesn't mean they won't.

"The threats made up 'til now are low level. But that doesn't mean we can take them lightly, not with what we're getting into just ahead of us. Everyone needs to be made aware now of what's going on." My eyes scan all the men around the table. "Make the calls to your other charters, we'll do the same to ours." I make sure I lock my eyes on Vincent's when I speak again, knowing that we're treading water with each other, but also knowing we have no other fucking choice. Enemies usually use love against you. "It's time to do whatever it takes to protect what we love most."

I grip the handle of my bike, twisting until the drag from the engine sucks me into my seat. I need to put a thousand miles on her—escape it all. Aint no feeling like it.

The answer is always the same. Busy head? Ride. Secrets to bury? You ride. A cluster fuck of emotions causing you to spiral? Just ride until the fucking veil lifts enabling you to think again.

Unless there isn't time. In which case, you're stuck under it.

I pull up outside number seventy-seven and kill the engine. I take a minute just sat trying to process everything. The way I handled things with Costa and Vincent didn't start off how I'd planned. I let them get under my skin. Let him in my head. I've never allowed anyone to do that.

Well, maybe one.

Now Mollie's back, I can't help but assume that's why I'm

losing my grip on things. I need to figure it out fucking sharpish. If I don't, we'll end up uniting our chaos, and there's only one way that ends.

Pushing the front door open, the house is shrouded in darkness. Doesn't look like Mads made it downstairs at all today. I knew she wouldn't. I should have come by sooner to check on her.

I don't bother kicking off my boots as I make my way upstairs. Dean's been gone four days. We'll know soon if they have sufficient evidence to charge him or not. It's pretty unlikely he'll get off given the charges, but I can hope.

Pushing the door open to the bedroom, the slow rise and fall of Mads' chest lets me know she's sleeping. Finally. Dropping her off the other night was devasting.

I'd put her in her car and drove her back. Not once did her tears lessen. When she didn't move, I cradled her in my arms and put her into the bed myself. No words were spoken. She wouldn't talk. Didn't utter a single word to me as I removed her shoes and coat. Her eyes just remained closed… like she was protecting herself by blocking it out.

Pulling the door to, I hear her stir. *Fuck.*

"Dean?" she whispers hurriedly. I feel shit for waking her. She props herself up on her elbows quickly, looking for the man she needs as I step into the room.

"No, it's me," I say.

Her head falls, and she slowly lowers herself back to the pillow.

"I'll get you some water." Turning, I leave the room again and head to the kitchen. Walking back a few moments later, I find her turned on her side, away from me. "Here you go." I place the glass on the bedside table.

Mads wipes her fresh tears away, her hair damp and crumpled, a few strands sticking to her cheek where she's been laid on them. I don't know what to say or how to comfort her. Mads and I, we've always just gotten along with jokes and sarcasm. Both of which have no place right now.

I sit on the bed near to her. "He'll be okay," I say softly. Mads gives me nothing. No acknowledgement of what I just said. I can't help the exhausted breath that comes from me. "Mads?"

Blinking her eyes, she eventually focuses on me when I say her name one more time. "What?" she says.

"I said, he'll be okay."

Sitting up slightly, she pushes the pillows behind her back to get comfy. She gives me eye contact for the briefest of moments. A tiny hint that she heard what I said.

We've done this before; sat together, me telling her he'll be alright, that nothing would stop him coming home to her. But she looks away from me, resting her head flat against the pillow. "Even you don't believe that."

Her words land heavy, like dropping an anchor into the ocean. They drop and keep going until they crash against the floor. I can't answer, can't even give her some smart-arse reply because she's fucking right.

Dean had no identity the minute he got arrested. Affiliations and brotherhood don't count. Ideology and power are what rule. If he's not protected, he's a sitting duck.

My heart starts drumming in my chest, my palms suddenly sweaty. I open my mouth to speak but Mads beats me to it. "He knew, didn't he?"

I drop my head, apparently giving her my answer. Of course he knew they were coming for him. We didn't know when exactly, but he had preparations made.

She turns her head away, pulling the duvet close to her face, trying to block me out. "Please, leave me alone."

With a sigh I stand, knowing I'm not wanted. Mads doesn't look at me, and I hate myself for what comes out of my mouth next. "It's time to go, Mads."

CHAPTER FIFTEEN

MADISON

I must have heard him wrong. "What do you mean?" My voice all but cracks as I ask.

"Uh, Dean… he wants you away from all this."

I bite my tongue, literally forcing my teeth down so I don't scream. "Why?" I manage to force out.

Travis flusters as he tries to explain why I supposedly can't be here; in the house I've practically lived in every day since Dean and I have been together.

"If you're going to tell me it's not safe, I need answers." I sit up straighter waiting for Travis to tell me what's going on.

"Jesus fucking Christ," he says quietly, his hand raking over his beard. "He's right, Mads. It isn't safe right now. We need to get in front of whatever's going on before we get in deeper…"

"Deeper?" I push when he doesn't continue. When he refuses to say anything more, I move to lay down, dropping my head to the pillow. "I'm not going anywhere. Not until he comes back."

Travis takes a heavy, hushed breath. "He warned you might make it difficult."

"Come again?" I say, wincing as I sit bolt upright, cupping my bump.

"Slow down there," he says, leaning forward to see if I'm

okay. I try to brush him off but he doesn't allow it. "Look, I know exactly where your head's at." He moves to sit next to me. I wonder how and whether it has anything to do with Mollie? "But you can't let it beat you. Dean *will* come back, mark my words. For now, we need to do what he asks. Otherwise we complicate shit."

I can't help the hint of sarcasm that escapes. "*We* complicate shit?" He smiles but I add, "I'm still not leaving until he gets home." His smile fades as I lay myself back down.

Travis rubs his face before speaking. "He was pretty fucking clear, Mads. Packed a bag for you and everything."

He did *what?* "Where?"

"It's at mine. Has everything you'll need in it."

"I can't just fucking leave, Travis. I need *him*."

"Yeah, we all do." His phone ringing from inside his cut makes us both look to his chest.

"Who's that?" I ask.

Travis looks at the phone. "Yep," he says, swiping his thumb across the screen, holding his other index finger up to me. The bed bounces slightly as he stands his full weight to his feet. I hang on to every movement; from his eyes, every deep breath he takes—anything that'll give me some sort of clue as to what's happening.

Holding the phone away from his face, he looks at the screen then moves the phone back to his ear. "So, Monday morning? Yep. Okay."

Something's not right.

Travis hangs up. I watch as he sends a text to someone. Putting his phone back in his pocket, he starts walking towards the door. He pauses looking back over his shoulder. "Get dressed," he says. His voice is devoid of emotion. Before I can get any words out, he closes the door, and I hear him go downstairs.

Reaching the bedside table, I turn the alarm clock towards me. It's just after seven in the evening. I've been in bed all day.

Swinging them off the side of the bed, I try to stretch my legs. They ache. From the tips of my toes all the way to my hips, they ache.

I look down at my bump before I stand. Tiny knocks can be felt against the inside, underneath where my fingers now lay. What do I do? Who knows where I'm meant to be going. I don't want to leave. But I also don't want to do anything that may jeopardise whatever Dean has planned.

I wish I knew what that was.

Grabbing my dressing gown from the back of the door, I walk downstairs, the bravest face I can muster pulled firmly in place.

Travis sighs so hard when he sees me. "Mads, for fuck's sake just please, help a brother out. I have a job to do."

"I can't," I say, my tone resolute but soft. "I have a job to do, too. He'll need me, Travis. You know that."

Travis holds my gaze.

I take the final step, moving closer to where he's sitting on the sofa, holding his phone. "What's happening Monday morning?" I ask, referring to the call he took.

His eyes move between mine. "It's—"

"—I want to hear it from Mollie."

My interjection has Travis looking like he could throw me across the room. His eyes drag in the corners, and I see his jaw tighten.

"I'll go with you, wherever Dean said, but not until *Mollie* tells me what's going on." His silence makes my stomach start to turn. I carry on, praying I'm not digging myself a grave. "I know you said not to mention her, but try to put yourself in my shoes. Please, Travis."

He throws his phone to the table, then covering his face with both hands, he rubs his eyes. "Go back up those stairs and get fucking changed."

"Hey, don't talk to me like that."

"No!" he barks. "You don't talk to *me* like that. Listen to what you're being told to do." His reaction to me mentioning Mollie's name proves there's a connection there.

I laugh. Like a deranged woman who should really read the room, I laugh. "I forget you do that." He gives me a look that suggests I should explain myself, fast. "Just blindly follow the leader."

The grunt as his rage is barely kept under wraps makes me shiver. "This might be a game to you, Mads, but lives could be at stake here. So go get changed, and for once in your life stop challenging every decision we fucking make."

Lives could be at stake here. "I know it's not a game, Travis. It's my fucking life too." He lets out a sigh. "I still need to hear it from her."

"Why's that so important to you?"

"Because she won't lie to me! She won't try to hide the truth because she doesn't know me."

"And I'll do everything in my power to keep it that way!"

When he shouts, I jump back, and I see him regret it.

Blowing out a breath, he stands. "Look, do as I say, please. I'll put the kettle on, give you some time, but then I need to get you out of here."

My body slumps, defeated in shock. "Where are we going?"

"You're going south, be with Bex for a bit." I can't complain about seeing my best friend. But my home is here. Travis stands, and I see his phone light up on the table.

Thinking on the spot, I say, "Can you grab me some biscuits with my tea?" quickly distracting him.

"Sure." He smiles, then turns and leaves the room.

I grab his phone from the table, my eyes flicking to the kitchen doorway. The passcode on the screen lights up. *Think. Think.* Heart rate booming, I press six digits, praying I know

Travis well enough. The phone unlocks. I shake my head at his stupidity to use all zeros.

Hearing his footsteps pad on the wooden floor, I quickly scroll through the names in his phone. I send myself the only 'Mollie' in his contacts. The fridge door slams shut making me jump. I quickly lock the phone once the message is sent and place it back on the table.

He walks back in holding out a mug for me to take.

"Thank you." I take the mug in both hands, then he passes me the biscuits.

"Don't be long. We've got a long drive ahead of us."

Nodding, I turn and walk back upstairs. I chuck the biscuits on the bed and place my mug on the bedside table. My phone is plugged on charge. I quickly snatch it then open a up a new message.

Me: Mollie? It's Mads, Dean's other half. I need your help. Please, if this is you, can you talk?

It takes a few minutes of me pacing the room before my phone vibrates in my hand.

Mollie: Mads? Is everything okay?

Me: Thank God it's you. Can I call?

Mollie: I can't take a call. Text is better. Where are you?

Me: I'm at Dean's house. Are you able to come here? It's important.

There's a slight delay before her next message comes through.

Mollie: Are you safe?

Me: Yes, I'm safe. I just need answers. I don't have very much time

Mollie: Okay, I can come to you

Me: Are you sure? Thank you.
Mollie: He still at 77?

I question how she knows that before sending my reply.

Me: Yes
Mollie: Be there soon
Me: Text me when you're outside

"How you getting on up there?" Travis calls.

I jump locking my phone and chucking it on the bed. "Fine," I shout back, as I aimlessly throw on clean underwear, my comfy trousers, a top and a black jumper. My hair is also scraped into a high ponytail. In the bathroom I brush my teeth, still with absolutely no intention of leaving this house.

Five minutes later, Mollie texts.

Mollie: I'm here

She mustn't live that far away.

I put my phone in my pocket and as quietly as I can, I make my way to the front door. Apparently, I'm not that quiet.

Travis stands at the bottom of the stairs, staring at me as I come down. "What're you up to?" he asks. He looks me up and down when I give him a blank look.

"Nothing, I just need a bit of fresh air before we go. Give me a minute?"

"I've given you plenty. Time's time, let's go." He opens the front door, facing me. The way I feel my face turn similar to that of a beetroot, has him slowly turning on the spot.

"Travis, wait!"

Too late. His shoulders slump when he sees Mollie stood at the front door, her hand raised to knock. Without a word, he closes the door on her, then turns to face me. He holds up his thumb and forefinger an inch apart. "This close. I am this close to losing my shit with you. We're not even an hour into the time we have to spend together, and you've already pulled this shit."

I brush past him, opening the door.

"Are you listening to me?" he shouts, but I manage to catch up with Mollie who's walking away.

"Mollie!" I reach her, extending my arm to stop her. I spot Lynn in the window. Giving her my best *everything's fine* smile, I mentally remind myself I need to let her know about Dean. She'll be worried.

"You didn't say *he* would be here."

Mollie's words pull my attention back to her. "I'm sorry, I just..." I pause, looking over my shoulder, hoping Travis remains inside. "No one will tell me what's really going on. The guys, they... they keep blocking me out, and I feel like... like..."

Turning, Mollie's brown, all-knowing eyes meet mine. "Like you have no control," she says discouragingly.

With a stark awareness of what she said, I suck in a big breath then wrap my arms around my body, nodding my head in agreement.

She lets out a small laugh at me, slightly shaking her head, her eyes glancing at my tummy. That's the second time she's done that since I've met her. "Can I give you some advice?"

I nod.

"You're already too late to take control of what's happening. Ride it out."

That's not what I thought she'd say. "Why would you say that?"

The side of her cheek sucks into her mouth. "Because I didn't," she says bitterly. Sad.

I take a step closer to her. "Travis?"

Mollie looks at the front door to Dean's house, her eyes narrowing with annoyance at his name.

"What happened?"

With a huff, Mollie shakes her head, looking to the ground. "What did you want to ask me?"

With her change of conversation, I decide to leave whatever happened in their past there, and ask about my future. "When's Dean coming home?"

She sniffs, tucking her hair behind her ear. "I updated the club half an hour ago." That would have been the call Travis took. "He was moved to prison. His hearing's on Monday."

I hesitate. "What's the charge?"

Mollie's slow to answer, just the same. "Suspected murder."

Slowly, my eyes close. Every muscle in my body tightens.

"Bail won't be granted, Mads."

Mollie waits for my eyes to open. I can't see her clearly for the tears swimming like puddles. "What can I do?"

Her lips part as she goes to speak, then looking over my shoulder, every feature on her face stiffens.

"That's enough!"

I spin on my heels seeing Travis storming towards us. "This aint fucking happening!"

"Travis, wait!"

He ignores my shout, stepping past me towards Mollie. "You need to go," he says, his shoulders broad, his chest puffed out. "Do what you're being paid to do, then leave. You got no business coming here."

Mollie frowns. "I told him I don't need his money."

"Ah, that's right. Mr Big Bollocks keeps you nice and sheltered in that fancy high rise of his."

The sound of Mollie's palm connecting against the side of Travis' cheek makes my eyes widen.

"You need to do that every time we see each other?" Travis riles, smiling and cupping where his skin must be stinging.

"Stop acting like an arsehole, then I won't have to. Outlaw or not, I'm not fucking scared of you, Travis."

I step forward, making sure Travis can see me. What difference it'll make, I'm not sure.

"Whatever you're trying to achieve here, it won't work," he angrily chides at her, his jaw clenching when he's finished.

I look at Mollie as she replies. "I stayed because Dean asked me to. I'm not trying to achieve anything—except saving your president from living the rest of his life behind bars."

And that's when I feel the wavering in my chest, the tightening in my lungs as I try to breathe. As if a stampede were trampling all over me, I feel caught under the weight of a possible future. A future without Dean.

A future without my VP.

My aching legs fail to hold me as black spots prick in my head.

"Mads!" Travis shouts. I feel his arms catch me before I fall to the ground.

When I wake, the three of us are inside the house. A cold tea towel is flush against my head, my legs slightly raised where I lay on the sofa. "She's waking up," I hear Mollie say.

"No thanks to you—"

"Enough." My voice is soft where my head is pounding. Their bickering won't help.

Mollie strokes my arm by my side. "I think we need to take you to the walk-in centre, Mads."

"No, I need to take her to the other end of the fucking country, then get back here ASAP."

"That's unrealistic, Travis," Mollie says. Relief fills me momentarily. "She needs to been seen by a doctor before she goes anywhere."

Sitting upright, I take the towel from my head and try to stand. I wobble, my head spiralling.

"Woah, steady," Travis says.

"Come on." Mollie hooks her arms under mine to hold me

steady. "I'll drive you there."

"Fuck," I hear Travis mutter as we walk towards the door. I hear him grab his keys. "I'll ride behind."

We pull up outside the walk-in clinic just on the outskirts of the city. The sky is dark, the air heavy and cold. Travis pulls up next to Mollie's car.

"I'm sorry."

Turning my head, I look at Mollie.

She stares out the front window. "I shouldn't have been so blunt earlier."

Unbuckling my seatbelt, I pause before opening the car door, my gaze moving out the front window like hers. "Don't be. I asked for the truth. Maybe I can't handle it anymore. Finally reached my limit." I try to smile, but it drops quicker than a lead balloon.

"The goal posts for your limits will never stop shifting in this life."

My head turns to look at her, but she doesn't return it. Words are lost on me. Has she been in my shoes? Now's not the right time to ask. I simply open the door and manoeuvre myself out. "You can wait here, I'll be fine," I say to Travis, as he places his helmet over the handlebars on his bike.

Mollie opens her car door and steps out.

Travis looks at her. "I'll see you in, if you don't mind?" he says.

Too tired to argue it anymore, I nod and accept his arm which he holds out for me. These two probably shouldn't be left alone together anyway.

Once inside and booked in, we sit side by side in the waiting room. A cloud of doom sits above us. Neither Travis nor I speak for the longest of times. It scares me; that I brought this all on myself. I haven't thought about who I'm carrying. Haven't eaten. I've barely drunk anything in four days.

A selfish wave of sadness washes over me. Lifting my hand

to cover my face, I can't stop the tears rolling down my cheeks.

"Hey." Travis lifts his arm and pulls me into him. "None of that, come on." It's a soft touch for such a hard man.

After a few moments, I lift my head back, wiping my damp cheeks on the end of my sleeves. "I'm sorry." He keeps his arm wrapped around me, giving me the comfort I need. "Do you think he'll come home?" I ask.

His dark eyes close. I don't know if it's my asking or the situation itself. An eternity feels like it passes between us before he answers me. "Do you believe in a higher power, Mads? Something bigger than all of us?"

His question comes out of the blue. I sit a little straighter, still under his hold. "You heard the story about how I was conceived, right?" I ask with a small laugh. He doesn't answer. When I look at him, he hasn't moved, his eyes are still shut, his head rests against the wall. "Do you?"

A small smile stretches across his face. "My kind of church is a much darker attraction, Mads."

"Of course it is."

He laughs at my words, opening his eyes to look at me.

My right hand moves to my bump where the baby knocks.

Travis looks down. "May I?" he asks.

"Uh, yeah. Sure." I sound more uncertain than I feel.

Moving my hand, Travis moves his and rests it over the curve of my belly button. The baby kicks, and we both look at one another. "Felt that one." He smiles, and it warms me to see him happy. "Does it feel weird?" he asks.

The tiny kicks make me need to itch where it tickles. "It certainly doesn't feel anything like how I expected."

"Dean told me he thinks you're having a girl."

My smile is genuine this time. "He told you that, huh?"

"Told me he knew before he even found out you were pregnant."

My eyes fill. I bite my top lip in an attempt to control my emotions. "He had a dream when the Saviours had him. He's been convinced ever since. Carries the picture from the scan everywhere he goes."

Travis smiles. "You're turning him into a chick, you know that?"

I slap his arm, and he laughs. He takes a deep breath, and I sense him trying to piece together what he really wants to say. Our eyes lock. "When it comes to you and this baby, I've honestly never seen him happier." I smile as he speaks. "But he can't be *that* man for what he has to do next. He knows it, and I think deep down you know it, too." I don't look away from Travis.

A member of staff walks past.

Travis watches him and waits for him to be out of ear shot before he looks back at me and whispers, "It'll get him killed."

I can't help but feel like a fight for our love is going to start. "How do I let him without losing him again?"

With a sigh, Travis lifts his arm for me go back under it.

I rest my head on his shoulder, not saying a word.

"You hold on tight. Pray... to whoever you have to. He'd die for you," his hand moves to mine, squeezing it tight, "so you live, for him."

CHAPTER SIXTEEN

DEAN

Present day - Monday

Thud. Crack. Thud. Crack.

I try to brace myself for the next hit, but the fresh stab of pain leaves me unable to move. Like holding your fingers to the flame, the harsh hot burn of my final decision, weaves itself through my bones.

They make to leave the room, their backs turning to me. I try to speak but all that comes out of me is a pitiful groan. "Wait," the officer who started all of this says. I see him turn in between my laboured blinks. When the blackness lifts, he's stood over me. "One more before he leaves for his hearing."

Thud.

The heel of his polished shoe strikes me on the temple, sending me to oblivion.

Six days ago

The torment of hearing her screams as I'm pulled outside leaves my muscles shaking. The anguished loud cries puncturing my chest. *What did you expect?* Not for it to instantaneously ache like it does.

I'm led to the back of a police car and swiftly driven to

the nearest station. There's just enough time for me to mentally think over everything I asked Travis to do. I know it's a bitter pill for him to swallow. But he needs to get it down. We need the new business if we're to remain in control.

Being escorted inside police custody, I stand at the booking desk. They take my name, my belongings, even my belt. The angry sounds of buttons being slammed on the keyboard makes me raise a half smile as they go through the motions.

One officer repeatedly looks at me like he has some issues. He's a similar build to me, less hair, broad shoulders. From the corner of my eye, I feel his look of disgust land on my cut. Eventually, I give him the eye contact he seems to crave.

He frowns shaking his head at me, rolling my thumb over the inky sponge to take my fingerprints. He lifts my hand, pressing the pad to the paper, and I watch him, knowing his eyes are going to jump to my face again at any minute.

There it is. "You know, last time someone looked at me this much, I got laid," I throw at him, my arrogance attempting to mask the ache in my chest.

He ignores me and carries on with his job.

Offering no resistance, it doesn't take long before they lead me to a cell. The door unlocks, and I walk in with a little help from my new friend. I stumble, turning to look at him.

He gives me a sinister smile. "Take it off," he says.

"What, no foreplay?"

Unexpectedly, he spits in my direction, his gob landing on my cut.

A misty red heat rises within me causing my nostrils to flare. I raise my eyes to the camera in the corner of the room.

"Temporarily out of action for repairs," he says, letting me know that *temporarily,* he thinks I'm his bitch.

I don't reply, too pissed off with this prick's lack of respect. It's come a hell of a lot sooner than I'd expected; me being tested, but there's nothing I can do in here. I'm guessing this guy knows it. "Your cut, take it off." His words he grinds due to my lack of movement. "Fucking now you worthless—"

"Yeah, yeah." I know. My cutting him off only serves to piss him off more. Still, I don't move.

He nods. "Fine." His slightly less bulky frame is across the room with his iron stick ready and raised. If I could punch this guy in the mouth, he'd already be down. All I can do is turn, protect my head, and hope the patch on my back is enough to hinder some of the blow that's about to strike.

His baton hits the top of my arm, causing it to instantly go limp by my side. *Fuck.* That fucking hurt. He strikes me again, then again on the back of my leg, forcing me to kneel. "That's better," he chides.

My teeth bite down as he stands over me. The waves of agony feel like blades have reached the bone in my leg. I huff out a breath I didn't realise I was holding before I suck for more air, desperately trying to breathe my way through the pain. I pull it in through my nose and let it out through my mouth when he hits me again. "Feel better?" I ask.

My smart mouth earns me another whack to the back of my leg. This time, my breathing has quickened, adrenaline suddenly overflowing in my veins. "Take off the motherfucking cut," he tells me again.

I steady myself, still knelt to the floor. "No," I laugh. I know I'll have to, but every fibre of my being really doesn't fucking want to. This is their way of stripping me of who I am.

Taking it off me was inevitable.

His heavy hands grab for my collar, and he pulls me to my feet. "I said, fucking, off!" He rips and pulls at me, jostling me about the tiny cell we occupy. Pulling it off my weak arm first, the prick manages to wrestle the leather off my back.

Now I get why he went for my arm.

With our struggle, the pain has started burning brighter. White hot flames so raw, start flickering in my vision. I bite the inside of my mouth to give me something else to focus on. When I start tasting copper, the distraction starts.

I watch on as the officer inspects my cut in his hands. He stows away his baton as he speaks. "Appears to have some dirt on it." He brings my pride to his mouth, then he spits on the flash across the front.

Prick.

He laughs as my face contorts, then strides to the door, victorious. He never once looks back. The door simply closes, the heavy sound of it being locked behind him, echoing down the corridor.

I'm not sure how long I stand there for. It's only when I see a red light on the camera start flashing in the corner of my eye, do I move to sit on the bed. I try not to show my discomfort as I roll to my back, one side of my body completely numb.

The hell they're going to put me through will be nothing compared to what will happen inside if I don't sit down with The Saint as soon as I arrive.

Three days ago

Once I'd spotted the tattoo on the man I killed, and he'd disclosed he'd been released with instructions, I knew I needed someone on the inside.

I never expected it to be me.

Mollie unexpectedly coming back was a blessing and also a curse. I couldn't stop the inevitable, so I took a chance and asked her to defend me, making sure things were in place for those I love. Am I worried it's a murder charge? Something less serious would have been ideal, but no point hiding from it. What other choice do I have? Ripper members we have currently residing in prison are all so spread out, it's just pure bad fucking luck they're not where I needed them.

She didn't want to get involved, but Mollie was never going to see me go down for this. We have history.

Police transferred me to His Majesty's Prison this morning; at the end of their allotted time to hold me in custody. Now I wait until my hearing on Monday.

Stood over the toilet, I lean my head against the wall as I struggle to piss, courtesy of the welcome party I received. Looking down, the sprays I manage to pass are discoloured. This isn't good. My jaw also aches and my shoulder's on fire.

The bleakness suddenly seems so broad.

After I was jumped, I laid on the floor for ten minutes before I was able to get myself up. No one helped me, and I didn't expect them to. But on my own, inside my own head… I couldn't hide from it.

It's a bitter irony that in order to survive what's to come, I'll have to unleash that part of me that used to consume me. That anger and violence that put me in here, I'm going to need it.

When I gingerly move back to my bed, I think of Rocco, then of Jack. Stupidly, I then close my eyes and think of Mads. This is going to hurt her; the not knowing what the hell is happening. Telling her about a potential murder charge was never an option though.

I don't want to fucking be here. Now that I am, it might as well fall on me to find who's sending threats. If I can survive until Monday when I go to my plea hearing, I'll stand a chance. I just need to sit down with The Saint fucking sharpish.

Forty-six hours in police custody was rough, but compared to life in here, it was a walk in the park. Anyone who says otherwise is either dumb or hasn't experienced it. It's numbing. Soul destroying.

Hell.

It's the mind that suffocates your soul.

Staring at these blank walls, I stupidly allow myself to imagine the scenario of Mollie *not* actually being able to save me from this place. All I can do is hope that this time history will actually fucking repeat itself, and for once in my life I'll get a win.

A life without Mads. Or my kid. Or my club... Mollie's good, but I'll need her to be a fucking magician if I want to go home.

When I wake on Sunday morning, the tips of my fingers are numb. I can't tell how long I slept for—or if I even properly slept at all. All I know is there was one face I held onto. One image that reminded me of why I'm not already dead.

The lights in the cell flick on, and I blink my eyes open. Putting the picture of Mads away in my mind, I sit up with a yawn, using my good hand to rub my face. Then I remember to check if my cellmate is awake. He's not there.

Fuck. He and I haven't exchanged proper words yet, but having him here would have been a damn sight better.

Here we go.

When the door opens, an officer—presumably starting his day shift—walks in with an envelope. He bends, placing it on the floor about a foot into the cell. He then turns and leaves.

I look down at it, then slowly move off my bed, my arm still hanging heavy by my side. Picking it up with my good hand, I go to stand, only for the door to fly open, and a foot to catch me off guard in the ribs.

The envelope skims across the cell floor as I roll to my back.

"Rise and shine. Solicitor will be here soon." The prick winks at me then shuts the door behind him.

I get up, grab the envelope, then sit back on my bed. On the front there's a stamp saying 'approved items'. Slowly opening it, I find the picture from my wallet. That's all there is.

My heart starts drumming. Rather than feel emotional, seeing it fills me with an unexpected influx of determination and confidence. A confidence that, no matter what they try to throw at me, I won't let them beat me.

After breakfast, I wait in a separate room for Mollie, my head in overdrive. When the door opens, seeing her instantly makes me think of Mads. I swallow the lump as I stand to greet her.

"Don't get up," she says, immediately dropping the papers in her hand to the table.

I pause mid-stand, then sit back down, cradling my arm.

She notices, taking a seat opposite me, fixing her suit jacket.

When she sighs—the noise a symphony of pain, I hate that I don't dwell on it more other than asking, "You good?"

I'm a fucking idiot. Of course she isn't.

"Dean." Her voice is bordered with doom as she looks at my arm. "What happened?"

"Nothing. I'm peachy," I reply. Darkened eyes assess me, but not once does she look me in the eye. "Mollie?" I say after I see her rub at her wrist subconsciously. She doesn't say anything. Her eyes move down slowly, and I see her go back to *that* place. "Don't," I whisper, trying to keep her here with me.

After a beat, I watch as she switches off her emotions. That uncanny ability to shut it all down in order to survive. She stops rubbing her wrist, covers it, and the next time she looks up, the woman I need is here with me. Mollie opens the folder in front of her and begins talking. "The bullet I warned you about."

I take the picture in my hand.

The next one she passes is of Travis' van. It's no longer distorted. Even I can make myself out. "They think they have enough evidence to charge you, Dean." Her voice is sombre. "This is real now."

I nod, knowing.

"What else is going on?" she adds, catching me a little off guard.

I look up raising a brow at how she can still know me after so much time away. I half smile. "Need to find someone inside," I tell her truthfully.

Her eyes pin on mine. "And if you do?"

Beat him. Cut him. Whatever it takes. "I need to ask him why he's threatening Sodom Saviours." I can see Mollie thinking, her lips pulling tight across her face. "Anyway, tell me what's happening with the case," I say.

She nods a little hesitantly, getting back to why she's here. "They know six men are missing, and they have that bullet." Our eyes meet again. "Conditional bail looks unlikely. You need to tell me everything, so I can try to find a way out."

I instinctively look up at the camera knowing they can't legally record this. "It fell apart the minute we got there. I did things my way and fucked it all up."

"Doesn't surprise me."

I smile with a sigh. There's a glass of water on the table. I take a sip. "Travis got me out. Another brother was there, but it was Travis who laid most of them down to save me." My eyes look up. Mollie frowns, and I shake my head, seeing the memories of that night and the days that followed like a carousel of pictures in my mind.

"How'd he do it?" she asks.

We look at one another. Mollie's face is tight, her emotions living so visibly on the surface. It's like an avalanche waiting to fall the way she carries them all. "I went in, took on five of them like some chump. I was blinded by my hate, Mollie. I'd lost Mads, Jack..." I struggle to elaborate on how I felt finding out that Jack was no longer on this earth with me.

Rubbing my face, I try to steel my composure. "When one of them mentioned him, I stabbed him before another one knocked me out. I came to, his hands around my throat. Travis shot the man on me, then turned and shot another as he went for Beats who was coming in at the back of the building, a petrol drum in his arms. He dropped the drum trying to protect himself, leaving two of them inside."

Mollie keeps watching me as I recall the events that unfolded that night at the mill. "He and Travis took out the last two when they ran like fucking cowards."

"Where were you when this was happening?"

"On the floor." Wishing in that moment that the air had been robbed from my lungs.

"Police report *six* missing persons."

"The sixth was outside—before I went in. I took him out there."

"Right," she says. "So, once the five inside were no longer able to talk, who brought the sixth man in?"

"I did," I tell her. She doesn't ask, but I sense Mollie waiting for me to continue. "We covered what we could in fuel and lit the place up like it was fucking bonfire night."

A moment of silence passes between us. "Why didn't you clean up. Like last time?" Her voice is hushed. The past still very much her present.

I sit back in my chair. "We went into lockdown later that day. There was no time. Saviours had threatened everyone close to us."

"I'm sorry."

"Don't be," I reply. "I don't need your sympathy, Mols. What I need is for you to ensure I get out of here."

She sighs. Hard. "I can't see the light at the end of the tunnel." I stare at her. "Your *hopes*," she says the word loosely, "to survive and get back out with the information you want, aren't very realistic when you're in on a *murder* charge. You do realise that in order to get you out, we'll need a miracle?"

I let that sink in. "Just because you can't see the light, doesn't mean it isn't there." Mollie looks at me hard-faced. I lean forward. "Now's the time to be the woman you left to become."

She takes a moment, then picking up her pen, she clicks the

tip. "What else do you need from me, besides working miracles?"

Simple. "She's with Bex now for a while, but make sure Mads is okay?" Travis will protect her life when I can't physically be there, but my girl will need someone who's been in this situation before. Emotionally.

Mollie smiles, but it doesn't reach her ears. "Sure."

"I need you to keep the club updated as well. Will mean talking to Travis." She eye rolls me, and I smile thinking of my girl. "Think you can manage that?"

"You want me to keep things civil?"

I nod.

"Then I need something in return."

I raise an eyebrow at her.

"When this is all done... if we can somehow get through this... I might need your help."

I immediately straighten my face. "Everything, okay?" I ask.

"Yeah, I'm fine. I just... need your help with something, but it can wait."

The look I give lets her know she better not be lying to me. She mirrors it as if to tell me to get fucked. "Deal," I say. "But if you need anything sooner, you let the club know. Whatever you need, Mollie, you come to us."

I'm interviewed with Mollie by my side. Her only instruction: to answer 'no comment' to everything they ask me. It's clear this isn't going to be a walk in the park.

After she leaves, I wait in the room to be escorted back to the cell. I'm in desperate need of a piss and know I've probably got a long weekend ahead of me, just waiting to hear that I won't be granted bail any time soon.

The door opens, and I hear two sets of footsteps approach me from behind. With my back to the door, I wait for them to tell me to stand so they can take me back.

My eyes dart over my shoulder when no one says anything,

but before I can get a proper look at the officers behind me, two hands fly over my head and pull me back by the throat.

Whatever he's using to try to suck the life out of me, it cuts in deep just above my Adam's apple. I tense the muscles in my neck as I try to wedge my fingers between my skin and what feels like an electrical lead.

Coughing and spluttering, the other officer steps forwards and lands a punch to my ribs. I can't brace myself for it—can't even fucking retaliate or kick out for how this prick behind me is holding me in place. All I can do is concentrate on not losing consciousness as he starts raining blows to my side.

When little stars begin to threaten, I refuse to let myself slip away. Using all of my energy, I push myself backwards with force, throwing my head back as far as I can into the officer's chest. He can't hold my weight. I clatter to the floor, taking the chair with me.

Rolling to my front, I manage to push myself to my knees as the door opens again, and someone else steps inside. I blink, desperately trying to line my vision in case there's another one joining the party.

"What the fucking hell's going on here?" the new guy shouts.

The officers in the room catch their breaths, both looking at me as they stand straighter. "Fucker came at us when we tried to move him back to the cell."

The new guy looks around, his eyes scanning the scene before him. It's pretty fucking clear what's just gone down in here, especially now that I can't stop coughing, holding my hand to my throat.

I look up to him once I've gained some composure.

"Take him back to his cell," he whispers.

The officers nod and follow their instructions, dragging me from the floor and throwing me in the other room.

"Don't lay another finger on him until we're instructed," I hear the one in charge mutter as they close the door behind me.

Instructed?

I shake my head. Worry and doubt start to plague me. Fear starts gripping at my insides. It twists its way into my head, so intertwined with my demons and their mocking voices, that for now—in this very moment—I begin to lose sight of that tunnel. I begin to lose sight of *why* I thought I could do this.

I see the lady on the lake. Trapped.

My future is in Mollie's hands. I've entrusted Travis to take care of my girl. What if I never see my child? *Stupid.* I hide my face in my hands, wondering why whenever I think I've found my place, the universe decides to shit all over me?

The third wall goes up, and suddenly I can't see what I'm doing. I can't see my purpose. It's going to take a lot more than what they've given to break me. They don't know I'm fighting what's on the inside. No amount of torture or punishment they dish out will come close to what I can do to myself.

Monday morning, my cell door opens. My breakfast is placed in the room rather than me having to go the food court for it. I don't get up. Instead, I stay sat on the bed, my elbows resting on my legs, my hands locked together. The officer who kicked me stares me down, a slight pause in his step when he notices me sat motionless.

That's the reaction I wanted.

I had Mollie call the club so that word would get to Travis of my hearing this morning. Mads will be south by now. No way she could show up to my hearing this morning. I wouldn't want her to see me like this.

I have to keep focused, and seeing her won't help.

A long night of no sleep and torturing myself made a consciousness shift occur. I plagued myself with Doc's words from my first therapy session. *In remembering who you truly are, the light of awareness will emerge.*

Remember who you truly are.

I've been patching at old wounds trying to be a new me. With the help of Mads, I've tried my hardest to fix how I function. But last night, I realised covering old wounds won't help me through this.

I don't need permission to be who I truly am. *I do bad shit, have done bad shit, and will continue to do bad shit until all the other shit goes away.*

"Bring that to me," I tell the officer still stood in my doorway.

"The fuck you talking to?"

I cock a smile, my eyes slowly raising as it widens. No more fear. No more doubt. "I'm fucking talking to you."

He strides into my cell, trying to swipe the tray at my head.

I jump to my feet, dodging the prick's advance, and hit him straight in the mouth, like I should have done the first time he walked in here.

He squeals loud like the fucking pig that he is. Amongst the food spread over the floor, his fingers then reach for the red alarm on the wall.

"It's too late for that," I tell him, entering the dark place where it doesn't matter how or why I'm doing what I'm doing. I'm just doing it. Possessed.

Dragging him back, I flip him over then straddle him, plunging my fists one by one into his face. I pound his flesh, thumping his skin until his blood is dropping from my knuckles.

The cell door swings open, and three more officers run into the room. They drag me off the man, pulling and pushing me until they have me where they want me. They kick and they hit, one of them grabbing his baton and striking my body repeatedly.

That's it boys, do your worst.

CHAPTER SEVENTEEN

MADISON

Monday morning, I arrive at the clubhouse a little after 7.30am. It's early, but we have an hour before we need to leave. I knew I couldn't stay at the house. Without Dean there, it doesn't feel right. I woke up at the crack of dawn, my head pounding. I text Travis asking him to meet me here before we leave.

Walking in, I'm surprised someone's already here to have opened up.

As if answering my question, Red walks past right on cue. Ah yes. Of course she wouldn't miss this day.

I don't give her any eye contact as I walk around the bar and grab the kettle. I decide to make some breakfast even though I'm not hungry. The thought of what today might hold turns my stomach, but more to busy myself, I carry on searching for food. Maybe Travis will want some. If I can find anything.

A door opens down the corridor. Fully expecting it to be Red again, I walk to the fridge grabbing the milk, not really paying much attention to who it is. When I do look up, Lauren's stood there.

Her blue eyes look lost. Her shoulders, drooped. The look on her face, exhausted. "Lauren?" I question, quickly snapping out of my mood and moving closer to her. "What the hell are you doing here?" I look around as if the answers will appear.

"Uh, the lady let me in. I swung by the house but… I need to talk to Dean. Is he here?" Her voice sounds tired.

"Come and sit down," I tell her.

We move to a table and I pull out a chair for her. She takes off her tatty coat and rucksack and sits, yawning as she does.

"You look exhausted," I say gently.

Lauren twiddles her fingers, playing with a large ring on her index finger.

"What's going on?"

She semi huffs, her body language instantly shifting to defensive mode. "Can I have some food and a drink before you start questioning me?"

Raising my eyebrows at her, I let out a breath. "Only if you agree to tell me everything and not leave this time?"

She slowly nods, defeated.

I give her a half smile, then stand and go to the kitchen. I make two cups of tea and search for some food, constantly checking she's still sat at the table.

Red walks in, audibly huffing when she sees me in here. Ridiculous.

"Where's the food that's not going to give someone a heart attack?" I ask, thinking out loud as I open and close cupboards.

"It's a clubhouse, not a five-star hotel," Red says popping her hip, watching me.

"Right." Bacon will have to do. I click on the grill and grab a tray, slapping enough pieces on for Lauren and Travis.

"You not lining that first?" she asks.

"Thought this was a clubhouse? What does it matter?"

She blows out her breath then moves to a drawer grabbing some foil. I notice she's wearing less makeup today, her face looking naturally pretty. "Because I'll be the one cleaning it up, that's why."

Reluctantly, I open it and place the bacon on top. I consider asking about the change of appearance but think better of it. We just about tolerate each other. We're not friends. Not by a long shot.

"Here," I throw the foil back at her, catching her off guard.

"Bitch," she glowers at me under her breath.

I can't help but smile as I pick up the teas and head back to Lauren.

Twenty minutes later, Travis is now here. He was grateful for the food. He was also pleased to see his little sidekick back. Watching the two of them was heartwarming.

Lauren burps, wiping the back of her hand across her lips.

"Feel better?"

She nods appreciatively.

"Looks like that's the first proper thing you've eaten in a while?" Her eyes raise to mine. I can tell it is. I place my hand on hers on the table. "Time to spill."

"Okay, but don't be mad, swear to me," she blurts out.

"Okay, I swear," I reply wide-eyed, shocked by her sudden change of pace.

Lauren drops her head. "I... I haven't had anywhere to stay for the past week."

"What?" I fire at her.

"Mads you swore."

Holding my head in my hands, I then look to her. "O-kay. Why have you not had anywhere to stay for the past week?" I ask, my hands held open.

"It's complicated."

Tell me something I don't know. Shit. How am I going to tell her about Dean? "Try me," I say.

Lauren begins by telling me how after she ran away three months ago, she and her older brother Jay were jumping from youth hostel to youth hostel, trying to steer clear of their uncle.

That was certainly the last I knew of her whereabouts.

She goes on to tell me how Jay had found work at a local takeaway place not far from the hostel, but one-night last week, he didn't return home. "He was meant to be back at seven," Lauren says. "He was bringing dinner home for us. I waited and waited, but I knew something was wrong. He's never late. Come eight o'clock, I couldn't wait anymore. I tried calling him but there was no answer. I even went to his work to check he'd shown up. They said he left at the end of his shift, like normal."

"Where do you think he is?" I ask.

Lauren shrugs, looking down. "At first, I assumed Dean had something to do with it." I give her a curious look. "I was so angry when I saw him. But I could tell he was telling me the truth that he hadn't seen him." Lauren lowers her head. "I assumed someone had come after him, finally found us, you know?" I nod my understanding. "We had a pact. If there was any danger, or anything was to happen to either of us—and we were lucky enough to get away, we would meet at the park near the common."

Now I know how Dean ran into her. His morning run is the same route every day. "Which is where you ran into Dean?"

She nods. "I'm not dealing like he thinks." I frown because I know she wouldn't do that again. "I made sure to go there, my stuff packed ready to go at the crack of dawn. I saw Dean as he was heading back."

I think for a minute. "Lauren, why not call one of us? We would have done anything to help you, you know that."

"I know. I just… I panicked—going to Dean's. My uncle will work out I'm here eventually, but I don't want to hurt anyone." A tear creeps down her face. She wipes it away as if she's not allowed to cry. "I guess we just got used to looking out for us." I can see her tougher exterior. The time away has hardened her. "I know Dean took something from my bag."

I incline my head. He never mentioned anything. "What?"

"A key."

"To where?"

"To the only other place I knew I could go that wasn't here."

I frown, even though I'm trying hard not to. "Which is?"

She gives me a hard look as I silently will her to tell me. "It doesn't matter now. I tried not to be a burden in your life, Mads. But I have nowhere else to go. I'm all out of options. And I'm tired."

My heart constricts. "You are not alone," is all I say.

She grabs me and holds on tight. We stay like this, both of us grateful to have the other back.

Pulling us from our embrace, Travis tries to not-so-subtly cough from behind us. "Uh, Mads? It's time to go."

"Where are you going?" Lauren asks.

I look at her wiping her tears off her cheeks. "I'll explain later. You'll be here when we get back?"

She nods her head, and I'm filled with happiness, followed by immediate sadness that the reality is Dean won't be coming home. I can't let myself think about it. The thought kills me.

"Give me two minutes," I tell Travis, standing out of my chair. He nods and unexpectedly, I go in search of Red. "Can I have a word?" I ask when I find her.

She's busy getting the kitchen ready before the guys arrive. "You want to talk? Usually you just look down your nose at me. What's changed in the past half hour?"

"I've looked down at you because you're infatuated with the man whose baby I'm carrying."

Scowling, she replies, "You're wrong, but if he didn't care about me, why hasn't he gotten rid of me? Made me leave or some shit?" She carries on wiping glasses.

"He doesn't want to see you without a job. He's a decent man." My mind trails. He's about to have a hearing on a murder charge, but his heart… his heart is the purest I've known.

Red stops as if thinking the same. "So, what do you want from me all of a sudden?"

"I need a favour," I say.

She laughs shaking her head. "Honey, I'm not teaching you how to give hand jobs under the prison table."

I stare at her. My face blank. Expressionless. *Don't rise to it.* "See the girl out there?" I motion towards Lauren who I catch fist bumping Travis. Their small gesture makes me smile.

"Yeah, what of her?"

"I need you to keep an eye on her whilst we're out. Don't let her leave. Let her sleep or keep her busy if you have to." I turn back to her, waiting for her reply.

"You're serious?" she asks. Not moving, she can tell by my expression that I am. "Fine," she mutters.

Walking away, I then stop myself by the door. Slowly, I turn around to face her. "Thank you."

Red looks up, shocked, then after a minute she simply nods her head.

Sitting in the reception area, I look at the clock. Mollie went into the courtroom an hour ago to meet with Dean. I haven't seen her since getting the all-clear Saturday night, but I don't think she'll be surprised to see me.

After not moving for four days then with having to see the doctor, time had run out to take me anywhere. Until I know exactly what's happening, I refuse to leave. I'm holding on, even though I know deep down Dean isn't getting out of here.

I look up at Travis.

He holds a coffee out for me.

"Where'd you get these?" I ask looking around.

"Vending machine. I'll tell you now, it's shit coffee."

I sigh, but I'm grateful for the warm brew now heating my hands. Stroking my thumb across the top of the lid, I ask, "What happens next?"

Travis sighs. "Normal process is charges will be read against him." He doesn't say anything more. He sips his coffee staring dead ahead.

"And then?"

"Mads, what do you want me to say?"

I quickly swipe the tear at my eye, then sip my coffee, turning my head away from him.

"It's a murder charge," he sighs. "He'll be refused bail and kept in custody until his trial starts. Could be weeks. Maybe months." Closing my eyes, I force myself not to completely lose control. "Heads up," he says, making me sit bolt upright.

Mollie walks out of a room.

"You ready?" he asks me.

I don't reply. Instead I stand and make my way to her.

"Mads, what are you doing here?" Mollie questions. Her eyes have a red glow directly under her lids. She looks between me and Travis.

"What is it?" My voice is dry and burning.

Mollie looks again at Travis, and my eyes follow. The way they glare at each other is intense.

"What's going on?" I ask urgently.

She looks directly into my soul. "He's about to be escorted inside."

Shit. My stomach bottoms out. I feel like I'm going to faint. Allowing the tears to fall but taking steadying breaths, I manage to speak. "I need to see him."

With a sigh, Mollie drops her head. "He thinks you're already south." I swallow my sadness. "I didn't tell him about the other night."

I nod. Grateful. "Did he say anything else?"

Mollie shakes her head. "No. Are you sure you want to come in? I'm really not sure it's for the best, Mads. Travis?"

He sighs, stood behind me. "Maybe she's right," he forces himself to say. "It won't do him any good to see you right now."

I take in a breath. "It won't do me any good if I *don't* get to see him."

Mollie looks at her watch.

I start to turn before Travis can try to talk me out of it.

"Right," is all he says, his voice flat. "Make sure you get him out," I hear him order. Travis then leads me into the courtroom, his hand turning my shoulder.

We sit hidden towards the back. There aren't many people here, three or four sat on the other side to us. I look around spying the door Dean will come in through. A glass screen sits in front of where it's obvious he'll be stood behind.

My heart's hammering. My chest rising and falling irrationally as men and women in suits start entering the room. The sombre mood they all carry signifies the severity of the charges about to be read. I look at Travis, but he doesn't say a word.

A door opens, making me look down. I see Dean. His hair is dishevelled. His face drawn out and tired like he hasn't slept. The way he's carrying himself... Something isn't right. Is he hurt?

Please God don't let him be hurt. As if hearing my thoughts, Dean looks up through the glass, spotting Travis. He sits, then his face turns grave when he sees me.

CHAPTER EIGHTEEN

DEAN

As soon as I see her face, the mixture of emotions I feel is so fucking hard to comprehend. I don't move. Rooted to my spot, the physical pain doesn't come close to how heavy my heart feels when I see her start to cry. I can't quite make out her face, but the way Travis comforts her, it's obvious.

What is she doing here? She should be far away, not able to see me like this. He knew what I wanted. He knew I needed her to be away. And Mollie? Did she know?

I just about catch someone saying all rise, but I'm still frozen on the spot. Mollie whips her head around to look at me on the other side of the glass cage I'm stuck behind.

My eyes snap to the magistrate who's entering the room. With my hands cuffed down in front of me, I try to stand as straight as I can. Through the pain in my bones, through the fire roaring through my chest, I look at him, shutting down everything else.

This is going to break her. But it can't beat me. I need to survive in order to get back to her. I'm here to say two words and get back to it. Meet The Saint. Find the source. Hope Mollie gets me out.

The magistrate asks me how I plead.

"Not guilty," I say.

He briefly looks up at me, then looks back down at whatever's on his desk in front of him. The courtroom sits whilst he asks both Mollie and the prosecution a bunch of questions—none of which register with me.

After what feels like an eternity, he asks me to stand again. "Given what evidence will be being brought forward, I have decided this case be sent to trial. The prosecution and defence both have six weeks to build their cases. The defendant is to remain in custody until his trial begins."

Just as he bangs his gavel, I catch a tall figure in the public viewing box stand and leave before anyone else. Quickly, I look at Mads, but before I see her face properly, I'm ushered to stand and dragged through to the holding cell.

Perhaps it's for the best. Perhaps not being able to see her one last time will make it easier.

I'm escorted to the main room where I was searched upon arrival. Two officers stand by my side. They take me to the transport vehicle and drive me back to the prison.

Walking back into my cell, I see my cellmate is here. I give him a nod of my head, and he jumps down from his top bunk. I wonder what he's going to do. "How'd it go?" he asks, catching me off guard. Considering he's hardly been around and we haven't spoken properly in the past three days, why's he so chatty now?

"Exactly as I knew it would." I dump my grey jumper issued by the prison onto my bed, then sit holding my head in my hands, grimacing at the pain in my shoulder.

"You have anyone there?"

I sigh. "It doesn't matter." Best I don't think about it.

He nods understanding. "I'm guessing by the tats you're the biker they've been talking about?"

My cellmate moves, now folding his arms stood in front of me. He's a big guy—bigger than Travis. I heard he was charged with first degree murder. Of his mother. Apparently killed her with his bare hands.

"They?" I look up to him.

"The men who talk in this place." He pauses, then holds out his hand. "Luke."

Rather than say anything, I lean forwards with another grimace, taking his hand in mine. I grip my shoulder, rolling it back a few times.

"You need to get that checked."

"I'll be fine."

"Sure you will, tough guy." I look at him scrunching my eyes. "No offence," he adds. He moves to the corner of the room, taking a piss in the loo we share, hidden behind a small protruding wall designed for privacy. I hear him washing his hands. "I'd make it a priority to go see the doc."

His raven hair shines in the sunlight coming through the window when he walks back into view. Our eyes lock, and I understand his instruction.

Later that afternoon, I'm sat in the small health clinic within the prison. The nurse who did my assessment before coming in here deemed my inability to piss properly and the bruising on my body, severe enough to get checked over.

Examining my torso and right leg, the doctor constantly gasps and sucks in her breath at the damage I've sustained in three days. I'm given painkillers before she asks me where the bruising came from.

"I fell," I tell her.

She pauses filling out her form, having checked the range of movement—or lack of, I have in my shoulder. She eyes me then looks away quickly.

How many bullshit stories has she heard?

"Right, all done," she tells me. "You'll be allowed back every day for the next week so that I can administer the paracetamol and ibuprofen together. Some stronger anti-inflammatories might be needed as well if the swelling doesn't go down."

"Thanks," I say.

She stands and knocks on the door.

It opens then closes, and I'm left on my own sat on the bed. When the door opens again, a tall brute of a man walks in instead of the officer who should be here to escort me back to my cell. His head is shaved, his face round and full. The black ink stretching across his neck trails up past his ear to the top of his eye. He smiles at me, his face authoritative and solid. "You took your time."

Face to face with him now, anger starts washing over me. I feel the small waves start to run through my body, warming my blood. "*I* took my time?" I query, wondering what the fuck he's talking about.

"Been waiting for you to cave. They done you pretty good this morning."

The Saint may be many things, but straight to the point he is not. The corner of his mouth lifts. He points to a note which I see has been left on the table. Picking it up, he reads it, smirking every now and again. Then he looks at me. "Blood in your piss?" He sucks his teeth. "They weren't supposed to go that hard on you."

With a huff, I swing my legs off the side of the bed, my palms flat on the mattress either side. Fuck, I ache.

The Saint screws up the note then chucks it back on the desk. "You needed to see me?" he asks. Moving to the doc's chair, he spins it, sitting one leg either side, his front against the back. "Officially, I'm in solitary. This was the only way I could facilitate a meet."

"And unofficially?" I ask, my voice low.

He pauses before answering, his eyes inspecting me. "You pay the right price; you can do or get anything you want in here."

I see. "And what is your price?" I ask him, knowing I'll

need to play by house rules if I have any hope of finding the information I seek.

"You are smart, considering you don't reside in here often."

"Just smart enough so I don't have to," I tell him.

The Saint blinks, his dark eyes staring through me. "You'll know my price when I need something."

Closing my eyes briefly, I then look up to him.

With a wicked smile, The Saint wheels his chair closer to me. From where I sit on the bed, his head still manages to meet my chin. "What is it you need from me?"

"Protection."

He nods. "Vincent mentioned protection. Said threats have also been made," he looks me square in the eye, "to the Saviours."

He's not wrong. "That's right."

His eyes widen, waiting for me to elaborate. "Anything *I* can help with?"

I slip down off the bed giving him no option but to wheel himself backwards. "No."

He laughs. "And just a second ago I thought you were smart."

Shaking his head, he quickly stands, pushing the chair away. His comment leaves me annoyed. I feel myself getting irritated by the way he carries himself. "I run this fucking place. If the source was in here, don't you think I'd know? Vincent would have asked me to look into it."

My stare is hard as I try to a get a read on him. "Maybe this is something you're unaware of? Just like Vincent." I know what I saw and what I heard in the barn. "The men making the threats came from here."

"What makes you so sure?"

"One of them told me. Right before I slit his throat. Vincent would have known that if he'd got his hands dirty."

The Saint laughs. "Sounds about right."

I let out a breath. "I need you to let me find the source myself. I can't do that if I'm getting the shit kicked out of me every day."

There's a grin spreading across his face. "That was mostly to get you in here." He gestures around the room.

The beatings from the guards may have been him, but until he removes the red light over my head, I can't expect them to stop altogether.

"Why not ask me to look for the source?" he adds.

I smile. "Maybe I have trust issues."

"And yet you go into business with the men you hate most."

I know I'm being a hypocrite when I reply, "We had no choice."

The Saint laughs again, throwing his head back. "Rippers had no choice but to get into guns? Guessing it was join them or let them get immeasurably rich?"

"It was more than that," I say. I turn on the spot, looking up to the ceiling. "Working with them was about protecting what's ours and keeping everyone safe. Too much blood was spilled before we came to an agreement."

"And now?" he asks.

"Rippers will allow them through our county lines, but they don't stop. They pay the toll to pass through, just like always. We're not involved beyond that."

Standing off the chair, The Saint walks towards me. "A lot appears to have changed for the Rippers in the past few days."

What the fuck's he talking about? "Meaning?"

"Meaning, I heard you're loading and transporting now."

"That's not what was agreed," I bite. My insides start boiling, my ears ringing.

Face to face, he holds his hands up. "Don't shoot the messenger. Vincent said Costa changed the deal when they sat down together."

Why the fuck am I only finding out about this now? "I need a burner," I tell him. I need a fucking line to Travis as soon as I'm back in my cell.

The Saint dips his chin to his chest and with that, I make my way to the door. I'm two steps away, my hand raised to knock for the officer stood outside to let me out.

"Hold up," The Saint says quietly, stopping me in my tracks. "What do you know of this Costa?"

Turning around, I look at him. "He's Irish. Could source military weapons."

The Saint nods. "Heard he's a big player. Got a lot of money coming in from somewhere."

I let out a huff of my breath. "And Vincent wanted in on it." I'm thinking out loud. I can tell when I see him looking back at me curiously.

"And you couldn't let him."

It *is* as simple as that. "Not when they plan on going through our turf, no," I reply. After a beat I say, "Look into him? Anything you can find, I want to know."

The Saint dips his chin. The dreaded feeling that I need to know everything about everyone seems to hit me in the face. "I'll start with the Irish and be in touch."

At lights out, I sit in my cell staring at the scan picture. My thumb absentmindedly strokes over the face of the baby. *Three things you love.* My girlfriend. My unborn child. My club. *And the other three things.* Me. Myself. And I.

What would I change if I could? My mind trails as the cell door opens. Luke walks in and pushes it to behind him. "Courtesy of The Saint," he says in a low tone, reaching underneath his jumper and pulling out a pair of rolled up socks.

I extend my hand and take it from him. Sitting up on the bed, swinging my legs off the side, I unroll the socks finding the burner phone I requested. That was quick. I look up to Luke and nod my thanks.

"He knows what he needs," he says.

Already? "What is it?"

Luke walks towards the door, checking no one's outside. "The Irish." His voice is quiet. "They're going to intercept your first gun haul with the Sodom Saviours." Jesus Christ. "Seems they're not a big fan of this Costa."

How the fuck has he found this out so fast? "What does he need from me?"

Luke looks at me a little sincerely. "Rippers need to stop that from happening."

My body stiffens. "I'm not sending my men to fucking slaughter." Hot flames dance in my eyes. My bones burn, my skin's immediately clammy.

Dropping his head, Luke hesitatingly adds, "He also said he forgot to ask how Madison was? And the baby." He speaks so soft and slowly, it doesn't match his size or the threat being made.

Biting the inside of my lip, the taste of copper instantly coats my tongue. I try with every ounce of my being not to, but I stand, moving my body closer to Luke. Tension suddenly swims between us.

I slam him against the wall, my hand around his throat. I don't care how fucking big he is. My lips part, and I fight the fury within as I speak. "Don't mistake my lack of position in here as weakness." The heat engulfs me, my fists naturally curl tighter.

Luke simply stares at me. "Thought you were smart? Figure something out."

"He threatens my family again, he'll see just how fucking smart I am." My face remains flat, my eyes holding his gaze. Luke doesn't say anything as fear and doubt scratch away inside my brain. Not that I'd show it. I need to think fast.

"Listen. Nobody would think about crossing The Saint. He's

got men doing all his work for him. Vincent's lucky he's an old friend. Without that tie, his club would be asked to take the risk. You do this, you're good in here."

I huff. He thinks *that* highly of himself that he can pick and choose who lives or dies? No one holds that kind of power. I turn away from Luke bringing the phone up to my face. There are no other contacts on here, no nothing. I dial the digits I want to ring so desperately, but immediately delete them for the ones that will send me deeper into my darkness.

CHAPTER NINETEEN

TRAVIS

Luckily we were sat at church when Dean rang the club burner we use. Staring at it, the boys can hear for themselves what's going down. I'm not sure how I could have relayed all of what we're hearing.

"How many charters are we going to need to protect that cargo from being intercepted?" Beats asks.

From down the line, Dean replies, "All of them."

The way the air leaves the room leaves me breathless. I feel a booming in my chest; my heart picking up pace. It's not impossible to call everyone in, we just need to figure out how to facilitate it without attracting the attention of the law.

I run a hand down my face. "You sure? That's going to bring a lot of heat." My thumbs push either side of the bridge of my nose.

Dean's silent as we hear other voices talking in the background. "Very least you'll need the east coast charters. Call Sonny, he can get the other nomads on standby."

"And the Saviours?" Skitz asks.

We hear Dean sigh. "Assume they don't know. We tell them, they'll assume we're lying. We don't tell them and somehow manage to protect the transport, they'll owe us."

A few heads nod in agreement. "Okay, but the first

shipment's moving one hundred and forty-five miles. That's a shit load of miles to chaperone something we don't want anything to fucking do with." I can tell by Skitz's face he hates this.

"I agree," Len says.

No one speaks for a moment. "We don't have a choice," Dean eventually admits, his voice completely devoid of emotion.

"Boss?" I say, after we're left looking at each other around the table, waiting for him to say something—anything as to what we're going to do.

"Take me off speaker," he says flatly.

I pick up the phone and walk out the room. "You good, brother?" I ask him, making my way to the top of the stairs.

"Your uncle still own that farm of his?"

My head hangs low. Thinking of my relative has my insides churning. "Yes."

"Reckon he can give us one of the vehicles? I might have a plan."

We haven't spoken in years. "Don't see why not," I reply.

"Find out then let me know on this number."

"Okay." Dean stays on the line, his breaths turning heavy. "Dean?"

"Why the fuck was Mads in court earlier?"

Heaven help me. I shut my eyes. "There's no stopping that one. Had she not been in her condition, I'd have just chucked her in the car. But..." my voice trails, "she needed to see you."

Dean sighs. "I'm entrusting you with her life, Travis. Anything happens to her—"

"—Nothing's going to happen to her. You have my word. You need to give me yours that you'll look after yourself in there?"

Just when I think he's going to say more, the line goes dead. I let my head hang, my gut feeling telling me I'm losing my president, and more importantly, my brother.

"That's all of it." The door to the lorry closes, the latch, locked. "You have the route locked in?" Another of Costa coffee's minions asks me. I haven't seen this guy before.

"Down to every last turn."

"Good. He was very clear. No stopping. You have your man drive east without any fucking about."

I swallow the need to knock this prick out as I nod at him.

The docks along the west coast are quiet. At three in the morning, the only people here are the Saviours, my brothers, and Costa's man.

Beats, The Joker and Skitz take off their gloves having offloaded a dozen large wooden crates into the back of the lorry. Skitz in particular looks exhausted.

I look at him as he wipes his brow. "What is it?"

"Them," he says, pointing at the lorry. "Them fucking boxes weigh a tonne. You sure we're not ferrying rockets rather than just guns?"

Costa's man stops in his tracks having checked the shutters are locked. I notice him padlock it. *Fuck*. "Just guns?" His eyes roam over all of us individually. "Let me make this real simple and clear for you, gentlemen. These *just guns* don't arrive on time, your club owes us the total value of the contents."

"Which is?" I ask.

He grins wickedly. "More than you can afford, sweetheart."

Turning, he makes his way to Vincent and the other Saviours who helped load up the lorry. I call him a cunt under my breath as I feel the phone vibrate from inside my cut. I check no one's looking as I step around the lorry out of sight.

Unknown number: Everything set?
Me: We're good
Unknown number: Let me know when it's done

I don't hit reply to Dean. I stow away the phone, then grab my own. The guys have all checked in. Everyone's in place. Fuck, I wish Dean was here. No time to dwell though. Now's the time to execute his plan.

Costa's man hands The Joker the keys.

I give him the eye signifying everything's set.

He climbs in, and Beats does too. "Call me if there're any problems."

I assume Costa's minion is talking to me. I turn and see Vincent mounting his bike. "What's going on?" I ask looking back at him.

"They're going with you." He doesn't say anything more. He turns, climbs into the car he arrived in, then drives off. *Shit.* How the fuck are we to switch lorries if Vincent and Billy are here? This wasn't part of our plan or our agreement.

Billy gets in the lorry besides Beats. Vincent's engine starts.

The Joker's wide eyes catch mine, peering from his side mirror. He checks my expression wanting to know what to do. There's fuck all we *can* do. We'll have to carry on as planned.

I nod again at him, then climb on my bike, putting on my helmet. "You knew you were coming with us?" I shout to Vincent.

"Not until just now," he says with a shake of his head.

I can't tell if he's lying or telling the truth. My palms are sweating as I bring my engine to life.

We head east on faster roads enabling us to move the cargo quicker. The Rippers are well spread along the route placed at check points. Each point will call the next until the cargo arrives at the port. Fuck knows how I'll handle Vincent and Billy now that they're with us, but the plan is to stop, switch the lorries, and move the cargo.

Half an hour into the journey, my phone rings. Our signal lets me know it's Len up ahead. They're set.

The Joker flashes his hazard lights twice, and I know he's

ready. He starts indicating to take the next exit as planned.

Vincent jolts his head to me, then looks back to the lorry. His eyes are frantically trying to work out what's going on. He revs his engine, but I manoeuvre my bike before he can get around me. I can't let him fuck this up for all of us.

At this speed, on these roads, I can't tell him what's going on. He wasn't supposed to be here—*this* isn't meant to go down like this. I raise my left hand, signalling for him to look at the lorry joining the road we're on.

Understandably, a look of confusion mixed with anger dons Vincent's face. Even from behind the neckerchief pulled up over his mouth and nose, I can see it in his eyes, the way they scrunch together behind his glasses.

The identical lorry continues to merge into traffic as we—Vincent included, follow the cargo full of illegal weapons.

The Joker pulls to a stop on a hidden side road.

Vincent stops his bike just ahead of mine. Reaching into his cut, he withdraws a gun, pointing it directly at me.

"Wait!" I shout.

"Tell me what the fuck you're doing, right now!"

I cut my engine. "Put the gun away," I say holding my hands up. "Put the gun away and I can explain what the fuck's going on."

His eyes dart to The Joker and Beats as they quickly jump down from the lorry. The Joker has his gun aimed at Vincent's head.

"Stop!" I shout at him.

The Joker's eyes jump between both mine and Vincent's.

"Vince, put the fucking gun down!" I yell once more.

"Where's Billy?" Vincent asks, still pointing his gun at me but looking at The Joker.

"Out cold," Beats says, holding his jaw. "Had no choice but to knock the cunt out once he tried stopping us."

Vincent suddenly points his gun at Beats. He's outnumbered

and he knows it.

"Vincent, we don't have the fucking time for this. We've got to get the guns off that and onto another vehicle!"

As I say it, Mop pulls to a hasty stop right beside us. Len, Captain, Riggs and Skitz all jump out the back.

With no way out, Vincent lowers his gun, then moves to check on Billy.

"Bolt cutters, Mop!" I order, as he jumps out of the livestock lorry we borrowed from my uncle. It's not fucking subtle, but given where we live it'll blend in perfectly.

"Start explaining, right fucking now!" Vincent stomps his way towards me.

Mop breaks off the padlock, then throws up the shutters. He jumps on the back of the lorry, and I move to help him start switching the cargo to our vehicle.

"The Irish," I say, as I climb on the back of the lorry. "They're thirty miles east, waiting to stop this vehicle and take the guns."

Vincent's eyes blacken. He remains silent.

"The decoy will be intercepted. Nomads will ring once they see it happen."

"And this?" He points to the lorry I'm in. "Why not carry on in this. Why the fuck are we switching here?!"

"Because, dickhead, they're looking for this!" I swing my arm gesturing towards the lorry. "Once they find out someone knew, they could search high and low for this one."

"And that?" he asks, watching the Rippers quickly load up the crates onto the livestock vehicle.

"That will deliver Costa's guns."

"Fuck, me!" Skitz cries.

We all turn our heads to look at him.

"I swear to fucking Christ himself, I'm too old for this shit!"

"I know you don't believe me, but you've got no choice right now. We need to get these fucking weapons to the port." I turn and help Mop lift a crate from the lorry, then walk up the ramp onto the next. Skitz wasn't lying. These crates must be crammed with heavy artillery.

We work together in twos, moving the crates as quickly as possible. Vincent doesn't help. He calls his men, letting them know what's happening and to be ready for a new vehicle arriving at the port we're dropping off at.

With one left, I climb on the lorry with Mop as the others get ready to leave. The lorry shakes as the front door opens then closes.

Billy. He's awake. I hear him tread around the back of the lorry at pace.

"Billy, NO!" The way Vincent cries out makes my heart jump to my throat.

I turn, instantly feeling a thud hit my chest, a loud crack shattering my ear drums. Dropping to my knees, I pull air into my lungs, looking down and seeing blood seeping through my shirt. *Motherfucker shot me.*

I fall forwards, my palms flat against the steel floor. *This also wasn't part of the fucking plan.* My vision blurs. Trying to stand, I realise that's a stupid idea when the floor starts moving like a conveyor belt beneath me.

Just as I feel myself start to sway, Mop grabs me and steadies me. "Sit down! Don't move!"

I try to brush him off, but he knocks me back against the inside of the truck. He rips open my cut. "Shit, Trav... you lucky son of a bitch."

Some of the guys rush over to see what's happening.

Mop pulls out the burner, completely blown to smithereens in his hands. "This saved your fucking life."

My head falls back against the inside of the lorry, and I take a steadying breath, wheezing as I try.

The Joker and Beats are busy working Billy over as Vincent

tries to rip them off.

"Tell them to stop, right fucking now," I splutter.

"Fuck him. I need to check the wound. Looks like you've got shrapnel in there." He prods and pokes at my chest forcing more blood to leak.

After I feel myself not completely losing consciousness, I bat him away. "Stop fussing."

Mop smiles holding out his hand to help me to my feet. "You go back in this. Riggs can drive you—"

"We carry on," I say.

"But—"

"But fucking nothing. We've got shit to do. Let's go."

He rips the bottom of his shirt, stuffing it against the small hole in my chest to stem the bleeding.

Grimacing, I then step down from the lorry with a thump. The second my feet hit the ground my head spins.

"You're stubborn, you know that, right?" Mop says, hooking his head under my arm, guiding me to the livestock lorry.

Vincent helps Billy as he staggers to his feet. His eyes bore into me.

I return the glare. "Mop, you take my bike. I'll take your place in the lorry. Beats, you drive us to the port."

Mop nods and chucks him the keys.

"Billy, you're with me."

He spits blood on the floor, his eyes momentarily looking away. He then looks at Vincent who nods for him to go.

Yeah, that's right, fucker. You shoot me, you get to ride up front.

Captain climbs up in the now empty lorry with Len. The two of them drive off, heading back to the depo. They shouldn't get picked up.

The rest of us carry on with our plan.

Arriving at the port just over an hour later, the look on Costa's face as we pull up in our not-so-inconspicuous choice of transport, is verging on feral.

Armed men in suits surround us instantly. Costa doesn't move as they usher us to line up in front of him. The way they're pulling and pushing us about, it's starting to really piss me off.

Costa looks at my chest. "Complications?" he asks.

"Nothing that can't be sorted," I grimace, pulling my shirt that's now sticking to my skin.

"Anything I need to be aware of?"

Me and Vincent exchange a look. "No," Vincent replies.

"What happened?" Costa asks.

I open my mouth to talk but Costa turns to face Vincent.

Vincent slowly looks towards him, and I wonder if he's regretting getting into this shit. This guy's a first-class prick with too much money and power.

"Why don't *you* tell me?" Costa asks him.

Vincent explains what happened and how we stopped the cargo from getting stolen.

Costa turns, whispering something into his other right-hand man's ear. I recognise him from the clubhouse. Starbucks. He makes a call, stepping off to one side just out of ear shot.

Sonny called me bang on the halfway point where the Irish planned to hit. Using other vehicles, they forced the lorry being driven by two of our nomads off the road. Masked men surrounded it, then opened it up. The second they realised they'd been duped; they fled the scene and the nomads took off.

"Where's my original transport vehicle now?"

Vincent looks at me.

I look at Costa.

Costa raises an eyebrow.

"Taken to a depo further north from here," I start. "Figured you'd want that somewhere else in case it was still followed?"

Costa's lip raises in one corner. He clicks his tongue then swivels on his heels rather dramatically.

His right-hand man comes back, and I'm guessing he confirms everything Vincent relays.

Turning back to me taking a step closer, Costa smiles. "And how was it that a man in a Ripper cut came to know of this... ambush, rather than the man wearing the Saviour cut?"

"We had no—"

Costa raises his finger, forcing Vincent to stop talking, keeping his eyes on me.

Guessing that's my cue. "My president. That's how."

"Interesting," he says, dragging his hand across his face.

"Why?"

His cheeks turn red. "Appears my fellow countrymen have found out about our business."

I'm guessing they're not friends, judging by the way I start to see steam blowing from his ears. He then snaps his fingers, the back of the lorry is swiftly opened, and the crates are counted for but not opened. A nod between one of the men on the lorry and Costa is made.

Collectively, we watch on as his men offload the crates onto the boat bound for Amsterdam. I wait until Costa comes over once we're done. "You," he says pointing at me.

I reluctantly stand, trying hard not to pass out due to my chest still very much bleeding.

I notice Vincent edge closer, wanting to hear what Costa's got to say.

"You should get that checked." Costa nods towards my chest. I don't reply, I simply look at where a hole now sits just below the flash on my chest. When he laughs, I'm not really sure how I should be reacting. "That. That right there," he says. "That's what I need. Someone with some fucking stomach."

Vincent then steps closer.

"Change of plan," Costa tells us. Me and Vincent exchange a look. "Rippers MC will now take point for my cargo."

My temper ignites like a furnace. Pure hatred and anger bubble just below the surface. "We don't want any part of that!" I exclaim, my chest suddenly surging with a sharp stabbing sensation.

With no regards for what I'm saying, Costa turns and begins to walk away.

His man steps closer when I try to follow, the tip of his gun pushing into my front, making me grit my teeth.

"This isn't what we voted," I shout behind him.

The Rippers walk up to stand by my side.

Costa looks over his shoulder. "Better take it to your table then. Details of your next transport will be confirmed soon." His car door closes and he drives off. Fucking, gone.

Without saying a word, his men leave following behind him. I turn slowly, looking for Billy who's going to feel every ounce of my frustration. Seeing him stood by the bikes that are here, I take off. When I reach him, I spin him around, his eyes momentarily widening just before my heavy fists begin breaking the bones in his face.

CHAPTER TWENTY

MADISON

This morning's been intense in the most overwhelming of ways. Travis called in the early hours after being shot in the chest by Lauren's uncle. A phone in his pocket saved his life, but seeing the blood when Jess patched him up had my nerves fried.

He wouldn't let me call an ambulance.

Outlaws. A gunshot wound. I should have known he wouldn't have it. And apparently, I should have known not to suggest it. I had to accept what happened and not question the fact that these men are supposed to be working together now, even though they're shooting each other.

I wonder at what point I question the giant lorry they showed up in?

Still, my heart was galloping for another reason entirely. Lauren was in the other room asleep when the guys arrived at the clubhouse. Jess and I had arrived after Travis called, and although she was never in any danger, simply knowing Billy was close to Lauren was too close a call.

I know she feels safe here, but she's going to stay with me now. Jess suggested it and she isn't wrong. Lauren needs stability; to be doing normal things that kids do. Not overhearing outlaws talking about being shot. I'm not ashamed to admit I even offered her ice cream and movies every night to convince her it's for the best.

In the other room, she grabs her things whilst I wait by the bar for her. "Everything okay?" I ask Travis as he stomps towards where I'm sat.

Dennis the Road Captain comes over too, following behind. "No, sweetheart, everything is not okay." I hear Travis sigh as Dennis talks. "It's all gone to shit." He moves to sit on a stool. "Prospect!" he booms for Legs to come to the bar.

Legs hurries towards him. "Sup?"

"Don't fucking *sup* me, boy. Pour me a fucking drink."

Legs laughs rather stupidly. Even I can see that. "It's not even nine."

Dennis' eyes travel the full length of Legs' body. Travis and I remain silent, waiting for Legs to be torn into. "Everyone drinks at this hour," Dennis says, more to himself than anything.

"I don't drink," Legs replies lifting his shoulders.

"Do you want to patch into the club, lad?"

Like a fool, Legs nods his head.

"Then don't ever fucking question me again."

Legs reluctantly moves behind the bar and pours Dennis his drink.

I look at Travis, widening my eyes. "I'm taking Lauren back to mine. She's going to stay with me for a bit."

We move away from the others. "Need my help?"

"No." I grab my things from the table hearing the bedroom door open. "I'll sort it."

Travis clutches at his chest.

"You going to be able to ride?" I ask him looking at the blood still staining his clothes.

"It won't stop me."

Of course it won't. "I'll take Lauren to grab a few things."

"Okay. You call me if you need me."

I nod my head. "And you call me if you hear from Dean?" He frowns, and I sigh. "I need to see him, Travis. I know you don't want me to—"

"—Don't push this anymore. I won't ask him to put your name on the visitor list. See you later."

With that, he turns and makes his way to the other members who have congregated by the bar.

I'm left standing on my own. Depleted.

Travis might refuse to help me, but I refuse to accept I have to stay away. Pulling out my phone, I quickly type out a message to Mollie.

Me: Mollie, how are you?

She replies instantly.

Mollie: Fine, Mads. Everything okay?
Me: Actually, I need a favour. When are you next seeing Dean?
Mollie: 11am. What do you need?
Me: You think you can put my name on the visitor's list?
Mollie: No. I can't do that.

My heart drops. Then I realise how selfish I'm being, asking her to break the rules for me. Someone she doesn't even know.

Me: I'm sorry. I shouldn't have asked.
Mollie: I get it. Believe me, I do. But I can't. I'm sorry.
Me: Don't apologise. Just, promise me you'll bring him home?

Mollie doesn't reply.

Lauren and I grab the things she'll need for staying with me. Some new clothes, toiletries, a few other essentials. I even take her for a haircut before we buy some food for later. All the while we're walking around the shops, guilt well and truly nestles itself deep inside me. I should never have asked Mollie to put my name on the visitor's list. Not only could she get into trouble, it goes against her and Dean's confidentiality.

Arriving back at home just after lunch, I spot Mollie's car waiting outside. Lauren and I get out, moving to the boot for our shopping. I hand her some bags, then we make our way to the door. "Give me a minute," I say to her.

Lauren goes inside.

Mollie's car door opens, and she stands, closing it behind her.

"Mollie?"

Dropping her head, she steps closer. "I needed to apologise to you, Mads."

"No, it should be me saying sorry to you. I never should have asked for what I did."

Mollie holds out her hand with a piece of paper.

"What's this?" I ask her.

"Can you get there for 1pm?"

"Today?"

She nods her head.

"But I thought... Why change your mind? Is he okay?" My heart pounds fast. I'm hot in anticipation of what Mollie's going to say.

"He asked how you were, but I think he needs to see for himself." Mollie looks down at her feet. "I get the feeling his mindset very much depends on how you are."

The tears roll down my cheeks. "He's going to be pissed off with both of us."

Mollie smiles. "I don't care."

Heading to the prison, my nerves are completely shot. Excitement mixes with unease as I park my car and walk inside. The thought of seeing him up close after the heartache that was yesterday, makes my feet move faster.

The rigmarole one needs to go through before being allowed to see someone is intense though. The piece of paper Mollie handed me told me everything I needed to know. On it is Dean's prison number, and a list of what I can and can't do once inside. Tears threaten when I read that minimal contact is allowed. It isn't much, but being able to feel him, to touch his skin, breath him in. I'm suddenly desperate.

After being patted down and having my belongings taken off me, I'm made to walk through a security arch, and my identification is checked. My hands shake, the back of my neck is cold and clammy. I have nothing to hide, but the stern faces of the staff and the way they carry themselves, makes the nerves rattle my bones. Is this how it always is?

A tall police officer escorts all visitors to the visiting room. We follow him like sheep, each being directed to a table. I sit facing the same way as everyone else. In silence, we patiently wait for our loved ones to walk in through the door separating this room from the prison.

Like any situation where you decide to do something for yourself, my mind begins telling me I've made a mistake. That coming here might set Dean back ten paces. That seeing me might somehow destroy him and make him vulnerable.

Travis is going to be so mad that I didn't listen.

Hearing a baby cry, I look to my left seeing the young mother I followed in here, sat with her two children. The baby fusses in her arms as her toddler sips from his cup, pulling on her clothes, demanding snacks.

I watch as she blows out a breath, trying to juggle everything. With nothing but admiration for her, I smile to myself.

She looks at me, and I fluster being caught staring.

"This your first time?" the mother asks me.

I nod.

"Don't be alarmed if he acts differently. Just let him know you're okay. Even if you're not, don't let him see it. They won't survive if they think you're not alright."

The corner of my lips twitches. A bitter half smile is all I can raise.

An iron door then clangs open, and an alarm simultaneously sounds. My eyes stay fixed on the mother for a moment longer. Her facial expression changes as she silences her emotions.

I turn my head when the prisoners start to file into the visiting room. My mind's racing, my body now unable to relax. He's coming. My VP.

When I see him, his steely eyes scan the room, presumably looking for Travis or another member of the club. Dark purple bruises taint one side of his face and under his neck. I could see them yesterday, but seeing him this close, they appear so much worse. The air I need, I don't seem to be able to breathe in. The urge to run to him—to hold him in my arms and never let him go, causes tears to fill my eyes.

His head swivels past me, then I see the moment he realises it's me here. His eyes move back, and I stand slowly, my fingers gripping tightly to the others.

Dropping his shoulders, his head then drops to his chest.

"Move, Carter," the officer by the door instructs. Dean's inability to move is causing a bottleneck.

A man pushes past him, knocking him forwards a few steps. Dean doesn't even look at him. His eyes are now locked with mine. They soften with every small step he takes towards me, the greenness outshining the black the closer he gets.

I can't stop the tear that trickles down my face. All I can do is stand and wait for him.

When he stops in front of me, his eyes close. His forehead dips to mine, and I lean into the contact. I breath him in, drinking in the fresh pine I smell every day, even without him around. God, I miss him.

My heart dances when his lips then push to the top of my head. He keeps them there, and as if he needs more of me, his hands slide to either side of my face, scrunching my hair in his fingers.

The touch of them against me releases a million tingling goosebumps to blanket my skin. The sensation makes my breath get caught in my lungs. Before I can freefall into him, Dean tilts my head back. He looks deep into my soul, his thumbs stroking underneath my eyes, wiping away my sadness. "You shouldn't be here."

"I needed you." My voice shakes, but not once do I look away from him.

Letting out a sigh, Dean pulls me into his arms. He holds me tight, and I wrap my arms around him, pulling him as close to me as I physically can. "I'm guessing Mollie put your name on the form?" His hand strokes my hair as he talks.

I smile against him, my eyes closed, feeling well and truly in my safe space. "Don't be mad."

Pulling back, he looks down to me, his eyes wider. "I'm furious." I can tell he is. My arms are still wrapped around him, but I see his eyes look at my bump. "How's my girl?" he asks softly.

I take his hand in mine and place it across my bump. Gently caressing across my skin, I look down, too. "The baby's fine," I say. "I have another scan later this week."

Dean's eyes and nose crinkle as he smiles.

Straying my gaze, I look at his neck. I can't help but run the tip of my finger over his skin where it's marked. "What happened?"

As I ask, an officer walks past us.

Dean turns me, his hand protectively across my back as he guides me to my seat.

My eyes flit from Dean to the officer.

The man in uniform looks hard faced and angry. He watches us, and I'm now all too aware of everybody else in the room. I couldn't see them stood so close to Dean.

Sitting opposite him, I put my hands on the table.

Dean scoops them in his, his hold on me much tighter than I was expecting.

"Dean?" I say, wanting him to talk.

He lets loose a breath, shutting his eyes. "I don't want to talk about anything in here. Don't ask me again." His words are harsh. His tone, indifferent.

"Okay." I swallow the lump now in my throat.

The mother next to us passes the baby to the man sat opposite her. Both Dean and I turn to look as the baby makes a saddening noise.

When Dean looks back to me, his eyes drop down. He can't see my bump from where he is, but a flicker of worry flashes across his features.

"That can't be us," I whisper, knowing he's thinking the same.

His hands tighten around mine. "I won't let that happen, Mads."

"How?" I ask, my voice rattling. *Don't cry*. "It's already happening. You're in here. Not at home, with me." I can't imagine having to bring our child here to see him. I don't think I could.

It's as if strong hands are now wrapped around my throat. The air won't go in. I'm suffocating under the weight of this reality being projected before me. "What if you don't get out? What happens if they find you guilty, and you never come home?"

I'm becoming frantic. My mind running away from me. "Hey, shh, shh," Dean soothes. With my hands being held, I can't wipe away the tears that escape me. "Mads." I don't move. "Look at me, babe."

Taking a few steadying breaths, I purse my lips, dragging my eyes to look at his.

"My girl," he says when they connect. His thumb strokes over the back of my hands bunched in his. "I need you to trust me, more than you have ever trusted me before."

With a sigh, I pull one hand from his hold. I wipe under my eyes, piecing myself together. "Do you have a plan?"

He subtly dips his chin.

"Will you tell me?" He doesn't reply.

Looking once more at the woman beside me, she turns her head catching my eye. She hesitates to look away before wrapping her arms around her child. Kissing his head, she then wears a smile, although her body remains drooped.

The man opposite smiles back at her, thinking she's happy. But I see her sadness. It seeps from her pores like blood oozing from a wound. "What if your plan fails?"

Looking back to Dean, he leans forward with wide eyes, the contact with mine, steady. "I will not fail you, Mads." He truly believes himself.

"I don't want to be left alone," I say honestly.

A roaring silence ensues. Neither of us moves. The thought of waking up every morning without him breaks my heart. The thought of delivering our child without him holding my hand and telling me I'm going to be okay, destroys me. I don't want our child to know him from behind bars. I don't want our child to grow up not knowing the love that this man is capable of.

"You won't be alone. I *will* get out of here."

Looking at the bruises on his neck again, it dawns on me. "At what cost?" I ask.

Dean's chin juts out, his jaw clenching. "I don't give a shit about the cost, Mads. Whatever needs to be done to get me out of here and back to you and the club, I'm doing it. I told you I'd respect your wishes if you needed an out. But if you're in, I need to know it's with everything you've got, babe. You're in my blood and my bones. Without you, I'm nothing."

My fingers touch my necklace.

He holds my hand still in his, opening his other for me to take.

Instead, I lean forward. I run the tip of my finger down one side of his face over the stubble, noticing how long it's gotten. I then drift over the bruise on his neck. A sharp line mars just under his chin, from one ear to the other.

Swallowing the agonising, burning lump, I stop my hand on his chest and press my palm flat. "I trust you." His heart thumps under my touch. It's fast. Almost out of control. "Travis told me you'd die for me, that I need to live for you," he blinks hard, "but you need to live for you, too. You need to live for your child. Live, and come back to us. Come back to me and have your family."

He doesn't give me any words. His chest takes in a deep breath as he packs away his emotions.

"Your demons, the club… they can't determine how you live your life anymore," I tell him. "Only you can."

Dean takes a long blink, then points his chin to the ceiling. He's inside his own head.

After too long a silence, I speak. "I found Lauren," I say quietly, trying to pull him back.

Dean looks at me.

"She's going to stay with me for a while."

He smiles. "That's good."

I rest my chin in my palm, my elbow resting on the table. "She also asked for her key." I raise an eyebrow.

"What key?" The corner of his mouth twitches.

"Where'd you hide it?"

"I don't know what you're talking about."

"That's how you knew she'd come back, isn't it?"

Tugging his ear, he replies, "Still not sure what you mean."

I smile. "You do realise she slept rough before showing up at the clubhouse?"

"But she's back, that's the main thing," he says matter-of-factly, straightening his back. He's not wrong, I suppose. "When are you back at work?" he asks.

I sit a little straighter. "Back tomorrow. I'll get Lauren back in as soon as I can, but I don't want to force anything on her." Dean's eyes pull together. "Her brother's missing."

"Her brother?" Dean sits forward as he asks.

I nod my head. "Didn't come home one night. She was looking for him, the morning you found her."

"Is she alright?"

"She will be. I'll help her," I smile.

"You let Travis find him," he tells me, throwing me a warning look.

I pause. "Travis is really busy."

"That's an understatement."

"He seems stressed, too," I say, referring to everything going on with the club and the way he's been around Mollie.

Dean rubs the back of his head, tilting his head slightly to one side. "I can't imagine why." His voice is hushed.

I eye him sceptically. "You mean with the club, right?"

A cheeky smile spreads across his face. "The club, undeniably. But it's probably more Mollie."

"What's the deal with those two?"

Dean lets out a small laugh. "That's a whole story in itself. Just, go easy on him. Don't cause him any added stress."

My face is stonewalled. "I'll pretend you didn't just imply that *I* would make anything more stressful."

He leans forward, opening up his hands.

I lay mine in his, watching as his thumbs glide over the back of my skin once again. It feels heavenly.

We stay like this, talking about a whole lot of nothing. It's nice. Simple. Conversation flows like a river heading to the sea. We keep it light, talking about mundane things. Mundane things I wish we were doing together.

After nowhere near long enough, Dean looks at the clock on the wall, making me turn my head. "Five minutes," he points out.

I blink back my tears. Our time's coming to an end.

"No more visits, okay?"

My lip quivers as I try to speak. "What about the trial?"

"No, Mads. If it should take me longer to get out of here, I want to remember this. Not watching you from behind the glass. You go home. You stay safe. You *listen.* You grow my child and you live."

Lifting my hands to his mouth, he lowers his lips until they caress my skin. How am I supposed to live without him?

As he stands, he brings me with him. I'm pulled into him, our bodies close, his warmness blanketing me. Savouring him, he tilts my chin, then kisses me softly. I realise in this moment I would do anything to make sure he comes home. His lips hover over mine as he begins to pull away. "I love you." His hot breath hits my mouth, my lips instantly parting, wanting more of him.

"I love you," I reply.

The buzzer then sounds signalling the end. He steals one more kiss, then stands up straight.

I keep my hand on his chest until he's forced to walk away with the other inmates. Looking back one final time, he rounds the iron door leading to the prison.

CHAPTER TWENTY-ONE

UNKNOWN

"Zoom in. Freeze image. Move it to camera one." I look at the screen, knowing what's coming. A body bloated by water, the skin blistered and purged from the bones. "Who is that?"

My tech guy starts to explain. "A kid, nineteen years of age. Last seen leaving the city centre last Tuesday. Police found his body along the riverbed after a dog walker spotted him."

"Is his death related?" I ask. *Why the fuck would it be?* Looking back at the screen, the green and black of the boy's remains make my skin crawl.

"Hard to say."

"Bring up his profile."

Sean clicks the buttons, bringing up the boy's information.

My eyes scroll down the list. "No known affiliates?"

"No. None." Sean keeps scrolling. There's nothing. No family. No school mentioned. No record this kid even existed.

I suck in a breath walking away from the computers. Making it to the drinks cabinet, I pour myself a whiskey on the rocks, holding back the rocks. I sip, immediately pouring myself another.

Would Costa recruit child soldiers to run things? Or maybe this was one of the unfortunate ones. "Bring the network up on screen."

Sean clicks some buttons, bringing up what we've pieced together so far. "It's getting bigger."

I nod my obvious agreement.

"We know our lead's Costa. We also know that both MCs are now shifting the cargo across the country."

My eyes travel over the pictures of the members on the wall, stopping on one.

"This body showing up doesn't suggest he's unlawfully recruiting children, but I think it's safe to assume he means business. He isn't wasting any time getting this off the ground."

I tear my eyes away, looking at recent cases we think might be linked. Missing people. Dead bodies showing up in the area. We know he's backed by big money and the drop offs and pick ups are scheduled on a need-to-know basis. Which makes the fact we were so close to stopping the first one, really fuckin' irritating. We won't get that opportunity again.

Sean slaps the table in his own frustration, clearly thinking the same thing. "If we could find where the people are being sold from, that would be our best chance of stopping him."

"What else?" I ask, my tone clipped.

"We know most of the crimes are being committed overseas once they leave the UK. They're transported alive by private boats and jets to the highest bidders. He isn't working this on his own."

Tell me something I don't know, Captain fucking Obvious.

"Remind me why we can't just move on the man we know is fronting all of this?" Sean asks.

Because it's exactly that. A front. The notion of selling guns hides what's really happening. "No." Plus, this is personal.

"But if you cut off the head—"

"—I said no." I don't want to just stop what we know is really going on. I want to end it all. End all of them. Crush their world and leave no trace of them behind. Obliterate every last fucking one of them. Then, when all is said and done, I get the last man standing. And I end his life the same way he ended mine. I just need to find him.

"You're going to have to see him."

I let my head hang, swilling the drink around the glass. I know what Sean is saying is true. "Not yet."

CHAPTER TWENTY-TWO

MADISON

Six weeks later

I've been learning to live without him. Breathing without my air. Walking with no direction. One day everything we wanted was in the palms of our hands. Then, without so much as a look over its shoulder, time spread its wings and flew away. The world was no longer ours.

I don't dream anymore either. Nightmares. I have those. Nightmares about the birth going wrong. Nightmares about the baby coming too soon. About the baby not knowing it's father.

Apparently it's normal, but now at twenty-eight weeks pregnant I haven't slept well for just over a month. I want to; my body craves the rest. But my brain feels like a murky, over-filled bathtub. I'm desperate to pull the plug before I drown.

I won't hold it together forever. I know it in the deepest part of my body. And as ashamed as I am to admit that, I also feel glad that now I can.

Those first few weeks after seeing him, I came home with a renewed sense of purpose. I worked hard; keeping busy with overcoming the restructure, managing to keep all of our jobs. I had an injection of life to keep moving forward and to live for him.

But without Dean by my side, the days are getting harder.

Lonely nights are getting longer. Dull days, duller. I've filled my time busying myself around the club, and whilst it feels like a home away from home, he's still not here. To the outside world, I am me. But on the inside, a hollowness has taken form. A giant void now separates me from everybody else. Maybe it's survival? Maybe it's instinct. I don't know.

What I do *know*—what I've come to realise in days gone by, is that I'm incomplete. And whilst I have purpose, there's no direction.

Waiting in the car for Lauren, I hold my phone in my hand. No matter how many times I remind myself he won't be texting me, I still type out a message, hitting send whilst holding my breath.

Me: Come back to me

I stare at the screen like he could reply any minute. It's a ridiculous form of self-torture, but I can't stop.

We've spoken when he's called. But he's the one person I can't hide the truth from. He sees me so clearly. I see him. The last time we spoke, he knew. He knew my strength was dwindling. My ability to live in the not so normal world I now live in, dissipating.

In my mind's eye I could see him. The way he asked how the baby was but couldn't finish his sentence. The way he told me he loved me, but had to steel every drop of resolve he could find before he broke. Transparent.

The car door opens, and Lauren slides in. "Hey," she says happily, dragging me from my head. She dumps her bag in the footwell, and I smile at her.

"Good day?" My tone is flat. Always flat.

"You talk like we didn't see each other three times already." Her voice rings with a cheer that's new. I look at her, noticing her beaming from ear to ear. Pulling out her phone, her thumbs start tapping the screen as she sits back in her seat.

Idly, I watch her. "What?" She doesn't raise her head or move her eyes, but she can feel me looking at her.

I tuck the stray strand of hair behind her ear. "Nothing," I say.

Lauren huffs but smiles at the same time. "Just tell me," she says quietly, her fingers still rapping.

Dropping my phone in the centre console, I push the key into the ignition. "You already know." I stare ahead starting the engine, moving the gear stick into first.

Lauren rests her hand on top of mine gently. "I'm proud of you too."

I look to her, then she holds out her fist. I lift mine to hers, and we bump with no more words exchanged. Truth be told, I'm beyond proud of her.

She's back in school, much to everyone's surprise. None more so than her. We had meeting after meeting, phone call after phone call. Finally, after applying for her place at college, she's now focused and back in education after almost six months. Catching up will be a mammoth task, but if any kid is able to do it, it's her. And she won't be alone.

Alone. The word drips like a broken tap, dousing the flicker of happiness that skips through me.

Twenty minutes later, we pull up at the local shops. "What we having tonight?" Lauren walks around the car as she asks.

"What about that Risotto I made last time?"

Holding her hand to her face, Lauren pretend vomits in her mouth.

"Really?" I hold my hand to my chest as if pained by her actions.

She laughs, and it's like music to my ears. "Why don't we just let Jess cook?" she asks as we walk.

"Because she's *our* guest. We can't invite her over then have her cook."

I grab a trolley which Lauren takes from me. "At least we wouldn't be at risk from food poisoning."

"Hey!"

She skips forward with the trolley, getting out of my reach. "She bringing Axl this time?" My heart warms knowing how much Lauren has enjoyed getting to know my nephew this past month, even if the circumstances surrounding it are shit.

With a slight shrug of my shoulders, I reach for some stir-fry veg, deciding on the easiest meal to cook that I can think of. "Not sure."

"I hope she does." Lauren's cheeks lift as she keeps moving with the trolley. It's nice to see her happy. She holds up different items of food for my approval before chucking them in. "Can we get some of the real ice cream tonight?"

"Real ice cream?" I question.

"Not the fake stuff you need. I mean the proper stuff. The full fat dairy one that's going to make me feel sick."

"Why not," I say. "We should get some cookie dough, too."

"Oh, fuck yeah."

I say nothing, but cock a brow.

Checking my expression, she scrunches her face. "Oops, sorry." The biggest grin then spreads across it.

All I can do is shake my head at her potty mouth and her ability to get away with it. Although, given she spends every bit of free time she has hanging around Travis, I'm not surprised she's started talking like a middle-aged man child.

A middle-aged man child who's holding everything down in the wake of Dean's absence. I can't fault him.

It's stupid really—our new Friday night ritual. More of a necessity to try to dam the turmoil we all individually live with. Girls' night used to be about drinks and laughter and togetherness. There's still togetherness, it's just now coated with a thick layer of sadness. We make the most of it, how women do, but it's not the same.

"Look at this." The sound of Lauren's voice makes me turn to look at her. She's holding up the tiniest baby onesie I've seen. "You should get it."

"It's beige." Not pink how I pray it'll be.

"Yeah." She looks at me then back to the small garment before continuing. "You don't know what you're having. Beige is safe, suits boy or girl."

I smile but shake my head. "I want to wait."

The scrunch of Lauren's face makes me realise she's more aware than I give her credit for. "Didn't Jess say most people have all the gear by now?"

I chuckle under my breath. Most people. Most people aren't having a baby not knowing when the person they love will come home. Most people don't have partners facing life in prison on a murder charge. *Which is probably more of a reason as to why I should start buying.* But I can't. I can't do it without him. Can't stomach the concept of choosing the things we need without him. I don't have the strength, nor the will to do it.

Does that make me weak? Does that make me a bad mother already? Certainly feels like it. "Yeah, they probably do," I reply sadly.

Later that evening, once home and showered, we start plating up the food. Jess arrived a little after seven. She left Axl with Max, deciding she needed the break.

Grabbing our plates, we head towards the sofa. I slump, cupping my bump as I move.

"How was the check-up yesterday?" Jess asks. She clicks on the telly then nestles herself at the other end, her legs propped up on the coffee table.

"Yeah, fine." I feel the baby kick and instantly regret my positioning. "I need to pee." Placing my food on the table, I then make my way upstairs. I take some painkillers for the headache that's coming, then feel my phone vibrate. It's Travis.

Travis: Checking in

I wish I could check out.

Me: Thanks. All good here

Sliding my phone in my back pocket, I immediately pull it back out.

Me: How are you?
Travis: I'm good, Mads. You know me

Yeah. I do know.

Me: That's why I'm asking

He takes a minute to reply.

Travis: I'm good

I don't press him anymore. Even though I know he must feel buried.

Me: What time will you be back tomorrow?
Travis: I'm on the list to see Dean, I'll be back late afternoon. You still good to help out?

My fingers rub my forehead. I'd forgotten about offering to help at the clubhouse. It's the last thing I want to do. Most of the club are away further north, not back until tomorrow. It's clear even to a blind man the club's new business is taking them into uncharted waters, but they never turn down helping charities. That's why I volunteered to be around; make sure things are in order for when they get back. It just means I'll have to pretend everything's okay when the reality is so far away from that.

Me: I'll be there

Travis: Appreciate it. Anyway, enjoy girls' night. See you tomorrow

Me: Night

Taking the stairs carefully, one hand on my hip, I walk into the lounge. My phone vibrates again.

Mollie: Mads, sorry it's bit late. Are you home? I'm passing, wondered if you were about?

Over recent weeks, Mollie and I have messaged regularly. She joined Jess and I one Friday, but hasn't made another girls' night since. So when she asks if I'm free, naturally I feel pleased.

Me: Of course, come over

Mollie: Great. See you soon

I sit on the sofa, picking up my plate. "What we watching tonight?" I ask.

Jess looks at Lauren. "We can't decide."

"No," Lauren starts a little sarcastically. "Your sister is being picky."

With a laugh, I stab at my food, shoving in a mouthful. "Tell me something I don't know."

"I am not picky," Jess says, rolling her eyes with a look of indifference. "You're the picky one. I'm simply offering my opinion that Die Hard is a Christmas film, therefore we shouldn't watch it. Your tiny adolescent seems to think we can, seeing as we've sworn off chick flicks."

I look between them both. *Your* tiny adolescent, as if she belongs to me. I guess she has no one else. "It's a Christmas movie," I say siding with Jess.

With a shake of her head Lauren takes a mouthful of her food. "Fucking ridiculous."

I choke on a huff, and Jess does too.

Lauren casually crosses her legs where she's sat on the floor.

"You have got to stop hanging around with Travis," I tell her sharply. "I mean it, these evenings spent working on his bike or whatever it is you're doing there, it's turning you into him."

"Chill, Mads, it's all good."

Being told to chill by a fifteen-year-old really isn't something I like. "Lauren," Jess says, seeing my reaction. "Maybe just, rein it in?"

I know I'm guilty of it, but Jesus if the eye roll Lauren then gives me isn't the single most annoying thing I've seen today. I tilt my head to one side, my eyes wide in disbelief. "Right, what are we watching?" I ask again trying to distract myself, my tone firm.

We all take more mouthfuls of food as Jess scrolls through Netflix. "How about this?" She stops on something scary.

"No," Lauren and I say in unison.

"This?"

"God no," I say.

She quickly backs out of putting on a reality TV show. "How about this? We all love men who can dance."

"Yeah, those of us who are old enough." I widen my eyes again.

Jess throws the remote at me. "You choose then, seeing how I'm the picky one and can't decide."

"Fine," I muse. I scroll until eventually I feel the plate on my lap has cooled. "Urgh, why is this so difficult?" As I say it, there's a light knock at the door.

"Who's that?" Lauren asks.

"That'll be Mollie." I walk to the door as Lauren darts for the remote. When it opens, I notice Mollie looking more worn out than usual. "Hi. Come in." I step back, making way for her.

"Hi," Mollie says as she steps inside, freezing on the spot.

"Crap. I completely forgot you'd have company. You should have said you were busy." Her eyes flits between Lauren, Jess and me.

"Mollie, the only thing we're *busy* doing, is trying to decide what to watch." Jess smiles.

"You're welcome to stay. There's more food in the pan if you're hungry?"

Mollie smiles sheepishly, but steps forward as I close the door behind her. She removes her coat and her shoes, kicking them off by the door.

The small act reminds me of when I first came to this house. How clean and tidy Dean always kept things. I wonder what he'd make of shoes simply strewn across the floor. What would he do if he found them like that? Then a small smile raises because I know exactly what he'd do. He quietly pick them up, arrange them neatly, no words or fuss.

"Madison?" Jess says.

I look at her, then back to Mollie. Clearly I've been asked something and should be giving an answer. "What?" I ask.

"You zoned out there. You okay?" Mollie asks.

I smile as best I can. "Fine. Did you want food?"

Mollie's face scrunches slightly. "Is there enough? I don't want to put anyone out?"

I look at her deadpan. "It's stir-fry, you're not putting me out at all." With a smile, I plate her up and hand it to her. "There," I say also passing her a fork. "Drink? I don't have wine unfortunately."

"Boooo!" Jess calls from the other room cutting me off.

I search through the cupboards, spotting a lousy bottle of beer. "Or there's this?"

"That looks good to me."

We're chatting and talking about everything and anything, our empty plates left on the coffee table in front of us. None of us are watching the TV, except Lauren. If you count the few times she lifts her head out of her phone, as actually watching.

"So, where does your husband work, Jess?" Mollie asks looking down at Jess' wedding ring.

"He's not actually working at the minute. He's decided he needs *time to figure out what he wants.*"

I look at Jess and see the confusion in her eyes. I feel for her.

"Oh," Mollie replies unsure of where to look. "And where's he looking... when he tries to figure this out?"

Jess purses her lips. "That is the million-dollar question, Mollie."

My head swings to check Lauren isn't paying us attention. "You don't know anything at this point. All you have is your gut feeling to go on, that's it."

"And didn't Mum and Dad raise us to always trust our gut? He's going to leave me. I know it."

The word dad niggles in the back of my brain. "Yeah, they did," I reply. "But you need to talk to him. At least give him the opportunity to explain." Max may be struggling with what he wants from his life, but he would never hurt Jess or Axl.

"Since when did you become team Max?" Jess snaps.

"Since my sister gave me some pretty similar advice when I was in the exact same situation last year."

Her round eyes watch mine, then she smiles, slowly. "What about you then, Mollie? Any man dramas you care to share?"

I wish I could control the speed at which I look at Mollie. I'm not sure why I feel so nervous by Jess' question. In the relatively short time I've known her, I've come to learn that talking to Mollie about Travis is a sore subject. Curiosity had me asking more than once, but the woman is made of steel. Never divulges more than a few knowing looks.

"It's complicated," she replies.

"It's okay, you don't have to tell us anything. Ignore Jess."

Mollie's bottom lip rolls under the other. With a look down

to her hands on her lap, she whispers, "My husband died." I think back to when Mollie first came to the house. Travis was angry, throwing comments about her living with her partner.

All eyes including Lauren's look up. The atmosphere shifts as we all realise Mollie's struggle. "I'm so sorry," I comfort her. "I had no idea."

"No one did." Her head remains lowered, her fingers twiddling together in front of her. She goes to open her mouth but says nothing more.

"Lauren, up to your room," I tell her. It's clear Mollie needs to talk to other adults.

"But—"

"Now, please." Lauren huffs but does as she's bid. "I'll be up in a bit."

"I'm not eight."

Ignoring Lauren's smart tone, I look back at Mollie. There's an air of remorse surrounding her; her mouth is twisted, her nose crinkled. But she doesn't look... sad. "When did he die?" I ask.

"Before Christmas."

My heart drops, my body frozen. "Mollie, I'm so sorry."

"Me too," she says, and she smiles as though remembering him. "He had such a kind soul." She stares into space. "Saddest part? I couldn't love him the way he loved me."

Looking at Jess, she turns her body to Mollie, listening to our new friend opening up to us. "You didn't love him?" she questions.

Mollie tightens her lips. "I loved him. He just... he didn't have my heart."

I sigh. Someone else did. "Did you tell him?"

"He knew. I hated myself every day. Waking up and seeing him do everything for us without hesitation. I wanted to love him. I tried."

Jess and I exchange a look. "Us?" I ask her gently.

Mollie doesn't maintain eye contact with me as she sweeps her hair to one side, busying herself. Hesitation halts her before she takes a deep breath. "Mads, thank you for having me over. I'm sorry, I need to go." Her lip wobbles but she holds back her emotion. Steel. "Nice to see you again, Jess," she says.

Jess nods her head, not chasing her like I will. "Mollie wait, you don't need to leave." I stand when she stands, albeit slower to reach my full height than her.

"I do. I have a trial to get ready for. There's lots I need to be doing." She checks the clock then looks away. "I appreciate it—letting me drop in. I… I needed it."

She grabs her coat as she slips on her shoes. She's desperate to leave. Desperate to escape what she just told us. She's panicking.

"Mollie," I say softly. I place my hand on her arm, forcing her to stop. Her eyes travel up my arm, stopping at mine. "If you need to talk, I'm here." A look of regret flashes across her face. I step forward, hearing her heavy breathing.

"I shouldn't," she says turning to walk out the door. She stops, looking back briefly. "Thank you. I appreciate it. More than you know." With that, she leaves.

I'm left wondering if there's any happiness in this world. It seems so dire. So bleak. So tragic.

I turn to Jess, resting the back of my head against the door.

"Think she'll be okay?" Jess asks.

I push myself away from the wood, picking up the plates from the table. "I hope so." I really bloody hope so. Because I'm not sure my grip on this life can hold on much longer.

Us?

CHAPTER TWENTY-THREE

DEAN

Sometimes, I wonder at what point things really changed for me. The day I found my aunt murdered; her body slumped against that tree? The day my father left this earth, leaving me alone to fend for myself as a kid? Or the day I met the woman who decided I was worthy enough of her love. She gave herself to me completely. Accepted my life and gave me hers. She chose my darkness. Chose my life. Chose me.

I've relived every second of my time loving Mads. Every morbid day spent behind these bars, I've recounted every kiss, every touch, every single time I've had my hands on my girl. It's my lifeline. My purpose. My drive.

My fucking means of survival.

I thought seeing her would shatter me, when in fact all it did was make me even more determined to get out of this godforsaken den. Everything's backwards. I know that. My demons are guiding me, but without them, I'd be fucking dead already. So if the only way I can ensure I get back to Mads is by doing what I'm doing, I'll do it every damn day for the rest of time.

I'm no closer to finding the source, but I have to get home.

Feeling the last draw of air be sucked in through his nose, I press harder, ensuring that was his last. My fists clench the pillowcase taken from his bed. I hold down as tight as I can, my eyes never leaving the door as Luke stands at the threshold keeping watch.

I don't ask for details anymore. Details make way for a conscience. And having a conscience in here leaves room for error. Every scar I earn in here builds a picture of my journey. There can be no room for error.

Feeling his body finally slump, I remove the pillow from his face. I push it back under his head and close his eyes with the tips of my fingers. He looks peaceful. Calm. Free.

"Let's go."

Luke opens the door, and I pick up what I came for, stuffing it down the joggers I'm wearing. We check the coast is clear before walking away, like I didn't just kill a man for my own safety.

Luke and I make our way to the outside area. It's rec time. Most other inmates are out here too. With my back against the high wall, I bend my knee, resting my foot against it. "You think that's the end of it?" I casually ask Luke.

He sweeps his gaze over everyone. "Doubt it. But I think you know that already."

I huff. "A man can dream."

Luke drops his head, kicking at nothing on the ground. "Not in here. Dreams are for free men."

I smile to myself. "You're wrong. Your dreams will set you free."

The way Luke looks at me makes me wonder if I've missed something. "You're fucked up," my mate says.

"Why?" I laugh.

"Because," he shakes his head, his eyes narrowed. "You just fucking... did what you did, now you're out here talking about dreams and being set free. It's messed up."

I let out a laugh. I'd argue this is the least messed up I've felt for a while. "Says the man who did what *he* did."

"My mother was allowing men into my room at night to fuel her drug habit. What would you have done?"

It's not a question. I don't know the answer, anyway. My mother was my rock. She would never have hurt me like Luke's mother did him. "I just know what I want now, and nothing's going to stop me."

I've known my life would be spent with Mads from the first moment I laid my eyes on her. I've tiptoed on the edge, trying to balance both our worlds, but she deserves the life I'm going to be man enough to give her.

"Clearly. Heads up." Luke's words signal the exchange is happening like planned.

Two men dressed like us step closer. They stand side by side, acting casual.

"Boys."

They don't give me the same greeting. "You have it?" one of them asks.

A low grumble escapes me. "Not, hello, how are you or a thanks? Just, *you have it*?"

The one who asked lets out a breath, saying nothing. I suck in my cheek, but I lift the corner of my joggers so they can see.

One of them turns and nods his head. "Wait here," I'm told. "You, with us."

Luke slaps my chest with the back of his hand when he's summoned. "Don't be late for dinner." His joke makes me laugh as I watch him walk away with the men.

Left on my own, I wonder what updates I'll be graced with today.

"You gonna hand it over or do I need to go in there and fetch it myself?" The voice from behind me doesn't make me turn my head.

"You can't handle what I'm packing."

"Take it out."

I subtly remove the photos I was ordered to take, then hold them by my side.

The Saint takes them from my grasp. "Dozy cunt," he says. "Trust he slept well?"

"He'll be out for hours."

The Saint chuckles, looking at the photos in his hand. "Good."

"What do you have for me?" I ask.

"Nothing more I'm afraid."

I turn, looking directly at him, my face tight. Anger sets up shop deep within.

"I can tell that's not what you wanted to hear."

"No, that's not what I wanted to hear." I wanted information on Costa the moment I found out he was changing the way things were going to work. That was over a month ago now. "He sucked my club in deeper. You told me you could get me information on him."

"And I have." The Saint shakes his head, like *I'm* the delusional one here.

"Telling me what I already know, doesn't help." Travis established pretty quick that Vincent was in way over his head with Costa. And now by default, so are we. "What I need—"

"—What you needed, was the red light removed from your head. And have I, or have I not done that?"

My teeth grind together. "You've *held* it over my head." The prick.

"Tomatoe, tomato. You're still fucking breathing."

Looking him square in the eye, I picture watching the life drain from his eyes.

"Got one more in you?" One more? He said that last time. With malice, he raises his eyes to look at me. "You won't need to watch your back once it's done."

One more. Can I play the puppet one more time? "Who is it?"

He doesn't answer. He pushes off the wall and walks away. He knows he has me where he wants me, dangling at the end of the fucking string.

Luke and I sit eating our food. The divisions of this prison keep us segregated from most. Times like these, they're quiet. I shovel in the food thinking about my trial, also wondering when I'm next going to be called to carry out the greatest of sins. How the two contradict each other.

I've killed three men since I came inside. Three men whose lives I've taken all for my own survival. I don't want to do it again. But I know I have no choice. *There's always a choice.* I shove the fork into my food, stabbing the thing with too much force.

"Spill it," Luke says, making me look up.

I push the tray away, no longer hungry. "Spill what?"

"Okay, I know it's not been that long, but don't try to pull the wool over my eyes. I've spent every hour with you for over a month."

"Meaning?"

"Meaning, I know you." I raise a brow questioningly. "I know you always take a shit before you eat. You don't sleep. You're always carrying around that picture like it's keeping you going, and you say you're good with what you're doing when you're actually really fucking not."

Fuck me. "Perceptive of you, roomie."

"Well, it's not hard to see."

"What isn't?"

"That part of you. The part of you that's holding on to your humanity."

My humanity. I thought I'd lost that long ago. "Shut up and eat your food," I tell him.

He laughs slumping back in his chair. "I can't eat anymore of this." Luke pushes his plate away. He stretches, leaning back.

"Fuck. Where the fuck did everyone go?"

I look around noticing we're alone. "Maybe they all shit *after* they eat."

He smiles as the door opens behind him. I look up, and he turns around to see who's joined us.

The Saint. His minions following behind him. The feeling of the room immediately makes me wary. "Sorry to crash the date," he jokes.

"No problem." Luke stands as he speaks, turning to leave us to talk in private.

"You should stay." The Saint points for Luke to sit back down.

My fists have clenched by my side. Luke never stays. I quickly try to work out how best to get us out of this situation. I can't see a way. Luke eyes me, looking for direction. He knows something's up, too. I don't know why or how we came to this point of him listening or taking orders from me, but it's where we're at.

It's trust.

I give him a nod, and he turns taking one last look back at The Saint before he moves back to sit opposite me.

"Remember when you came to me, asking for protection?" I don't move. My eyes firmly locked on his as he shifts to stand behind Luke. "Well, you might have been right about the men who were sent to disrupt Sodom Saviours."

Might have been right? I know I fucking am. "And?" My heart's hammering my chest, but I keep the rise and fall of my breathing steady, not showing my unease. Is he going to tell me what he knows?

"As it turns out, the man you killed for Vincent," I struggle not to let out a laugh, "I knew him. Wondered what happened to him once he got out." He knew him? "He didn't bring much to this world," he continues, "had no ambition or drive for life. But in here, he was for want of a better word, obedient."

Hot heat swims through me. Jagged shards of anger start to pierce my calm. "Obedient," I repeat his word.

"Yeah. Did exactly what he was told."

I raise my finger, moving it between his minions. "Do they?"

"I shouldn't worry about them," he laughs menacingly. My gaze wanders to the men stood either side of him. "I want to see how obedient *you* are."

My move to jump out of my seat is immediate.

The Saint wraps his hand around Luke's neck, pulling him back tightly, catching me and him off guard.

With frantic hands I reach across the table, grabbing to pull Luke from him. "Ah, ah, ah," The Saint chides, yanking him back. "Sit the fuck down!"

His minions put me in my seat when I refuse.

"What the fuck is this?" My question earns me a whack to the face. I hear my nose crack before I feel the blood trickle to my top lip.

"This is you deciding what you want."

"What I want?" I balk sitting up straighter.

"Gonna need you to speed up your search for the source. *I* want the person who ordered a man who worked for me to threaten my family."

"Family," I laugh. "You were never a member." I taunt him pulling against the hands holding my arms behind my chair.

"Funny." The Saint flicks open a makeshift knife. His eyes look down to Luke then stay on me. "Just about as funny as this." He plunges the knife into Luke's side, forcing him to let out an ear-splitting cry.

"No!" I'm pulled back, shocked, my head savagely held in place to watch.

"Make sure you're fucking listening closely, boy. Here's what I need you to do next."

My breathing is quick, my eyes watching Luke's clothes turn a dark shade of crimson. He grits his teeth together, his eyes clamped shut.

"You're going to find the source for *me* now."

I shouldn't, but I let a low rumble of disbelief escape past my lips. "You mean The High and Mighty Saint can't find someone in his own house?"

A waste of time. That's what this has been. Played like a pawn on a chessboard, I've been used for someone else's gain. For what? *Survival?* The men I killed weren't to help me, they were to keep me in my proverbial place.

"Oh, I looked, but it seems as though whoever's behind this, really doesn't want to be found. A ghost, some might say, appears to be haunting us."

"How do you expect me to find someone where even *you* can't?"

His hand on the knife still wedged in Luke's ribs, twitches.

Luke grimaces, his back curling.

"It's not a question of *can't*. More like won't." I scrunch my face confused. "If I start digging too deep, people will begin to question how I let a man who worked for me, hurt my brothers on the outside."

"They're not your brothers!"

The Saint twists the knife, grinding it in Luke's flesh. "Continue running your smart mouth and your boy's gonna suffer more than he needs to."

I spit the blood flooding my lip to the floor, then close my mouth.

The Saint gives his men a knowing look. They let me go but remain stood close by.

I wipe the blood off my face with the back of my hand. The Saint doesn't let up, still holding Luke. Every part of me wants to reach across the table and end this. But I stay put.

"I have a reputation to uphold. Whereas you… well, you're nothing. So you *will* find out who released men to threaten the club. And you'll let *me* know."

"As simple as that?" I half mock, half ask seriously.

"Simple. As. That."

I let a beat pass. "How did you find out about the ambush so fast?" It's a question I've wondered since he ordered Rippers MC to stop it.

The Saint smiles. It's malicious. "I started digging into Costa like I said I would, and they told me—the Irish. Or more so, the Irish *man* I bribed to tell me, did. You met him this morning." He must tell by my face that a jolt of shock is shooting through me. "Those photos you retrieved? Pictures of his wife and kids. He truly was an easy one to make talk you know. Cracked within an hour of our first meeting. Even up until this morning, he proved very useful."

The Irish man ratted about the ambush to protect his wife and kids? Shame and guilt swallow me whole. I wouldn't rat. But his wife and his kids? *Fuck.* I get it.

"Does having loved ones make you weak?" The Saint asks.

Luke's skin has paled. His forehead beads with panicked sweats. Every muscle in my body tenses. "They give you something to live for."

The Saint's lips curl upwards mechanically. "Of course they do." He stands, slowly withdrawing the knife from Luke. The sickly noise of his tissue squelching turns my stomach.

Luke's hand automatically goes to the open area as his head drops to the table.

"Finish it."

I look up to The Saint, my lips parted with doubt. "Not a fucking chance." My tone is firm.

"Confident of you given the circumstances." The Saint stalks around the table, the tip of the blade he scrapes across the surface. "This is the last kill I need from you."

"No. He hasn't done anything."

"True. But he'll be the difference between you surviving in here, or you winding up dead. Remember, we run on fear and favours."

"Still no."

I'm struck from behind, one of the men's fists striking my neck.

My body slumps forward, just like Luke's. I'm still here. Still with it. Still vaguely aware of the voices in the room. My head swims like I'm on a fairground ride the way my brain washes from side to side. Round and round.

"Stay with me, boy. Almost over."

Lifting my head an inch off the table, I look at Luke. He's motionless, but I can just about see him still breathing. There's a woosh to his breath, the hole in his side desperately sucking in air.

"Luke." My voice is pathetic.

"Put him out of his misery," The Saint instructs.

"No." I can't. I won't.

Pulling a handful of his hair, The Saint lifts Luke's head off the table.

I'm suddenly grabbed from behind, one man either side of me, lifting me forward. They throw me on the table, my face so close to Luke's. I can hear his throat gargling as blood floods his lungs, drowning him.

"Finish him and it's done. No more kills. No more watching over your shoulder. You can find the source and live out the rest of your days in here in relative peace."

My eyes bore into Luke's face. If Mollie doesn't win my case and I'm sentenced to live out my days here, I'm not going to survive without alliances. But if she does, and I go home, could I live with myself knowing I killed my friend? *You haven't known him long. Do it! Don't let anything stop you from surviving. For you, for Mads. It's one more kill. Just one!*

"What's it going to be?" The Saint mocks my situation. My right arm is lifted, and the knife he used on Luke is forced into my hand.

I try to straighten my fingers, but the prick holding me swaps his elbow on my back for his knee. I can't move. He uses two hands to wrap my fingers around the handle.

The blood in my veins pumps loud. The rapturous beat drowning out everything else. "Are you strong enough to do anything for you family?" I barely hear The Saint's words. All I can hear is Mads. *Come back to me.*

The blade moves forwards against my will. I try with all my might to slow the movement, but I'm not in control. The edge pushes against the thin layer of skin under Luke's chin. Blood already starts to fall.

"End it," The Saint pushes again.

Jamming my eyes closed, I don't want to watch. I swallow hard, biding any morsel of time that I can salvage.

"Dean," Luke's hoarse voice croaks. I open my eyes. His head being held is unsteady, unable to hold his own weight. "Do it."

Feeling an ice-cold jab of annoyance, I press my lips together. "No," I reply in a clipped tone. "We don't have to do anything we don't want to."

His eyes swirl as he tries to focus on me. "Yes. You do."

I shake my head.

"Do it." With a splutter he chokes, sharply grabbing for oxygen. "Do it, then you'll be okay in here."

Okay in here? I might live. But I wouldn't be living. "I don't care about that," I tell him. There's only one place I want to live. If I can't live there, then there's no point.

"Liar." The corner of my lip twitches. "It's okay… I haven't known you… that long."

Staring at him, this fucker's joking with me as I hold a knife to his throat. And he thinks *I'm* fucked up. "That's messed up."

As I speak, The Saint grabs for my wrist with his other hand. "Enough!" he yells squeezing, thoroughly out of patience.

"Do it!" Luke shrieks coughing up more blood.

My time has run out. I'm about to take my friend's life against my will. I shout out, pulling back my hand as best I can as The Saint pushes forward. With gritted teeth, I'm unable to watch.

The split second before the knife's about to penetrate Luke's skin, a thunderous alarm sounds. The Saint's hand stops. Our heavy breaths surpass that of the drilling vibrations bouncing off the walls.

Letting go of Luke, The Saint lowers his face to mine.

The men holding me push my body flush with the table when I try to push away.

Black eyes then narrow with revulsion. "You're a dead man." I hold his stare, understanding his words on every level. I won't be going home. He stands straight as his minions let me go. Together, they make their way to the door, leaving us.

My heart breaks to hell. A putrid poison kills my soul. *This is merely what you deserve, you fucking idiot.* Looks like I'm learning the hard way again.

In silence, I get my breathing under control. "You should... have killed, me." Luke's voice is barely audible.

I push myself off the table, rounding it to him. "I know." I guide him to his feet, hooking an arm under his good side. "We need to get you to the nurse."

"I'm... sorry," he says.

We hobble to the door, checking left and right before we move. "Why are you apologising you soppy prick?" I drag him, virtually holding all of his weight as he stays in the present.

"You know why."

I stall, my feet almost coming to a halt. He's sorry? I'm the one who failed to keep my promise. Shaking my head, I pick up my pace, carrying him along the corridor towards the medical wing.

Two guards approach us. "Don't move!" they yell.

I stop, waiting for them to come to their senses and intervene. "He needs help!"

"What happened?" They then move to take Luke from me.

"I don't know? I just found him. Hurry! He needs fixing, quick!"

They scurry, guiding Luke through the door to where he'll get help.

He looks back to me, rendering me unable to move. He's sorry?

Every emotion a man could feel plummets into me, knocking me back a step. I brace myself, one hand on the wall, pulling at my clothes as I try to breathe. It's no good. As though my legs are then swiped from underneath me, I'm suddenly unable to stand. What the fuck is this?

Panic.

I'm struck by anger and pain. But more than anything, a raw, agonising sadness grips me from the inside, winding itself so tightly around my core. My body's bowed, my limbs shaking. I allow it to take over me, to consume me completely.

I'm not going to see Mads again. Not going to give her the life I promised her I would. I can't be the man I swore I'd be. *I'm sorry.* So fucking sorry. Sorry for letting the angel who saw my chaos, believe she could help my demons seek peace. Who was I kidding? Who the fuck do I think I am?

I don't need magic or miracles. I need my girl's arms wrapped around me when the dark gets too much. I need her close to me, living for me. Holding on for the man she needs me to be. She's mine. She always has been. Always will be.

I need to get home. But how? *Don't let fear and doubt get in your way.* Fear and doubt? Fear and *doubt?* Do I doubt myself? My ability to make it out of this? To make it out of here.

Holding my head in my hands, a million memories flash before me. The endless days I don't remember all blur into one. But that's exactly what they are. Memories. Not my present nor my future. My past.

The first day I truly saw a life worth having; a life worth *living*, was the day I met her. I knew it then. And I know it now. With every ounce of me, I fucking know it. I see Mads' face before me, and I know exactly how far I've come. Know exactly just how far I've managed to drag myself from my ruin, leading me to my home.

Running my hands over my stubble, my breathing settles, my body no longer trembling. What's the point of saying sorry if nothing will change? Life can change. We can change. *I* can change.

The smallest of smiles graces my face. I know what I have to do.

It's a fine line; the one I'm treading. The line between need and want. I *need* to be quick. Need to get this done. The alternative is unimaginable. It leaves me only one option. One opportunity to ensure my future. Whether I'm in here or free, The Saint needs to die.

Back in my cell, I sniff, wiping the blood from my face with my hand. God knows how long I'll have before The Saint sends someone to finish me. Lifting the corner of the flooring by our toilet, I pick up the razor blade Luke managed to get inside. That's all I need.

My cell door pushes open, and I quickly curl my fingers to my palm. The sting is instant. The warm liquid slips between the cracks. I flush the loo, then step out from behind the partition.

"Carter."

I pretend to rearrange my joggers.

The officer stands back, taking in my clothes. They're still drenched in Luke's blood having had no time to change.

"What the..." he starts, his hand moving to his belt that holds his baton and cuffs.

"It's not my blood," I say in a rush. "It's Luke's. I found him. He had an accident." I reckon I've got thirty seconds before I'm tossed to the floor and restrained. I don't move.

The officer withdraws his baton stepping into my cell, his eyes searching for Luke.

"He's in the medical centre," I quickly add.

With Luke's absence, the officer clicks his radio. He asks for the medical unit. I'm saved when they confirm Luke's there. He stows away his baton, stepping back for me to leave the cell.

"Where are we going?" I ask, aware my hand's bleeding, the razor still firmly in my grasp.

"Visitor. You had him on the list."

Travis. Right. I'd forgotten. "Can I wash my hands before I go?"

The officer still watches me closely, but he spies the blood.

With a nod, I offer him my thanks and step back behind the partition. I run the tap, simultaneously slipping the razor stealthily back in its place. When I stand, the cool stream of the water washes away my blood. I watch as it seeps down the plug, slipping away. Truth be told, I can't feel it. Can't feel the sting like I should. Only in my mind can the pain be felt.

If The Saint wants me dead, nothing will stop him. I let that play in my head until the officer steps into view, telling me to hurry up with a bang on the wall.

Drying my hands, I then follow him to the visitor room.

Travis sits waiting on the other side of the iron gate. When I see him, his eyes don't widen as they scan over my clothes. Given no time to change, I resemble something straight out of a horror movie. I don't know what's more worrying; the fact I'm covered in my cellmate's blood, or that my best mate isn't acting surprised.

I can't help checking my surroundings, taking in who's on shift as the bars clank open. There're two officers, neither of which I'm in good standing with. Just my luck.

One of them holds my gaze, his icy stare puncturing mine. It's unrelenting. Hard hitting. Deadly smug. *Fuck.* No doubt he already knows of The Saint's plan to off me.

"Rough day?"

He has no idea. I give Travis a blank look as I step closer, aware that time appears to have closed in on me much quicker than expected. My window to carry out my final kill has vanished.

"Normal," I reply on a sigh, indicating with a heavy heart just how *normal* the death and sickly sight of me truly is.

Travis' face flattens, but he slowly stands, his tall frame standing broad. His face suggests he's worried. But he's here. He's with me in my hell.

Holding out my hand, he grips it firmly then drags me into an embrace. He pats my back, and I mirror it, aware this is the last time I'll be like this with him. Suddenly, like I've been winded, I'm breathless, choking on the realisation.

I move back, pulling away from him. The man who will now take over my club. I look at him, desperately pressing down the misery that churns inside. That light at the end of the tunnel is now a mere speck. The last ember of life almost doused.

"Something I should know, brother?"

Words flee me. I shake my head, dropping to the seat. Once he's sat, having checked the guards over his shoulder, he waits patiently, giving me the time I need. The time I don't have. "I'm good," is the best I can do.

"Dean?"

A shiver of regret starts ebbing its way under my skin. What do I say in my final hour? How can I write my wrongs and explain what happens next? "Mollie." I look up and see a flash of surprise flicker across his face as I say her name. "I need you to speak to Mollie."

"You've got a fucking nerve." He's pissed. Angry. Seeing right through me.

"Just listen to her."

He leans forward. "*You* listen to me." The tips of his fingers steeple together in front of his face. He's serious. "I've not held everything down like I have for the past six weeks *for you*, for you tell me you're not coming home."

"Trav—"

"Don't fucking *Trav* me," he interjects shaking his head. "I don't want to fucking hear it. Do what you have to do and hang the fuck on. Your trial starts soon. And Mollie," her name rolls of his tongue with something other than hate, "*Mollie* will get you out of here."

I let the dust settle. Let the echo of his words fade away. "And if she doesn't?" She won't get the chance to, but I won't tell him that.

"She will, otherwise..." He trails off not knowing how to finish. He then drags a hand down over his beard, staring into space. "I need you, brother," he says after a long, drawn-out pause, his sadness obvious.

My shoulders slump, and I drag my feet back underneath the chair, pinching the bridge of my nose. The pain is still rife where it's split. I wince, jolting my hand away. "You've got this," I tell him. Because if any man can step into the shoes I failed to fill, it's him.

Travis' lips twist. "And what do I tell Mads?" he asks, his voice deflated.

My body goes cold. My stomach knotting with dread. I look

up, watching him as he reels internally. Is this where I give my goodbye?

Goodbyes make you think; make you contemplate everything you would or could have done differently. There's so much I should have done. So much more I should have given Mads. This goodbye shouldn't be coming like this. I've failed her, more than any man could have failed the woman he loves.

Picking up speed, my heart stammers. Guilt kicks my thoughts back to my past. Back to a time I was lost. Lost in the darkness. Lost in my head. Hopeless. And now? Now I'll move to her memories. I'll fade, but a part of me will live on through my girls.

My girls. Fuck, I wish I could see my girl grow. See Mads' face once she holds our child that I don't even know is a girl, but I *know* in my heart. I don't want Mads to wear my scars or carry my burden without me. But her sun. Her sun will keep on shining. Her light will continue to shine brightly. Even from the deepest depths of where I fear I'm going; it will be her light that shines through the cracks.

Travis simply looks at me. We exchange no words for the longest of time. We both feel the heaviness that comes with this final hour. We know where we've been together and what now lays ahead. As shit as it fucking is, there isn't anyone that could have stood at my side like he did.

When we do eventually speak, he vows to his promise; that nothing will happen to Mads. That he'll take care of my girl. Then we talk about the club and its future. The direction it will head and how best to keep it alive. I lay out the vision. The way I see things working, but ultimately, that's no longer my concern.

The officer behind us steps closer when our time is up. This is it. The end.

Over.

I stand with compliance, glancing at Travis as he too, rises.

"It was good seeing you, brother." I swipe my hand against his, pulling him close. Our grip is tight, but Travis, he tightens it, holding on to me with everything he has. I return it, closing my eyes, savouring the last good thing I'll have.

When we let go, an emptiness ensues. I'm forced to drink down the rising panic. I mustn't show him. Mustn't allow him to see my truth. He steps back leaving me, and I watch. All I can do is watch as he turns and leaves me on my own.

Just as I start to turn, I see the other guard stand. He's motionless, his eyes fixed on mine. "Sit down," he tells me coldly.

I hold his gaze not afraid to look away. If this is it, the moment The Saint uses another human to make sure I don't walk another day on this earth, well, I'm not going down without a fight. "I'd rather stand."

He grunts, a stupid look of disinterest striking his face. "You're a lucky cunt. I'd have rather seen your insides across this floor." His jaw ticks.

Lucky? I'm not sure whether I should attempt to claw my way out of here or sit, like I've been told. *Lucky?*

Choosing the latter, I move to the table, my eyes never letting either of these men out of my sight. The air around me is thick. It carries uncertainty. With every moment that passes with these two arseholes in each corner of the room, my worry intensifies. The ideas of what's about to go down in here multiply by the second.

I hear a door unlock. The jarring of the iron should make me flinch in my seat. But it doesn't. It comes like a full stop. Signifying my ending.

Unexpectedly, the two officers leave with haste, and I swing my head around, panic peddling over me. There's no one there. I wait as adrenaline starts to crash against my insides. It tumbles over me—again and again and again, leaving my body shivering, my mouth dry.

And still, I wait for someone to appear.

What the fuck is happening? A weird chill takes control of the hairs on the back of my neck. They stand on end, dancing in the woosh of air that comes when another door opens. I look. Listen. Wait. Whoever's coming, they're stalling for effect. They want me panicked. Want to see me sweating before they show themselves. It's working. I hate to admit it, but it's fucking working.

Taking a deep inhale, I steady myself, controlling my breathing. I look down at my hands, turning them over. Fresh blood seeps from the cut on my palm when I stretch my hand. For some reason, I stretch my hand open wider, relishing the tear of my skin. I watch the oozing blood trickle, leaving me. Then I stretch it some more, knowing this is the last thing I'll control.

When I curl my hand again, the light scuff of a shoe brushing the floor has me balling my fingers to a fist. I stiffen, my shoulders tensing tight. I can't see who it is. I think about looking at who's come to take me out.

Steady feet then hit the floor, and I know this isn't an ambush. This isn't someone coming in to end it all and get out sharpish. Men in here are too sloppy. Too quick. They crave immediate gratification where others have learned patience. This is an outsider.

To my left, the presence of someone begins to enter my vision, walking around the table. My eyes never look up. I wait until they take a seat opposite me.

I'm leant back in my chair. Then, as though every sense awakens on a beat of my heart, I'm suddenly numb. The blood in my veins, freezes. I'm stripped of words. Stripped of the ability to move. Even my eyes remain paralysed to the person sat in front of me.

"You?"

CHAPTER TWENTY-FOUR

UNKNOWN

Six months earlier

"We're sorry," they'd said, turning their backs on me. Gone. They weren't sorry. Never fuckin' are. The amount of shit they put us through, you'd think they'd at least recognise how much time and effort we put into this life. But no. We're like scrap; chewed up, spat out. Forgotten.

What happened this morning scratches like a broken record in my mind. Everything I have has been given to them. I sacrificed a normal life. A wife. Children. None of that appealed to me—not like this did. Now what? Now what do I do? When I get out of here, what waits for me?

The club? A dry sob threatens to leave me. But I won't let it. I don't want them to have the satisfaction.

Turning gingerly on the bed, I let my head drop to the pillow. It hurts. Bruised and broken.

Searching for sleep, alone in my thoughts, the subtle click of the lock makes me turn to see two men enter my room. They're not the same two who came by earlier.

My head thumps when I jolt, startled, wondering what the fuck is going on here? I said no visitors. I said I don't want to see anyone. I don't want people to see me like this. A man without purpose. Weak.

"Nice to finally see you awake."

I look up to the tall one. His face is sharp, his nose pointed. I don't say a word. Instead, I look between him and the other man as I slowly sit up.

"We need a moment of your time."

That's all I'll have now.

When I remain silent, the small one inhales a breath, shoving his hands in his pockets. He ambles around the foot of the bed, his chin down. "We have a proposition for you," he says.

Skipping between them, my eyes take in the two strangers. Both wearing casual clothes. They look like your average run of the mill soccer dads. Who are they?

The short one stops by my side. "We're aware of what happened this morning."

My teeth grind. My muscles tighten. With a long blink, I look up.

"We're here to change that."

This morning. That's when I was told I was no longer needed. Forced to accept my rehab will take me off the front line. I'm not moving to behind a desk. I gave up too much to wind up behind a fuckin' desk. "How?" My voice carries discern, but intrigue allows me to ask.

"Before we get to the hows, what we're offering won't be easy."

I can't help but laugh. "Because everything up until now has been exactly that."

The small man's lips pull tight. "It won't require a badge. You'll get no medal, no... recognition for what you'll have to do." My face tightens. "It will require you to operate in the shadows."

The shadows? "Is that where you two are?"

They both look at me. Their joint silence giving me my

answer.

"Why would I want that?"

"There's a virus spreading. We need to stop it."

A virus? "Who?" I can't tell if the sleep I need is dampening my ability to understand what these strangers are saying.

The tall one steps closer on the other side of the bed. He opens up his worn jacket, pulling out a large envelope. He uncurls it, pulling out a picture, then drops it on my lap.

Looking between both men, I then look down.

"Costa Affini," he says. "Backed by billionaires and gangsters. He's moving cargo into Amsterdam from the UK."

Costa? Like the coffee? What a stupid fuckin' name. "Let me guess. You don't know how he's doing it?"

Another picture is slapped on my lap. No expression across the tall one's face. "Intel suggests he'll move on criminal gangs, have them mule for him. At present, we know he's got eyes on these ports, but we suspect an underground operation will be set up imminently." Two images are fanned before me. With a finger, he points as he speaks. "This one is where it will set off for Amsterdam. And here," he moves his finger, "is the first location we think they'll load at once they're established. We had a man on the inside who confirmed Costa had been there."

"Had?" I ask.

His face tightens. "His death was unrelated; however, we've lost our advantage."

I pick everything up and hand it back to them. Given the location of the load, I can hazard a guess at which *gang* could be muling. I also know which one will avoid it. "I'm not seeing how any of this can help me."

With a disingenuous smile, the small one steps forward. "We know you're good at working alongside criminals."

"Meaning?" I snap, knowing full well what he means.

"Meaning... we need you to divide, complicate, unpick, and

put an end to what Costa's running. Because it can't make it here. We need to stop it before it gets into Europe and spreads wider. Otherwise we're fucked. They'll be no stopping it."

"What's he running?" I'm assuming drugs. Money. Guns. This isn't anything new.

The two men exchange a look. I know it. I recognise it instantly. Hate. "This." One final picture is placed before me.

Slowly trailing my gaze, what's on the image jumps out. My stomach flips, horror mounting with every second I look at it.

"Supply is low, but goddamn it demand is high."

There's evil in the picture. I don't need them to explain what I'm looking at. "Were they forced?"

"Yes. Unfortunately these were, but not everyone is. People will willingly sign up for this if the payout is big enough."

My head shakes as I try to make sense of it.

"Unlike most criminal organisations, Costa isn't part of the chain that just supplies the underworld. Medical doctors, lawyers, people of that calibre, that's who he's supplying."

What the fuck?

"This is why we need you."

Even with what I know of enterprises like this, I can't see how I fit the bill. "And what is it you think *I* can do? What difference can I make?"

The tall man pulls out his phone. "You'll have a drive that no one else will possess. It's an opportunity to stay in the game and put a stop to this."

Undercover. "From the shadows?"

He simply nods at my question.

I look down once more. The image of a child cut open. Lifeless. My skin crawls. "Why *me*?"

He steps forward, turning the screen of his phone in my direction.

"Who's that?" I ask. The picture of a man's profile looks back at me. You can't make him out. His face is unrecognisable.

"Check the time and date," is all the tall man says.

Pulling the phone closer, I see it. The day everything changed for us. Anger claws up my throat. The rally. The man in the picture was at the rally all those years ago. My skin prickles as adrenaline suddenly swamps my veins.

Past and present unite. My promise back then clashes with recent events. The accident is patchy. The aftermath of what happened, tricky to piece together. But I'll never forget the past. How could I?

Any scrap of composure I had flees me. "Who is he?" I force the words out as rage and hate suffuse.

"Former prospect. Presumably patched in. Never came back here as far as intel shows. That's why you missed him."

Missed him. The words sting like failure. I suck in a sharp breath. "Missed him?" I say harshly. My fingers tremble. The hairs on the back of my neck vibrate with every disbelieving breath of air I manage to take.

"He got away. We suspect he's now tied to Costa. Intel confirms he moved to the UK and ran in similar circles to other MCs, committing similar crimes. But he went off grid. *He* is how we know you'll say yes." More anger. More rage. More annoyance at their correct assumption of me. "He's tangled in that web somewhere."

"The image though?"

"It's all we've got, but we know it's him."

"How can you be so sure?"

"He's wanted for multiple murders, all with a unique brutality." He drops his head before he continues. "He's hidden. Unnoticed. All we have is an unconfirmed sighting that cropped up last year."

There's a silence lingering in the air around us. I study the picture, unable to fully make out the man's face. "Do you at least have a name?"

He sighs. "No."

All of the emotions from the past are driven home. They run deep, intoxicating me, surrounding me in a haze. I can't see. Can't think. Can't control the sudden desire I feel to hunt this cunt down and destroy him.

Bowing my head, I rub my eyes with my hand as if that will help me to see. I can't make sense of what my gut's telling me to do. Costa's actions are deplorable. But this man? This man was *there*. He unknowingly got away. I won't let that happen again. "What would I have to do?" My voice is grave.

"You say yes, from this point moving forward you'll no longer exist." *Live in the shadows*. "There can be no communication with your family. No one can know what you're doing."

The weight of what he's saying all of a sudden lands heavy. "What about—"

"—No one." I stay silent. Taking it all in. "We'll let you think on it."

They leave the room, and I'm left wondering. Wondering how we didn't know of him. It's like we've lived a lie. We may have kept our promise, just, but ultimately I failed. I'm a man without purpose who failed. All those years that passed with me assuming I'd done right by her. Well I won't fail her again.

This is the easiest decision I'll ever make.

CHAPTER TWENTY-FIVE

MADISON

It's Saturday afternoon. My body aches. I'm tired. So, so tired. Pregnancy seems to be taking its toll on my body. It's beautiful, if you count the fact I can no longer see my feet as that. My progress is good. The doctors are happy with the baby's growth. I need to go tomorrow morning for another scan and blood test, but I'm doing okay. For now.

Earlier this morning, I set up for the guys getting back to the clubhouse. I probably shouldn't have gotten here as early as I did. To be honest, I needed the space. Needed the quiet that could only be obtained here without anyone around.

Now that most of the food is prepped, the families and other members who didn't go on the run have started arriving. I can feel a sense of dread starting to loom over me. Travis should be back any moment. I know he went to see Dean before he was headed here. That's the only reason I'm waiting around. Waiting for the latest update on how things are with him.

Mollie walks over to me, stood in the kitchen. "Think that's it," she says, placing an empty crate of boxes on the side.

"Thank you." I look up. "Appreciate your help this morning."

She smiles genuinely. "You don't have to thank me, Mads. We're friends. I'm happy to." She picks up her coat and her bag from the countertop. "I better be off." Her eyes sink. She knows

Travis is due back soon.

"You don't have to leave because of him. You're helping us, Mollie. We want you to stay. *I* want you to stay." Mollie's become more than a friend. She is what stands between Dean coming home or him not. I need her to know that I see her as more than just his solicitor. "Mollie?" I say when she doesn't move.

"He won't like it."

I smile this time. "Since when do we care about what they like?"

With my words of solidarity, Mollie drops her things back down. "You set? For Monday, I mean." I hate the wobble of my voice.

She steps closer. "I'll do everything I can to bring him home…" Mollie looks off into the distance, her eyes coated in a light film of mist.

"Do you think you can do it?"

She sighs. "I've built a strong case."

Translated; it's not going to be easy. We stare at each other, a shadow of sadness wrapping itself around us. I drop my head, staring at the ground as I gather my wayward thoughts. *Not here. Not now. Contain it.*

A loud cheer of laughter runs down the hall, filling the entire main room. We both look up, watching as the men laugh and joke with one another. "Is it still as wild as it used to be?" Mollie sits on the stool, and I follow watching as the men start drinking. The music turns up in the background.

I nod. Then think. "You used to come here?"

Mollie's face straightens. Her lips pull tight. "You could say that."

I follow Mollie's eyes, her gaze is glued to the back of one of the girl's heads.

The girl, wearing tight jeans and a lace top that I would consider merely a bra, panders to the needs of one of the guys.

She tosses her long, dark, straight hair over one shoulder, then leans into him, her breasts pushing against him. I watch as her hand then slips, cupping his crotch as he whispers presumably filthy words in her ear.

I shake my head, rubbing the back of my neck, wishing the flames kissing my skin to die down.

When I look up, Mollie smiles, reminiscing. "We didn't need anything but each other."

Gravity lets go of her words, dropping them on me with force. "What happened?" I turn my full attention to Mollie.

Her eyes are still planted on the sex show, but her voice? It screams yearning. Like she's looking for something she can't find. Something she once had. "It died," she says solemnly.

"Travis."

She looks at me then, never actually acknowledging my admission of it being him. I can see it in her eyes though. I saw it the first moment I saw them together. It wouldn't have taken a genius. The chemistry and tension between them. It's obvious.

Her eyes are just slightly wider, her cheeks blushed with a tint of rose colour. "In the end, we wanted different things."

My heart swells as her eyes drift to my stomach. Like the sea leaving the shore, she withdraws, her mind taking her somewhere else. I want to reach out and comfort her. But Mollie isn't a woman who requires my tenderness. She needs me to listen. I get the feeling she hasn't had anyone to talk to in so long.

A tear wilts to her chin. Quickly swiping it from her face, the door then opens, and Travis strides in. He carries his helmet under his arm, adjusting the beanie he wears on top of his head. His gaze roams over everybody, looking through the crowds now filling the space between us.

There's a weariness to him. A bleak look upon his face. The smile I wore when he walked in, dissipates on a beat of my heart. For the first time since I've known him, he looks scared. The way he carries his large frame, usually so tall and strong, he's now so small. So engulfed in a weariness that seems to drag him down.

He glances up, disorientated, and our eyes meet. He then looks to Mollie, his lips all of a sudden curling tight on his face. His brows scrunch as he walks to us, his huge strides bringing him close in mere seconds.

We both stand. Both ridged. Both reading him so clearly. "What's wrong?" I ask rushed. Travis' chest rises and falls quickly, his eyes having never left Mollie. "Travis?" I ask again. Failing to pull his attention, I look to Mollie. Her face mirrors his. Broken. "Travis," I speak more firmly.

"Mads, I need you to go home."

"Home?" Why home? He asked me to be here. He asked me to help.

"What happened? Did you see him?"

Travis' sigh is immediate. I don't miss it. It causes a knock in my chest which throws me back a step. Tears fill my eyes. A hazy fog clouds what's right in front of me. Dean's lost himself. Buried himself in his darkness. I feared it would happen. Feared and knew it would happen. I *knew*. Because I've lost myself too. Because that's what happens when we don't have the other by our side.

"Go home. I'll be there soon." My lips part when I go to speak but his raised finger stops me. "Please. Just go home. Get Legs to follow you."

His eyes plead with me, and that's something I don't enjoy. Yes, I've tested him. I've pushed boundaries with him and Dean sometimes. But only because they're stubborn and controlling. This though, this is a situation where I fully understand I need to listen.

My heart's pounding. The tears I'm holding clog my throat as I move to get my bag. I give Mollie a look, swinging the strap over my shoulder.

She raises a small smile. "I'll message you," she says not moving.

Leaving the space, I walk away in search of Legs.

On the drive home, I can't shake the feeling that I'm stuck in reverse. Like I'm moving in slow motion, away from everything I want. Tears uncontrollably fall from my eyes. I keep wiping them away, but it's no good.

Intuition casts its unwanted veil over me. Why? Why now? What changed for Travis to have come back so shaken? Every bone in my body wants to drive to the prison to see Dean. Wants to demand they let me in. Let me save him, bring him back to where he needs to be. With me. With us.

Pulling up at the house, I sit, unable to move my body to the front door. My head falls, and my hands rest on my bump. I cradle it as the baby kicks. Each nudge sends fresh waves of confusion and heartache to bulldoze their way through me. I'm breaking down when I don't know what's happened. I should pull myself together until I know what's really going on. I should summon the strength instilled in my blood to remain strong.

But in the bottom of my heart, I feel it. Feel the pull towards a sorrowful truth that hides around the corner.

Legs taps the window, getting my attention. "Need me to come in?" His gentle voice stings me with melancholy. My energy zapped, I take him up on his offer, letting him open the car door and take my bag.

Lauren opens the front door seeing my tear-streaked face. Her face drops, and I manage to smile, hoping it's enough to pacify her. She steps back letting me in, and I turn catching Legs with his eyes on her, his arm outstretched holding my bag for me to take. Motionless.

I look to her and double take, seeing Lauren staring back equally charged.

Legs looks at me. "What?" he stammers.

"Nothing." I raise a brow before he shakes his head as if realising he's been caught.

"Need anything else?"

My eyes pull from Lauren, and I take my bag. "No. Thank you."

"I can stay," he fires back too quickly for my liking, possibly revealing his intentions.

"We're good. Thanks, Legs." Taking a step forward, I encourage the young prospect out of the house then turn to Lauren.

She stares at the door after him. "His nickname is *Legs*?" she asks curiously.

Closing my eyes, I gather myself. "It doesn't matter." Travis will be here soon. "I need you to run to the shop."

The way she looks at me. She knows something's wrong. "O-kay." Her tone is curious. "You, alright?"

Feeling another onslaught barrelling my way, I quickly walk to the kitchen. "Yeah," I lie, "just hormones."

Lauren follows me. "What do we need?" she asks tentatively.

Shit. Anything. *Say anything*. "Um, grab some milk. Some bread, maybe?"

"Maybe?"

I sigh. "Yes. Please," I turn to face her, "grab bread." Reaching for my bag, I open my purse and hand her some money, then watch as she turns and leaves. She closes the door behind her.

Then, and only then, do I let my grip go. My back sinks down the kitchen unit, my body slumped on the floor. I unravel. Still unknowing, but fully aware.

CHAPTER TWENTY-SIX

TRAVIS

"Why are you here?" My unblinking, focused eyes never stray from Mollie's.

"I was helping my friend."

I smirk, tucking in my chin. "Your friend?" I question.

"Yes, Mads. My friend. She needed help setting all this up."

I know the two of them have gotten closer, but I do not want them relying on each other. Mollie's got no reason to stick around now. No reason to remain close by. Not now that I know Dean's intentions.

He didn't have to say it. His half-arsed goodbye when I saw him only served to anger the beast within me. What am I supposed to do? Step into his shoes? Take care of his family? Run his club? That'll kill me before I even try to start. I won't break my promise, wouldn't dream of it. But I cannot see for the fucking life of me why Dean appeared to quit so easily. Would he explain it to me or give me any reason as to why he was covered in blood when he walked in? No, none. I sat there like an idiot, reeling internally at the sight of him. Reeling because I had to look him in the eye knowing that I wouldn't see him again.

Ever.

Just thinking that tears an agonising rip through my chest. It scratches and burns unapologetically, leaving me exposed. On edge. What the fuck am I supposed to tell Mads? I fear there'll be pieces no one will ever be able to fix back together once I do. Damn you Dean, all the way to fucking hell for putting this on me.

Taking a step closer to her, Mollie throws her shoulders back, her chin lifting as I invade her breathing space. My hands haven't stopped shaking since I left the prison. They continue to when I see her eyes narrow, her armour falling into place ready to spar with me.

Good. She'll need it. "Apparently, I'm to talk to you." My voice is thick and heavy as I incline my head to her.

Judging by the way her face tightens and her eyes never stop moving between mine, I'd say she knows full well what I'm referring to. Licking her lips before they part, Mollie takes a shaky breath. "What did he say?"

"You know what." I can't help the short way I respond.

I don't bother checking if anyone's looking, but Mollie does. There's a hint of worry in her eyes as she scans the room.

"He didn't say anything. Only that I should talk to you. Which I've simply had e—fucking—nough of. So spill it, quick, then get the fuck out and don't come back."

Her breathing quickens. Her eyes now a shade of maddening red. She shakes her head side to side. "You think coming back was easy for me? You think being here, seeing you almost every day is what I wanted?" Her voice is getting louder. "These past weeks have been hell for me too!" she snaps.

I smile taking another closing step towards her. Parting my legs slightly, I drop my face, lowering it dangerously close to hers. I let my hot breath hit her cheeks. I can tell it takes everything she's got not to breathe me in. "It's nothing more than you deserve."

A chink in her protective suit vanishes. "Deserve?" she grinds out. "I didn't *deserve* for you treat me the way you did." She pushes forward, but immediately stumbles back when I keep my vow to never accommodate her again.

One leg hitches to stop herself falling, one hand resting flat on the stool behind her. The slit in her skirt shifts, exposing her leg to me. I'm still stood over her, our eyes mercilessly locked on one another. I shouldn't, but when she looks down checking her leg and doesn't move it or pull away, I reach out, placing my hand on her skin. Her soft, inviting skin.

This woman. I hate her.

"Don't." Mollie's voice wobbles.

I don't listen. My hand glides over the surface of her leg, slipping its way to the top of her thigh. She doesn't want me to stop. Her chest rises and falls, bobbing her round breasts up and down.

When I reach the apex, my thumb sumptuously close to her pussy, she squeezes her legs closed. "I said don't." Her breath wooshes out of her like she's enjoying the feel of my hands on her body. It's been a long time, but she hasn't forgotten. How could she.

There may be hate, but one thing neither of us can deny is how good we fucked. Like animals it was unbridled, uncaged. Wild. She's thinking. Remembering like I am. "Are you sure?" I say in a low tone. My dick hardens as I move my lips to her ear, her back arching her breasts into me. "I can smell how much you want me."

Warm air hits my cheek as her lips part, her breath escaping her. I don't move, but I feel the twitch in her leg. Turning her head into mine, shivers scatter down my spine when her lips brush over my ear. "I'd rather die than let you fuck me."

And that's when the biggest smile I've had in days stretches across my face. It hurts as the skin pulls. "We both know that's not true," I growl.

Without warning, her left fist jabs me in the ribs. If it wasn't for the small hole in my chest, the pain wouldn't sting like it does, jolting me and giving her enough room to escape.

She stands grabbing her bag and hastily swipes for her coat.

"I need to know what Dean asked you to tell me." I stand straight clutching my side, willing my dick to settle.

Mollie doesn't reply. She moves to walk past me, but I grab her wrist, forcing her to stop. "I need to speak to him first," she says. "Make sure what you're saying is—"

I don't let her finish her sentence. Grabbing her neck with my other hand, I push her back to the wall.

She drops her belongings to the floor, her steps quick as both hands grip hold of my wrist.

I slam her back, her head hitting the paint with a thwack. "We're all out of time, Baby Doll." She grimaces at my pet name for her. "Now tell me what it is that only *you* can tell me. His last wishes? Is that what it fucking is? His last wishes?!"

"Yes!" she cries, her nails scratching into my skin. My hold on her isn't as tight as it could be. "He wrote it all down. A note for you. And one for Mads."

I grind my teeth, my jaw twitching. "Where is it?" I ask. Mollie doesn't say anything. "Fucking where, Mollie?" My patience is wearing so thin. She stares at me, her heart clearly pounding. Is she worried that this signifies the end? The end for Dean? The end of her time here?

As if reading my mind, her eyes glass over, but no tears fall. "I have it. At my office."

My hand around her throat flexes.

Silence then settles for a moment before she asks, "Now what?"

I aimlessly draw a few strokes with my thumb across her delicate neck. "You get it for me, today. I'll have to go speak to Mads." What the hell am I going to say? I don't know how or why Dean came to know that his time was up. All I know is that he was sure.

"Then?" A hopefulness seems to skate around the edge of Mollie's question.

I stop my strokes, dropping my hand to my side. "Then we move on." My heart feels heavy, my words holding significance. Stepping back, I turn to walk out the door. An unknown feeling suddenly buries itself deep inside me. Remorse? Regret?

"It wasn't my fault," I hear Mollie whisper.

She must feel it too.

Like a gas burner flickering on, the small flame in my gut is ignited. I stop walking. "What wasn't?" I know exactly what she's talking about, but she owes me this. Owes me this explanation after eleven fucking years of not knowing why she aborted our child and never said so much as one word *to me* before she upped and left. I try to steady my heart. Try to ebb the rush of every emotion trying to destroy me in this moment. It's no good.

"You know what."

Yeah, I do. "I need to hear you say it." It's all I've ever needed.

"I... I can't," she says after taking a breath. "You ruined everything."

The sardonic laugh that leaves me riles her. I step closer to her again, but this time she remains unprotected, no time to put up the walls she can hide behind. "I may have ruined your faith in love," Mollie lets out a sigh, "but I wasn't the one who turned my back on us. You did. The day you decided my life for me."

Her eyes pick up off the floor, looking directly at me. "I made a decision for us," she balks, tears filling her eyes as she frantically tries to blink them away. "It wouldn't have worked. I ran because you would never have changed."

"I did fucking change."

She shakes her head. "Travis, you wanted freedom and the club. Not a wife. Not a kid. If you changed, why don't you have either of those things now?"

I let out a breath. "Like you?"

Mollie falls to the wall, her back pushed flat against it. "Fuck you," she sobs defeated. She drops her head, and maybe for the first time since she's been back, the smallest part of me hates the way she looks so sad. "He died you fucking prick."

My eyes dart to her. When she doesn't look at me, I slide my hand to her chin, lifting it, slowly making her look at me. She fights me at first, but I hold her tighter, not letting her go this time. "He died? When?"

Mollie sniffs. Lines in her forehead scrunch together. "Do you care?"

I don't drop my gaze or my hold. "I care. Because now you know what it feels like to lose the one person you loved the most."

One tear. That's what I get. One single tear. It drops to her cheek as she closes her eyes, unable to look at me any longer.

"Apparently, it doesn't matter how far you run. You always end up back here."

Mollie sobs, and I let out a sigh. I pull away and walk to the door, resolute. I need to get ready for when Costa gives us our next shipment details. I can't get distracted. Not by her or by anything. This shit is all on me now. "Get me those letters," I tell her.

I walk out, not looking back.

CHAPTER TWENTY-SEVEN

DEAN

Once upon a time, I would have done anything for the man sat in front of me. He would have done anything for me. He was my brother. My best friend. The reason I started enjoying my life again.

But he's dead…

What I've never felt towards him is anger. Never felt infidelity or had an urge to jump across a table and batter him with my bare hands. They're the emotions residing in me at present.

Jack simply stares. He takes in my cut nose, the blood still dripping from my hand which now is squeezed so tight, the pain starts to throb. I can feel the beat of my heart against the opening.

A dizziness makes my head swim. Maybe it's the blood loss. Or maybe it's the fact I'm sat in front of a ghost. A ghost who haunts me. Taunts me. Talks to me every day, keeping me on my toes.

How is this possible? I go to ask him, but I'm robbed of all ability to form words. "Deano." Just the sound of his voice, even though he's never stopped speaking to me, leaves me wrecked.

The familiar ache I felt when I heard he'd died kicks back in my chest. "Why are you not dead?"

His face drops when I sound disappointed. I'm not, or I don't mean to be. But I'd just about buried him mentally. Just about let him go and come around to the idea that I'd actually lost him.

Anger burns my insides like hot coals. Why wouldn't he tell me he was alive and still fucking kicking? He could have called. Sent a message. Anything. He could have done anything to let me know. But he didn't.

Jack pulls at his jumper, readjusting himself. Nerves? He then draws in a long breath, steadying himself. "I owe you an explanation."

He's got a fucking nerve. "An explanation? You owe me more than an explanation. Try starting with an apology."

His head drops. "I couldn't tell you," he says hesitantly.

I massage the back of my neck with my good hand. "Couldn't tell me you weren't dead?" I can't believe he's sat here. My jaw locks, my teeth grind so hard against each other. "You're not sorry then?"

There's a pause. "I'm sorry I couldn't tell you sooner." He looks up at me, gaping holes replacing his pupils. "But I won't apologise for it."

I shake my head, torn. Something's different. Off. Something out of sorts. He's sorry but he won't apologise for it? "How've you managed to clear this entire room to sit down with me?"

I'd almost forgotten about The Saint wanting me dead.

Jack leans forward, resting his arms on the table. "You're in shock, but we have a lot to discuss."

Formal. That's what's different. He's direct. A man on a mission. Where's my carefree, take no shit brother? I guess a part of him really did die back in Oz. My mind torments me with the memory. "Mads is pregnant," I tell him.

He flinches.

"So yeah, we may have a lot to discuss, but I'll never see my family again. Forgive me if I'm not somersaulting with joy."

He leans forward with purpose. I frown, my guard still up. "What if I could ensure you saw her again?"

A twisted smile pulls my lips to my cheeks, a dreaded pang of misery jolting me. "You're too late." I won't make the night. My heart skips a beat, and I will it to stay in control.

"No. I'm right on time."

My head snaps up. "How?"

"The hows can wait, just know things have been taken care of." He ends the conversation bluntly with no room for negotiation.

I can't wrap my head around what he's trying to tell me, but flashes of my uncle reflect through his eyes. "Does Ronnie know you're alive?"

I see the pain hit him. It's undeniable. It seizes him, twists him, pulls him in different directions. "No," he sighs. So, Jack faked his own death and told no one. For what? Is he working? "We should talk about why I'm here." I don't speak. I simply wait. Jack links his hands, his arms still on the table in front of him. He takes what feels like an eternity to finally open his mouth and start explaining. "After the accident, I had visitors. They told me I was no longer on the force." He drops his head. Just telling me appears to hurt him.

"Why?" I ask.

"Didn't want to wait for my recovery. Rehab was going to take too long. They offered me a position behind a desk." He looks up. We both know he's better than being stuck behind a desk. Jack is front line, hands on. No way he would have accepted that offer.

"Is that why you didn't want us to see you?"

With a sigh he admits, "Partly." Only partly? "I was gutted. The force had been my whole life. You know that." I understand how much it meant to him, still doesn't make sense why he wouldn't see us. "I didn't want to see anyone because I was distraught. Then out of the blue, I had an offer I couldn't turn down."

"Must have been worth it," I huff. "Worth more than letting your grieving family know you were actually alive."

The way he looks at me, it sends a shockwave crashing through me. His eyes pin on mine, his face slightly lowered. Whatever he's about to say, I can tell he means it. "It was."

Leaning back in my chair, I let my body sag. Meanwhile, Jack's fists clench on the table. I don't miss it. He didn't want me to. He wants me to know how much his decision means to him. "Who was it?" I ask needing more.

"ASIS."

I narrow my eyes at him. He's working with the Australian Secret Intelligence Service? "Must be a big case." My tone is nothing but arrogant.

Jack's temples twitch. "Bigger than you'll ever be able to comprehend. Took me a while to get my head around it."

"But not too long that you couldn't see us before we left?"

"Enough," he barks at me.

I huff again with a laugh. "Or what, Jack?" He needs to start talking or so help me God. "Tell me right fucking now what was so huge you couldn't pick up a fucking phone?"

Mirroring the way I'm sat, the only sound I can hear is that of my own heart booming in my ears. "You made a wrong choice." His voice remains as tight as the air sitting between us.

"Which one?" I've only ever made one good choice in my life. "The list is pretty long."

"The one where you thought you were doing the right thing for the club. That fuckin' one," he hisses.

"Saviours?" I question, and he nods. "That was about peace, Jack. The deal was changed without me there. Co—"

"Costa," he simply says, finishing my sentence for me.

My ears prick up when he says Costa's name. "What do you know of him?"

Leaning forward again, Jack sighs then takes a breath. "I know you made a deal with the devil, Deano."

My stomach bottoms out. My eyes flare wild with terror.

"The club is soon to be on every federal radar from the US to back home."

Unsure of how to move or how to react, I let Jack's words sink in. How can this be happening? The move to work side by side with the Saviours was to ensure peace. We knew we'd be in deeper by moving guns, but this new deal... we could handle it. We brought in more men so we could run things smoothly. "How do you know Costa's the devil?" I ask.

"I've seen it with my own eyes." A haunted look sets itself upon him.

"That bad, huh?" I ask.

His body stiffens. "Worse."

Another silence. "Why you?"

"'Cause it was easy for me to disappear. No one would question it. I could work in the shadows. Bring this organisation to its knees."

I frown. "How? How are you going to stop him running guns? What's your plan here?"

Jack hesitates, his lips part but he stops himself. After what feels like hours, he finally speaks. "My plan is simple." He smiles. "Divide. Complicate. Unpick." He's focused. Each word he delivers ferociously, with lasers for eyes locked on mine.

"Divide?" I struggle to conceal my look of shock.

Divisions. Divisions appeared when the threats to the Sodom Saviours started. *A ghost, some might say, appears to be haunting us.* They were The Saint's words. *Divide. Complicate. Unpick.*

I couldn't have known Jack was alive, but I feel like a fool. I allow my head to drop. It's obvious. So bloody obvious. "It was you sending threats. Wasn't it?" My voice is quiet, but the ringing in my head is anything but.

Jack's half shrug and dismissive wave of his hand has me across the table in a flash. I land a solid fist to his nose, making his body curl off the chair to the floor.

He stands, shaken, taking a few steadying steps.

"This is your fault!" I shout, my fists curled tight. All of it is his fault. The charges against me were unstoppable, but everything that followed after the package showed up on the Saviours' doorstep is on him.

Jack. The dead man.

He tilts his head to the sky, blinking his eyes rapidly. Good. I hope it stings. Prick. I move to sit back down, my foot frantically tapping the floor.

Think. Think. Think.

Cracking his neck before he starts sniffing back the blood, he turns looking the angriest I've ever seen him. "Now we match," he throws at me flatly. He stalks back to the table leaning both hands flat. "I assumed you'd stay away from this. Then I found out you went into business with the *Saviours?* I couldn't fuckin' stand it. I did what I did to try and keep you away."

Heat floods me. My voice raises. "What you *did* was make them not trust us!"

"Exactly!" Jack pushes off the table holding his palms to the ceiling. "I thought with enough push they wouldn't let you in on the new deal. But low and be—fuckin'—hold, you go and get yourselves a front row seat!"

"Why does this mean so much to you? You've known what the club does since we were kids. Never once have you gotten this involved to stop us doing business?"

Jack sighs. "This goes bigger than simply running guns! You nosedived to the darkest depths of hell and you don't even fuckin' know it!"

I need a drink. A smoke. Anything to calm my shot to fuck

nerves bouncing all around me. "Then tell me! Tell me what the fuck is really going on here." I push to my feet demanding to know. "Tell me what was worth more to you than family!"

His eyes jump. His cheeks puff out. "It is fuckin' family! It's Mum."

What? His words get lost in translation. This is getting more complicated by the fucking second. "What are you talking about?" My head is swimming. I can't take this all in. How can this have anything to do with Aunt Linda?

Jack bangs the table then puts his fist through the back of the chair. It shatters into a million pieces, scattering across the floor. Rage has consumed him. Blinding rage that overtakes him. "We missed one. We fuckin' missed one." His voice is harsh. His words clearly stinging him.

"Missed one?" I think back to the event. The day that for years has plagued me. The promise we made never to let another woman get hurt on our watch, we've kept it. But missed one? "We killed the only man there. How do you know we missed one?" My blood is starting to boil. Tiny ripples of hot, steaming anger are pushing their way to the surface.

"He was a former prospect. Took off after..." Jack's voice trails. "They showed me a picture. He's unidentifiable, but the dates matched the person in the picture close to the scene. He'd been at the rally, Deano. He followed her."

"Who is he?" Because right now I know Jack's thinking the same as me. He's a dead man.

"I don't know. The threats were to flush him out and push you away... if I can stop Costa, I'll find him."

"What?"

Jack lowers himself to the remains of the broken chair.

I move and sit opposite him.

"The guy is close to Costa. I don't know how or where, but the two go hand in hand."

I sigh, my head starting to ache with the overload of emotions and information. "This is how they got you to play dead? Dangling a man in front of you."

Jack looks up at me through his lashes, anger still very much coursing through him. "I know what they showed me. I know that I need to stop that, then I find the man who killed my mother. And when I do. *I* kill him." Jack sighs, running a hand through his hair. "I know he's here. He was involved with the Saviours at some point. That's where you come in. Former prospect, it's likely he's patched in now."

Makes sense. Both clubs have recruited new members. But we've got tabs on everyone. Surely I'd know? I roll my bottom lip under my teeth. "He could be any one of them. But in case you weren't aware, I'm not going anywhere anytime soon." I hold my hand out, gesturing towards the blank walls.

Jack smiles. It's genuine. "In case *you* weren't aware, my new job comes with a few perks."

My face drops. My heart all but stops. I hold my breath, not quite wanting to believe what I think Jack's suggesting. When he suggested me seeing Mads, I assumed he meant bringing her in here. "What are you saying?"

Jack stands then slowly walks to the door he came in through.

I crane my neck towards him.

"It's time to go home."

CHAPTER TWENTY-EIGHT

DEAN

I'm back, babe. Staring at the house, I've almost made it. The place I long to be, my home, she's on the other side of the door. Relief settles deep in my soul. I feel like I can finally breathe easy. Six weeks and yet it feels like I endured eternity to get back here. I should be running to the door, tearing it down until I have her in my arms. But unease keeps me in my seat.

"What is it?"

I slowly look at Jack.

He sits in the driver's seat of his car, one hand on the steering wheel, his body slightly turned to mine. "Ten minutes you've been staring at the door. Why not go in already?"

Looking back to the house, my chest tightens. "When I go in, I'm not leaving her again." I look to Jack. "I won't do that to her."

Jack nods his understanding. "Family." He half smiles. "They're our greatest weakness."

"She's given me nothing but strength," I fire back.

"I don't doubt that." He raises a hand as if to apologise. "But there's a reason you're still sat here. You're doubtin' yourself."

Wrong. I'm not. "Until I know the full plan, I'm wondering what the cost to my family will be."

"The cost?" Jack questions.

Of course. He wouldn't understand. I'm new to these

feelings too. The feeling of loving someone so much you would burn the world to ensure their safety, then realising the world only needs burning when you're around. "If what you've got planned will take me away from her again, then I don't want it. I need to get out."

Jack lowers his chin then looks back up. He can hear it in my voice. I'm serious. I walk through that door I'm not leaving her again. "Even with what you know?" he asks.

"What I know?" I retort. I don't know shit. "I know we need to find and kill the man we let get away, of that I am one hundred percent sure. But whatever else is going on here, I need your word the club and my family aren't going to suffer under the weight of it."

"I get it, Deano, but—"

"Do you? Get it, I mean. Because from where I'm sitting, you're the one who couldn't call, couldn't get any word to me that you weren't dead." He's clearly got some muscle behind him, to be able to walk me quite literally out the front door of prison a few days before my trial. I don't doubt that what's happening is serious. But what it is, I'm still none the wiser.

Time spent with Jack should have lessened my irritation towards him. It hasn't. His lips pull tight, hating that I'm not on the same page. "I couldn't risk it. We need to make sure we bring Costa down properly. He's been recruiting, pulling people in left right and centre. There can be no fuck ups here. No wrong turns."

My eyes widen. "You said you sent the threats to keep us away." I shake my head. "Rather than call me before we got in too deep, you sat back and watched because you couldn't risk losing your man." My nostrils flare.

Jack stares at me. A man on a mission. Unable to see past what he wants. "If you really want your out, this is your only opportunity."

My *only* way out. "What about the Irish? Did you know they

were planning on ambushing the shipment?"

Jack takes a deep breath. "Who do you think told them?"

Jesus fucking Christ. I exhale, blowing out my cheeks. "You made this so much worse. *You* put us in the driving seat." My heart kicks, sending my temper rising. "One of them talked—ratted to protect his family," I spit staring him down, my face tight. Jack's eyes widen. "You didn't count on The Saint finding out, did you?"

Wiping a hand down his face, he looks remorseful. But mostly exhausted. "I expected the Irish to take the bait. I never expected *you* to intercept it, no," he says, lines scrunching across his forehead. "That wasn't part of the plan."

My lip curls. "That when you found out I was inside?"

Jack shakes his head.

My body slumps. "That was you. At the hearing."

He nods.

He could have protected me. Could have stopped The Saint and got me out sooner. But he didn't.

Words failing, I slowly turn my head to look at him.

"I know you're pissed off, but I couldn't risk you knowing about me too soon." His words hang heavy as he turns facing forward, staring out the window. "If it means anything, The Saint paid for what he did to you."

I huff with a slight shake of my head. "What did you do? And what about Luke?"

"I took care of it like I told you."

"Meaning?" I gawp.

"Meaning, The Saint's no longer in charge and your friend is safe."

I rub my beard, a slither of relief moving alongside more questions I want answered. I guess he really does have some pull. Slowly, I look back at Jack. He's looking at me.

"We have one shot to get this right, Deano. The guns being

shipped, they're a front for the real business. The ambush set things back, but it won't stop it. The next run *has* to be the last."

"What is, *it*?" I ask.

"Tomorrow. Please, trust me. You see it with your own eyes, you won't question the cost."

Dread. That's all I can feel. The desire to avoid something. I keep my eyes on Jack. What could be so bad? What could have him so hell-bent on annihilation? My hand lifts towards the handle. "And my trial?"

"Forgotten."

Just like that?

Jack looks at me. "Are you with me, Deano?"

I climb out, the bag of my belongings he returned in my hand. "I guess we'll find out tomorrow." I don't look as I close the door then hear Jack drive away.

Stepping inside the house, I take advantage of the only thing I can control in this moment. I kick off my boots, the simple task leaving me trembling with a familiar happiness. I gently place my things on the table then take a minute to myself, revelling the fact that I'm home and no longer in blood covered clothes. The lump in my throat I manage to swallow, holding my head to the ceiling. I let out the biggest breath. *Fuck*. This is overwhelming.

The situation surrounding my coming back is rattling my head. My gut's telling me to stop. To walk out of the house before we see each other and are unable to let each other go. But my heart? My heart's vibrating of its own accord. It doesn't give two shits about the circumstances. Couldn't care less for ramifications or details. It can feel the person it's connected to close by.

I haven't even seen Mads yet, but the smell of the house—*her* smell, it wakes my senses. Where is she? I suck in more air, making myself dizzy as I draw it into my lungs.

Slipping my cut off my shoulders, I chuck it over the back

of the sofa as I walk into the kitchen. She's not there. Turning immediately back around, I'm forced to double take at the leather now laid slumped on the floor. Must have slipped. I stare at it, then slowly move to pick it up, holding it in my hands. I dust a finger over the trim, contemplating a life without it.

The low rumble of Mads snoring upstairs has me turning my head. My girl. Sleeping. I smile then hang my cut on the hook, taking note of the mess on the floor by the door. Things have slipped.

I tread lightly, the stairs creaking in their usual places, but I hear no disturbance in her snore. With every step I take, her smell, the sound of her... it's intoxicating. I'm getting high off of her, simply by stepping closer.

At the door, I forget how to breathe. The tip of my finger touches the wood, and I slowly push it open, my eyes finding her through the dark of the room. Her chest slowly rises and falls showing off her swelling breasts. They've changed. Bigger. Fuller. Long brown hair fans across the sheets. I don't think I've ever seen anything so beautiful.

Tears. They don't fall, but they fill my eyes, blocking my vision. She's radiant. Her beauty evident. I lean against the door frame, shifting my hands to my pockets. Her body has changed so much since I last saw her, reflecting that she's growing my child.

I love it. And I love her unconditionally.

With a slight moan, she must sense my presence. "Travis?"

Or not.

She sleepily murmurs his name again, rolling onto her other side.

I know he has a key, so I smile, anticipating her reaction when she finds out it's me stood here and not him. I push away from the frame of the door, then slowly make my way towards her. "Mads?"

She grumbles. "Please, go away."

I smile to myself that she hasn't twigged yet. "Are you sure, babe? I sort of wanted to stay." My voice breaks through her tiredness, waking her.

I see her body stiffen, her shoulders hunching as if she knows I'm here but she's too scared to look. I hear her sob. "It can't be you."

Stepping closer, I walk around the bed into her line of vision. I click the bedside light on.

Blinking her eyes open, she just stares at me. I'm not sure how to react. Time freezes. My insides are burning. She doesn't think I'm real.

Pushing the covers off her skin, I see her bump. Her swollen belly makes goosebumps plague every inch of me. My heart swells. My thighs begin to shake. I'm not sure I can stand too much longer. "I came back."

Carefully swinging her legs off the bed, Mads pushes herself to stand in front of me. Her eyes drink me in, roaming all over my face. The cogs in her head bang loudly. I can hear every single second that ticks by, each one bringing her closer to me. "Dean?" She reaches her hand up, her soft skin cupping one side of my face.

I smile with the biggest sigh of relief. "It's me, babe. I'm here."

Mads folds, collapsing in my arms, and I catch her, moulding her body into mine. It's euphoric. The satisfaction of having her back in my hold, immeasurable. My hands scrunch in her hair causing her to moan in between her tears.

She holds me tighter, pulling herself closer, and I breathe her in. If it wasn't for her bump, I'm pretty sure she'd be climbing me.

Pushing my lips to her forehead, I tilt her head back, looking down at her. She's trembling. Her tear-soaked face is blushed. She doesn't wipe her face dry as her beauty attempts to steal my breath. I don't let it. "I've missed you." My voice is hoarse as my thumbs stroke the sides of her face.

"Am I dreaming?" The croaky words roll off her tongue, riddled with confusion. Her eyes start darting between mine, her top lip disappearing under her teeth. I feel Mads' knees start to knock against each other.

"Shh." I steadily walk her back to the bed, sitting her down on the edge.

Mads lifts her hands to her face. She's completely overcome.

I am too, but I need to make sure she's okay. "Let me look at you," I tell her.

Sniffing, Mads takes a breath, then wipes away her tears.

I kneel to the floor in front of her, brushing her hair off her face. I wait for her to look at me. "Mads." I say her name, my need to see her becoming urgent.

When she eventually looks up, she holds my contact, her bloodshot eyes full of tears. "I'm scared if I blink, you'll disappear." Her voice shakes, her tears fall. And it's me who suddenly feels weak.

My fingers squeeze her legs as I slump back to sit on my haunches. "Trust me, babe. I'm never leaving you again."

Every night. Every, single, night, I clung to the image of the face staring back at me. Every outline, every curve, every detail of it... it's what got me through. Ensured that I remembered I had something to live for.

Time seemingly pauses, stilling the air between us as we watch one another. Devouring her beauty, I'm completely taken aback. Someone must have made a serious mistake upstairs. There's no way I am deserving of the woman before me. As much as I have come to accept it, I still need pinching. Whatever it is that I bring to her, it's enough to make her stay.

The baby must kick for Mads looks down, breaking our focus. Her hand rests on her bump, her fingers elegantly spread across the material of one of my t-shirts she's wearing.

I shift my gaze, happiness rippling through me. I lift my hand as Mads lifts hers, making way for me. The second my palm bends over the curve of her bump, I feel the tender thump. It warms my soul. The knock enough to shatter me like glass.

I close my eyes, allowing the movement under my touch to unearth a type of joy I've not experienced before. Until I met Mads, I'd never questioned whether the life I was used to, was where I was meant to be. Every day that I've been blessed to call her mine, deep down I've known that *she* is where I belong. Right here. On my knees before her. *This* is my purpose.

The club has been my entire life. If I were to die tomorrow, the world would know I was a Ripper. But for the first time in my life, I'd rather be remembered for being her man. Her protector. Her saviour as much as she has been mine.

Back where I belong, in this moment, I am content. At peace.

"Dean?"

Not ready to open my eyes just yet, I lean forwards, gently resting my head against her tummy.

Mads threads her fingers through my hair, and I let out a sigh. Her touch is tender. I finally feel like myself for the first time in a long while.

Pulling my head back, I place a kiss next to my hand still on her. I look up and find her watching me. The balance we instil in one another, we were made for each other. "I love you, Mads."

Her smile reaches her ears. Happy tears now fall, and as she closes her eyes to stem their flow, I push up, cupping her face in my hands. Mads parts her legs allowing me to move closer to her.

I kiss her, lightly pressing my lips to hers. A saltiness coats where we're connected, her tears still in full flow. "Don't cry, babe. I'm here."

Lips parting, Mads takes in air.

I slide my hand to the back of her neck, holding onto her,

keeping her close.

Our foreheads touching, both breathing a little heavier, she opens her eyes, her hands holding onto my arms. "You came back to me."

I smile. "I made a promise." I kiss her again, angling her face toward me, pulling her closer.

Feeling her relaxing, finally believing I'm here, my tongue dips past her lips. Her taste. It's all-encompassing. As much as I want to lose myself in her, I know this isn't the right moment.

She's thinking the same as me. I can hear her heart racing. The fast pace at which her chest now rises and falls, tells me everything I need to know. "Never again." Mads tightens her hand around my arm, pulling back, forcing me to stop. We lock our gazes, the tips of our noses still touching. She's happy I'm here, fearful I'll leave again.

With a knowing sigh, I agree, "Never again." I stand climbing over her, laying myself down on the bed, my arms opened for her.

She shifts, tactically twisting her body towards me.

I smile watching her move. It's no longer as easy as it once was. I can't help placing my hands on her bump, and she curls her body into mine.

Mads wraps an arm around me, and I tuck her into me. I rest my head on her hers, kissing the top of her hair. As long as she's here, I know I'm good.

Shuffling my body further down the bed, my eyes suddenly feel heavy. The bed feels soft. My girl is in my arms. I'm surrendering to bliss, treasuring this moment. A moment I didn't envision ever having again. "I know who I am now." The words fall out before I fully register I've said them.

Mads pulls her head back, her chin on my chest looking up at me. She's silent for a long moment before she speaks. "Tell me what I'm thinking."

A weight lifts from my shoulders. The familiarity of this small thing between us makes me smile. "You want to know if I'm the man you need me to be."

She doesn't give me a reply. She doesn't need to. I cup her cheek, leaning down to meet her lips. I kiss her, then I hold her still, making sure she's truly listening. "I will prove to you that I can be the man you want to marry. One day, I'll leave all this shit behind me. You deserve more. My child deserves more. Don't give up on me, I'll get us there."

Mads doesn't say anything. She's as exhausted as I am. She simply kisses me, then turns her head back onto my chest.

I lean to switch off the light, then pull the duvet over us.

We find sleep. Together.

CHAPTER TWENTY-NINE

MADISON

Dim light shines through the window. It brightens the colours behind my eyes, sluggishly waking me from deep sleep. I haven't slept that well for weeks, shattered by Dean arriving home. To be honest, I'm still not sure it was real.

Blinking my heavy eyes open, I take in every ray of light. Without doubt, I've slept too long. It's Sunday morning. I have nowhere to be, but my body feels heavy.

I look to the empty space beside me, slightly lifting my head. Maybe it was a dream? Maybe I've finally snapped. Started conjuring up scenarios I desperately want. I honestly wouldn't put it past me now.

Then the sound of running water trickles to my ears, my senses immediately heightening. I push myself up with one hand, the other scratching across my bump where my skin stretches. Dean's woody scent touches my nose. I whip the covers back, swinging my legs over the side of the bed as quickly as I can.

My feet barely touch the ground as I scurry to the bathroom. I'm eager to see him. Desperate to make sure he's real and not just a figment of my imagination. I push the door open marginally, the steam dispelling enough for me to see him. His back is to me, one hand against the tiled wall, the other hanging lose by his side. He looks worn out.

He doesn't know I'm here. I steal precious moments simply admiring him. His muscled back, his toned thighs and legs. I've wanted to run my hands all over his body for so long, I'm almost petrified if I allow myself to move, I'll rush enjoying him.

I want to love him in slow motion, knowing I have forever to go.

The hot water cascades over his muscles. My eyes anchor on the way his body flexes as he moves to let the water hit the back of his neck then his face. I enter quietly, removing his t-shirt over my head, then dipping my body to remove my knickers.

He hears me then, my feet padding the floor as I step into the shower with him. I'm slow, perhaps a little hesitant when I see him wide eyed, lost in thought. "Can I join?" I ask.

He tilts his head, an affectionate smile beaming at me like sunlight.

I return it as I step closer. Stopping in front of him, I reach my arms up to lay my palms flat against his chest. The drilling rhythm of the spray matches the beat of his heart beneath my fingers. I refuse to ask what he's thinking. I lean forwards, kissing his chest, determined to take his mind off whatever it was.

Dean slides his hands into my now damp hair, gently massaging the back of my scalp.

I moan against him, my lips vibrating against his wet skin. Our bodies instantly heat. I press another kiss against his chest, my hands moving to his hips. They buck like they always do, and I smile feeling his arousal press against my skin. I straighten my spine, pushing my body into his.

"I'm not the only one who missed you," he purrs lustfully.

I look up, Dean's eyes are set on me.

He pulls me closer, tilting my chin up to him.

"I missed you more." I let my hand sweep between us as I speak, taking his cock in my hand. He's hard. So hard.

His eyes close when I tighten my grip. His breath hits

my cheeks, and his lips part as the water runs down his face, dripping onto mine. He's beautiful.

I start moving my hand, pulling stifled groans from his throat as I work him tenderly.

Dean shifts his stance, lowering his forehead to mine. "Not fucking possible."

I open my mouth, whimpering as he hungrily crashes his lips to mine. My back's pushed against the tiles when he guides us backwards. I throw my arms over his shoulders, and his hands move from my hair, trailing down along my arms. Without warning, Dean hooks his fingers under my thighs, lifting me to wrap my legs around his waist.

"Dean!" I protest all too aware of my increasing weight. "You can't lift me like—"

"Shh, babe. I've got you."

I try my best to get my point across when I feel him slide against my entrance. "Shit." The sensation of his soft tip stroking my pussy makes me squirm, halting any concerns I had. I dig my nails into his hard skin, and he groans, slowly filling me with every thick inch of him. "Fuck." I throw my head back, my chin raised high.

"Mads."

I hum my response lowering my head, knowing he wants me to look at him. We're back together. As one. Connected.

Blinking away the spray hitting my face, he pulls his hips back, then slowly pushes forward.

A drawn-out moan escapes me. My lips part, and he takes my mouth, his tongue sliding against mine. I pull him closer, my arms still wrapped around his shoulders.

We lose ourselves, and finally my mind feels free. Our history. What we've been through. What we have to come. All of it vanishes from thought, leaving me right here in the now. All there is is the want. The need. Hunger for one another. I've never seen anything as beautiful as him.

Dean's hands grip my skin, carefully holding me as he glides in and out of me. The steady rhythm makes me start seeing stars. The warming sensation between my thighs makes me arch my back.

I slip into a trance, enjoying every movement of his body against mine. The love I have for him, it surpasses any kind of emotion I've ever felt. It's too out of this world to put into any kind of words, and its only gotten stronger. Like they say love does when you're apart. It's hitting me in this moment like a hurricane in a storm, striking my heart, blurring everything as it consumes me without apology.

I'm momentarily blinded. Completely overcome by the full force of the love I feel. This reconnection of our love. What we have, it may not be perfect, but it's ours. I grip his hair never wanting to let go of him again.

Closing my eyes, I feel it coming, feel the shift in my emotions drawing closer as Dean tightens his hold on me, his mouth sucking and nipping at my skin as he buries himself deeper inside me. I'm overwhelmed, unable to suppress the hot tears unexpectedly rushing to my eyes and spilling over the edges. They hide behind the droplets of water running down my face from the shower.

When a dry sob heaves from my chest, Dean instantly stops moving, wiping my face and turning me away from the spray. "Mads?" His voice is full of worry.

"I'm fine." I suck in a breath, biting my bottom lip to stop it trembling.

"Babe." His full focus is on me. His soft words make my body slack in his arms. With one hand steadily holding me, the other scoops the nape of my neck, pulling my head to his. "I'm here," he reassures me. He kisses me, a deep kiss that has my back arching, my toes curling. Then he says, "We can stop," thinking

I'm overwhelmed. He's right. It is overwhelming. We've not done this for so long. But I don't want this to ever end.

No. Still inside me, I roll my hips, eliciting a deep rumble from his chest. I hold my hands either side of his face, looking down to him. "I don't want you to," I sniff. "I want you to love me," I look to his lips, gently brushing mine against them as I whisper, "and never let me go."

And then he's pushing into me, his hips surging forwards with a newfound determination.

I let out a cry, my lips parting against his. "Dean." My hoarse throat burns as I try to beg him for more.

More. I need *more.*

His hips pound at a forceful but steady rhythm, and he moves us back under the spray. The hot water beads off my breasts, massaging the tender skin. I moan, my nipples instantly pebbling as the water bounces off them. The sensation burns in my core as I feel my pleasure rising.

It comes with urgency. Hot flames licking me from the inside. I squeeze my legs tighter, feeling the full effects of him. His thick length, his heavy eyes, his strong hands. They control me, bringing my body to life.

Pulling me further onto him, Dean watches me intently, his eyes roaming over every inch of my body. Then with a grunt, his head tilts back. "I'm going to come so fucking hard, Mads."

My nerves tingle. The hairs on my arms vibrate as my orgasm rises.

Dean moves my hips, rubbing the soft spot inside me. Taking one of my nipples in his mouth, he licks the bud, then his eyes find mine as he bites down.

My whole body shakes. I let go, keeping heavy eyes on him as I come, my orgasm tearing through me.

Dean joins me, his hips piston pace to his release. When he lets go, he buries his head into my shoulder, one arm encasing around my head, his fingers twining in my hair. He holds me tight, emptying himself, breathing heavy.

When he's done, he lazily reaches for the shampoo as our breathing settles. "Hands." He kisses my neck before I hold my hand out, and he squirts some into my palm. He places the shampoo bottle back as I begin massaging his scalp, washing his hair as he watches me. There are so many questions I want to ask him, but I don't want this moment to be ruined.

"Tell me what you're thinking."

My hands stop. I pause, desperately trying to think of anything to say. "We need baby stuff." I start moving my fingers to distract myself.

"What have you got already?"

Again my fingers stop. "Nothing. I couldn't face it without you." My reply is honest and heavy. He knows how much I've needed him with me.

"I'll take you shopping."

My eyes drill to his. Given he's only just got back, I hadn't considered normal things taking place anytime soon. I can't stop my smile. The beaming look he gives me lifts my spirits. I kiss him, not once taking my eyes off his. My fingers then continue with their job as I pull my lips away. "Rinse," I tell him.

Still inside me, he turns holding his head back under the water.

I brush my fingers over his longer hair, making sure all of the suds are out.

"Your turn." He lifts me, guiding my feet to the floor.

I turn, tilting my hair back, allowing the water to soak me.

His fingers are gentle as he massages my skin, taking his time with his task. I close my eyes, relishing the sensation.

Once he's finished he washes my body, lathering my skin, his gentle hands gliding all over me. He pays extra attention to my bump, carefully bending and reaching the parts of my body I can no longer get to.

When it's my turn to wash his body, I don't ask about the new scars decorating his perfect skin. He knows I want to. I can feel his eyes on me as fresh tears cloud my vision. What happened inside?

"Come on," he says interrupting my thoughts, knowing exactly what's racing through my mind. He knocks off the water, then reaches for a towel, handing it to me.

I accept stepping out, only to hear the front door close from downstairs. "Shit," I half whisper, half shout.

"Who's that?" Dean asks.

"Lauren. I don't want her to see you. Not yet."

"Where's she been?" He wraps his towel around his waist, then runs his hands through his hair, brushing it off his face.

"She stayed with a friend last night, after..." I don't finish my sentence.

"After what?" he whispers.

I frantically dry myself, trying to wrap the towel around me at the same time. Feeling last night come and smack me in the face, my hands slow to a stop. "After Travis came by. Whatever he was going to tell me. He couldn't do it. He left, and not long after getting back, I sent Lauren out again to stay with a friend." She didn't need to see me in the state I was in.

"Babe," his voice cracks sensing my sadness. He steps closer, taking my face in his hands.

I look up to him, then hear Lauren approaching. I hold my finger to my lips, begging Dean not to say anything.

He smiles, a cheeky grin smearing over his face.

"Shh," I mouth.

He bites his lip on another grin, and it's the single hottest thing I've seen him do. It melts my insides.

"Mads?" Lauren shouts.

"Be right out," I shout back.

"Want a tea?"

"Please."

We hear her feet pad away from the door, descending the stairs. I let out the breath I was holding, leaning back against the door. "Thank God for that."

"What's the big deal?" Dean says. He steps back, walking to the sink, grabbing his toothbrush and squirting on the paste.

The big deal? "Don't you think everyone will have questions when they see you?" I say hushed.

Dean turns. "Do you?" The brush stills in his mouth. I nod, and he sighs turning back to the sink.

Does he really expect everyone to accept his arrival home like he only went away for a day? He's been gone a month and a half. People don't just get let out of prison for no good reason. Part of me wonders if he's committed a great escape.

Spitting into the sink, he dries his mouth then looks back to me. He steps closer, stroking the sides of my bare arms, stopping his hands at the back of my hair. He tilts my head to look up to him. "I can't give them the answers they'll want yet."

My eyes flicker. He knows how much I want to ask. "That doesn't fill me with confidence."

"It's not meant to." He drops the words like any other.

My eyes widen, inspecting him. "And me? What about the answers I want?"

With a heavy breath, he says, "You are not to worry about anything I have going on. You are my priority. I will not have you stressed, worrying about me."

Does he know me at all? Rather than argue, I contain my growing frustration. "What will you tell everyone?"

Dean kisses my forehead, then lets go of me. "As far as everyone is concerned, the trial has been dropped. I'm a free man." My eyes scrunch at his insinuation that he is *not* in fact, a free man. He sees, regretting his choice of words. "I'll make things right. You have my word."

Again, that doesn't fill me with any sort of confidence. I should just be grateful he's here—that he's home. But the subtle movement from within is a reminder that it's not just me I'm thinking about anymore.

With a smile, I gesture towards the door. "She'll have breakfast then probably crash in her room. Let me talk to her first, before you come down."

"She has a room now?"

"I hope that's okay?"

He turns looking at all the girly products spread across the vanity unit. "It's more than okay." He winks but I know he's going to tidy it as soon as I walk out the room.

Opening the door, I grab my dressing gown then head down to Lauren. "Something smells good." The waft of sugar and sticky, sweet pastry floods my nose.

"Breakfast," Lauren says pushing a bag from the local bakery towards me.

I move closer, inspecting it. Two glistening, sickly iced buns have my name on them. "Lauren, these," I lift the brown bag to my nose, sniffing them intently, "these are no good for breakfast."

She smiles. "But you're glad I got them?"

I tear open the bag, taking a large mouthful. Heaven. "Yep," I mumble.

Lauren places a cup of tea on the table.

"Did you have a good night?" I ask swallowing.

"Yeah. Alright I suppose. Saw an old friend."

I pause thinking she'll elaborate. She doesn't. "Oh?"

"It's nothing. How was your night? You seem different this morning."

If she only knew. "Uh, yeah. I got an early night and woke up feeling rested, I guess."

Lauren levels her penetrating gaze at me. I suddenly feel on the spot. "You feel, rested?" she questions disbelievingly.

"Yes."

Her lips part on a laugh. "No offence, Mads, but you aren't usually awake now, and I haven't seen you eat food like *that* before."

I pause mid-scoff before a floorboard creaks.

Lauren's head immediately shoots to the hallway. "Who's there?" Her eyes are wide. Shock and fear smear across her features. "Who's there, Mads?"

"Lauren." I stand holding my hands up, cursing Dean under my breath. "I wanted to tell you in my own time—"

"—are you cheating on Dean?"

I freeze. Shocked. But weirdly I admire her protectiveness. "No!" I shake my head with a stunned laugh.

"Don't lie to me. If there's another man here, I will hurt him!"

"Woah, take it easy," I sooth, trying to calm her. Another creak sounds from the hall. I let out a sigh, dropping my head. "You might as well come out now." I roll my eyes at his lack of ability to wait.

Dean's feet sound louder as he approaches where we are.

Lauren's jaw hits the floor the moment he comes into view. "What the fucking hell is this?" she shouts.

I open my mouth to scold her, but Dean beats me to it. "What the fucking hell was *that*?"

I slap his arm.

"Why? How? What the fuck!" Lauren says still startled.

I can't blame her. But still. "Stop swearing," I tell her, rolling my eyes purposely so Dean can see what he's done. He stands still, a slight line donning his forehead. "You deserved that one."

Lauren steps closer. "Dean, is that really you?"

He looks away from me. "It's me, kid."

"Shit." I shake my head at her. "Sorry. But… come on. He's

here!" Surprising both of us, Lauren darts forward, wrapping her arms around Dean.

I see him, his eyes are wide. He has no clue what to do. "Uh, this is a little different to how you last greeted me."

She pulls back, a spring in her step. "Yeah well, that was when I thought… when I thought you may have hurt Jay or something." She shrugs.

"Still no joy finding him?" Dean looks between us both.

I shake my head, moving to sit back down at the table.

Dean follows, sitting next to me.

"No," I say, my eyes glancing at Lauren.

She refills the kettle then takes a seat.

"Travis looked, but there's been nothing since he disappeared. Jay's phone's dead, too. Tried tracking it, but it's no use."

Dean and I exchange a look. "Tracking it?" I ask.

She shakes her head dismissively. "I've been learning how to access…" Her voice trails off when she looks between me and Dean. We're both wide eyed and waiting. "You know what, it doesn't matter. It's no good if his phone's off."

I'm really not sure what to say.

"So, school? How's that going?" Dean asks chirpily, if not to iron out the tension of our little hacker's admission.

"Great, actually. Thanks to Mads, I can finish my exams."

Dean's hand finds my leg under the table. "That's great."

He smiles at her, and she nods turning back to the kettle, making him a brew.

We watch her until she's done, then she places it on the table. "Right, I'll grab a shower, then we can go."

"Go?" I look at her.

She looks confused. "Yeah. The guys? Travis? They know you're out, right?"

"No. Not yet. I came straight to Mads. Haven't told anyone

else." His hand still on my leg tightens, and he leans forward placing a kiss on my lips.

"Gross," Lauren remarks.

I laugh at her disapproval.

"So we're not having a big party at the clubhouse for you?"

"Maybe some other time. I need a decent meal which only my lady next door can provide."

I knock his leg playfully.

"Plus, I kind of want to—"

"—No, come on!" she cuts Dean off. There's excitement in her voice. "Please, it will be good for everyone." She's really pushing this. I can see a joy I've not seen in her before, it lights up her face. "I can sort it out. Trust me."

When Dean looks at me for backing, I look back to Lauren. "Maybe she's right? Things haven't exactly been fun around here."

"That's an understatement," she throws in.

"You know I hate parties." Dean rolls his head back. It's two against one. He's already lost.

"Too bad. I'm calling Travis now." Lauren holds out her fist, and I bump it before she goes off to find her phone.

Rubbing his face, Dean genuinely looks tired.

"It'll be fine," I reassure him. "Everyone will want to see you. Lynn has missed you too."

He smiles sitting straighter. "I'll go round later."

Kicking my chair, he uses his foot to spin me towards him.

I let out a laugh, jolting in my seat.

With both hands, he drags my chair slowly closer to where his legs are parted. "The only person I have missed," he dips his finger under my dressing gown by my neck, skimming it down exposing one of my breasts, "is the one I want to spend all day in bed with." The tip of his finger brushes over my now hard nipple. He circles it leaning forward, placing a kiss on my chest.

We're stopped when Lauren's loud banging feet hammer the stairs. I quickly cover myself, feeling my checks flush with my need.

"There it is." She snatches her phone from the counter, then turns and leaves, completely unaware.

Dean looks to me. "A night away. That's what you and I need."

"You just got home," I point out to him, giving him a wry smile.

He pulls my chair an inch closer. "And I'm a man starved." His hands glide up my legs underneath the soft material of my gown. "I want you in bed, on your back at my mercy."

"As your whore?" I joke.

He looks at me seriously. "As my girl. I've missed *my girl*."

My face drops, his words making my heart skip a beat. He tucks my hair behind my ear, his eyes searching the depths of mine. Licking his lips, he then kisses my chest, his hands gripping my thighs tighter.

A subtle moan creeps out of me.

"I've missed your smell." His lips travel to my neck, forcing me to lean back, giving him room. He grazes the delicate skin with his teeth before gently sinking them into me. One of his thumbs then drops to my inner thigh, pushing flat against my clit. "I've missed your taste." His tongue then licks up my neck, finding my mouth as his thumb starts small circles.

"Dean."

"I've missed the way you call out my name when you come."

My hot breath runs wild as more banging footsteps are heard upstairs. I clench my thighs together.

Dean smiles against my skin. "You girls have taken over my house." He leans in again, skimming his soft lips over mine.

The smell from his shampoo has me closing my eyes, taken aback by how mind-altering he is. "Better get used to it," I say.

He looks at me closely, deep in thought once again. "Or we could move?"

I pull back with a jerk, studying him. "This is your home?" My voice is full of curiosity.

"Babe, *you* are my home. I'm serious. We could get away from it all. Buy somewhere bigger, fill it with babies."

The speed at which my heart soars into outer space steals my breath away. I feel lightheaded. The pull of what he's suggesting has me throwing my body at his. I can guess where this is all coming from. Being away from me, from us. He's filled his mind with thoughts of our future. But he shouldn't be here. That harsh realisation has me pulling back slightly. "Are you sure you want that?" I ask seriously, one hand cupping the side of his face.

He's silent. Sweeping my hair back, he stares at me. "More than anything."

CHAPTER THIRTY

DEAN

I pull out my phone when it pings from my pocket.

Jack: Where's best to pick you up?
Me: Clubhouse
Jack: Be ready for 1pm

I let out a sigh noticing the time already. It's just before lunch as we pull up outside the clubhouse.

"Who's that?" Mads ask.

I tuck my phone back in my pocket. "No one." I don't miss her lingering eyes on me.

All morning I've tried to work out what Jack would be showing me today. I've toyed with ideas of what could be so bad, he would literally turn into a ghost in order to bring it down. I've got nothing. Drawn no conclusions.

"I'll go in and make sure they're there." Lauren opens the car door, darting to the rear entrance of the clubhouse.

"She's keen," I point out.

Mads smiles softly. "It's nice to see." She dips her head, looking to her hands on her lap.

I move my hand to the back of her neck, stroking my thumb across her skin. "What did she mean earlier?"

She looks at me, her eyes quizzical.

I raise a brow. "I overheard her this morning. The not sleeping? Not eating properly?"

Mads drops her head again. "It's not been easy, Dean."

"I know, babe." Pulling her closer, she leans, and I kiss her. "But I'm here now. Okay?" Our foreheads touch, and we stay like this for a long time.

"We better go in." Mads eventually breaks the silence.

I kiss her again before letting her go. Getting out of the car, I walk around to open the door for Mads. I hold out my hand, and she takes it as I guide her to her feet.

"Ready?" she asks.

"As I'll ever be."

We walk inside, the door opening to a raucous silence as they all see me. I feel Mads' hand squeeze mine. I momentarily feel unsure of what I should do. My heart hammers in my chest, and I look around wanting to find Travis.

I see him stood resolute by the bar, Lauren by his side. She's beaming from ear to ear. He on the other hand looks like he wants to kill me.

Mads lets the door close behind us. It's only then the clubhouse cracks into resounding cheer.

Mobbed. It's the only way to describe it. I keep my hand firmly on Mads, making sure none of these shitheads barrel her over as they crowd around us. I eventually manage to get her to the bar, stopping by the man I want to see most.

Travis pulls out a stool for Mads, then looks at me. "I spoke to Mollie. She didn't say you were getting out."

Oh, he's really pissed off with me. Probably because I gave him a final goodbye, then showed up the next day. It's fair. His jaw twitches, and I try my hardest not to smirk. "You so much as smile and I'll throw you through the fucking window."

I can't stop it when he reads my mind. It stretches across my face.

"You're a prick. You know that?"

Nodding, and still very much smirking, I hold out my hand.

He stares at it then slaps his hand in mine, dragging me into an embrace. "Missed you, brother."

As if they were waiting for it, the music then starts up, and the atmosphere changes.

An hour later, the drinks are flowing. There's food for everyone, games of pool on the go upstairs. The family I'm going to walk away from, they've shown up in force to welcome me home. An inkling of guilt sweeps over me, but I can't let it take hold.

Jack will message any minute. I know this moment of happiness and togetherness is going to be broken. But for what? To drag us out of the hell we're apparently unknowingly in. Can it be that bad?

My phone pings a text.

Jack: I'm outside

I squeeze my arm around Mads tighter, moving my lips to her ear. "I need to dip out for a bit."

As predicted, a stark look of horror smears itself across her face. She leans away from me, her eyes narrowing.

"It's fine. I'll be back soon."

"Dean?" She glances sideways, checking if anyone's watching us. I can hear her heart pounding in her chest. Can smell fear radiating off her. "Where are you going?" she whispers for only me to hear.

Honestly, I have no clue where Jack could be taking me, or what he's going to show me. "Meeting an old friend. Don't worry."

Mads recoils instantly. "Last time you told me not to worry, I was left on my own."

I can tell by the drop of her face and the way her body

droops; my actions have scarred her faith in me. But feeling my phone vibrate, I know I have to go. I have to get the club out of the mess I got us in before I have any hope of having the life I want.

I stand, kissing her forehead, not giving myself time to change my mind. "I'll be back soon, I promise." My heart tugs wanting to stay near to her, but my feet carry me out of the building unnoticed.

As I approach the main street, a few cars are parked up along the curb. I expected a blacked-out Mercedes or some other standard issue government car when Jack dropped me home yesterday. But when I spot the blue truck further down the road, I start walking.

I open the door, and Jack looks up from under the hood of his baseball cap. "I still think the government should hand out better vehicles than this."

"They do, but the ute's more my style."

I let out a sarcastic laugh as he shifts the truck into first and pulls away.

We drive for almost an hour, heading towards the coast in relative silence. There's plenty we need to catch up on, but nothing I can bring myself to say.

"We're almost there."

I look at Jack then back to the road. He pulls the truck down a narrow path, pulling to a stop near an estuary. I eye him, wondering what the hell we're doing here. "What is this?" I ask.

"Down there." He points to what appears to be a disused lifeboat hut. "Come on."

We jump out of the truck, treading across the squelchy sand. Jack pulls back one of the rotten wooden doors, and I follow him inside.

It's dark, the stench of rotten eggs, seaweed and a musty scent hangs heavy in the air. No doubt it's coming from the crate sat in the middle of the hut. I pinch my nose stepping closer, noticing the crate is the same as the ones we inspected when Vincent first brought his deal to us.

"You recognise this?" Jack asks smacking the top of the wood. I don't reply. He knows I do. "These are the crates Costa uses to transfer the weapons."

I grind my teeth. The smell of the enclosed space is beginning to make me feel sick. Where's he going with this, and why doesn't he seem to be affected?

"Do you know how many people can fit inside one of these?"

Terror. It's unmistakeable. It almost unmans me the second he mentions *people*. "I can tell you if you like."

I give him a hard stare, willing the anger rising in me to lay low.

"Seven. That's the most recorded to date in one of his shipments."

Bile rises to my throat. People? Shipments? No way seven people could fit in the crate. "Jack?" I plead for more information.

"Sean."

From out of the shadows, another man steps forward.

I naturally reach for my hidden knife.

"No need, Dean. He's safe."

"One of you, is he?" My eyes dart between them both.

Sean seems to wait for Jack's approval to step closer. Once he gets it with a dip of Jack's head, he places a tablet on the box.

"These images," Jack starts. My eyes haven't left Sean yet. "They're not for the faint hearted."

Peeling my eyes to the lit-up screen, I lower my hand, taking a step closer. When I look down, fear stabs my heart. "What am I looking at?" I know what I'm looking at; corpses with body parts missing. A child with a missing eye. A grown man with a slice across his abdomen. "What the fuck is this?"

Jack steps closer, swiping to an image of one of the crates filled to brim. "Organ trafficking." My eyes don't leave the screen.

"This might look like dark underworld business, but those people you're looking at, they were sold to the highest bidder; a doctor overseas."

I'm stunned into silence as I try to let this travesty sink in.

"Those who need money, be it through poverty or wanting a better life, willingly sign up to give away their organs, in exchange for money or safe passage."

"They willingly signed up for this?"

"Not all of them." Jack purses his lips. "*These* people did. But some are collected from the streets. Provided they don't drink, don't smoke or partake in any major drug use, they're the perfect candidates to be shipped."

"Perfect candidates?" I ask bewildered. The putrid smell coming from below adds to the bile rising in my throat.

"Through either grooming or social pressures, they're lead away, and we never see them again. But we know through intel we've obtained they're all auctioned to the highest bidder on the dark web."

"The highest bidder?" I ask.

Jack nods. "Once they've been bought, they're transported to their buyer."

My mind whirls. I need to get out of this fucking hut. "And you know where they ship them from?"

Jack frowns. "We knew where the *first* one was being shipped from. Once someone's bought, they're taken to where the cargo's leaving, then they're moved out of the country."

My heart stammers, but my hands are cold and clammy.

"Once the organisation's established itself; they'll branch out. Find new pipelines. Usually scumbags like this buy big businesses to facilitate more people being shipped; air strips, haulage companies, those sorts of things." Jack looks at me and his face tightens. "I know this is a lot... but time, Deano, we don't have much of it."

This is fucked.

I scrunch my eyes, still looking at the horrific image on the screen. Pieces of this messed up puzzle click into place. "Were there ever any guns?" I gesture towards the tablet.

Sean steps forwards. "They deal guns alright, but that's not their plan for you. Not in England."

Both men remain silent. The air shifts. I look between them both. "The run that the Rippers intercepted?" Jack's straight mouth and slumped shoulders tell me what I don't want to believe. "So we escorted innocent people, dropping them off to some sick fucks who *bought* them, all for their insides?" Again, silence.

I lift my hands to my head, unable to stop the anger now. I wasn't there, never saw the procedures, but it was my fucking decision. My decision to get into this business. My decision to intercept it—to *protect* the crates all so they could be sold to monsters.

Anger and fear spark anew inside me. "This is..." I stop myself from passing all the blame. "If you hadn't informed the Irish of that haul, Rippers would never have been made to stop it."

Jack shakes his head, letting out a sigh. "If you hadn't stopped the ambush, you wouldn't have been forced deeper." His voice has raised, and it does nothing to quell my temper.

I turn to look at him. "The Saint gave me no choice. I played his fucking game to find the person making the threats. And low and be-fucking-hold, I found him. And not only did I find him, I killed to find him. To survive so that I could get home."

The door seems to get further away as I turn to leave. My *home* is pulling me away from this hut. From all of this shit. It takes all my strength to remain at walking pace and not run.

"Look in the crate!" Jack shouts.

I keep walking.

"I said look in the fuckin' crate and tell me you can walk away."

Before I know it, I hear Sean call out his name just as Jack grabs me, hauling me back inside. "Fuckin' look, Dean!" Jack shoves me forward, but I turn to throw a punch, landing it square on his jaw. He hits me back splitting my lip, the blood instantly filling my mouth.

I charge him, knocking his heavy frame to the floor, his baseball cap flying off his head.

"Just look in the crate!" Sean hollers.

I don't look at him. I bury my fist in Jack's ribs before striking his face. Once I look in the crate, there's no going back. I just know it.

In some fucking karate style move, Jack pulls my arm, bringing me closer to him. He lifts one leg, swinging it over my head, and rolls me to the floor. I'm unable to move, pinned down by his long limbs. He elbows me in the ribs, then squeezes me tighter.

My chest rises and falls rapidly, my lips parted as I spit my blood to the floor.

"Just look in the crate you stubborn prick," Jack says.

I move to get free, kicking my legs out in hope I connect with Jack. I don't. "Get the fuck off me!"

"You need to look!" Jack fires back.

"Why?!"

My shout silences him. He's still pulling me, holding me in place when I hear him take a breath. "Because... because I fuckin' need you!" I still. "You hear me! I can't stop this without you!"

"You've done a pretty good job of finding out everything you have so far without me. Why now?"

Jack lets me go, and I jump to my feet. I turn, desperately wanting to hit him again. I raise my fist, but he doesn't get up.

He lets out his breath, his head falling back to the floor. "I need to get on the inside, find where they're collecting people."

I frown, lowering my fist slightly.

"We can't pinpoint where the next shipment will leave from."

Jack then rolls with a grunt, moving to push himself off the floor.

I spit my mouthful of blood on the ground.

"No two runs leave from the exact same location," he continues. "It's how they stay hidden. We got lucky with the first one, ASIS knew he would set up there, but since the fuck up with trying to pick it up, we have no idea where the next one will come in. More and more of what's in there," he points to the crate I'm still yet to look in, "will keep showing up."

"And the only way you get *your* guy is to put an end to this?"

Jack's eyebrows lower. I can see the vein pulsing in his neck. "This," he says, striding to the crate and flipping off the top. "This is what happens to the ones who don't get sold or get sick in transport."

I eventually make my way over to him. The smell hits harder the closer I get. Peering inside the crate, anger pulses through my veins. I have to swallow my frustrations, try to tame the tumour of resentment growing inside. "Why's she like that?" I ask, forcing the words out.

The girl's body lays at an odd angle, her features sunken into her skin. Her wet, tangled hair trails over her face to her eyes that are stuck half open. The coldest of shivers traces down my spine. It's as if her ghost itself knows I'm here, staring at her corpse.

Sudden flashes of Lauren and my child crash through my mind. This is someone's daughter. Someone's sister.

The familiar tightening of what was no doubt an anxiety attack, rises to my chest. I look away, stepping back, subtly trying to draw some fucking oxygen into my lungs.

Breathe, Dean. You fucking idiot, breathe.

"When a person is found to have lied about their physical state," Jack starts, "or gets taken ill or dies in transport, they're no longer viable to the buyer. It's not as common in the UK, but this isn't the first body we've come across like this since Costa set up camp here. The first was a young fella, late teens. This girl we think is roughly the same age."

"Does she have a family?" I ask quickly.

Jack looks at me. "A missing person's report was filed. The mother may have filed it."

Pinching the bridge of my nose, I shake my head, unsure whether I'm hearing Jack right. "Then tell me, why is she rotting in a crate and not being sent home to be buried?" I suck in harsh breaths through my nose.

"We can't get involved."

I sigh at the inhumanity of it. "*Can't* get involved?" Can't take her body, leave it close to where someone will find it at the very least? "It's desolate around here, no one will find her."

"The body needs to be put back where we found it." Jack's serious. He fires his words at me like he's using a bow and arrow. The pinch of his tone silencing me.

I take a pause. "And the boy?"

Jack frowns at me. "*We* didn't find him. Dog walker did. He had no next of kin. No family. No nothing."

My eyes meet Jack's. "What did they do with him?"

"He was given a pauper's funeral. Buried in what's known as a common grave for those who die alone, unclaimed."

Unclaimed. It's sounds so… lost. "Where?"

"Why does it matter?" Jack asks sternly.

"Because it fucking does," I quip. There's no denying who the boy sounds like. A missing brother I promised I'd help find.

Sean steps forwards having not spoken a word since Jack and I were wrestling on the floor. "Here." He shows me what appears to be a police report. The cemetery is close to home.

"Now what?" I ask.

"First, we put her body back where we found it. Then, you help me get someone on the inside of Costa's organisation. We shut this down before it grows. I've gone as far as I can. I need you now, Deano."

Staring at the heavens, I imagine my life away from this darkness. I can see it, just. But my fingers? They don't reach the light. "Do either of you have a smoke?"

Jack grimaces, but Sean steps forward. He hands me the packet and a lighter.

Stepping outside, I draw the nicotine deep into my lungs, holding it in for the longest of breaths until it burns.

"Deano?" Jack says, as I throw Sean back his smokes and walk away.

No way I'm helping dump that girl's body on a fucking beach.

Once back at the car, we make our way to the clubhouse. "Drop me off here," I tell Jack.

He doesn't bother to ask questions. He mounts the curb, pulling the truck to a stop. We sit in silence until he leans forward, jerking his thumb to the clubhouse up ahead. "What's the cover story?"

I look up, pulling down the sun visor, assessing the damage to my face. "I'm going to tell them."

Jack sighs. "You can't," he says sternly but flat.

I slam the visor shut. "I have to."

Jack rests his hands on the wheel. "If we blow this... if we miss this opportunity to stop it right now, then they go further underground, and we never catch them." He rubs his chin harshly with his hand. "We're so close, Deano. So fuckin' close." Sitting back in his seat, he adds, "I didn't lie to my dad, didn't sacrifice *everything*, for it all to go to shit now."

I wait for him to stop breathing so heavy. "Is this really

about what Costa's doing, or just your pure fucking desire to get the man we know killed Linda?"

"Fuckin' both!" he snaps. "You saw it with your own eyes. We can't let this shit continue. And as for..." he trails off staring ahead. "I want a normal life."

I slowly turn my head to look at him.

"I had a normal life, I know that. I mean a family. A wife. Shit, maybe even a kid, you know?"

I look down, knowing exactly what he means.

"I have given up so much, worked so hard... and for what?"

Nothing. "You can still have all of those things," I assure him.

A gloomy shadow casts over him. "No. I can't. At least, not until this is done."

After all these years, the pain still lingers. It's manifested itself so deep within our blood, the only way to make sure we ever move on is to put an end to it. Once and for all. I'm not sure why or how we never knew the real truth about one getting away. Rippers MC went to war after Linda died. We killed. We fought. There were no questions asked as to whether we got the men who actually took her life. They were one and the same. You wore a Saviours' cut. You died.

Simple.

But to find out that one of the men physically responsible is alive, out here, close to my home. That has to be stopped.

"I *can't* do this without you." Jack's statement, I feel it to my core. We went together. Found her together. We end this, together. For her. Shutting down Costa is a bonus.

"I know."

"Then please keep this to us. Or at the very least a man you trust with your fuckin' life. You bring *love* into the equation; you'll bypass the hate and the burning anger needed to see this through. I've had your back for life, I need you to have mine now."

He's asking me not to tell Mads. He's right. I hate him for it, but he's right. I bring her into this, she'll do everything she can to keep me out of it. And to get out of it like I want to, this has to be done.

"For life." My words are barely audible. I open the door, climb down, and don't look back.

Walking to the rear entrance of the clubhouse, soft singing reaches my ears as I walk past the garage where I last left my bike. Stood just out of sight, I catch Lauren humming to herself. I wonder what she's doing in here? I can't help taking a minute just to listen, enjoying the sudden flare of peace it brings me. "What's going on?" I make her jump as I show myself.

"Fuck!"

I laugh, taken aback. She sounds like Travis. "What are you doing?" She has various tools out, scattered across the floor.

"I'm tuning her up."

"Tuning her up?" I query. "What needed tuning?"

She wipes her hands on the bottom of her jumper, looking at my bike as she talks. "It wasn't running quite right. I flushed it out and put in new fuel, replaced the air filters, too. I'm considering cleaning the carburettors, and you might want some new brake pads soon."

"Oh." I'm not sure I was expecting her to reel off all of that. "How do you know how to do all of those things?"

She looks nervous. "Travis. He showed me."

Explains the boisterous language. "This is what you've been doing whilst I've been away?"

She nods bashfully.

My lip twitches with gratitude. I draw a smile, ironing out the lines across her forehead.

"He's been teaching me, so I can start earning my keep."

Earn her keep? "Lauren, you don't—"

"—I asked him, Dean. I want to. I'm not afraid to work."

I check her expression. "I know." I was the same. Didn't want the handouts. Didn't want the attention. I was happy to work for it. "We're your family now, Lauren. Whether you like it or not, you're stuck with us. And family look out for one another. That's all I'm saying."

She smiles and shrugs her shoulders. "Not like I got anyone else." She then turns, looking down, pretending she's looking for a tool she needs.

"Still nothing on Jay?"

Lips pinched together; she shakes her head side to side.

"I'm here now. I can start helping Travis to find him."

"You won't find him."

I frown, my insides sinking knowing where I'll look first. "What makes you say that?"

Lauren turns to look at me. I can see her chewing the inside of her mouth trying to stop herself from crying. "Because I can feel it. He disappeared before you left. Too much time has passed."

I hold out my fist to her. "Come on, let me get you a drink to say thanks for looking after the old girl."

Looking at my hand, Lauren widens her eyes, embarrassed for me. "Can I have a beer?" she asks brazenly.

My lips pull straight, and I drop my hand quickly. "A coke. You can have a coke."

She humphs, rolling her eyes, but accepts my offer. "Might want to get Mads a coke too."

I raise a brow.

"She was *not* happy you left so soon, *and* then stayed out for three hours."

I look at my watch as we start walking. *Bollocks*. "Did she say anything?"

"She didn't have to. I can just tell. You are definitely in the doghouse."

Great. "Listen, I'm taking her away for a night."

"Yeah?"

At the door I push it open, holding it for Lauren to walk through. "Yeah. Tomorrow. Think you can stay here? Or I'll have Travis watch over the house."

Lauren laughs. "I'd love to watch you tell him that."

Again, my brow hits the top of my head. "Meaning?"

"Meaning, big guy needs a break." We take a few steps down the hallway leading to the main room. "You know he got shot, right?"

I jolt. My feet coming to a halt.

"Oh. Maybe you didn't. Um, don't tell him I told you." She bolts ahead, scarpering out of my firing line.

My head pounds with the events of the day. Travis got shot?

CHAPTER THIRTY-ONE

MADISON

"Want another?"

I look up from my empty glass.

Talia lifts the nozzle for the soft drinks, wiggling it in the air.

"Why not." My head thumps relentlessly. I try to rub my temples, but what I really need are some painkillers. For the first time in a long time, the pain in my ribs also chose tonight to make a reappearance. I feel heavy. Tired. Fed up with feeling pissed off that as soon as we got here, Dean upped and left to meet an 'old friend'.

I want to ask so bad what's going on. But emotionally, I'm drained. I need to go home and sleep. He's home. Above all else, he's back where I need him.

"Looks like it's going to be a late one."

I look up to Talia.

"Got more members arriving."

I turn and look to the door. "It's Sunday," I comment, still getting used to their lifestyle as a mass of men tumble through the door.

"They'll be partying through to next weekend."

I turn back to Talia.

"Prez is back. Best fucking news they've had for a long time.

But you know that."

I rake a hand through my hair, my head aching at the touch. "Shame he couldn't be here to enjoy it with them."

As I say it, I spot Talia looking over my shoulder, a sly smile spreading across her lips.

Two hands then appear either side of me, slowly leaning against the bar.

I look down at the tattoos, a sudden craving for the hands they're painted on to be on me. Sitting straighter, I feign disinterest. "How good of you to show." I sound a lot more confident that I feel.

Scooping my hair in his hand, Dean sweeps it off my neck.

I should stand and walk away, give him a piece of my mind somewhere private. But Jesus if his nose nestling into my neck, his warm breath hitting my skin, doesn't leave me glued to the stool I'm sat on. I blink the longest of blinks as desire and want stir within my belly.

"I think I need to apologise." The sexy edge to his voice makes me think of all the ways I'd like him to.

He kisses my neck gently before I smile to myself. "You think?"

Dotting his lips to my ear, I ignore the temptation to roll my head back into his shoulder. He knows exactly what he's doing. Even after six months, even after the time apart, we still have this. Him in control. Me letting him take it but pretending to hate it. "I know I do." His voice vibrates against me, goosebumps scatter up my arms. "Let me make it up to you."

"Make what up to me?" I remark, trying to sound nonchalant.

"Let me take you home." Dean slowly spins me in my seat.

I manage to keep a straight face when I look up at him. "Everyone's here, for *you*."

"I don't care about everyone else. I want to lose myself in my girl."

I would love nothing more. "Sounds like you have a problem," I laugh. "Look around you."

He looks knowing I'm right, then sighs. "Tomorrow. I'll give you all of me tomorrow. From the moment I wake you up, to the minute I take you to bed."

I stand pushing my body and therefore my bump into him.

He splays his hands across it, his thumbs lightly gliding back and forth.

You only have to look around the room to see how much the men here love him, how grateful they are that he's home. I'm sure like me they have their questions. But tonight, they only want to enjoy him.

Dean takes my face between his hands, his thumbs stroking my cheeks. "My fucking sunshine," he says softly, making me smile.

"From the moment you wake up."

"To the minute I take you to bed," he promises. He pulls me to him, kissing me, and I let out a moan as I close my eyes, accepting that tonight's going to be a late one. "I'll get one of these shitheads to bring me back." He kisses my cheek.

Only then do I notice a scent of the seaside on him. Where was he when he was out? "I can pick you up." It's not like I'll get any sleep anyway.

"I'm not having you drive back here late." He silently drinks me in.

I eye roll his overprotectiveness but offer a warm smile. "Fine."

Taking me again, his lips push to mine, his fingers curling into the back of my hair. "You'll call if you need me?"

"Yes," I tell him, pushing him away as I notice a few eyes on us. "Now go."

There's a bang on the bar next to us. "Red, two glasses,"

Travis orders.

I turn seeing Red now working the bar.

Travis lifts a bottle of vodka in between himself and Dean. "I want to drink this and forget the last six weeks. You good with that?"

Dean nods to Travis. What Travis is offering is simple. Drown the memories. Forget. "Is it true you got shot?" Dean asks him, catching us both off guard.

I assumed Travis would have told him by now. Travis sucks his teeth. "Sort of," he answers.

"Sort of?" Dean replies with a chuckle.

I scoff at Travis' placidity to the fact a bullet—had it not been for a mobile phone, would have torn its way directly through his heart.

"I'll fill you in, brother." Travis pats Dean's back. It's nice seeing them back in each other's presence. He then whistles, and Legs makes his way over.

Looking between us, I see a flicker of uncertainty swipe across Dean's face. His time away is potent. He doesn't know our routines.

"Legs will see Mads and Lauren home safely," Travis informs him, also seeing him looking lost.

Dean keeps me close to him as he places a kiss on my temple. "Okay," he says, almost unsure.

Red slides two glasses to Travis who grabs them and walks away, heading towards the sofas in the corner of the room.

"You going to be alright?" Dean whispers for only me to hear, looking at Red. He kisses me once more on the cheek.

"I'll be fine. Go."

Giving my bum a light squeeze, he turns and joins Travis, slumping himself down into one of the sofas.

I look to Red. Her eyes don't track him like they usually do. Instead, they're fixed on me. "Everything alright?" I ask unsure of what to say.

"Yeah."

Maybe she's waiting for me to leave? I'm not certain. I grab my bag as I sip the remains of my coke, looking at her, only to notice her hair's changed. I take the time to observe her. It's no longer the shade of trampy red. I like it. The auburn strands curl under chin in an elegant way. There's a word I never thought I'd associate with her.

I slow down my sipping, making it look like I simply need a breather. "That your natural colour?" My eyes flick to her hair.

She shrinks, but I don't miss the twitch of her eyes. Is she nervous? She looks at me, her body shifting, her words coming at me all defensive. "Yeah. What of it?"

We may not always see eye to eye, but I know when someone's hiding their vulnerability. "It looks nice," I tell her truthfully.

She huffs pulling her head back, then stops, noticing I'm being serious.

Her words tell me one thing, but the councillor in me knows there's more to it. "You can talk to me."

Red laughs, moving to collect a tea towel, aimlessly busying herself. "The day I talk to *you,* will be over my dead body."

Letting out a sigh of doubt, I finish my coke then hit the glass to the bar. I lean forward grabbing a napkin, and reach into my bag for a pen. "You don't have to be so defensive," I tell her as I write my phone number down. "I'm simply pointing out that you don't seem to have anyone to talk to. So, if you change your mind and manage to pull your head from out your arse, I'm actually a pretty good listener."

I toss the napkin her way but she remains quiet, offering me nothing. Instead, she stares blankly at it, a look of confusion shimmering in her eyes.

Even if she doesn't care to admit it, the environment she

works in is not for the faint hearted. You need balls of steel and a solid wall of glass protecting you from the men in here. It shouldn't be the case, but this many alpha males and a woman like Red… I hear the comments she gets; I see the way some of the guys look at her like she's a piece of meat.

Turning, I swing my bag over my shoulder. Drained.

"Why are you being nice to me?" she asks.

I immediately stop and look back. "I just told you to pull your head out of your arse, that wasn't very nice."

Red smiles for the first time. It suits her.

I relax my shoulders. "Because I see you, that's why. The changes you're trying to make? I get it."

Red takes a step closer, slowly picking up the napkin and folding it in her hands before she looks up at me. "Thank you."

Giving her a small smile, she then turns and walks away, and I'm left feeling hopeful.

Back at home, I take some painkillers for my headache, then slip into the shower once Legs has left. In my comfy clothes, I make me and Lauren some dinner. She opts to eat upstairs so she can revise, whereas I settle on the sofa.

My phone pings a message. Before I can reply, it starts ringing in my hand.

"You look like you've seen better days," I laugh answering the FaceTime call.

Bex huffs. "Don't, I feel so tired."

"You, okay?"

She smiles. "Yeah. Just wanted to see how you were."

I place my plate on the table, then sit back running a hand through my hair. "I'm fine. Got a headache, but things are good. She dropped yet?"

"That sucks. Uh, yeah, I think so. I'm feeling heavier, definitely. How about you, what's the midwife said?"

"My blood pressure's still high. I have to go on Wednesday

for another check-up." I smile to myself knowing Dean can now come with me.

"The check-ups once a week now?"

I nod. "Pretty much."

"That's good. And reassuring I imagine?"

"Yeah, it's lovely seeing the baby."

Bex takes a sip from her mug. "Still in the dark as to what you're having then?" I nod and she smiles. "That blows my mind."

"What?" I ask curiously.

"That *you* of all people are happy not knowing the sex. I had you down for finding out, having it all ready and set up months in advance."

I can't stop my face from dropping. I would have if I'd been able to. Up until this morning, the thought of buying anything without Dean was out of the question.

"Shit, I'm sorry."

"Don't apologise," I say quickly. "We'll go this week. It's school holiday's where we are. I'm only working a few days, then we'll go."

"Jess and your mum helping?"

Shit. I haven't told Bex or anyone for that matter that Dean's home. I'm not sure how it will go down. My eyes look anywhere but at my phone in my hand as my heart drills, making me come over all lightheaded.

"Madison?"

"Jesus, Bex. I don't know how to tell you this..." Slipping up on my words, I take a breath.

"What is it? Everything okay?"

I rub my face. "I," my voice quivers. "I hope so."

"You *hope* so? What's going on? You're worrying me," Bex says with a shaky breath.

"I'm fine. The baby's fine. It's just... it's Dean."

"Have you spoken to him recently?"

You could say that. "Uh, yeah, actually. He's home." I should have delivered that better.

Bex's mouth widens into a giant O. "He's what?!" She bolts up straight. "Did I hear you right?"

Eyes wide, sweat starts forming on the back of my neck. "You heard me right."

She gawks. "Does Jess know?"

I stare back at her, hot tears now dotting my vision. I shake my head.

"Jesus Christ, Madison."

It hits me hard, seeing her displeasure. I know she's about to reprimand me, make me see how messed up this all is. "I know," I say before she can start.

"What? What do you know?"

"I know what you're going to say." I hold my head in my hands hating that I snapped at her.

"And?" she says more calmly.

The smallest fragment of embarrassment grips me. "*And* I know he shouldn't be here, because nobody just walks out of prison two days before their trial starts, but..."

She waits. "But you're glad he's home."

I nod, holding back my tears. "I am not stupid," I manage to say, "nor blind."

"I never said you were."

"I know something's going on, but I cried myself to sleep every night, Bex, willing him to walk through the door, waiting for him to call, to text, anything. He came home. That's where I need him to stay."

Bex, who has always been my voice of reason, sighs, dropping her head. "I get it," she says softly. "And I know how hard the past few months have been for you. I've no idea how you've kept it together like you have."

I swipe under my eye, trying my best to smile as she speaks.

"But Dean was arrested for *murder,* and now he's *out?* Something is clearly not right with that. Please, just let that sink in."

Knowing it shouldn't, because she's absolutely right, an irritating itch scratches a nerve, forcing me to frown. It twinges, forcing an unsettling emotion to reside in me. The hard truth she delivers, I no longer want to hear it. "Okay." It's honestly the best I can come up with as my defences go up.

Bex assesses me as best as she can, staring at her screen.

I stand grabbing my plate from the table, and make my way to the kitchen.

"I've upset you," Bex says cautiously.

"No. I'm fine. I just have a headache, that's all." It's not a total lie. It's just not the whole truth. Annoyance is running rife.

"Okay then. Will you call me tomorrow when you feel better?"

"Maybe," I say, recognising how harsh I suddenly sound. I don't like it. Not with Bex.

"Okay." Her voice is flat.

"Okay." I'm unable to say anything more. I smile my goodbye then press the end call button.

Guilt. That's what I immediately feel once I hit the red circle on my phone. I am a shit friend.

Me: I'm sorry x

Her reply is instant.

Bex: Me too. We'll speak before I see you x
Me: Okay. Night x

Tapping my phone against my chin, I remember the message I received before Bex called.

Mollie: Hi, it's me. Fancy a visitor?

I'm tired, but going out might clear my head a bit. Perhaps Mollie can help put my mind at rest.

Me: I can come to you?

Mollie: Sure. I'm flat 50, last building on the left past the station.

Me: See you soon

Mollie's place really doesn't take that long to get to. Having made sure Lauren was okay before I left, I park up and enter the building, wondering if Mollie grew up in the area. The flat I'm now riding the lift up to, really doesn't suggest that she did. It's a stone's throw away from the terraced houses and cobbled lanes, yet it screams inner city living.

With modern amenities, marble floors and spotlights brighter than the sun, everything about it reminds me of Mollie. From how smartly she dresses, her job, her tough exterior. All of it.

The lift dings, and the doors slide open. I step out and walk to number fifty, finding the door already slightly ajar. Having buzzed me in, Mollie knows I'm on my way up, but I feel less than comfortable just walking into her place. I try to knock as best I can, only for the door the start opening.

I call out her name, willing her to appear. She doesn't. I take a look behind me, not liking the silence or the stillness of the hallway. Seeing no other option, I walk inside, closing the door gently. "Mollie?" Still nothing.

Wiping my feet, I'm not entirely sure whether I should just go and find her. My eyes roam around the entrance. Beautifully decorated, there's an air of cosiness as my eyes scan my surroundings. The flowers sat in a glass vase underneath a large mirror give off the smell of early spring. The colours are feminine, the pretty sight making me take in a deep breath, filling my lungs with the rich, sweet smell.

My eyes continue to trail over her things as I step forward. A bunch of keys are in a small dish. Beside that I spy a family photo. I bend to take a better look, but a knock from down the hall makes me stop.

With a guilty fright I stand up quickly, turning on my heels to see Mollie. "I did knock," I say panicked, my finger pointing to the door as if that will attest to my being found out.

Mollie smiles, slowly brushing her hands on her thighs as she moves closer to me. Once she reaches me, her eyes fall to the photo. She smiles looking down, then collects it in her hands, tracing her index finger over the glass. She takes a deep breath. "This was taken six years ago." Her face lights up.

"May I?"

She hands me the photo, and my stomach clenches at the sight of the little boy. My suspicions were correct. Mollie has a child. His dark hair is messy, the front a little bit too long as it falls in his face. "What's his name?"

Without a shadow of doubt, Mollie's breath hitches as she blinks profusely. "Riley."

I look back at the photo. My heart swells noticing his familiarity. The little boy has round chubby cheeks, his head's tilted slightly upwards, trying to gaze at the grownups stood above him. There is so much love bouncing between the three of them. My only thought in this moment is how on earth has she been coping without her husband?

"I'll put the kettle on," she whispers gently before I can ask.

I place the photo back down then turn, following her.

In the kitchen, I stand on the other side of the island in the middle of the room. "Have a seat," she says.

Pulling out a stool, I shrug off my coat and sit down.

"Milk? Sugar?"

"Please." I smile pulling out my phone, checking for any

messages. Placing it on the counter, I rest my elbows down and look around.

"There you go." She holds out her hand, passing me the mug.

I immediately take a sip, letting the warmness sooth me.

Mollie takes a seat opposite me. "So, Dean's home?"

With a slight smile, I take another sip of my tea then place it down. "Apparently so."

Mollie shakes her head. "I'd love to know how." She looks off to the distance, her brows knitted.

I think the same, also worrying what that means for Dean. "Have we got any way of finding out?" I wonder.

Mollie checks my expression. "I had a call telling me the case was dropped. That was it. No explanation, just done. Finished. I haven't heard from Dean to know if anyone came to see him, talked to him, nothing. I've worked pretty hard putting a case together, you know? And for what?"

I'm not sure I do know. The closest I can think of is putting together Lauren's case, only for her not to show the day we expected her. But I can imagine, and I know how hard she's worked to make sure he doesn't serve time. "Do you think it's..." I struggle to say the word. "Is it legal?" I blurt out, "him getting out I mean?"

She nods. "Has to be. No other way he comes out without being immediately on the run or picked up again."

I slump, and Mollie taps her finger on the counter. "Would he?" she says to herself.

"Would he what?" I ask dubiously.

She scratches her head in thought. "Would he rat?" I scrunch my eyes. "Would he work with the law for his freedom?" she clarifies.

My mind whirls. I really don't think he would be capable of going against the club for his freedom. But would he do anything to ensure he came home to me? My hands shake, a coldness travels from my head to the tips of my toes. Without a doubt, he wouldn't let anything stop him from doing what he wanted.

"Shit," I release on a sigh.

"Shit, indeed."

Reality settles in between us for a second. Thrumming my fingers against my mug, I can't help letting out a huff. "How did you do it?"

"Do what?" she asks, scepticism rife in her voice.

My eyes roam over her face. She doesn't give anything away. "It's clear you know how to live my life, Mollie."

Mollie drops her head, not looking at me. Resting her hands to her forehead, she then brushes her hair behind her ears, blowing out her cheeks. "You love him?" she asks briskly.

I nod, giving her a confused smile as I wait for her to continue.

"Then I told you. Ride it out. Your only other option is to leave, which we both know you won't do." Her eyes dart down, hinting to the baby.

I chew the inside of my mouth, contemplating my response.

I rode out the time Dean was away. Does that mean I now have to sit around and wait for it to happen again? I can't do that. Not with the baby coming. I won't. "Is that what you did?"

Mollie's stark look back at me suggests I've hit a nerve. I hold my ground, not budging on where I stand. I need to know how I help Dean. "I did what I thought was best for my family," she says boldly.

"Which one?" The words fly out of my mouth before I have any chance of stopping them. *Shit.* She's taken aback. "I'm sorry," I quickly add, cursing myself internally. That was a low blow.

Mollie remains quiet. I've worked out her secret. The boy in the photo looks nothing like the man stood behind him. He looks like someone else we both know. "Does Travis know?" I ask.

She gives me another knowing look before her face

unexpectedly plummets, her voice heavy with emotion. "Mads, I'm not ready to talk about this." Fear stares back at me. A truth has come out. She's wanted to tell me—someone, for a while now, but it doesn't come easily. It hurts.

I'm not sure how long we sit in silence for, but looking at Mollie, it is undeniable she's savvy with club life. Her admission to once loving Travis is a clear indicator she knows what I'm going through. I don't know the whole truth, but she needs to know she has me.

I get up and walk to her, wrapping my arms around her without hesitation. I've been there, the crippling loneliness... she's been fighting this for too long.

After a while, she leans into me, her hand resting on my arm around her.

When I pull away, I look to her, and she smiles.

Mollie then swipes the corner of her eye, changing the conversation. "Think you can get him to talk? Dean, I mean? Get him to tell you anything that I can look into."

She's asking me to help her. To find out what's really going on. A lifeline.

I sit back down. If anyone can find out who or what is behind Dean's release, it's her. With a firmness to my voice, I reply, "I'll make sure I get something out of him. He's at the clubhouse now with the guys."

Mollie gives me a knowing half smile.

"He'll be back late but leave it with me."

We finish our teas in relative silence. I don't dwell on the fact that I haven't asked more about her son. Each time we spend time together, we get closer. The trust builds.

CHAPTER THIRTY-TWO

DEAN

Fuck me. I've drunk too much. The fresh air makes it abundantly clear as I step outside to light a smoke. I watch the tip glow amber, feeling the burn of the flame on my thumb. The delayed reaction to the pain has me grimacing, sucking the skin between my lips. I curse my lighter flipping it shut, then shove it in my pocket as my feet stagger on the spot, my eyes rolling to stay open.

I haven't drunk anything in nearly two months. I'm glad I made the arrangements for tomorrow before I started drinking. I was half-cut one quarter into the bottle, let alone the whole thing. Now I'm fucked. All I want to do is go home, roll into bed with my girl and sleep. Because last night was the best sleep I've had in a long while. I crave more of it. Crave more of Mads in my arms, her skin against my skin, her body pushed up to mine.

I'll be no good to her tonight. I'm far too pissed to worship her the way I should. The way she deserves. But tomorrow... today? Tomorrow? *What bloody time is it?* I pull out my phone. It's two in the morning. Fuck. *Today,* Mads gets all of me. No club shit. No Jack. Just Me and Mads.

I notice she's sent me a message.

Mads: I love you x

That was sent two hours ago. My stomach knots as I remember seeing the text she sent when I was inside. Her plea for me to come back to her. She knew I wouldn't reply, but she sent it anyway. What have I done to her?

Trapped her in my shitty existence, that's what. But I will get her out of it. Me included. To see the other side, I'll have to risk it all.

The thought of Mads not being able to sleep whilst I've not been here for her is unrelenting. I was the same, but I don't care about me. What I care about is the mother of my child getting the rest that she needs. She doesn't need any of the added stress this last mission will bring. *Mission?* I'm not fucking Action Man.

I scoff, then jump out of my skin noticing Travis stood behind me, a bottle of Vodka in his hand. "Jesus!" I bellow. "You trying to give me fucking a heart attack?"

He looks around, standing motionless. "Why are we out here?" he asks confused.

I look around as best I can, one eye open. "Beats me?"

"Beats… wasn't he taking us home?" he says.

I swing my head back to the door, my brain rolling in my skull.

Beats is stood slumped against the wall, his limp dick in his hand as he takes a piss. Travis looks. We watch on as Beats then flops into the bricks, his body slumping to the floor with a thud. We grimace at the same time. "I don't think so." I'm definitely not that drunk.

"Then who the fuck is? And why the fuck are we stood here?" Travis gripes. I don't answer.

Looking down at my hand, I lift my smoke to my lips, drawing the nicotine in.

Travis lifts a hand to me. "Thought you were quitting?" he asks.

I pass it to him. "You about to give me bitch advice?"

He sucks, blowing out a white plume with his head raised to the heavens. Between heavy blinks I watch as he laughs, holding the bottle out by his side. "No, I'm giving you Vodka."

My body recoils. I still accept and take an unwanted sip, surprised I don't shudder as it goes down. "So, no luck finding Lauren's brother?"

Travis rolls his head. "No."

I take another sip from the bottle, hating every second, baring my teeth as I swallow. "I think I might know where he is."

"Where?" Travis slurs.

I don't know how to explain that yet. "What are we doing here Trav?" I say after a moment.

Travis shakes his head, his free hand pulling at the back of his neck. He knows I'm not talking about being outside.

"Because from where I'm sat, what we do keeps hurting people."

He turns his head to look at me, his gaze surprisingly focused. "That's because you have people. It didn't matter before. Now, every fucking thing matters."

He's been shooting doubles all night, needing to forget the last six weeks, needing me back to lead us through this storm. I need to tell him it only gets worse. That what we've done is sell our souls to the King of Hell, and I'm not sure how we get out in one piece. If it wasn't for Mads and the fact she's pregnant with my kid, I'd burn it all down. Easiest solution. Total fucking annihilation.

"I ruined her faith in love."

Travis' statement has me turning my head. Again, my brain swirls. So, *he* needs some advice. "Mollie?" I ask knowing.

Travis doesn't reply. He sniffs before pinching his nose. "Actually you know what. Forget I said that." I probably will given the state we're in. "It doesn't matter." He shrugs as if he didn't just finally admit how he feels about her.

"Mate?"

"No," he holds up his hand waiting for me to pass him back the bottle, "just don't."

I hit the bottle into his palm, and he pushes it to his mouth, throwing his head back as he chugs the clear, harsh liquid down.

"That won't take the pain away," I tell him honestly.

A white van pulls up in front of us, and I look at Legs as he gives me a thumbs up. Guess this is how I get home.

"Worked for you," Travis says throwing the now empty bottle to the floor, smashing it to smithereens. He then staggers away before I can tell him my plan to leave the club. To leave him. I think about following him, given where his head's at, given what happened between *them*. Their loss. Their pain. They're living with their own demons. I'll only make it worse if I go back inside.

Legs pips the horn, startling me. I want to slice his head off for making my brain crash against my skull.

Dragging my body to the van, I open the door and climb in, giving him a look that suggests if he wants to see tomorrow, he best drive me home. "Make sure he's okay when you get back." I slap the window with my palm, drawing his attention to an out-cold Beats still lying on the tarmac.

"Uh, sure, boss." He doesn't move. He looks at Beats through the window, then back to me, probably wondering if he should be doing something to help Beats now. We probably should, but I want my girl.

I hold my palm to the sky, trying my hardest to focus on him. "Drive," I slur.

Before I know it, I'm back at mine, lighting another smoke before I step inside. Legs drives off, and I lean back against the wall, gazing up at the moon. Thinking.

The decisions I need to make now will set the course for my future. Jack needs his guy. We need to stop Costa and the fuckers buying people on the black market. How the fuck I do that and survive, I can't piece together in my drunken head. But when I do, I need to make sure we don't mess it up. We can't allow this to go on any longer than it already has.

The front door opens.

I turn around seeing Mads stood watching me.

There's silence. The whirring in my head stops. The fear, the doubt, it vanishes. She is my way out. "You coming in?" Her voice is tired. She needs me to sleep.

I throw my dirty habit onto the road, happy to oblige. Then I turn, stagger, and quickly realise... I'm *fucked*.

"Dean?" Mads rushes to me, hooking my arm over her shoulder.

"I think I drank too much."

"No shit."

I look down to her. "Sherlock."

She smiles up at me. She is fucking beautiful. Glowing. The pull of her lips has my heart warming. My dick, twitching.

"Do I need to ask if you had a good night?" She guides me through the door and straight up the stairs. We go slow. I may be three sheets to the wind, but I'm still aware I need to be careful with my precious cargo.

"Travis," I start. "He's going to hate me for what I have to do." Why am I saying this out loud?

"What do you have to do?" Mads asks the obvious, still guiding me.

"Betray him." I don't know if she can hear my thoughts. I hope not. I'm going to leave him. Leave him behind. But he wouldn't be alone. "He's in love with Mollie," I say.

She looks at me for a long moment then lets out a small sigh, sliding one hand up the banister as we move. "She's in love with him too."

My eyes are closing, but we reach the top of the stairs and

walk into the bedroom. "Do you love me?" Why the fuck am I asking that?

Mads stops me by the edge of the bed. "Why'd you ask?" She pulls my cut off my shoulders and places it on the chair. Walking back to me, she stands in front of me, her fingers slowly rolling the bottom of my hoodie into her palms.

"You won't marry me," I reply displeased.

Mads pulls my hoodie over my head then does the same with my t-shirt. "I love you." She makes my heart sing. Her fingers trail over my new scars, her eyes darting between them. I hear her breath hitch as she sees me. The real me. "Still, after everything we've been through, I love you." She places her palms flat on my chest, her eyes looking up. "You will always be my VP."

I smile taking her head in between my hands. For a women who was once hesitant to declare her love, now she doesn't stop telling me. She has stopped calling me her VP all the time though. I know that's because things have changed and I'm now in charge, but when I hear it roll off her lips, it only serves to make me want to devour her.

"What did you call me?" I need to hear it again.

Her lips reach her ears, knocking me for six with her beauty. "My VP," she purrs, knowing what it does to me.

Changes or not, what hasn't changed is the way I love this woman, and the way she still loves me after everything I put her through.

Holding her, my upper body starts to sway.

"Come on. Bed," she orders.

"Fuck, yes." I sway some more now unable to open my eyes. My cock might want to have its way with her, but the rest of my body is starting to shut down. Alcohol has well and truly wheedled its way into my system.

"Not for that." She taps my arm as if telling me nice try, subtly pushing me towards the bed.

Mads pulls back the covers, and I slide in. She pulls off my jeans, and I help by raising my hips. Then I slump, the mattress feeling like a cloud, moulding to my body.

I feel Mads climb in next to me. She shuffles her body to mine, and I lift my arm for her to come close to me.

Even through the drunk fog, the smell of her shampoo fills my nostrils. I breathe it in, pushing my nose to her hair as I kiss her. Her hand traces circles over my chest, the sensation relaxing me, sending me to sleep. I manage to ask her one more time, "Marry me," before I give in and surrender.

When I wake, my scratchy throat and banging head tell me what I already know. Last night, it felt good being back with my men, but I drank way too much. Far more than I have in recent weeks, anyway.

My heartbeat pulses in my skull. I place the heel of my hand over my eye socket. *Fuck.* It pounds even harder. I need painkillers. Today is meant to be about me and Mads. Fortunately, I've managed to wake before the snoring sleeping beauty who's sprawled across my chest.

Shower. That's what I need. Then she gets the best of me.

I carefully roll her off me, then make my way to the bathroom. I look drawn out as I stare at my reflection in the mirror. Grabbing two paracetamol, I turn on the tap for some water. I gulp and I slurp, my mouth drier than the Sahara desert.

I take one last look at myself before I shower and make my way back to Mads. She's turned on her side, the duvet over her head where she's buried herself in my absence. I drop the towel around my waist, then duck under the covers by her feet.

This'll be the best wake up she's had in a long time.

Skimming my lips over her ankle, I work my way up the back of her calf to her knee, over the curve of her hip to her bulging belly. My hands rest flat on the mattress either side of her as I hold my weight, bending my body over hers.

She moans quietly, her body turning on before she's fully awake.

I keep going, worshiping my way from one side of her belly to the other.

Mads slowly rolls to her back, her arms bending behind her head as she stretches. I watch as she arches her back, bending her legs. She knows I'm here, but her eyes don't open. "Morning," she whispers, her voice laced in sleepy lust.

I dip my fingers under her knickers, pulling them down her legs and dragging them off her feet.

Her head rolls to one side, and I catch her peeking at me. Placing my hands on her knees, I keep my eyes on hers as I push her legs flat to the bed. I lick my lips when I look down, seeing her perfect pussy already glistening for me. I'm about to feast on her. Make up for the lost time not spent losing myself in her. My mouth waters wanting to be on her. I can practically taste her from here.

"Dean, we need to... oh," she moans, her voice hoarse, her eyes still not fully open.

Dusting my hands down the insides of her legs, I lower my mouth, pressing my lips to her clit.

Mads shakes at my touch.

I dot another kiss before my tongue flits across the nub, forcing her body to tremble.

"Dean," she moans louder. But it's not the name I want to hear her cry.

Using two fingers, I slide them either side of her clit, tenderly massaging the sensitive skin, my thumb stroking against her entrance.

"Oh, God."

No, he's not taking credit for this. I groan, slipping both fingers inside her, watching as she draws me in, her body starting to wriggle under my touch. I lick over her clit again, then suck the sensitive nub into my mouth.

Arching her back higher, her bones vibrate as I push further into her. I hold my fingers in deep, sucking her clit at the same time.

Mads cries out, throwing her hands to her hair. "Dean!"

I work her clit harder. Sucking. Biting. Rolling my tongue over and over. She's desperate for movement. Desperate for me to fuck her and send her over the edge.

Her hips start to rise, trying to pull back on my fingers still buried inside her.

I give her what she wants, twisting them as I withdraw, then pushing them back in, pulling a drawn-out moan from her. Fuck, the sound is breathtaking.

She clutches the bedsheets, curling her fingers as her clit starts pulsing against my tongue.

Feeling the soft spot inside her, I circle my fingers, gently stroking her.

"Dean!" Her hands fly to my hair, tugging me against her.

I moan on a lick, my tongue completely flat against her, and I look up, unable to see her face properly over her bump. It makes me smile. My girl. My life. She's making me a dad.

I groan as her clit swells, and a rush of desire makes my cock hard. I bite down, listening to her lose her breath.

"Shit, VP, I'm… I'm!"

That's what I wanted. I bite down again, pumping my fingers. She unravels, her pleasure coating my face. I bury myself, soaking it up, licking her until she's shaking, her body unable to take anymore. She tastes so fucking perfect.

When I push up on my hands, her eyes are closed. I climb her, my body possessing her like a caveman. I want—no, I *need* to be inside her. Right now. Lowering myself, enclosing her head with one hand, my cock naturally finds where it wants to be. I practically tear my t-shirt she's wearing off over her head, twisting it around her wrists, binding them together.

I hold them above her head, my legs holding my weight off her belly as my hips start to move. She's mine. All I can think of is claiming her. Owning her. Loving her. I push in deep, forcing her to arch her back. Her eyes roll into her head, her lips parting wide. I dip, taking her mouth, my tongue finding hers. It twists with hers, coaxing its way in deeper.

Our heads turn, lips crashing, teeth clattering. "I thought about you." I pull back, then ram myself home. "Like this." Thrust. "Every." Thrust. "Fucking." Thrust. "Day." Thrust.

With a whimper, she turns her head into her arm, hiding herself as I drive us both crazy. "Harder," she pleads.

I pull out, tactically rolling her to her side, one hand on her bump as I move her. "Not harder, babe." I sit on my knees, pulling her arse closer to me. I raise her leg, hooking my arm underneath, supporting her, watching as she opens up for me. It steals my breath; her body dampened with sweat, arms still above her head on the pillow.

I line my cock with her pussy. "You need it deeper." I choke as I slip inside her again, my lips parting, watching as I fill her completely.

"Jesus, VP!"

I hit her sweet spot again and again, bringing her whole body to life, covering it in goosebumps.

Mads straightens her back, her tits now bunching together.

Unable to keep my hands off her, I roll her nipple between my thumb and finger, pinching and flicking, eliciting the most seductive of moans from her as my hips steadily push forwards and back.

Then I let go, driving home, chasing my release. I need to come. Need to come so hard I'm momentarily blinded by need. The need for nothing else to matter except what we're doing right now. Loving each other. Quietening the noise around us.

Tiny specks start entering my vision as the orgasm that's going to tear through me starts taking hold. "Don't stop," Mads begs.

Oh, I won't. Pushing up on my knees, I enter her so deep, feeling her walls clamp down, her body stiffening instantly. Then I buck, pounding into her like a man possessed. I'm out of control, fucking her hard and fast. Lost in her.

"Yes!" she screams, and she shatters, wave after wave of her release coming out in shakes, cries and moans.

It takes me, watching her stumble over the edge into her pleasure. I grunt with one last thrust of my hips, then a roar rumbles from my chest, my fingers pinching her skin further onto me. "Fuck, Mads." I spill, filling her with my load, admiring her as my hips slowly come to a stop.

I'm spent. She's spent. I collapse to the bed behind her, pulling her into my arms, spooning her. I nestle in, and she frees her hands, holding my arm around her. She holds me tight, like she's never going to let me go. I don't want her to. Ever.

After breakfast, we drop Lauren off in town to meet her friends, then I take Mads for the first part of the day I have planned. This family life, driving her around. I love it. But I'd be lying if I said I wasn't itching to get out on my bike. I need to put some miles on her. See whether Lauren's fine tuning has helped keep the old girl in shape.

"Where are we going?" Mads asks.

I take her hand, pulling her into my side. "We need baby things, don't we?" The way she looks at me, I see her eyes mist, the emotion taking hold of her.

My phone pings, and I quickly check the message, smiling to myself. "This seems like a good place to start," I muse, rounding the entrance to the massive shop filled to the brim with baby paraphernalia. It's mind blowing to say the least. "They look like they can help, too."

Mads' mum and Jess are both stood waiting for us. They beam at Mads when they see her.

Mads' hand tightens in mine.

Jess was shocked when I called her last night after Mads left the clubhouse. She bombarded me with the questions I'm sure Mads is desperate to also ask. I ignored them all. More importantly, she filled me in on Mads not being able to do anything like this without me here. It stung, adding to the growing list of things Mads hasn't done whilst I was inside. It also adds to my decision not to tell her what's really going on.

I need her focused on my baby.

Jainey, whose locked gaze on me suggests she really has some issues, steps closer to us.

"Why's my mum staring at you like that?" It appears it doesn't go unnoticed.

"Probably because I shouldn't be here."

Mads' head drops, making me feel shit for pointing out the obvious.

"Babe." I stop, forcing her to turn towards me. "It'll be okay." She doesn't look at me. I take her chin, holding her still. "I promise." I kiss her gently, then turn her, walking her towards her family.

We walk up and down every aisle at least twice. I liked the first buggy we chose. The first cot we picked out. But Jess makes sure we've measured, tested and checked every item. Looking at Mads, I see her happiness, her face beaming. And that's what keeps me going.

My phone rings from in my pocket. "Hello," I answer, catching Mads look up at me. I give her a smile, stepping out of ear shot to take the call. "What is it?"

"You picked your man?"

"My man?" I answer Jack.

"The man you trust to bring into this?"

I sigh rubbing the bridge of my nose. "Yeah," I say confidently. There's only one man in my mind. I know he's going to hate every second of it, especially when I tell him I want out.

"Meet me today." He doesn't ask me.

"I can't today." Last thing I want to do is upset Mads on the day I promised I'd give her all of me. I'm already walking a tightrope, needing to meet Lauren in a short while, but it will be worth it.

"I need to know I can trust your man," Jack says sternly.

I balk, taken aback by his statement. "Really? My trust, that's what you need to check." There's anger in my tone as I force the words out, trying to keep my voice down.

"Don't be so precious, Deano. I want to make sure, that's all." So black and white. Detached.

End game. Remember the end game. I look down spotting the tiniest pair of shoes. Why does a baby need shoes? I gingerly look up, not seeing Mads. "I need to know."

He takes a breath. "What?"

"Will my family be safe? What if this goes wrong." If we don't catch the guy responsible for Aunt Linda, Jack will never let this go. My thumb taps the edge of the white shoes hanging on the rail.

I hear Jack moving, there's rustling in the background. "We do this right. They'll never be in danger again."

"Then we're done?" I'm referring to the shit storm we allow to hang over us. Because it's draining, living in the past. I need peace. I only get that one way.

"Then we're done."

I look around again, grabbing the shoes off the rail. "There's an old farm. I'll bring him there tomorrow, 11am. I'll text you the address."

CHAPTER THIRTY-THREE

MADISON

Did I just hear that right? Tomorrow. 11am at a farm? What the hell is going on? I watch as he ends the call, only to make another. The thrum of my heartbeat in my ears distorts my hearing. I can't be sure of who he's talking to. I quickly rummage through my bag, pulling out my phone, typing a message to Mollie.

Me: He's going to a farm? Tomorrow, 11am

Mollie: Did he say why?

Me: I didn't hear

Mollie: I think I know which one. It has to be Travis' uncle's place

Me: What do we do?

No reply but she's read it.

Me: Mollie?

My heart leaps to my throat. We have no idea what is going on or whether Dean meant what he said.

Last night in his drunken state, he didn't realise his blunder of telling me he would betray Travis. I managed to keep it together, even though my insides were in turmoil. Surely he wouldn't betray the man he left to look after me? The man he entrusted with my life. His brother. And betray? What does that even mean?

Once he was asleep, I messaged Mollie in a panic. She called me, telling me it would be fine. But I know her well enough now to know when she's lying. After some persuasion, I managed to convince her not to act on anything without me. We have to try and remain level-headed if we're to find out what's really going on.

With a drop of my head, my heart suddenly feels uneasy. If Mollie still has any feelings for Travis, I don't doubt she'll do anything to protect him.

"Look what I found," Dean says cheekily, making me jump.

"Jesus, don't do that." I quickly drop my phone in my pocket without him seeing.

He takes me in his arms, pressing his lips to my head as he holds up a tiny pair of baby shoes.

Heart fluttering, I can't help but sink, my body dropping into his as he holds me. His smell makes me momentarily stand down.

"Where's your mum?"

Shit. I don't know. I walked off trying to eavesdrop on Dean's conversation. "Urm," I look around. "There." I point to Mum and Jess looking at various breast pumps and sterilisers.

He chuckles to himself. "I think they're enjoying this more than you."

I try to smile, watching them totally engrossed. But it's fake.

"Mads?" Dean pulls me closer. Distracting me further.

The baby kicks, and my mind's pulled back to him, my hand lifting to my bump.

Dean lifts his hand, cupping and feeling it for himself. "Baby awake?" he asks.

I nod my head. "Awake and apparently wanting to start their own football team."

"Come on. Let's go see what they've found now." His hand on my back guides me to Jess.

She shows us some contraption designed to suck the milk from me. "It looks like something a cow would use." I sound so deflated, having enjoyed this so much when we started. Being here with Dean, my mum, Jess. It's so thoughtful of him. Now it's clouded. Overshadowed. "Sorry. Headache." I rub my temple, definitely feeling one coming.

"Coffee?" Mum suggests.

"Yes. We can come back after a break," Jess points out.

At this stage, I don't care what we choose. I know Dean liked everything I liked. He won't worry for colour or size; he'll just want me happy. My heart sinks. He's here, but really he's not. His mind is far away. Distracted by the something he's not telling me.

"Yeah. That sounds good," I say flatly.

"You ladies go."

My eyes suddenly dart to his. He's leaving? My hand tightens around the strap of my bag.

"I need to step out. I'll meet you in a few hours." He nods at Jess like she knows the drill. What the actual fuck is happening?

Another kick from the baby is like a pipe bursting. I drop my head, the tears hijacking me. Damn myself for not controlling it. And damn him for making me feel like this.

"Right. I'll just grab these few bits," Mum says, not noticing me crying. She walks off, and Jess follows.

"Babe?"

I sniff. "Don't *babe* me, Dean." I wipe underneath my eyes.

His face falls. Those heartbreaker greens glint with their own sadness at seeing me upset. He said from the moment I wake up to the moment he takes me to bed.

"Where are you going?"

He lets out a breath, taking a step closer to me. "I need to see someone."

"Now?" I interrupt him.

"Yes. Now," he says with conviction, throwing the shoes on the nearest shelf. It startles me. He's serious. I don't hear that tone often, only with the guys. He doesn't want to be questioned. Well too bad for him. "I know this is messed up, Mads. When I can, you will know what you need to know, but right now is not the time."

I want to slap him. "Right. So when will it be a good time to tell me? The next time you get arrested? When someone comes after you? When you next *kill* someone?" My voice is far too loud for where we are, but I can't control it.

Dean takes my elbow, clearly thinking the same thing. He pulls me outside, turning me to look at him, pressing my back against the wall. Lines crease his face. His teeth grind. "Do you think I'd do anything to jeopardise you or my child?" I don't reply. I know he wouldn't. But he would himself. "Everything I have to do next is for you. For my kid." His face is in front of mine as he forces out his words, his body dipped so we're level. I watch his temple twitch, feel his warm breath hit my face in short, sharp bursts. His frustration, clearly spiking.

I frown at him, wishing we were so far away from this life. That he wouldn't *have* to do anything next for me.

"I know this is hard, but I have to make tough decisions and take responsibility for our life together. The one we fucking deserve, Mads." He slides his hand against my cheek, standing straight.

I raise my chin, his touch immediately dampening my temper. "The goal posts keep shifting for us," I tell him.

He presses his head to mine with a sigh. "I know. But please, hold on for me."

I swallow hard when he pulls back, giving him the best look of understanding I can muster. From the very first kiss, I've been losing my mind for this man. I don't want him to go. "Stay here with me." In a desperate attempt to keep him here and away from anything that might be dangerous, I grip his arms, pulling him closer.

He sighs, dropping his head.

I'm powerless. It's not enough.

Dean kisses my head. "I'll meet you at the hotel."

My face scrunches tight. "Hotel?"

Those greens light up at my confusion. "You're beautiful when you smile."

I didn't realise I was. "What hotel?" I ask again.

Invading my personal space, he takes my head in his hands, then he slides them into my hair, making me shiver. "The hotel we're staying at tonight."

His fingers gently pressing into the back of my head make me relax. "How am I supposed to get there?"

His face drops a fraction. Tilting my chin up again, he gently presses his lips to mine. My insides collapse. "I'll call you when I'm on my way. Jess will drop you there."

I roll my lips tasting him on me. "Okay."

He takes me in before he turns, and I watch him walk away. Each step he takes, I feel the urge to follow him increase. I quickly check my phone. Still nothing from Mollie. I push off the wall, my feet daring me to go. To stop him. *Do it.* One-foot raises, my heart going into overdrive as I lift my heel off the ground.

"Madison?"

My foot instantly goes back down. "Mum?"

"You okay, sweetheart?"

I turn, looking back to where Dean walked away. He's gone. My breath expels, and I chew the inside of my mouth trying to squash the way my heart aches. Where's he going?

"Fine. Can we grab that coffee now?"

She walks to me, looping her arm under mine. "I know just the place."

The waitress places our coffees on the table. I don't pull my gaze away from the passers by outside. The state Dean came home in, I've seen him worse. Once. Last night was no way near as bad as that. But it was a reminder I'd rather not have had.

"Sugar?"

I look at Jess holding up two sachets. I smile, pushing my mug closer to her, then check my phone. Nothing.

She tips in the sugar, stirs, then looks at me as she pushes it back. "Want to talk about it?"

My eyes drop. "Can I say no?"

Mum leans forward. "It's good to talk about it." She places her hand on my knee. "And," she strings out the word, "you have no choice."

I let out a huff, sitting up straighter. My hands go to my head, rubbing my temples. "I don't like the feeling of being helpless."

Mum gives me a knowing look. "It doesn't get any easier." I frown. "I'm sorry," she says. "I don't mean for that to sound so morbid. I just… I mean, together or apart, the decisions new parents have to make are the most difficult you'll *ever* have to make."

Jess and I exchange a look. We've heard Mum's story—of how she asked Rocco to let her go. But we don't know how she and our dad lived with that. How hard that must have been for both of them. I take the opportunity to finally find out. "Did Dad know early on?"

I see her think back to when she and our dad, Michael, were married. She picks up her mug taking a small sip of coffee. "He always knew." Looking out the window at the front of the café, she loses herself in thought. "He loved you. There was no denying you weren't his, though. You have Rocco's eyes."

I smile back at her.

"Dad must have found that hard," Jess says.

Mum gives a slight nod. "The first few weeks were the hardest. We hardly spoke. Barely touched one another. Like ships in the night, we simply existed."

"What changed?" I ask, knowing they had a happy marriage for many years.

"You did." My eyes start to fill. "You brightened each day and brought us together. Then Jess came along and suddenly we were parents to two beautiful girls who stole our hearts and turned our world upside down."

"Who was more annoying?" Jess asks with a laugh.

"Oh, you were by far," Mum says instantly. We all laugh. "Could never get you under control. You were unruly whenever I took you out the house. That time you poured an entire can of blue paint all over yourself when Dad took you to his work," I laugh, picturing it, "you looked like a bloody Smurf. Explaining that in A&E didn't go down well."

I hold my tummy, remembering the pictures Dad took on his polaroid. Head to toe in blue paint, yet he still managed to grab the picture of Jess before he took her to hospital.

"Then there was that time you shoved polystyrene balls in your ear," Mum continues.

I snort, unable to control it.

"The nurse had to suck them out with a mini hoover. You know they found a rock in there, too?"

I wipe underneath my eyes, the happy tears ruining my mascara. "Oh God, stop." My tummy jiggles, bouncing up and down like a space hopper. We eventually settle, then I start up again when I make eye contact with Jess. It takes a few more minutes before I manage to keep myself together. "That feels good," I confess, stretching my back where my stomach has cramped.

Mum then looks at me seriously. "When was the last time you laughed like that?" She knows I'm unable to answer. Mum's lips pull tight. “It doesn’t always have to be doom and gloom. You’re allowed to enjoy yourself.”

Picking up my mug, I take a sip, licking at the sugar caught on the rim. “I know. There hasn’t been much to laugh about, that’s all.”

“But he’s home, darling. Smile about that.”

But he shouldn’t be. “For how long though?” I say out loud, rather than to myself.

Jess looks up, her face grave. “How did he get out? I asked, but he didn’t say.”

He wouldn’t. I want to tell the truth and let her know something else is going on. But to everyone else, “The trial got dropped,” is what we’ll say.

Jess frowns.

I don’t want any more questions. “Anyway, I’ve already had a lecture from Bex. Everything you’re thinking, I’ve already thought myself, so can we move on?”

Mum’s face drops.

“You're telling me to smile and laugh when the reality is, unless he changes things drastically, I could be left on my own to raise his child, either sat on the other side of the visitor's table, or stood over his grave.”

My words silence them. *Shit.* My blood pressure spikes. The hairs on the back of my neck stand tall. Neither of those are options. The thought alone turns my stomach.

“I get it,” Mum says solemnly.

Sadness swipes at me, sucking my energy with it. “Christ, Mum, I’m sorry.”

She places her mug on the table. “You don’t apologise to me.” She takes my hand closest to her in hers, doing the same to Jess with the other. She motions to Jess, then to me. “Sometimes, saying I love you means you accept that person for exactly who they are. You hold on to them and never let them go. And other times, it means you love them enough *to* let them go." She squeezes our hands, looking between us both. "It will come and go, and if you're lucky like me," her blinks suddenly quicken, "then maybe you'll find it more than once."

I smile at her, placing my other hand on top of hers.

"There's only one person who can find you through the storm, though." Mum looks at no one in particular. "Only one person who can make you fall, pick you up and make you feel alive like nothing else matters. Take it from me, that person... they never leave."

Quiet. We're all quiet. Still. Until Jess says, "Jesus Christ, Mum," her voice thick with tears. Jess takes her hand away, picking up a napkin and blowing her nose.

"I didn't mean to make you cry, Jess. Oh, I've gone and stuck my camel's toe right in it."

I look up at Jess, my eyes wide in horror. Then I'm blindsided by uncontrollable laughter. I slide down my chair, Jess doing the same, unable to breathe.

"What? What's so funny?"

"What the fucking hell are you talking about?" Jess gasps, her eyes soaked.

I feel my face redden, my eyes aching from not being able to open them.

"Camel's toe? What, is that not right?"

"Really, really not." I snatch another napkin, trying to catch the tears streaming down my cheeks. "What on earth possessed you to say that?" I almost choke as I ask.

"I thought that's what you say when you've put your foot in it?"

Jess laughs harder, banging her hand on the table. "Well, why didn't you just say *that.* Why'd you have to go bringing a woman's vagina into it?"

Mum's face drops so fast, I almost lose full control again

when she realises. "A woman's vagina? Jess, stop. I told you; I can't take you anywhere."

I wave my hands in front of me, a silent beg for her to stop talking. I'm saved from vaginas by my phone vibrating. I get my breathing under control as I read the screen.

Lauren: Hope you have a good night tonight. You need this x

I look down at my phone, smiling happily, still wiping my face.

Me: Thank you. Hope you had a good day? I'm sure we'll be back first thing x

Lauren: No rush. Travis will be here later. We're getting Chinese.

Me: No Die Hard x

Lauren: LOL. See you tomorrow x

I put my phone away, noticing I still haven't heard from Mollie. Maybe I shouldn't have text her. A jab of guilt stops my laughing as I contemplate what's the right thing to do.

Half an hour later, Jess and Mum drop me off at the hotel I'm supposedly staying at tonight. Our shopping trip for baby things ended in disaster. We are still yet to buy one item. I already feel like the world's worst mum. With thirteen weeks left to go, I should be more prepared.

"Looks fancy," Jess says, walking to the boot of her car.

It does look rather grand for one night away. Hopefully he'll be here soon. "What am I meant to do?"

"Don't be so stupid," Jess starts. "Go in there. Enjoy yourself. Run a hot bath, eat their fine food and rest. For the love of God, rest, Madison. Before the baby arrives, sleep as much as you can."

I smile, appreciating that one small speck of freedom I still own.

Mum rests her hand on my shoulder, making me turn to

look at her. "I'm a call away, if you need to talk some more."

"Thank you." I hug her, holding her tight.

"Will you do me a favour, if you don't mind me asking?" Both Jess and I look to her. "When you see your dad, please let him know you love him."

"I do love him," I rather defensively reply.

"I know you do, sweetheart. But men… they need to hear it. They need you to tell them over and over, otherwise they feel like they're not needed. They'll pull away rather than simply talk. Understand?" She's not making excuses for my dad's lack of communication, but she's telling me to be mindful.

"Understood."

With that, I say my goodbyes and check into the hotel. I look out of place. No bag. No partner. Just me. I'm given a key, the room already paid for, and shown to our room. When I push the door open, the vast space has my jaw hitting the floor. Dean really pulled out all the stops.

A queen-sized bed with pure white sheets is to my left. A mini bar and a wall-mounted sixty-inch screen TV are to my right. I step into the room. Giant windows overlooking the city are dead ahead. They stretch from ceiling to floor, fine drapes hanging either side. Luxury.

"You have a massage booked in thirty minutes, Mrs Carter."

"What?"

The concierge looks like he's seen a ghost. "You have a massage booked—"

"—No, what did you call me?"

Quizzical eyes take me in. "Mrs Carter. Apologies, that was one of the names on the booking."

I stand, astonished. "Uh, no. Don't apologise." I just didn't realise I'd gotten married. "Honestly, it's fine."

He looks at me unsure.

"You know what. Can you cancel the massage? I'm not

feeling too good. Wouldn't want to pass anything on."

"Certainly. Can I fetch you any room service?"

I smile. "Now *that* you can do."

Feeling pretty pleased with myself, I start running the gigantic bath, having ordered as much food as I can off the menu. I'm not hungry, yet I found it necessary to order one of everything, just in case something took my fancy.

Might as well enjoy this.

Dean still isn't here. He has fifteen minutes until he's been gone two hours. I've kept my eye on the clock. As much as it paralysed me with happiness, he still gave me his surname without me knowing. I feel petty enough to hold it against him, even if he strolls in here one minute late, he'll know about it.

Tick tock, Mr Carter.

I hear my phone ring from the bedroom. "Hello," I answer, removing my shoes and socks, sat on the edge of the bed.

"Babe."

I look at the clock. "You have thirteen minutes to get in this room."

There's a moment of silence. "Or?" he asks suggestively.

"Or I take it back."

"Take what back?"

"Nothing," I quickly say. "Where are you?"

"Just parked your crappy Fiesta."

"My crappy what now?" Twelve minutes.

"I'm buying you a new car. That thing's too small."

My lips stretch. "Really?"

"Yes. No complaints." Right. "How was the massage?" he asks.

I move the phone away from my ear, putting him on loudspeaker, dropping it to the bed. I push down my leggings and knickers, feeling an odd sensation as I look to the massive windows. It's like the world could be watching, but for some reason, I don't care. "Didn't go."

"Oh," he says disappointedly.

"Mrs Carter didn't feel up to it." I hear him take in a breath. "Figured you can do it for free, if you ever get here, that is."

"I'm working on that."

"You have," I look at the time on my phone, "eleven minutes."

"It will take me longer than that to get there."

"Well, you shouldn't have booked somewhere with no parking." I hear his teeth click in frustration.

I walk into the bathroom.

"Sounds good, doesn't it?" he says.

"What?"

"The surname." I smile, rolling my eyes. It sounds better than good. "That a bath running?" he asks, desire in his voice.

"Uh huh." I place my phone by the sink next to the ice bucket currently holding my bottle of water. Petty. "It's huge. Has mirrors all around it."

"Are you naked?" he breathes harshly.

I lift my t-shirt over my head, unclasp my bra, then drop it to the floor. "I am now." I look in the giant mirror as I step into the still running bath, the warmth making me moan. I purposely make my noises sound more seductive.

"Jesus, babe. Don't do that down the phone. You're killing me."

I peer at the time on the screen. "Nine minutes. Better start running, VP." The groan I hear when I call him that tells me he's turned on. "Or I might have to start without you."

"Mads," he strains. His breaths are quick, his voice filled with need. Want. Desire.

"I don't think I can wait," I tease. I slide down into the bubbles, the hot water biting at my bum.

"Tell me what you're doing."

I look down. My nipples could cut glass. My skin is riddled with prickles. "My nipples are so hard." I cup both breasts, tweaking my nipples between my fingers, my touch sending ripples down my spine, pleasure blooming. "I'm touching them."

He swallows. I wait. "Keep going," he says, jolting me to carry on.

I hum. "I'm squeezing them how I like it." I pinch, rolling the buds between my fingers until tingles starts to dance in my core. I close my eyes, knowing from his silence he wants me to keep going. "That feels so good," I moan. Still there is silence. "VP?" He gives me a low growl. "Seven minutes."

"Don't. Fucking. Stop."

I blush. "I need you inside me, VP." Trailing a hand to between my legs, I gasp, slowly and gently slipping two fingers into my pussy. "I'm so wet. Please, hurry." My other hand cups my breast as I begin circling my clit, my legs parting wider.

My attempt to make this a joke has failed. There's no way I can stop myself now. I roll my nipple between my finger and thumb, pinching it hard as my back begins to arch.

"Talk to me, Mads."

I only moan louder as my fingers plunge inside once again. Then I pump, not managing to get as deep as I need.

"Mads!" Dean shouts, the hotel room door bursting open with a bang.

I jump with a fright, my heart racing. The orgasm I was in hot pursuit of races away.

The door slams. Dean appears in the bathroom doorway. He's breathing heavy, but not out of breath. His hands grip the sides of the door frame, propping himself up.

"Dean! You nearly gave me a fucking heart attack!"

"I couldn't wait in the hall any longer."

I look at him startled. "Outside? You've been outside the door *this whole time?*" He smiles like some sort of handsome pervert. "Well?" I pull myself to sit up, but he quickly makes his way to the side of the ridiculously large tub.

"No, no, no," he breathes. "You need to finish what you started."

"Dean?"

His thumb is on my lips as he bends his body over the side of the bath. "Shh, babe. I want to see you lose control."

Fuck. The way he talks to me has me fighting for air. My need to let him feel all the things that went wrong with this day can be paused for the moment. I need this. And so does he.

He trails his hand from my mouth to my breast. It sits just out of the water, my nipple still hard from the temperature of the water and the man before me. The way he squeezes and kneads my skin feels impeccable. He has me closing my eyes, rolling my head back in no time at all. I want him to kiss me. I need his mouth on me, his body close to me.

He notices, leaning down, lapping his tongue with mine.

I can't help the whimpers that escape me as I pull him closer, both my hands either side of his face. "Get in here," I order.

He pulls away, undressing at the speed of light, freeing his rock hard erection. Lifting one leg, he places his foot in the tub. "Fucking hell!" He immediately turns on the cold tap. "That can't be good for the baby. A bath this hot will smoke her out."

I scoff and roll my eyes. "Don't be such a drama queen."

Dean splashes me with cold water, making me shriek. He smirks mischievously, a playfully wicked grin dragging his cheek higher as he looks at the bucket of ice on the side. "Lie back," he tells me.

I move as carefully and seductively as I can.

He turns off the tap, then reaches for the bucket, discarding the bottle of water before he grabs some ice.

I look at him. Heat and flames dance in his eyes.

The tub's big enough for both of us to lie down, but he

climbs over me, hovering his hand above my chest. His eyes flick to my nipple as he lowers the ice to my skin, slowly skating around the swollen bud.

I bite my lip. The nip of the ice leaves a pinching sensation against my warm skin.

Dean traces the cube over my other breast. I arch my back as he begins a trail to my mouth, the cold bringing me out in goosebumps. When he slides it over my lips, moving slowly, tiny droplets fall down my chin. I let my tongue catch them before he lifts his hand allowing the droplets to drip freely.

Our eyes never break contact as he starts swaying his hand, dropping the water, purposely missing my mouth. Then his mouth's on mine, his hand slipping to cup my jaw. He holds me still, our warm lips tangling together with the cold. They dance as he licks, sucking me into him, devouring me.

When his hand lowers to between my legs, my back arches, my legs spread wide, my hips begin to rock.

He consumes me. He's steady, taking his time with my body as his fingers gently fuck me. I moan as Dean holds himself up with one hand before he scoops me, turning and rolling so that he's submerged under the water.

I sit between his legs, my back flush with his front. "Open for me." Dean kisses my neck as I part my legs, holding my bump as I move. He hooks his legs under my knees, pinning them wide against the sides of the bath. I'm at his mercy. He's in control.

Leisurely, he begins gliding his hand down my front. He doesn't stop until the very tips of his fingers are brushing my clit, and I'm squirming against him for more.

"Dean," I moan, turning my head up to him.

He cups my neck with his other hand, holding it back as his tongue pushes past my lips.

I reach up, gripping his hair, pulling myself closer to him. Needing his cock inside me. Moaning against him, he starts circling his fingers, and my mouth opens wide. It's instant. The rush of heat, the pull in my stomach. "Please," I beg.

"Please, what?" He kisses me again, his hold on my neck tightening as I start rolling my hips in time with the strokes of his fingers.

"VP. Please, fuck me, right now."

He smiles against me. "I want us to watch."

Turning my head, both my arms go behind his neck. My head rolls into his shoulder, and he holds me there, momentarily stopping his fingers as he grabs his cock, placing it at my entrance. "Are you ready?" he groans in a deep voice against my ear.

"Yes," I reply, my breath all hot and wild as I look at us in the reflection of the mirror.

His hips push up, and we watch, seeing the moment he fills me.

A rush of heat rises from my toes, all the way to the base of my neck. I moan loudly, my lips parting. I can't look away from what we're doing. It's so hot.

We watch as his cock moves back and forth, slipping in and out of my pussy. I grip his neck, pulling him closer as his hands push my hips down onto him. "My girl. Look how good you take me."

His words put me in a spin. "VP." My back curls, and he begins circling his fingers on my clit. Swiping. Swirling. Flicking. Pinching. Every touch, every bit of movement has my mouth opening wider, my hips trying to rock for more friction. More filling. Deeper. "Harder."

Dean's hand tightens around my throat. "Are you close, babe?"

"Yes," I breathe lustfully.

His teeth nip my neck then kiss the area. "Good," he rumbles. His hips thrust faster. His fingers move with more determination. Every inch of me is being controlled by him, taking everything he has to give. He pounds on, hammering me towards my release.

I feel so full. So complete. So completely his. Our groans mixed with the sounds of the water slapping the side of the bath, light up fireworks in my head. Colours jump and sparks ignite before me. I cry out, digging my fingers into his neck, pulling his hair as I come, letting go. Warmness then consumes me. My eyes close and my muscles relax, leaving me limp.

Dean roars, joining me, his hips jerking before they still. I feel every twitch of his cock as he empties himself.

When he relaxes, he holds me close to him, breathing against my skin. I can't talk, can't even move to tell him how much I love him.

CHAPTER THIRTY-FOUR

MADISON

I wake in the lush bed, Dean's arms curled around my body. My hair's damp. The towel's still wrapped around me. Lavender and bath soap radiates off his arm. I can't help but lower my nose, filling my lungs with the calming scent as I pull him closer, my eyes still closed.

I need to get him to talk. I need to find out what's really going on. If I have any hope of keeping him away from what Mollie suggested he may have done, I need to know sooner rather than later. I need to end this. He can't leave me again. I won't let him.

Making me jump, the baby kicks.

Dean's hand moves to cradle it. "She's going to be a fighter," he says softly, waking from his dozed state. He buries his face in my neck as he speaks, undoing my towel as his hand strokes my stretched skin.

"Will you come with me Wednesday?"

Dean kisses my neck. "Wednesday?" he questions.

Inclining my face towards his, he lays his mouth on mine. "I have a scan," I tell him once he breaks away.

Dean lifts his finger to my face, brushing my hair away, stroking my cheek to under my chin. "I wouldn't miss it for the world."

Joy unfolds like a flower in spring. I lift my hand to cup the side of his face. "Thank you."

His eyes narrow, his lips pulling tight. "Why are you thanking me?"

I shrug. Why am I thanking him? He should be there. "I don't know."

Dean's eyes move between mine. "You're doubting me."

It's not a question. "No, I—"

"Don't ever doubt the love I have for you, Mads. It's the only thing I'm sure of."

My heart stammers. My hackles rise, suddenly defensive. "It's not doubt, Dean." I steadily roll, lifting to one elbow. I look down to him, now laid on his back.

His hand brushes my hair off my face.

"It's fear," I say, my voice gravelly. "Fear that I'll lose you." My tears brim.

He swiftly wraps an arm around me, pulling my body to his.

I lay my palm flat on his chest.

"Lose me?" Dean wraps his fingers around the back of my neck. "You couldn't lose me if you tried."

I raise a half smile. "You'd find me through the storm," I whisper.

He smiles, not fully knowing but understanding what I'm talking about.

"I know something's not right." He frowns. "Is it bad? Will you get hurt? Dean, I can't have you leaving me again."

"Babe," he coos, calming me. Dean pushes me to my back so he's looking down at me. His eyes and his hand move to my bump. He takes a few moments, stroking my skin before he leans down and places a kiss above my belly button. "What happens next for me," he looks up, "I don't have a choice. I have to see it through. But I have told you, everything I do from here on out is for you. For my child." I go to open my mouth but he cuts me off.

"I want out."

Out? He wants out? From the club? "Out?" I ask shifting my head on the pillow.

He nods.

"How? I thought you said there was no way out?"

He closes his eyes. This decision he's made clearly doesn't come lightly. The club has been the most prevalent thing in his life. Until me. Until our baby. "I want you. I want peace."

I smile listening to him.

"I'm almost done. I'm *so* fucking close."

At what cost? "You once told me you wouldn't give it up." I don't know why I say it. I don't know why I'm questioning it. This is what I want. This is something I've wanted to hear. Him, me, peace. Family life away from the carnage.

"That was before you told me you were going to make me a dad. A *dad*, Mads." He shakes his head, still looking down at me. "You're about to give me something I never thought I'd have, and something you've only ever seen in your dreams. One day, our reality will be far better than any of our dreams, babe. With my life, I promise you that."

I cover my eyes, both palms flat to my face. His words sink into my soul, my heart daring to hope for our future. "With your life..." My voice gets lost in the silence surrounding us.

Dean pulls my hands away from my face.

My eyes are soaked, my throat burning from trying not to let my cries be heard. "You are enough as you are, Dean. Your life, it doesn't mean anything if you lose it trying to be free."

I see tears fill his eyes. They won't fall like mine. But I see them. I see him. "I will never be free from my demons, Mads, not if I don't do this."

His demons? This is more than fighting physically? "Why are they still chasing you? Tell me why, please." I sob as I ask him to help me understand.

"No."

"No?" My voice wobbles.

I watch his face drop, the line across his head indicating his pain. "If I run, they chase me. I jump, they fly. I try to drown… they'll drag me to the surface."

I lift my hand to his face trying to calm him.

"This is what you chose when you told me you loved me that very first time. That first moment you dared to love me, this is what you got." His green eyes narrow, and my hand freezes. That sternness again, rearing its head. "I tried giving you an out, and still you chose this. You can't leave me now. We may have a long way to go, but *you* are why I fight. *You* are the gravity that keeps pulling me home. You know I can't do this without you." Dean's voice rattles, his hands trembling.

In the blink of an eye, frustration kicks inside me. A solid wall of anger blocks my ability to give him what he needs. Reassurance. Love. Calm. Why does it feel this heavy?

He leans down to kiss me, but I turn my head. "No," I speak softly. I shimmy my way to the edge of the bed, swinging my legs off the side. "I didn't choose this." I stand, and he draws back, staring at me.

I don't care that I'm naked. I don't care that the windows are behind me. Maybe the world needs to hear this; God knows the man I love does. "I chose you, Dean. Not the club." I point at him. "I chose, you. And I will keep choosing you until the day I die. And even then I'll choose to be wherever you are."

He shifts to sit on his bum, his legs bent wide. Elbows resting on his knees, the sheet covers his lower half. He runs a hand through his hair, then he huffs so loud serving only to piss me off even more.

"You can't do this without me," I say with a sarcastic laugh, "yet you treat me like I'm not strong enough to handle it."

His head snaps up. "Strong enough. You think I don't know

you're strong enough?" Flames of anger dance in his eyes. His face tightens. The ground feels like ice underneath me. "It's your fucking strength and love that saved me. I would never have made it back here without *your* strength."

I step closer to the bed, my eyes fixed firmly on his. "Then tell me how you got back here? How did you come home to me?"

His jaw ticks. I don't miss the slight narrowing of his eyes. "Why are you pushing this?"

I laugh, rubbing at my head. The baby then kicks, feeding off my stress. I look down, sucking in some air. "Because a part of you is growing inside me," I say tiredly, still looking down. "You think I'm going to let you put yourself in danger? You think I wouldn't do anything to protect you? To make sure we never have to live another day without you. Not knowing whether you're okay or still *breathing*?"

A tear slips from my eye. I quickly swipe it away, trying to prove my point of how strong I can be. For him.

Without a word, he stands off the bed, the sheet falling from around his waist. I swallow, begging my eyes not to fall. Dean steps to me, his bare chest level with my eyes. If it wasn't for my bump, I'd be able to press my lips to his soft skin.

Putting his hand flat on my chest, he slides his fingers around my throat, scooping some of my hair as he goes. He angles my chin up to look at him, his thumb twitching, clearly he wants to hold me tighter than he is. And for the strangest of reasons, I want him to.

I lean into his hold. Tempting him. Begging him.

The corner of his mouth twitches. "You dragged me through hell last time." He leans in closer, his lips now close to mine. I'm desperate for him to take them. My knees tremble. My head's dizzy with ecstasy. "I won't let you do it again." Then his hold on me is gone. He turns, walking his gorgeous arse away from me towards the bathroom, his muscles flexing, showing off their definition as he moves.

I'm left breathing heavy, my mouth unexpectedly dry. I hold where his hand was, wanting it back on me. *Needing* it back on me. "Don't walk away from me," I goad, hoping he'll come back. I wait until the red mist dispels a little. He doesn't reply or give me any signs of hearing me.

My phone then pings from the bedside table, making me move with purpose.

Mollie: We go to the farm tomorrow. Together? We can't get involved. We just watch. See what he's up to

My breath gets caught reading her message. Go to the farm tomorrow? Follow Dean? Find out what he's up to? I frown hearing the toilet flush, hoping I can drag something out of him before then.

Me: Okay. I'll call tomorrow

I eventually stomp my way closer, following his path. I push the door open, seeing him stood at the sink, washing his hands. He's gorgeous.

"Tell me what I'm thinking," he says cooly, his eyes lifting to me in the mirror.

He wants me to listen. He wants me to submit. To promise I'll let him finish what he thinks he needs to do. But until I know what *it* is, he isn't getting his way. "No."

"Just like that?" he smirks.

"Just like that," I reply sardonically.

He stands straight, turning to me, his cock semi-erect.

My mouth dries. My heart hammers my ribs relentlessly. I want him. I want him so bad. We stare each other down in this battle of whose love is strongest. There isn't anything else *but* love in this moment. It's passionate. Ferocious. Powerful. It's the kind of love that'll never go away. The scars run too deep.

Scars. My eyes trace over his—new and old. I need to touch them, let him know they don't scare me or put me off. I love him for who he is because he's mine. All mine. And I am his.

"I can hear your thoughts," he says lustfully.

I cross my arms in defiance.

He smiles.

Bastard.

"Want to hear what you already know?"

I lift my chin trying in vain not to acknowledge his growing arousal.

He wraps his hand around his shaft, gripping himself at the base.

My lips part, my breath escaping.

"I'll take your silence as a yes."

"Take it anyway you want," I bite back. Is this what we're doing? Who'll crack first. A standoff for control. He'll control me with his body, try to distract me like he does. But I want him to tell me what's going on.

His hand tenderly strokes all the way to the tip of his now glistening cock.

I lose my breath, but I stand straighter. As if that will help.

"I'm in control here, Mads. But you want me to lose that control with you." Another stroke. I want him to lose control *and* talk. "You think you can pretend not to want this?" Stroke. "Babe, look how needy you are." His dirty words make my nipples harden as I tighten every muscle in my body. "You want me to put you against the wall and fuck you until you're screaming at me, begging me for more."

I swallow the lump in my throat, squeezing my thighs. Imagining it. His dominance. His power. Yes, that's what I want. As well as his words, I want him to do what he wants with me.

I make sure to keep my eyes locked on his as he stalks towards me, dragging his hand back down his full length. I hear him let out the smallest of moans, seeing his temple twitch.

"Are you done?" I manage to say.

He cocks a brow, stopping right in front of me. My back's up against the frame of the door. The cool of the wood bringing my naked body out in goosebumps. He might know exactly what I want, but I can't let him win.

I push forwards, feeling his cock press against my skin. He hums, and I look up to him through my lashes, blinking as though I'm about to surrender. He wants me to cave, to drop to my knees like I could so easily do. Instead, I turn and walk out of the room.

I'm breathing heavy, almost at the bed when his hand grabs the back of my neck. He steps close to me, my back against his front. One hand goes to my hip, the other holds me under my chin. "There's only one way you get what you want here, Mads."

I wrestle to get my jaw free. "Oh yeah?"

"Yeah." Wet kisses fall off his lips against my neck. Each one makes my back arch further. I feel him behind me. Hard. Ready. "I will make you come over and over, but you have to promise me one thing." His fingers on my hip grip my skin harder. His hand around my throat then trails between my breasts. He rolls his palm flat against one nipple, then scoops up the other breast, rolling my nipple between his fingers.

"What?" I say on a shaky breath.

He pulls my nipple until it pings back from his hold, forcing me to moan. My head rolls back, and he repeats with the other side. I moan again, closing my eyes. "Like that, beautiful?"

Yes. Oh God, yes.

His other hand raises, and he pulls both nipples at the same time. They're tender but the feeling is euphoric. My legs tremble, my pussy's soaked. He does it again. "Do you want to come, Mads?"

"Yes," I pant, his fingers still rolling.

He pulls. Rolls. Pulls. Rolls.

"Please." He's going to win.

He kisses my neck again, and I can feel him smile. "No more asking about prison, or me getting out."

My eyes immediately flick open. The small high I was riding at his touch, suddenly forgotten. "I want to know."

He lets go of me. I feel lost. My body's buzzing. I watch him walk to the chair in our room. It's black leather with a scooped back. He pulls it out, turning it to me. Without a word, he taps the back for me to come and sit down. I don't move. He places both hands on the back of the chair, leaning forwards in silent warning. He holds my gaze, looking at me, one piece of his hair falling down the front of his face.

Shit. I want to walk to him so bad. I squirm, biting my bottom lip.

"Sit," he instructs firmly, his voice low and commanding. He definitely holds the power in the bedroom.

My body betrays me, taking the lead, walking forward before my brain has made up its mind. I walk to the chair, turn, then slowly lower myself.

"Good girl."

Jesus. He's never called me a good girl. I don't want to give him the satisfaction of knowing how much that lit up every nerve ending I have. Everything is heightened. Every breath he breathes, I hear a thousand times louder. My heart starts pounding in my chest. I'm pretty sure I'm about to die by the rush of excitement flowing through me.

Gentle fingers strum under my chin, angling my head back against the chair to look up to him. Dean takes my mouth, my lips parting, allowing him to kiss me deeply. My tongue explores with his, then he sucks my bottom lip between his teeth, nibbling as he watches me.

I pant. I'm so turned on right now, I need him to make me

come. "Dean."

"Shh," he breathes. His fingers glide over my top lip, then the bottom. I open for him, and he dips his fingers inside.

My tongue licks, my lips closing around them, our eyes never breaking contact.

Once they're wet, Dean immediately pushes them against my clit, and I spread my legs wide, arching my back as best I can. He circles, pressing his lips back to mine. He's controlling me, leaning over me, working me to my release. But he won't give it. Not unless I agree.

"No more asking." He kisses me hard, cupping my chin harder, circling his fingers faster.

Pleasure runs wild. My core burns. "No," I breathe.

He stops.

I'm breathless. Needy. My body tight with the sudden loss of his hands on me.

He takes me in, moving around the chair so he's in front of me.

I close my legs instinctively.

He kneels, resting his palms flat against my knees. He tries to part my legs, but I offer up some resistance. "Stop challenging me."

"Tell me the truth," I reply firmly, my breath still not fully caught.

Dean parts my legs with little effort, holding them wide. He looks down. Rolling his bottom lip under his teeth, those green eyes look as though he's about to feast on me.

I wriggle against the back of the chair, trying to sit up. As much as I want it. I also want the truth.

"No." His hand lands on my chest, holding me down.

"Dean!" I try again to move, but he presses me harder.

"Don't. Move." His head dips, and I lose sight of him behind my bump.

Cool air then blankets between my parted legs, and I bite my lip, stopping the groan of pleasure that tries to escape me. I throw my head back, feeling his wet tongue slide straight up the middle. My body slumps. I'm pretty sure he's going to win.

Flicking over the swollen nub, two fingers dive in my pussy.

"Oh fuck," I cry out, my fingers digging into the leather.

He sucks my clit before he swaps his fingers for his tongue. The sensation has me collapsing with bliss in the seat. "Are you with me, babe?"

"Hmm," I moan, unable to talk.

Dean's tongue is relentless. Every flick, lick and suck from him has me rocking my hips into his face. Hot heat swims in my belly. My toes tingle as they curl. I'm going to come. "VP," I mumble, turning my head to the side as he increases his speed, edging me closer.

"No more," he says quickly, before he's back on me, his fingers fucking me with tenacity.

I want to say no. I need the truth. But now, I need to come. I'm sweaty, my body starting to shake in anticipation of my impending orgasm. There's no way I can say no now. No means this stops. And this can't ever stop. "Yes," I whimper.

I push myself up straighter, wanting to see him. He looks up, his eyes on mine, and I watch as he slowly licks me, his nose moving side to side as he spreads me. Two fingers are then back inside, teasing the sweet spot. "Yes," I groan louder.

He stands bending over me, carefully pulling me into his arms. I wrap my arms and legs around him as he walks me back to the bed. He lays me flat, guiding my body as I lower to my back.

Lifting both my legs, he bends them, holding them wide at my knees. He lines himself up, then enters me, his cock filling me to the hilt.

"Fuck, Dean." One hand scrunches into my hair. I need to let go. Need my release. "Please."

Pulling his hips back, he groans, watching when he then pushes back inside. I hear him hiss as I arch my back, the weight from the baby and him filling me combined, makes me feel so incredibly full. "Say it," he tells me. He draws back, holding just the very tip inside me.

"Yes!" I cry.

He drives home. "Say it," he pushes past gritted teeth. He draws back again, this time holding himself still.

I need him to fill me. I try to push back onto him.

"Tell me, Mads."

I try to prise my eyes open, but it's no good. "I won't," I choke out. "I won't ask."

Slam. He drives so hard my whole-body jerks. Again. I need that again.

Slam.

I bite my lip, gripping the sheets around my head, smiling as I reach a new high. "Yes, Dean, just like that!"

Slam. Slam. Slam. He doesn't stop. He keeps his rhythm. "Mads," he cries. He grips my legs tighter, fucking me hard and unforgivingly. He's careful of the baby, not fully losing control with me, but dominating my body so I know he's serious. I mustn't ask again. I mustn't ask him how he's out. "Together, babe." The sounds of wet slaps and our moans vibrate the air around us. "Take me with you."

My body tightens. My orgasm washing over me in one hot wave. "VP!" I cry. "I'm coming!"

He drives home, and I don't hold back as I moan through my release, gripping the sheets.

He does the same, grunting as his hips shudder, letting go. Dean folds his body over mine, planting kisses on my chest and my neck as we breathe our way down to settle.

I turn my head, holding him close. I don't say anything. Neither does he.

Once we've recovered, he pushes up on one hand to look at me. His eyes are relaxed and sleepy. Content. "Get dressed." Another kiss lands on my lips before he pulls out of me, holding his hands for me to take.

I do, and he pulls me to sit up. "Dressed? Where are we going?"

Dean smiles. "Somewhere. Just trust me."

Half an hour later, we're pulling up in my perfectly sized Fiesta on the outskirts of a beautiful little village. Cobbled streets lead my eyes towards a trickling stream with an old stone bridge curved over it. A white iron gate stands at the end of someone's garden; their small cottage backing out onto fields of green and rolling hills.

Engulfing. That's how I'm finding the feeling of joy that this unknown place is bringing me. I smile seeing tall green trees dancing in the sunlight. An old pub on the corner with people stepping inside. Children playing in the small park opposite. A dog running down the road without fear of being hit by cars.

I don't know what it is, but this place brings me immediate peace. "It's beautiful."

Dean smiles, getting out the car. He walks around to my side, opening the door and holding out his hand. He pulls me to my feet. "I'm glad you like it."

I frown with a smile. "Why?"

He laughs, tugging my hand. "Come on. Let me show you."

We walk past the pub, past the village shop and the park. Only the sound of children laughing and the water trickling can be heard. I squeeze Dean's hand in mine, and he looks at me.

He smiles, rubbing the back of my hand with his thumb. He's happy here.

Tapping feet hitting the cobbles come up behind me. I turn around, looking down, seeing the black and white Border Collie go trotting by, stopping to look back at the two of us before he runs off. My heart swells. I don't recall a time I've ever felt this happy. Me. Him. Our family. I've envisioned it. "This place." Other words escape me.

"I know," Dean says. He looks content as he nods his head, leading me to a large cottage further down the road. The antique grey painted on the outside looks neat and clean. Tumbling flowers hang either side of the door. It screams cozy and warm. Safe.

"What is this place?"

"You like it?" His expression looks hopeful. His eyes sweep over my face.

"Dean, I love it. But, why are we here?"

The brown wooden door opens, and a man steps out. "Mr and Mrs Carter?"

I look to Dean, rolling my eyes.

He smiles rather than scowls.

"If you'd like to come inside."

Dean holds out one arm, the other he places at the small of my back, and I keep my eyes on his as I follow the man in.

The cottage is all open plan. Bright light pours in through bifold doors on the back, leading to the garden full of flowers, plants and fresh cut grass. A large wooden table sits in the middle of the dining area, low hanging bulbs drop in the centre. The walls are painted white. Everything white and wood. It's homely.

"You like it?" Dean whispers, his lips pushing to the back of my head.

I turn, bewildered. "It's gorgeous. But?" I smile shaking my head. "Is this what I think?"

My heart runs wild when I see his green pool's brighten. "You want it? It's yours."

"Dean," I choke, my breath getting clogged in my throat. I gawk at him, completely overcome.

"Would you like to see the three bedrooms upstairs?"

presumably the estate agent asks.

I look to him, then back at Dean. He waits. Waits for *me* to decide.

After earlier, I feel a little lost. Whether there's more to know or more to come. I know in this moment what he's trying to give me. He wants to give me peace; the life he wants. The one he more than deserves. And I want it, too.

CHAPTER THIRTY-FIVE

DEAN

We arrive home the following morning, having spent the rest of our night away in frustrating bliss. Bliss because I declared I wanted to buy us somewhere to live.

Frustrating because, even on the drive back to the hotel leaving the tranquillity of the little village, over dinner, another bath together, Mads didn't ease up on trying to find out what's going on. I dodged giving any real answers, keeping her sated with orgasms and sleep.

Sleeping next to her is the best. Especially after we'd celebrated the new house. Our own place. A family home, one not shrouded in history and memories. Ghosts.

I met Lauren and showed her the place. I'm not ashamed to say I wanted to gauge her reaction and get her opinion on whether she thought Mads would like it first. Poor kid didn't twig it's for her too.

Rounding the table, I pick up my things. "I'll be back later." I lay a kiss on Mads' head, feeling her tense.

"What are you doing today?"

I move to check her expression. She wants to know if I'm doing anything dangerous. I *could* tell her about Jack. About taking Travis to meet him. About how I'm going to tell the club what's going on. Or I can protect her. "I need to catch up with Travis about work," not a total lie, "then we have church." Again, not a total lie, but still. I'm risking my friendship with him. He'll kill me when I tell him I want out. "Should be home around five," I tell her.

Mads rubs her temples, a clear sign she's overthinking. Stressing. "Right."

I sigh dipping my front to her back, pressing my mouth to her neck. "Everything will be fine."

She huffs, and I can guarantee she just rolled her eyes.

"What are your plans today?" I ask.

Mads pushes her chair, and I step back. Rejected. "I need to meet with Vivian, call Bex about going to see her and then I'm meeting Mollie for coffee." She busies herself, making a cup of tea.

There are a few things there I need to unpick. "When are you seeing Bex?" If the next run with Costa gets confirmed anytime soon, I'll need to be here. I won't be able to travel anywhere with her. But I don't want her away from me. Panic spikes. And Mollie? "And why are you meeting Mollie?" I add.

Mads gives me a look. The one I know means I'm asking stupid questions. "Me and Jess are going to Bex's baby shower this weekend, and I messaged Mollie because we're friends. She was here when you weren't." There's venom in her voice. I see her instantly regret her choice of words. She bows her head. "Sorry."

I can't be mad. "Where are you going for coffee?"

"Town," she says stirring the spoon, still rubbing her temple with her other hand.

I tap my cut, checking I have my phone. "What time? Maybe I can take you or pick you up."

Tapping the spoon on the edge of the mug, Mads turns slowly, leaning back against the work surface. "Eleven," she says, eyes honing in on mine as she takes a sip.

Did I miss something? The inside of my mouth takes a

beating as I gnaw on it. Her brown eyes slice through my thoughts. Same time I'm meeting Travis. I won't be able to take her. "I'll meet you back here then."

Her face creases. "Fine."

"Why are you being so short with me?" I ask, drilling her with a frown of my own. I'm not being ridiculous here. She is definitely not happy about something.

"You know why."

Right. We're still on this. She wants to know. "Mads."

Before I can say anymore, she's walking past me out the kitchen.

I reach out grabbing her wrist, and turn her into my body. No matter the mood, her body reacts. "Listen."

"No, you listen," she counters.

I cock a brow, stunned, but smile cheekily. I can tell by her brows knitting together, I should probably stop.

"You're driving me crazy and you've only been back three days."

"I like driving you crazy."

"Stop," she sighs. "Please, just stop."

I lose the grin and widen my stance, bending my legs to bring my face level with hers. I must have done something right to have her love me the way she does. I brush her hair off her face, curling my fingers into the strands behind her ears. I get a small moan from her, her eyes closing. "Soon."

Kissing her, I make sure to leave my mark before I go. I possessively push my tongue into her mouth, standing straight, her head rolling back as I claim her. I hold her head steady so she can't escape me—can't ask me to share a truth I simply won't yet. Maybe once we're out, then she can know. But the truth hurts, and I'll never hurt her again. I'm going to give her the world and more.

A short while later, I arrive at the clubhouse, fucking sick of driving. Thankfully, we're riding out to meet Jack this morning. I haven't fed my addiction for two wheels in so long. I don't feel right. Turning off the engine, I reach inside my pocket for my smokes. I light one, feeling some of the tension leave my body, then step out, going in search of my bike.

Hearing his bike drawing closer, I worry how Travis is going to take my wanting to leave. I checked out on him once not too long ago. He won't stand for that again. Not a chance.

He pulls up, shifting his gaze to me as I draw back the shutter where my bike has been.

I nod my chin to him. "The kid kept her in good nick?" I say, gesturing towards my bike once he kills his engine.

Travis nods holding up his hand, motioning two fingers towards him.

I step closer, passing him my smoke.

"Kept her busy, you know."

I smile. He is definitely smoking more these days. He sucks on it as much as I did.

Seems like I was blessed with a curse of having people who want me around. I used to think I had no one. I've learned enough to know that simply isn't true. Never was. Travis is stressed, and me not being here was the cause. What will he be like when there's no more of this? No more of us, running this club together.

I have no fucking clue how I'm going to tell him. "We should quit."

I look at him, and he huffs looking down at the cigarette, pulling another draw from it. "Yeah, but unlike you, I don't have another vice. So this will do me." Another vice. He knows damn well he could have another vice if he wanted it. He's just too stubborn to let her back in. "What time we riding out?"

I look at my watch. "Best get going." I pull the cover off my bike, smiling on the inside as I swing my leg over the saddle.

We ride to the old farm Travis' uncle owns. There are pigs and a few vehicles kept here when they're not being used. Travis was reluctant to come here, seeing as his uncle and he are not on the best of terms. The terms being that Travis hasn't kept in touch since his family asked him to reconsider joining the club years ago. It was an easy decision to make back then, but I feel my face fall when I silently question whether it was worth it.

Riding in first, I dock my bike and look around for the truck I suspect Jack's still driving.

"Come on. Explain what the fuck is going on," Travis demands.

The quiet mind I gained from riding is suddenly full of screaming voices. My head throbs. "Do you want the good news or the bad news?"

He laughs. "You fucking prick." I drop my head. "You drag me here, of all places, to tell me bad news?"

I step off my bike, running my hand through my hair. I need to get it cut.

Just as I go to speak, a vehicle I recognise pulls into the courtyard. *Fuck.* My insides rattle. They've met once, but that was years ago. I know exactly how Travis will react once he sees him. I'm instantly regretting this.

Holding my breath, I watch as Travis looks to the truck, then to me as he works this all out. I don't miss the subtle straightening of his cut and flash of a gun. Great. Just what we need.

"Have faith in me, brother."

Travis looks to me as the truck door opens. Jack steps out, closes the door, and walks to the back of his truck. He stops, then casually leans against the boot.

I turn to Travis, double taking, seeing him unimpressed and looking murderous.

"He's dead."

"Apparently not," I reply scratching my beard which is in equal need of a trim.

"What the fuck is this, Dean?"

I gear myself up for the standoff of all standoffs between the two men I care about most. Neither of whom I can see standing down if things turn sour. "I know," I try to reassure him, because I really do know how messed up Jack being here is.

There's nothing I wanted more than for Jack *not* to have died. The days and the weeks after hearing he'd gone were some of the worst I've ever experienced. And the man who picked me up and talked some sense into me, he's the one who's standing off his bike, looking like he's ready to strangle someone if he doesn't get answers, fast.

"One of you talk," Travis jeers.

My lips part, but I struggle to put it into words.

"Travis." Jack steps forward, his tone calm.

Travis remains wordless, his eyes flick to me before going back to Jack.

Jack senses his hesitation, edging himself closer. "Been a long time."

Travis huffs. "The fuck is going on here?" His voice raises. "When you called yesterday, didn't it occur to you to mention that your fucking cousin had risen from the dead?"

"Travis—"

"—Don't." His eyes relax but his body still carries tension. Travis drags his hand down his beard, mentally working this all out.

"He got me out," I confess. Unsure of what to do with my hands, I shove them in my pockets. Nervous.

Travis leans forward slightly. "And?"

"And, now we're here," Jack concludes stepping closer. "Need to make sure I can bring you in on what's going on."

Travis smiles but it's not real. "Bring me in?" he says angrily, his eyebrows lifting. He turns to look at me. Judging by the way he's starting to shake, maybe Lauren's right. I need to give him a break. I've asked too much of him lately.

"I got us into some shit, brother." Confusion spreads across his face. "Costa," is all I add.

"Costa? What's that coffee loving prick got to do with Jack being back?"

Jack laughs to himself, and we both look at him confused. He smiles. "That's what I called him."

Travis doesn't react. Doesn't so much as take a fucking breath. Jesus Christ. "Costa isn't dealing guns," I say, pulling Travis' attention to me. "The shipment we intercepted." Travis stares, waiting for me to go on. I sigh, gesturing to Jack. "Show him."

Jack steps forward holding the tablet which details the grim reality we've got ourselves wrapped up in. Wrong. What *I've* got us wrapped up in.

Travis takes his time processing everything he's being told. I let Jack take the lead, outlining to Travis what he told me. He's saved witnessing the inhumanity of the girl's body, but his reaction is the same as was mine. He lunges for Jack, his fists raised.

Managing to get my body in front of his, I push Travis back, both palms flat against his chest. The only reason I manage to move him the inch it takes for Jack to step out of the way, is because of his gunshot wound.

My mind suddenly struggles to comprehend losing Travis. As if getting a massive kick up the backside, I shove him harder, determined to make him see sense. "Enough!" I bark.

He stumbles, equally just as shocked that I managed to hold him off. "So, what are you suggesting?" Travis shouts throwing his arms up in the air, shaking me off. "How are we supposed to believe we have any fucking chance of shutting this down?"

"By getting inside," Jack answers him. "We find their haul before you move it; then they have nothing to sell. We need to be ready before they confirm the next shipment."

"The next shipment will come in a matter of days," I fire back.

Jack shifts, scowling. "One man. You only need to risk one man." *Shit.* He's lost his fucking mind. "We have to get a man on the inside. Someone who can get a message back to us. We're running out of time, Deano. And choices. We're running out of choices."

He's panicking. Panicking he won't get the man he so desperately needs for Linda. But what he's asking? It's too far-fetched. Too unrealistic to believe we could infiltrate Costa's set up and bring an entire organisation down so soon. He knows all of us, has seen all of us.

"Getting a man inside will take time. Trust would need to be built."

"We don't have fuckin' time!" Jack presses.

"I know that!" I yell. "But we can't rush into this half ready. Everyone will lose."

"This is fucked," Travis adds his piece, turning and walking to his bike. He's heard enough.

"Where are you going?" I shout to him.

"I need to clear my head before we take this to the table."

"The table?" Jack's eyes dart to me. "Deano, you take this to your table and they vote against it..." his fists are clenched, his face grooved. "If you vote against stopping this, I'll have no choice but to—"

"—to what?" Travis interrupts him.

I look at Travis. No way the club will vote against stopping this. Bringing the Saviours into it, that's a different matter. Jack will hate it, but I can't do this without the club fully on board. And I can't lose Jack again. My gut's telling me without Vincent on board, more blood will be spilled trying to bring this to an end. He'll fight me at every turn to ensure he has his hand in the jar of the gun trade.

Except he's not in the gun trade. He's in the pit of Hell, same as me. Helping some cunt ship people for someone else's gain.

The weight of it is simply too fucking much to handle. My conscience won't allow me to let this continue, and my past won't ever let me free. We need to kill the man who changed everything for us. I'm stuck between a rock and a hard place.

Jack and I are chasing the same dream here. Every bit of me hurts for him. And I know he'll be hurting for me.

"Travis is right." They both stop to look at me. Feeling my phone vibrate but ignoring it, I stand straight, knowing we need to take this back to *everyone*. We need to build any broken bridges with the Saviours. I exhale. "However you think you need us, Jack, this next part needs to be done our way. Club won't vote to stop it, but we bring everyone in. I'm their president. No fucking way I'm doing this without them knowing the truth."

"We need the Saviours on board," Travis backs me up, making Jack look the angriest I've ever seen him.

His face drops. "What are you suggesting?" Jack folds his arms.

I run a hand through my hair. Thinking. "Come to the clubhouse."

Jack balks. "I can't go there." Granted, a dead guy showing up, ex-police, now working for secret service, it's going to raise a few questions about where I stand on things. But we don't have a choice. "Rocco made it pretty fuckin' clear I was a man your charter couldn't trust."

"Rocco isn't here anymore. I am. You may not have met them all personally, but out of respect for Ronnie, they'll listen to what you have to say." More importantly, they'll listen to me. I look at Travis now sat on his bike, ready to leave. He's nodding his head in agreement. I turn back to Jack. "I'll call you with a time."

Jack levels me with a look I'm all too familiar with. He's with me, but he's still very much a man on a mission. He's going to have to keep that in check if he wants this done. Without a word he steps forwards, embracing me with a hard pat on my back. His entire body is tight, riddled with his uncertainty.

Travis and I then watch him leave; the air heavy and still between us. "When we first made the deal with the Saviours, I told you things would get messier. Nothing good comes from working with them."

I drop my head.

"Organ trafficking," he says flatly. "How the fuck did *we* get into that."

Turning to face him, I slowly pick my helmet off my bike. "Because I made the wrong decision. I wanted peace, but I never saw this coming."

He sighs running a hand over the top of his head. "None of us did. When we voted this in, none of us could have predicted this shit."

We both wait, unmoving, mentally assessing our next move. "Honesty." My eyes find his as he speaks. "When we get back. Total fucking honesty, that's what's needed." My heart drills at the word. "They won't like bringing in Vincent any more than needs be, but you were right, Saviours owe us. We've proven they can trust us."

"You and me, we can sit down with Vincent after we've taken this to the club." Travis nods at my order and slips on his helmet, but I don't follow suit. My head's spinning.

"Dean?"

I look up.

"It's not just the club you need to speak to."

I know in the deepest pit of my soul what he's referring to. I just can't see how I tell her what's really happening. And right now, he and I have something else we need to do.

I roll my shoulders, picking up my glasses, managing to squash everything else. For now. "I think I know where Lauren's brother is."

Wiping my face, I push open the door to the clubhouse, heading towards the bar. The past few hours were grim, but we checked the grave Sean showed me. It wasn't Lauren's brother. No one will know what we did, but at least it means he's still out there. Somewhere.

"What time we sitting down?" Travis asks stretching his back.

I pull out my phone. One missed call from Mads. Shit, I ignored it earlier. "Uh, now," I reply flustered. Is something wrong? My heart anxiously gallops as I press the button to call her back, only to hear a phone ringing up ahead. I step closer to the rings, seeing Mads and Mollie sat at the bar, Red serving them. Are they all talking? What have I missed? "Mads?" I call her name just as she's about to answer my call.

The angry lines on her forehead wrinkle even more when Travis steps closer behind me. She looks worried all of a sudden.

"Why the fuck is she still around?" Travis asks distastefully.

I don't look over my shoulder at him. I'm too busy concentrating on Mads who's waddling closer to me. Definitely waddling. Beautiful.

"Where have you been?" Her voice is raised, her eyes wide.

I can't help giving her a questioning look. "With Travis."

Her wild eyes look to him, then to me. I see her deflate a little.

"Babe, what's wrong?"

"Wrong?" Mads puts one hand on her hip, waiting for me to explain—I don't know the fuck what—and I widen my eyes, slightly thrown aback.

The main door opens. Beats, The Joker and a few others are

arriving for church.

I check my watch. I don't know what I've missed or what's going on, but I've got to get this done. Now. "Is the baby okay?" I check, because if something's wrong, Travis will have to take the lead. If not, whatever has my girl in a spin will have to wait.

"The baby's fine, Dean. Tell me where the fuck you've been."

Slightly baffled by her sudden tone, I take a step closer to her. Her voice is loud. I see a few heads turn our way. What happened whilst they were having coffee? "You knew where I was. With Travis." Her eyes begin darting between the two of us again. "Why are you acting crazy?"

"Crazy?" she shouts, repeating me.

I move, putting my hands on her arms, trying to still this rage that's apparently come from nowhere.

"If I'm acting crazy, it's because you're driving me that way." I roll my eyes. "Don't roll your eyes at me, I'm talking to you."

There it is. The outlaw in her. "I'll let that slide," I say, not sure how to handle this. My voice is stern. I'm deadly serious. My men are arriving, about to receive the shittiest fucking news I could deliver, yet I'm here, arguing with Mads, something we never do. Something we've only done in the past few days. And why's she here anyway?

"Or what?" she challenges.

I double take. Every muscle, every fibre of my body, tenses. I see Mollie shift, and Red turns, continuing with her work.

Travis pats me on the back, ignoring Mollie and everyone else as he heads upstairs for church.

Stepping forward, Mads doesn't move. Not one step back as I tower over her. Challenging. Taking her elbow, I tactfully take my time turning her, and move her somewhere quieter, out of earshot from everyone else.

I open the door to the bedroom, holding it open as Mads walks past me. She doesn't give me eye contact. As soon as the door's shut, she's in my face. My back hits the door, shocked.

"Where were you today? And don't lie to me!" Her finger is in my face making me feel like a schoolboy, as opposed to a fucking outlaw.

"Put your finger down."

"Talk."

I try to walk forward, but her feet are planted like cement. She knows I'm not pushing her. And she sure as shit isn't backing down from whatever fucking one she's on right now. "You talk. What the fuck happened over coffee?" I ask firmly.

She laughs. "I didn't go for coffee." I see her face turn redder. She's working herself up, her temper no good for her or the baby.

Calm. That's what I have to do. Keep her calm. Talk to her. *Tell her what's going on.*

Shit. Jack. He'll be heading here soon. I need Mads gone. Need her away from here. If she's going to find out about Jack, that needs to be at home. Just us and him. It broke her as much as it did me thinking he was dead. She sees him alive; she'll fly off the fucking handle.

Like now.

I reach in my pocket, pulling out my phone. I check the time of my missed call from her, noticing it was when we were stood with him. She didn't go for coffee. *No.* She wouldn't have. She couldn't already know. Could she?

"Where were you today?"

Her faces tightens, but she one hundred percent turns the anger in her veins down to a simmer as soon as I ask. "What?" she asks, and I see it. I see the moment she realises she's given herself up.

"You followed me?" My blood starts to boil.

She takes a step back. "No."

Oh, she's *not* stepping back now. There's no backing away from this, not until I know what the hell went on. She keeps moving her feet back, but I keep my front to hers, not allowing her the breathing space she's searching for.

"Why are you lying?"

"Why are you?" she counters quickly.

"I'm not, and I asked you first."

She frowns, squaring her shoulders.

"Mads? Did you follow me today?"

"No." She looks anywhere but my eyes. "Not exactly." She's backing down.

"Not exactly? Then what *exactly* did you do?"

The backs of her legs hit the corner of the bed. There's no way out now. "Dean," she says, her voice now devoid of any hostility or anger.

"Sit." I put my hands on her shoulders, guiding her arse to the bed. She lets out an over-the-top huff, but she's all out of challenge. I stand for a moment, waiting for her eyes to look up to me.

When they do, I kneel, my knees sinking into the carpet before her, her eyes staying on me the whole time. "Tell me what's going on," I say. I rest my hands on her legs, my insides still very much rife with fear that Mads may have seen Jack. And more to the point, she followed me thinking what? That I was doing something I shouldn't? *What if I was?* A harsh lump swells in my throat.

Mads sniffs, and I tighten my fingers on her legs. She's desperately trying to keep herself together, to show me how strong she is. I know just how strong this woman before me is. It's the reason I love her. The first night she stood up to me, it started the fire in my soul. It's what starts my heart beating so fast, I get high just by simply looking at her.

Placing my hands on her bump, I feel the baby wriggle. I look down, needing to make sure she focuses on this. Not me. Not her need to know everything. This. Our child. "Why did you follow me, Mads?"

Wiping her eye, Mads looks directly at me. She pales slightly, making my stomach drop.

"Why were you there?" I ask again.

She sighs, and the tears fall. My strong woman cries. Because she saw. I know it. Saw the fucking ghost I didn't even consider her finding out about until we were through the storm.

I wipe her cheeks then lean closer to her, kissing away her sadness one tear at a time. "Babe." I speak softly, hoping she talks. "Tell me."

She shrinks, her body sagging. "I overheard you. In the shop. You said you were going to a farm at eleven."

"How did you know which farm?" I ask calmly.

Her eyes shift to mine. "Mollie."

"Mollie?" I question.

Mads nods.

Of course Mollie knew about the farm. But how did she know? "You called her?"

Slowly nodding, Mads looks to her bump. It's as though she's thinking the same as me. She shouldn't be putting herself in any danger. "I called her when…" She doesn't finish her sentence.

"When what?"

Her top lip disappears under her teeth as a tear runs to her mouth. "When I thought you were going to hurt Travis." She drops her head, and I jerk away, totally confused.

My lips part, but I'm unsure why, because anything I thought I was going to say in response to her ridiculous claim, gets lost. "Travis? Babe, why the hell do you think I would hurt him?"

"You told me. When you came home drunk. You said you were going to betray him."

As if his ears are burning, a knock comes from the door. "Dean. We're at the table," Travis' low voice rumbles. He needs me.

I scrunch my face. I don't remember telling Mads I was going to betray him; at least not how she thinks, anyway. "I haven't told him I want out."

I feel her anguish. See the look of hope mixed with uncertainty take hold. Her relief turning to guilt, colliding with the notion of normality. *Our* normality. The thing we crave the most.

"I have to go." I stand tilting her chin to look at me. "We'll talk later."

I wait for her to smile. When she does, and her lips stretch, I relax a little.

My attempts to protect and keep her safe… she's going to challenge them if she suspects so much as a whiff of anything that might take me away from her again.

But that face. Those eyes of hers, so wide and transparent. My girl's living proof if I keep my face to her light, the demons will stay where they belong. In the shadows.

CHAPTER THIRTY-SIX

DEAN

I call Jack, but it goes straight to voicemail. I get his hesitation to want to come here, and I get even more why he doesn't want this opportunity to slip from our grasp. But we can't carry out this plan of his without every one of my men on board. We went into this new business with Costa together. We see it out together.

I message Vincent asking him to meet me and Travis later, then put my phone back in my pocket. Taking a deep breath, I push open the wooden door to church. I don't know why I feel so nervous. Probably because I know I want out.

My brothers look up. Their eyes watching and waiting for me to take my place at the head of the table.

Stepping in, I shut the door behind me, then take my seat.

Travis leans forward, slowly pushing the gavel across the table.

My fingers lift to pick it up as Beats bangs the table. He does it again and again until others start joining him.

I lift the wooden instrument as all hands thump the wood, excitement that I'm back taking over. Smiling at their show of brotherhood, I then slam the gavel down. Their drumming slows, and I look at each and every one of them. "I missed you shitheads too."

They laugh, and Travis pats me on the back.

This is our first sit down since I got out. Somehow, I have to find the strength to tell them what I got us into, and that I need them to help get us out. I suck in some air. "Feels good to be home," I say truthfully before continuing, "but I need to be straight with you."

All of them look my way.

"It's no coincidence I'm sat here. My trial didn't get dropped as you heard." A deathly silence descends like a thick fog. From seconds ago being so loud, not one of them now makes a noise. "It was Jack."

I see wondering eyes looking to one another. "Jack?" Dennis asks scrunching his face. "Ronnie's boy?" I nod. "Thought he passed?"

I drop my head, then reach into my pocket. "We all did."

"Ronnie knows?"

I shake my head slightly, pulling out and lighting a smoke. "The only men that know about Jack being alive are in this room. I know not all of you have met him personally, but we need to keep it that way. Ronnie can't know about Jack. Not yet."

"He'll want to know, Dean," Captain says.

Being an older member, he's familiar with my uncle from his earlier days at the club. "I know," I reply, "but we have to get down to some business that involves him. I need all of you to know, Rippers are in some serious shit."

Any joy they were feeling gets zapped out of the room upon my words.

I bring them up to speed with everything they need to know. From the contents of the shipments to the fact Rippers have been pulled in to stop it. Some want war; The Joker, Len and Skitz. Others want to do this quietly. All of us want this to end.

The task of being their leader never stopped being hard, even when I wasn't here. "We need a plan to find their haul before we move it. And we need to make one quick." I browse their faces, lighting yet another smoke as I do.

"Going to need more than just a plan. You'll have to call our supplier, up our personal order," Travis says.

I nod. "I'll call him. You reckon triple it?"

Travis agrees, dipping his chin.

"Riggs, all bills paid, fees collected?" I query. He nods. A triple order won't come cheap. "We'll meet with Vincent later, see if we can scope any way inside."

Travis nods as Captain laughs impassively, leaning around Beats to see me. "Inside. Like mission fucking impossible? We don't stand a chance trying to do what you're suggesting, Prez, especially if we're asking Saviours to join us."

Beats chews a toothpick, nodding his head. "Never going to happen," he says to himself in agreement.

Letting out a puff of smoke, I look to Captain who sips his beer. It's not my suggestion; to get inside. I would do what the guys achieved last time, intercept and lose the cargo. But Jack wants his man. And long term, do we really want this popping up again?

Mop runs a hand over his face. "We need a show of force, brother," he says, silencing the room.

I look up, seeing him resolute.

"We've gone into this whole fucking thing trying to maintain power and keep the peace. But by doing so, Rippers are slowly being pushed out." He sighs rubbing his head, not looking at anyone else around the table. I keep a straight face but see everyone else silently agreeing with him. "Costa walked in here, told us what to do, and like pussies we agreed. For you. For this club."

Our eyes meet, and I feel my body tense. Blame. Weakness. It shines bright in his eyes. I scratch my thumb along my bottom lip, sitting forward. My mind's screaming at me not to blow a fuse. "We voted it."

"I know, brother. But we voted to allow them to transport guns. Not this. Now things have changed."

The goal posts, as Mads put it, have shifted. I'm not stupid. "What are you proposing?"

"I'm proposing we find what we're looking for, then get rid of them all, not try to infiltrate them. We have, what, a week—if we're lucky, before the next shipment will be confirmed?"

Travis nods, knowing better than me how this operation ran last time.

"I say we just go find him and wipe him off the map."

Everyone stays quiet, waiting for me to talk. "War will destroy everyone. Stocking up our own supply makes sense, but trying to wipe everyone out? No good can come from that."

I take a sip of my beer, my brain shutting down, unable to see any way out. I pull at my jumper, feeling it tightening around my neck. *Not now.* Why the fuck does this keep happening to me? The last wall goes up in front of me, everything around me turns black.

Fuck. Fuck. Fuck. Air. I need air, desperately. I don't know myself anymore. Whatever the fuck this is, I'm going out of my mind.

I dart from my chair and make my way downstairs. Practically kicking the door open, I step outside, my eyes adjusting to the light as my vision shakes, doubling everything in front of me. Show me some mercy. "Please," I pray to no one, my hands resting on my knees as I bend over. My ship is sinking. My world burning down. The impossible has never seemed so impossible. My mind feels like an enemy. Leaving me choking, it's determined to make me suffer at every fucking bend.

"Dean?" I hear my name, but I don't look up. I keep my eyes shut. I can't see past the walls. How many times is this going to happen? My life, this *fucking* life. It's taken its toll. "Dean." I need relief. "Dean!" The voice shouts louder, making my eyes dart open.

Breathe. Breathe. Breathe.

Pulling my gaze from my feet, I look up. Legs is watching me, his face weary. Standing straight, he scans me all over. I realise I'm seconds away from panting like a dog, my back fully pushed against the wall, so to speak.

"Everything okay?"

Jesus Christ. *No*. "Yeah."

I'm not sure if he's buying my bullshit. "Thought you were at the table?"

My hands are shaking. "We were—we are," I correct myself, rubbing my eyes to clear my vision. I need to get home. Being there is the only place this doesn't happen. I need to sort myself out. This shit isn't fucking normal. "Be in in a sec," I tell him.

He nods, turns to the door, then pauses with it open. "Beer? Something stronger?"

This kid. Trying to make sure I'm alright. I don't really want either. "Something stronger." I step forward taking in some oxygen, my legs seeming to work. That's good.

"I'll bring it up," he says.

Dragging myself inside, I make my way back into the room.

Legs walks in a few minutes later, a whiskey in his hand. He places it on the table as I finish explaining to Len why we need the Saviours on board. "I know I allowed this to come to the table," I look up trying to gauge all their expressions, "but I never thought it would get us wrapped up in anything like this. I only wanted peace. For our club, for my family."

"We know, brother," Captain says, trying to reassure me.

"If we can find out where the next shipment is going from, then maybe we can intercept it, change it, I don't know. But we need to end it, and that won't come without risk."

"The risk is what makes it fun."

I look at Beats, giving him a half, knowing smile. "Let me talk to Vincent, get Jack to show him what he knows." If I'm lucky, this could be the start of peace between both clubs, not just here but across the other side of the world. Our charters find out we pulled this off together, peace could follow for everyone, even Ronnie. "Meet back here tomorrow morning." I nod at Travis then bang the gavel.

The men filter out, but Legs remains stood in place. Travis waits, seeing him hovering. "You good, Legs?" he asks.

Legs steps closer to me still sat in my seat. "What business are we shutting down?"

I look at Travis before moving my gaze back to his. He wasn't sat at the table. "The one with Costa."

"It's not what we thought," Travis adds, leaning against the door.

Legs moves to sit opposite me, and I watch him, wondering what appears to be troubling him. "The panic attack you had." I feel Travis' eyes boring into my head immediately. I refuse to look up. Panic attack? Why the fuck did Legs say that. "I used to suffer with them too."

I look at him, held hostage by the fact this kid was put through the mill before he found the club, but wanting to strangle him for exposing my recent shortcoming. "Legs, spit it out, whatever you're trying to say." Because I need to get the hell out of Travis' path.

"I'm guessing it has something to do with the transporting?"

I frown, leaning in. "How do you know?"

Travis steps closer.

"The crates they moved; Skitz was whinging about how heavy they were when he got back, right? Said he almost put his back out."

Travis huffs to himself. "That's right, he did whinge."

"Travis got shot, then with everything going on, us waiting for the next shipment, you not being here, it just didn't seem like the right time to bring it up…" Legs bites his nail, thinking.

"Go on," Travis tells him.

"It's probably nothing, but Skitz also mentioned a stamp on the boxes… Parkway Shipping, I think?" He waves his arm at Travis.

"Fuck, that's right. That was the company name."

"Well, the place I crash at, that's close to the Parkway site he mentioned. Had no reason to think much of it, but I figured if we need a way in, we could go there, see who's picking them up and where they're headed?"

The way Travis and I look at one another, you can tell he's thinking the same as me. We've been thrown a lifeline. A starting point. "That's fucking brilliant, Legs."

Travis looks at me. "We can track the delivery, find out where they'll load the next cargo. Good work, boy." Travis slaps his back.

"One of us can scope it out later," I say to Travis as Legs stands to leave the room.

"You won't get close." His words stop me. "Only the desperate hang around there. You show up, you'll raise suspicion."

I shake my head. "I'll figure it out." Because I know exactly what's coming next.

"I can go."

Of course. "No," I tell him.

He turns, his chest not puffing out how I imagined a young man's would when being told no. He's calm. "I can get close, put a tracker on the crates or something."

A tracker? "I said no."

He frowns but doesn't answer back before turning and leaving me and Travis.

We sit in silence before Travis lights a smoke. "Boy might be right on this one."

"No. We can't have a kid going into this."

"He's a kid to us because we're pushing forty."

I huff. "Speak for your-fucking-self."

"Boy wants to patch in. This could be his opportunity."

"Travis—"

"Panic attacks?" His deep-set eyes lift to mine.

I sigh then bow my head.

"You ever going to tell me about them?"

Fuck no. I don't even know that's what they are. "I'm fine."

He takes another drag from his smoke. "As always."

Letting out another breath, I pull out my phone and chuck it on the table. "We can't have Legs go into this."

"Why not?"

"*Why not?*" I counter. "Because he's too young."

Travis considers me for a moment. "How old were we when we patched in?"

I lean back in my chair. "That's different," I reply, knowing it isn't. Legs has no family. We're it for him.

"Why?"

"Because it fucking is."

Travis leans closer, rolling the tip of his cigarette around the rim of the ashtray. "It's the fucking same and you know it."

Rubbing the back of my neck, I feel my mood start to shift. Is this it? Do I tell Travis I want out? It's on the tip of my tongue, but I can't. I need him fully focused if we're to get out of this godforsaken mess. "He's not going in alone. Not a chance I'll allow that."

"I never said he'd go alone. But if what he's saying is true, he'll have to be the one to get close."

"Then what?"

Stubbing out his smoke, Travis rubs his face. "Then we take

the haul and wipe them out."

"That won't come without repercussions." Repercussions I can't afford to have.

"Provided Sodom Saviours are with us, we can find new business with them. Either that, or you leave the past well and truly behind you. Chat to Ronnie and call a complete seize fire. Lord knows he needs it, the way I hear things have been churning for him."

Ain't that the truth. I nod picking up my phone. "I'll up our order, have it secured before we meet Vincent."

Travis nods then leaves, closing the door behind him.

I hit call to our supplier.

"What?"

I hold the phone away from my ear as the woman's voice shouts down the phone.

"Where's Daniel?" I ask, also wondering why the hell our usual supplier isn't answering the phone. I hold it out in front of me, checking I have the right number. I do.

"Dead!... Dean?... Is that you?"

I let out a sigh. "Fuck. Yeah, Ray, it's me. I need your help."

"Where the fuck's Rocco?" she barks.

"Dead," I let her know, wishing he wasn't.

"Motherfucker!"

I don't beat around the bush. "I need to triple our order."

There's a pause. Even she knows we only ever order what we need for personal stock. "Is this gonna blow up in my face, Dean? I swear to Hades I will skin you alive!"

I laugh under my breath. "No. Always a pleasure, Ray, say hi to the chuckle brothers for me." Then I hang up, holding my phone to my top lip.

The pressure keeps mounting. The road so far has been nothing but twists and finding out some pretty hard truths.

Stopping Costa. Getting out. There's still work to be done.

CHAPTER THIRTY-SEVEN

MADISON

Having said goodbye to Mollie as we left the clubhouse, I decide to stop in at work. My desire to know what's going on with Dean may have increased tenfold, but seeing his reaction to us following him... I don't want that again.

The view from Mollie's car wasn't great, but she was right about the farm. A field full of pigs, a few tractors sat in an open barn; the place was pretty quiet until Travis and Dean showed up, followed by a truck. A truck so similar to Jack's back in Australia, the sight of it put me in a spin.

For the briefest of moments, I could have sworn it was him. But it couldn't have been.

I must be losing my mind.

Grabbing the painkillers from my top drawer, I feel Vivian watching me like a hawk. "Problem?" I ask, closing the drawer and turning to her.

"No problem. Just, kids aren't in school for another week, and we could have caught up over the phone, so I'm wondering why you're really here?"

"Um," I stall, picking up a file from my desk. "Needed to get everything together before I go on leave." I shake it in the air.

Vivian pouts. "You have a little over a month before you go on maternity leave. Don't give me that crap, Madison."

I snap my eyes to hers. I actually don't have a reason for coming in, other than to give myself something to do. "You can be so rude sometimes."

"I know," she laughs deviously. "Everything okay with Lauren? Is it Dean?"

"What?" I rub between my eyes. "Uh, yeah, Lauren's absolutely fine. Things are going well at home and at school. It's her birthday soon."

"She doing anything for it?"

I'm not sure. It's crossed my mind a few times to bring it up with Lauren, to see what she wants to do. But she'll be turning sixteen, free to do what she wants. She might not want to stay with us anymore. She might want to leave and search for her brother, and what sort of position will I be in to stop her?

"Mads?" Vivian asks upon my silence.

"I guess she'll see some of her friends, I don't know."

"So it's Dean?"

It's *always* Dean. I fear if I share what's going on, it'll only open up questions I simply don't have the answers to. She's going to find out eventually, but, "It's hard, that's all."

She gives me a sympathetic smile. "I bet, love. But you won't be alone, okay? You've got all of us."

"Thank you." I smile, waving her off as she leaves. I check my emails, make sure nothing more requires my attention, then I head out.

Arriving home, I close the door, kicking off my shoes. My phone pings a message from Jess confirming our plans for going to see Dad and Bex. I really should call her before we travel tomorrow after my scan. I have no reason to feel pissed off with her. Everything she said was true; something clearly isn't right with this entire situation. Dean being home. His shutting me out.

I wipe my face, mentally drained, and decide on a shower. There's no ignoring the more frequent headaches I'm getting, or the fact my body seems to be swelling at a rate of knots. I know at the check up tomorrow they're going to tell me to take it easy. I can only laugh at how stupid that sounds. *Take it easy.* Like that's the easiest thing to do considering who I'm in love with.

Towel drying my hair, I look for a pair of Dean's joggers I've not seen for ages. I open the wardrobe spying the bag he packed for me when I was to leave to stay with Bex, at the top. I reach up, curious, then pull it down letting it drop to the bed. That seems so long ago now. I can't believe I've left it so long to sort.

Actually, I can.

I unzip it, finding what I was looking for. There are enough clothes to have been away for a week. I pull out the joggers, chucking them and everything else in the washing basket when a rattle of something at the bottom, catches my attention.

Pushing aside the clothes, I find a key with a skull and crossbones keyring. *Lauren's* key. So he *did* take it from her bag all those weeks ago.

I hear the front door open, hoping it's him. Within seconds, I know it is. I hear him move my shoes to one side, then hang up his leather. It makes me smile. "Mads?" he calls.

"Up here."

He makes his way up, stopping at the door. His eyes slip down my body, the towel still wrapped around me.

"Are you okay?" I wasn't expecting him home so soon.

He pushes off the frame, slowly stepping towards me. My soul takes flight when he invades my space, his chest expanding as he looks down at me. "I am now." Leaning down to kiss me, I smell the smoky stench, trying hard to ignore it as my head twists, our kiss deepening.

"Dean," I breathe. He hums, not wanting to stop. "Brush your teeth."

He smiles. "You're getting bossier." Tapping the tip of his nose against mine, he steps back and heads to the bathroom.

I use the time he's out of the room to quickly change, not wanting him to get distracted. After earlier, we need to talk.

When he comes back in, his forehead wrinkles.

"Come sit."

Disapproval gleams in his eyes that I'm no longer easily accessible, but he moves, sitting on the bed.

I take a seat next to him, relishing the relief in my ankles. "I'm going to stay with Bex after my scan tomorrow. I'll be back on Sunday." Dean tilts his head, looking at me, but I don't look at him. "Remember when I asked you to come back to me, and you promised *never* to leave me again?"

He places a hand on my leg, holding me above the knee.

"It's been three days and I already feel like I'm losing you."

"Mads," he tries to stop me.

"Please, let me finish." His hand momentarily tightens, then relaxes. "I need you to know, that loving you is the easiest thing I've ever done." Liquid pools in my eyes and my throat turns thick.

Dean leans to me, lightly kissing my shoulder.

I look to him as he moves back, our eyes and souls connecting. "I will always choose you because you will always be my VP. But whatever you think you're protecting me from, you're only making my determination to find out more, worse."

He sighs, dejected. "I know. I'm making this so much worse for everyone."

"Call me selfish, but I don't care about *everyone*. I only care about *you* being with us."

Fretful eyes jump between mine and my bump. "My family comes first, you know that."

"I do. But sometimes, you have to put yourself first *for* your family."

Dean lifts his arm, and I nestle my head against his chest, wrapping my arm around his front. "I just want to see you free,"

I whisper. "From your demons. The pain. All of it. I want to make you happy. To make you feel so loved, you never doubt yourself ever again."

"Babe." I hold him tighter as he strokes his hand up and down my spine. His chest rises as he takes in a breath. "This shit with the club, I need to put an end to it. Once it's done, we're free."

I look up, still in his arms. Taking him in, I see the conflict in his eyes. "Why do you need to end it?"

He sighs. "We didn't know what we were getting into," he locks eyes with me, "but I *will* get us out of it. Once that's done, you and me, babe... we go."

I sniff back my tears. "What's the business?"

He shakes his head. "You'll have to trust that I'll tell you when I can."

Trust. I've been holding this in. "I *do* trust you, Dean. But you need to get this done before the baby gets here. If that means I need to step back to let you finish this, then that's what I'll do."

"Step back? Babe, you can't leave now," his voice raises in panic.

"I'm not *leaving*. I just... I need to let you breathe." I feel him tense. "With me around, you'll do everything you can to protect me, when what you need to do is get business done. And I need to think about me." I drop my head, my mouth turning dry with what I'm about to say. "I thought I saw Jack today. That's how crazy I'm making myself."

Dean sighs, rubbing his eyes.

"I'm sorry, I should never have followed you."

He turns, and I sit up when his strong hands cup my face. "No, I'm sorry. Tell me what you want, Mads. How can I make this better?"

I place my hand on his chest. "When everybody else needs you, I want you to choose yourself."

His face pulls tight, his eyes darting between mine.

A few moments of silence then pass. Dropping my face, I push myself closer to him, my hands holding his leather tightly.

As if trying to keep his emotions in check, he runs his fingers over his eyes, pinching the bridge of his nose. "I wish it was that simple."

"I know. But, perhaps if I put myself first, you'll see it can be done." He searches my face when I look up to him. "The last thing I want to do is leave your side, but we have more to think about now."

He squeezes me into him, splaying a hand on my bump, making me sit back. "That's all I've ever wanted, for you to put yourself first." Dean pushes his lips to my head. "Although now that you are, I think I prefer you challenging me."

He chuckles as I laugh. "I love challenging you. But this is me thinking about you. About us."

He smiles, giving me a wink. "Strongest woman I know."

I push my lips to his, sitting up straighter, making him kiss me deeper.

He holds my face tight, his thumb stroking my cheek.

"And you'll do it? Get what you need done so we can be free?" My lips brush against his as I ask.

"Have I ever let you down, babe?" His breath is hot against my face. I can feel his need—his desire to love me taking over. He holds me close to him, turning my head, lowering me to the bed as his gaze cruises over my face.

"Never."

We lay still. Both quiet until his phone rings from his pocket halfway down his legs. I laugh watching him trying to find it. "Yeah," he answers, still laid on his back. He then bolts upright, looking down to me. "Okay, I'll be there. Give me half an hour."

I refuse to sit, bending an arm underneath my head as I watch him arrange his clothes.

"Travis," he says.

I smile because I didn't ask. He pauses, the realisation catching up. I can't help but laugh at him. "Do you know about him and Mollie?" I ask out of nowhere.

He frowns, probably thinking the same. "What about them?"

I feel my nerves fray. This isn't my news to tell, but I wonder if Dean knows. "I think they have a son."

His eyes widen before he closes them shut. "A son?"

I nod at his question.

Dean looks like he's seen a ghost. "Does Travis know?"

I shake my head. "I saw a photo at Mollie's place. The little boy looked just like Travis. She didn't confirm it, but it was clear she was in pain. She said she wasn't ready to talk about it."

He rubs his face deep in thought, his hand stroking his beard. Like a history they once all shared finally makes sense. "She asked me to help her with something when this is all done."

"You think it's to do with this?"

"Has to be. Fuck." He lets out a breath, sitting back on the bed. "Explains why she came back, but I don't get the timing."

My face drops. "Her husband died at Christmas. She doesn't have anyone else."

He closes his eyes. "She came home," he whispers as he slowly stands. "Keep this between us."

I nod, but silence stills us for a few moments. "What did Travis want?" I ask, bringing Dean's attention to me.

His jaw stops ticking, his frustration ebbing away. "Got to meet back at the clubhouse. Then meet the Saviours later."

I sit up. "Will Billy be there?"

"Yeah. Why?"

"He can't know Lauren's staying here. If he finds out, he could have her taken. He came close once, Dean. I don't want him knowing."

He nods his head in thought. "It's her birthday soon." I don't see what that has to do with it. Dean must see my confusion. “I’ll sort it.”

“Meaning?” I ask, my face tight.

“Meaning, I’ll sort it.” With that, he kisses my head and starts towards the door, double taking, looking back to the bed. I follow his gaze. “You found it then?” He walks forward, picking up Lauren’s key, a guilty but somewhat satisfied expression on his face.

“You’re a bad man, Mr Carter,” I tease.

With a smile he leans over me again. “No, babe, just *your* bad man.”

CHAPTER THIRTY-EIGHT

DEAN

I arrive at the clubhouse and make my way to Travis by the bar.

"Where'd you go?" he asks briskly.

I eye him. "Where'd you think?" I check my messages seeing Vincent confirming to meet later at their clubhouse.

"You tell her about Jack?"

I give him a look, letting him know to leave it.

With a sigh, he then takes a sip of his beer. "Legs wants to go check these crates now."

Looking at my watch, every part of my mind is screaming at me to hurry and get this done. We don't know when the next shipment will be confirmed. What I do know is that Mads being away tomorrow until Sunday, gives me the perfect opportunity to have this squashed with her safe. "Okay. Where is he?"

Usually behind the bar, I look for him, but see no signs he's around. "He went to collect what he needs. Trackers, shit like that."

"Right." Fucking kids and technology. This better work.

Twenty minutes later, Legs arrives at the clubhouse, and the three of us set off in a work van towards the site. Leaving his cut behind, Travis and I run through with Legs what he has to do. "You think you can place a tracker on one of them without being caught?"

"One? I have hundreds of them." He pulls out a bag filled with tiny chips no bigger than a fingernail. "I'll get these on as many as I can, then if they go different places, we can track them all. These are all wired to my phone."

Travis and I exchange a look as he parks the van out of sight from the main depo. The large facility has six-foot iron gates all around it, barbed wire curled around the top. I don't like the idea of Legs doing this. "Maybe I should go." Anyone sees me, I have a better chance of jumping that fence than Legs does.

"You know how to activate the trackers once they're in place?"

I turn in my seat, silent. *Fuck.* "Don't get caught. You even suspect someone's made you, I want you back here or you call."

I see him smile like a smartarse before he quietly opens the door and walks towards the site.

"This is where he crashes?" Travis asks looking out his window.

"That's what he said."

We see an older man stagger on his feet along the pavement. He's clearly drunk, ambling along to no place in particular. "Not very homely."

I swing my head looking out the windows. There's nothing here except a few buildings and different business facilities. I can't see any signs of somewhere you could stay.

Sitting back, disheartened, I look at my phone. My heart starts its usual staggering rhythm and I will it not to bury me in panic. *Not now*. Come on kid, hurry up. I check my phone again. Nothing. Fuck.

"You're making my skin itch. Stop."

"Fuck off." I want to jump out the van and see what he's doing for myself. "We don't have eyes on him."

"Your stress is fucking bouncing around the van. You're

making *me* nervous." I shouldn't have let Legs go in alone. One hundred trackers all needing activating. Boy's in way over his head. We all are. "Look."

My head darts to where Travis points.

"There he is." We watch Legs stalk around a dozen crates, stopping at each one in turn. "Now calm yourself before you give yourself a heart attack."

"I'm already having a heart attack."

He sighs. "What the fuck are you going to be like when your kid gets here?"

I scowl. I'll be murderous. On edge twenty-four seven. Happy. Sad. Verging on a breakdown. Fucking *all* of it.

A loud bang has us jolt in our seats. We look up, spotting two men pulling open the gates to the site. "Should we go?" I ask.

"No, Miss Daisy. We stay fucking put."

I punch his arm. Prick doesn't even flinch. "There!" I bark, looking out the front window, my prayers answered.

Legs ducks behind the back of the vehicle piled high with crates. He keeps his head low, out of sight.

"What's he doing?" Travis' voice has raised.

Legs looks at the crates, then to our direction, then back to the crates, sizing them up.

"Don't fucking do it," Travis grates reading Legs' mind.

I hold my breath as the men climb in the lorry, shutting their doors. We look back to Legs. He's gone. "Shit."

My hand reaches for the handle but Travis pulls me back. "We'll follow it." We watch the lorry pull out, and he starts the engine. "I'm not patching him in. If he fucks this, he's out."

"Out? He'll be fucking dead."

We wait until the lorry leaves, rounding a bend, then slowly pull away after it. We take the turn but are immediately thrown forwards when Travis slams the brakes, coming head on with another lorry pulling in. "Cunt!" he shouts, slamming his hand against the wheel.

"Move the fuck out the way!" I hold out my hand to the driver.

He beeps his horn, shouting at us. A few people appear from nowhere, watching the commotion as the driver sounds the horn again.

"Go back before this prick draws attention to us."

Travis grumbles putting the van into reverse, quickly moving us out of the way.

The driver of the lorry moves forward, shaking his head at us.

We go to move, but fuck me, we're jolted again as lorry after lorry file in after the first.

"What the fuck is this?"

"Get us out of here," I rush, urging Travis to go back the way we came in. Blood surges around my body, my fist clenching tight. "What the fuck was he thinking? I told you I should have gone in!" I'm going to kill him. If he doesn't show up dead first, I'm going to rip his head clean off.

Connected to Bluetooth, my phone starts ringing through the van's speakers. My teeth grind against each other, my mind reeling on how we're to find Legs. "Jack," I answer.

"Deano? What's wrong?"

How can he tell so fast? "Prospect doesn't want to patch in, that's what."

Travis flings the van onto the main road, pressing the accelerator to the floor.

I continue, "Kid knew where the crates were leaving from. We got him close to attach trackers, but he's fucking gone. Jumped on the back of the lorry carrying them."

Jack's harsh breath doesn't go unheard. "And what the fuck does he think he's going to do on his own?"

I scrunch my eyes, pissed off. "He thinks he can help get

inside information, which, correct me if I'm wrong, is exactly what you fucking wanted."

There's a pause. "Where is he now?"

"If I fucking knew that, we wouldn't be having this conversation, would we?"

Travis speeds trying to join the traffic heading in the direction of the lorry.

"We're trying to find the vehicle now."

"Fucking, Christ!" Travis yells. We hit standstill traffic, no sign of the lorry up ahead.

"What is it?" Jack asks.

I grunt sending my fist into the glove box. "Meet at us the clubhouse—"

"I—"

"—I don't want to hear it, Jack. We need everyone there, including you." I'm not having the blood of a kid on my hands. "We need to find him."

I hang up, flexing my wrist as white-hot pain emanates through the bone. "I'll call Vincent, tell him to meet at the clubhouse. This has all got to happen right now."

When we make it back over an hour later, tempers are high. Saviours arrive at the same time as us, the look on their faces is pure confusion. Vincent approaches me. "Why did you change the location of our meet?" He assumes a set up? An ambush?

"Had no choice," I throw at him, making my way inside.

Seeing the Sodom Saviours walk in lifts a few of my men from their chairs.

"Table. Now."

They all file up upon my order, their eyes lingering on each other as they pass by.

"Care to explain before we sit down?"

I turn to Vincent, throwing Legs' cut on the table as Billy brushes past me. He'll regret that. "Need to end our business," I say to Vincent, managing to keep calm.

Vincent's eyes retrace their path to mine. He's sees I'm serious, then pulls out his gun, aiming it at my head. We haven't got time for this.

"Not sure what you think you're going to do with that. Especially in here." He can't shoot. He also doesn't have the balls to take me out like that.

Travis pushes closer, both sets of men dangerously standing off with each other.

"This deal is not yours to end." Vincent's teeth grind. I see rage grip him.

"This *deal* you brought to us, it's nothing like you thought. Saviours and Rippers are soon to be on federal radar. We need to bring it to its knees before both clubs go down."

The gun still raised, jolts forwards. "We need the money."

"No, you want the power. They're two very different things. It has to stop, and only we can do that."

"What is *it* exactly?"

Right on cue, Jack appears in my line of vision. All eyes turn to him. "Drop your gun," he tells Vincent. The look on his face is malicious. Overpowering hatred swells inside him. He despises The Sodom Saviours. Has watched us fight them for decades. Almost died because of them. *Did* die, because of them.

Vincent lowers his weapon allowing everyone to breathe.

"*It,* is the end of Sodom Saviours if you don't agree to destroy Costa and his set up."

Looking at Jack, his temples twitch at a maddening rate. "Before you explain what's going on, I have a man missing. We need to get him back first," I tell him.

"Don't expect us to help," Vincent butts in.

My lips pinch. "He's helping our fucking cause." Provided he's in one piece and not hurt. Why the fuck did he jump on the back of that lorry?

"The cause we don't know a thing about?" Vincent scoffs. "This is fucking typical—"

"The only thing that's fuckin' typical, is that at the centre of every bit of trouble Rippers have had, your fuckin' club was always there." Jack's losing control. His face flashes red, his eyes narrowing.

"It's not like they didn't deserve it."

Jack's final straw snaps. He snarls, crashing into him, sending Vincent flying.

I move to intercept him, but I'm thrown back, my spine crashing against the bar.

Travis picks up one Saviour coming toward him, throwing him like Hulk across the tables and chairs.

Fists are flying, all of us pummelling whoever the fuck we can get our hands on. Crazed. Over the top. Violent.

I look up when someone calls my name. "Motherfucker." I whistle, drawing the attention of all the men towards the man —no, *boy,* standing watching us like we're the crazy ones. "I'm going to kill you!" I make a grab for Legs, but he jumps out of my way.

"I'm sorry!" He takes a wise step back.

"You fucking will be," I shout. "Why'd you take off?"

"I heard them talking about where they were going. Figured I'd just go see for myself."

He shrugs his shoulders, and I swallow my anger. "That was the whole point of the trackers." Breathing heavy, I turn to Travis. "Take it off him."

Travis steps forward, grabbling with Legs' cut that he must have picked up off the table when he walked in.

"Wait! Wait! Okay! Look!" Travis holds him by the scruff as he begs for us to listen. "Just look at my phone!" With a push forward, Legs dives into his pocket, pulling out his phone, turning the screen towards us. "I found them, okay?" He speaks laboured breaths, but his voice is calm. "I found some of them. Women, men. A kid."

My frightful eyes hone in on the screen. "Where was this?"

Jack steps forward, lowering his face to the screen. I hear him take in a sharp breath of air. "Fuck," he says barely audible.

I look at him, then to the phone. My eyes drag back to his. "Is that him?"

Jack nods, his eyes wide.

My stomach flips, and I look back at the screen in his hand, my heart racing. The image isn't clear, but I notice the man's wearing glasses. "We've got him."

Vincent swipes under his bleeding nose as Legs continues. "The lorry went to an old airfield by the river."

Jack swallows, steeling his composure as he pulls out his phone, opening up one of the apps. He zooms in. "Explains why bodies keep showing up on the beach. River runs for one mile before hitting the sea." He looks at me. "What else?" he asks quietly, turning to Legs.

"Each person had a tag assigned to them. Keep going." He signals for me to keep swiping through the photos. "There was Rohypnol as well. Guessing for when they move them?"

"And this?"

"That's the form." He steps closer. "It had all their names on it. I overheard a few men talking. Two days time, they get auctioned on the web, then they get moved."

"Which is when we'll get informed of the shipment, I guess," Travis adds, piecing things together. "How the fuck did you find out all of this?" Travis snatches the phone, looking for himself.

Vincent finally speaks up. "What does he mean, auctioned? People?"

"It's the dark fucking web," Jack snaps. "You're in organ trafficking now. Happy?" He cocks a brow, and Vincent's face drops like lead.

"You knew?" Vincent asks me.

I look to Jack. "Only once I got out."

Vincent's eyes follow mine. "That was you?" he asks Jack.

Jack rolls his shoulders, giving him a nod.

"Guessing it was also you who offed The Saint?"

Stunned, my eyes meet Jack's once more.

Vincent wouldn't make the link between Jack and the threats. But The Saint? Jack had him killed? "He got what he deserved," he answers sternly, keeping his eyes on mine.

"Hmm. Was only a matter of time, I guess. He always did take it too far. So, now what?" Vincent asks.

"Now?" Jack puts his phone away then rubs at his shoulder. "I'll go inside, get my name on that form."

I give him a bitter laugh. "You're built like a brick shit house. These people come from poverty." My heart kicks. A lingering sadness gathers. "I'll go." What choice do I have? I'm only a bit smaller than Jack, but this is my club. These are my men. I can't expect them to do anything I wouldn't.

Travis scratches his beard, biting back his need to kill me. I can see it in his eyes. "Motherfucker." He stands. "I'll go. Poverty or not, I'll carry every damn one of those people out of there."

Sadness swallows me, a gaping hole drawing me in. He can't go. "No. I'll do it," I tell them again.

"You have a fucking family waiting for you, dickhead." Travis turns, striding away. I feel my panic rising like a tidal wave.

I catch up to him, yanking his arm, pulling his back to me. I'm unable to stop the words from pushing past my lips. "So do you," I say quietly so only he can hear.

Travis freezes. Silence. I'm a dickhead. A *selfish* dickhead. "She isn't my family." He turns as he speaks.

"No, but her son might be."

Drunk on rage, he grabs for my cut, pulling me into him.

"What the fuck are you talking about?" he spits.

"She has a *son*, Travis. Looks just like you." I swear I see tears cloud his vision as I whisper his truth.

"That's not possible." He shoves me back, turning again, this time making it to the door.

"It's too late!" Legs shouts halting Travis. All heads turn to Legs. "I already put my name down."

What the actual fuck? "Kid, I swear to God..."

"No point arguing, Prez. I fit the bill. My name's on that list."

"They'll know you're a Ripper."

He shakes his head. "I never went on that run, and I was watching Mads when Costa came here. He and his men never saw me."

"Fuck," Travis sighs before taking heavy steps towards Legs. He jabs his finger into Legs' chest. "No fucking way you're patching in now." He then makes his way up the stairs, the weight of what I just told him, suffocating.

"Two days, I need to be on the dark web. I have a friend who can help me. She's good with this stuff."

She?

"She can hack the system and you can follow me."

I sigh, so completely lost in the storm. "We need to get everyone to the table. Work this out properly. You," I look at Legs, "don't give me another reason to kill you."

Sheepishly, he nods and begins following the guys as the door opens.

Red and Talia arrive to start their shift.

I bump into the back of Jack stood motionless; his eyes fixed on the Red devil stood by the door. I look between them.

She definitely blushes, then dips her head, shy.

Oh, no fucking way that's happening. I push him, making him miss a step and knock into Legs.

"What's this?" Red shouts, making Jack turn way too

enthusiastically back to look at whatever she's holding.

"That's mine." Legs takes two stairs at a time down to her.

Every bone in my body shakes. My insides flip. Hot heat swims from my toes to the back of my neck. I pat down my pockets. Lauren's key, no longer there. "What do you mean that's yours?"

He runs back to the bottom of the stairs. "My key. Been missing since..." He looks up, seeing his life flash before his eyes.

CHAPTER THIRTY-NINE

MADISON

"And you'll call me when you get there?" Dean's hands knead my bum, working their way up my back.

With my arms around his neck, I stand on my tiptoes, my lips pushing to his. "Yes. And you'll have your phone if Lauren needs you?"

"Yes. She's with friends until Friday, then she'll be back." Another squeeze.

"That's right." I kiss him.

"Come on," Jess shouts from her car.

"Don't miss me too much," I tell him.

He cups my face, my feet falling to the ground. "I'll only miss you when I'm breathing."

He studies me, and I get the horrid feeling he's memorising every inch of me. Worry flashes across his face, the line on his forehead, telling. "Dean." His eyes wander to mine. "Everything, okay?"

"Yeah," he sighs, his body tightening.

"I trust you, VP."

He pulls me closer, cradling my head to his chest. I feel him relax a little as Jess beeps the car horn. He kisses my head. "I'll see you soon."

"Be safe." When I look in his eyes, my heart suddenly stammers. It's like he knows danger's waiting for him. My bottom lip wobbles when I see the first night he helped me to my feet. The way he dragged his eyes over me. How I lost my breath when he lifted me onto his bike. I smile, but it fades. "Promise me," I quickly add.

"You have my word." He walks me to the car, then opens the door for me to climb in. "We're almost there."

"I love you." I smile.

He closes the door, and both Jess and I watch him walk away. "Everything go okay in there?"

Putting my seatbelt on, Jess starts the engine. "Usual. I've got to take it easy. Baby hasn't grown much in the last two weeks. I have to go back on Monday."

Jess places her hand on my knee. "It'll be okay."

I squeeze her hand before she places it back on the wheel. "I know."

What I don't know is whether Dean's worried for me, or for what he's got going on with the club. I shake my head. Who am I kidding. He'll be worrying about everything.

Not acknowledging the fact my heart already aches to be near him, I turn to Jess in my seat. "How's Max?"

"Better," Jess says. "He's going to change his job, maybe take some more time off before he decides what he's going to do."

"That's good."

Jess humphs. "Yeah. Would be better if he could hurry up and decide though. I feel like I've been a single parent for the past few months."

I look out the front window before I look back at Jess. "Maybe once we get back, you two should get away for a bit? Just the two of you. I'll watch Axl."

She smiles. "You'd do that?"

"Of course. Makes sense to get away before the baby comes

and I have no free time."

Jess laughs. "Zero free time. You can kiss goodbye to tight skin and bladder control as well."

"Sounds—"

"—then of course, there's the leaky boobs, hair loss, crying for no reason. Weight gain. Low sex drive." Her dropped face says it all as she looks at me. "Sorry."

I laugh. "I hadn't thought about all the other stuff to be honest." My minds drifts.

"You'll be fine." Jess smiles a little. "It's worth it. All the shit we as mums have to endure, it's all worth it."

Sitting forward, I turn on the radio. 4 Non-Blondes *What's Up*, plays through the speakers.

"Dad used to love this song." Jess sings, turning it up.

"I remember."

Thinking wistfully to myself, Jess nudges my arm after the song finishes. "You nervous about seeing him?"

Nervous? "No," I tell her truthfully. Nothing will change for us. Regardless of paternity, I know nothing different. My childhood memories don't involve Rocco. They involve the man who tucked me in at night. The man who read to me. Took me to after school club, taught me how to ride my bike and play catch. I can't wait to see him.

We arrive at Dad's later that afternoon. Forever and a day seems to have passed since we last saw him. Nothing inside his house has changed. Bar a fresh lick of paint, the halls are still graced with family photos and memorabilia from his days playing cricket.

As he places some nibbles on the table, he sits himself down, wiping his nose with his hanky. His faced has aged. His hair greyer than I remember. "It's good to see you girls," he says with a snivel.

"Dad." Jess stands, wrapping her arms around him. "Why

are you getting emotional you big softy?"

He swipes his eye as Jess rubs at his back. "I'm not," he lies, shoving his hanky back in his pocket. "It's just been so long since I saw you. You both look," his eyes flit between the two of us, "you both look so grown up."

"You do too, Dad," I say pointing at my hair as I widen my eyes towards his greys.

"You cheeky..." We laugh, and I shuffle myself from the sofa, making my way to him for a hug.

I give Jess a nod. "I love you," I tell him, squeezing my arm around him.

He squeezes me tighter. "You don't know how much it means to hear you say that."

I lean back so I can see his face. "Actually, I think I do."

His lips roll, stopping himself from crying. He then coughs, steeling his spine. "Nothing's changed, has it? Because, I spent every day loving you like you were my own."

The elephant in the room is addressed, and I appreciate him not beating around the bush. "*Nothing* has changed." I sit on a chair close to where he sits.

I want to ask him so many questions about my childhood. About how he raised me knowing I wasn't really his. But considering everything I've come to learn from Mum about Rocco, it's clear what the underlying factor is here. "It says a lot about someone, to be able to love and raise someone else's child as their own."

He smiles. "It was easy." He lifts a thumb over his shoulder towards Jess. "She was the pain in the arse."

We break out in laughter, the mood lightening somewhat. Jess moves to sit down, scooping up a handful of crisps before she does.

"The hardest part," my eyes dart to his, "was hearing you were moving up north. It wasn't giving you your name, or having to watch you grow up looking nothing like me. It was feeling like I lost you."

My eyes mist, tears clogging my vision. Sadness swells in my throat. That must have been so hard for him. All alone down here. "My name?" I ask him.

Dad sighs. He lifts his drink, taking a sip before he places it back on the table. "Your mum. She was hell-bent on calling you Rose. I just knew... could tell why she wanted that so bad. We fought, but eventually we compromised. I chose Madison, but Rocco, he chose the name Rose."

My tears fall. I rest my elbow on the table, holding my head in my hand.

Jess places her hand on Dad's shoulder.

The overriding emotion coursing through me is one of sheer sadness and heartache. I feel pain for my mum; losing the man she truly loved. I feel pain for my dad; raising a child that wasn't his. And I feel pain for Rocco; for giving up what he loved to keep them safe. "If he hadn't left, then I wouldn't have had you as my dad. I wouldn't have Jess. Who knows where I'd be or what I'd be doing."

Jess smiles, and I look up to her, wondering what on earth is making her grin like she is. I see her eyes fill. "You were always going to meet Dean." She says it more to herself than to anyone else.

I look at her, my eyes squinting.

She shakes herself out of thought. "Don't you see? You were destined to meet him. Whether you grew up there, or down here with us. Either way, you would *always* have met him."

My heart bursts. Like stars exploding in my veins, Jess' words send a surge of happiness to flood my soul.

"Jesus, she's right." Dad leans forward as I struggle to keep my emotions in check. I smile, my cheeks burning as he wipes away one of my tears. "Guess nothing changed. You got the ending you deserved."

I sniff, wiping my face. "Almost." Once the baby's here and Dean's out of the club, then we get our ending. We're so close to the finish line.

"You need to tell me all about him."

"He's fucking gorgeous," Jess butts in, again lost in her own thought.

I look at her bewildered as my dad slowly cranes his head.

"What? No harm in saying the truth."

I laugh at her. "He'll be your brother-in-law one day."

"Only by half," she says with a wink and a grin spreading wide.

"Marriage? You want to marry this man?" Dad asks looking back at me.

Not want. Will.

I already said yes.

CHAPTER FORTY

DEAN

I'm the president. When it comes down to it, I have to take responsibility. For the club. Lauren. Legs. Mads.

Me.

Grabbing a shower before I head out, I let my head hang, the hot water massaging the back of my neck. Fuck, I already miss her. Four days is nothing compared to the time we were apart, but she's been gone two hours and I already want to call. Like the night sky without the stars, I'm empty without her.

Taking her to the scan, I've never felt more needed. More loved. More in the place I know I'm meant to be. The baby never stopped moving. Little wriggler's on the small side, but she certainly doesn't lack strength. Like her mum. It's yet to be confirmed, but *she* will be my saving grace.

I could look in my wallet and see it for myself, but something inside me tells me not yet.

I turn off the water, watching the last remaining drops fall off my face. What lays ahead is not going to be easy. Everyone has to play their part. One wrong move, one fuck up… then I don't get what I want.

We won't stop Costa.

This shit won't ever end.

Grim as it may be, I am not prepared to let my future slip

away again. Last time was too close a call.

I run through the plan one last time. It only works if I can confirm the final piece, getting Travis' uncle on board. They haven't spoken properly in years after things turned sour. He may be family and helped us before, but he'll need some reassurances we won't destroy his livelihood if he's to agree.

Stepping out the shower, I dry off and change. Legs is going to hate every part of this day. Stupid kid may *fit the bill,* but Lauren's key? I couldn't talk to him. Ignored the little prick until the fire dancing in my head was tamed.

Fucking, Lauren. She was staying with Legs before I stole her key? *His* key. The thought makes me want to rage. If Mads were here she'd know how to handle this. I'm too out of my depth. Too old to be worrying about teenagers.

Mads can't find out about Legs' friendship with Lauren. Not a chance. Nor can she *ever* know that I'm going to have to ask Lauren for help. Legs is already walking a fine fucking tightrope. He so much as breathes too loud near me today; I might kill him.

After getting Mick to agree to loan us a truck and his barn, I meet Travis at the clubhouse. He's quiet. Hasn't spoken a word to me since I arrived. My visiting his uncle and telling him about Mollie's son has clearly brought up the past for him.

He downs his drink, places the glass on the bar, then turns back to the laptop he's working at.

"You want to talk about it?" I ask.

He turns, and I lift an eyebrow. He bangs his fingers on the keyboard, eventually looking from me to the screen. "What time is she getting here?"

I take a sip of my coffee. So, he doesn't want to talk about his uncle. "Any minute now."

"And Legs?"

"He's busy."

Travis eyes me curiously but doesn't question it. His phone

pings, and he pulls it from his pocket, reading the screen. "Shipment's confirmed. Tomorrow, midnight."

"Location?" I ask.

"Legs was right," Travis starts. "Pick up's at an airfield further north. Then we drop off same place as last time."

I quickly shake away the desire to drive to Costa and put a bullet in his brain, end all of this now. Once those people have been auctioned tomorrow, it's our job to get them out of there before we're expected to ship them across the country.

"I can't fucking find a thing." Travis slams the laptop shut.

Fuck. I was hoping he'd be able to access the dark web before we needed Lauren's help. I can't believe I'm about to drag her into this. "What *have* you found?"

He stands from the stool and rounds the bar, pouring himself another pint. "Nothing. Not even a sniff. I don't get it." He walks back around the bar to his stool.

"You ever think we're too old for this shit?" I ask quietly. Why? Why the fuck did I ask him that?

He looks at me, his face blank. "What you getting at?"

Getting out. "Nothing." I look at him. "Just weird that we're enlisting the help of kids to do this shit."

"Speaking of kids, where the fuck have you been?" Travis nods his head.

I look over my shoulder, a wicked grin plastered on my face as Legs makes his way towards us. He's covered in sweat and dirt. Soon to be tears, too.

"You look like you've seen better days," Travis says.

Legs drops to a chair, his body sagging where he sits. "I have."

"Did you do the bikes?" I ask. He nods. "All of them?" A nod. "The gutters?" A slow nod. "Toilets?"

His eye dart to mine. "You're serious?" he says sounding broken.

I don't even smirk. "Deadly."

He reluctantly drags his sorry arse from the chair, then heads to start his next task.

Lauren chooses that moment to arrive. The pair look at one another, a familiar smile exchanged between them. And that's when I step in, signalling for her to come over.

Grabbing the straps of her rucksack, she walks to us, breaking their eye contact. "Big guy." She holds out her fist, and Travis bumps it with his.

I smile to myself. Then I immediately drop it when she looks to me, remembering I'm mad I didn't know about her and Legs' friendship.

"What's up with you?" she asks, sensing my mood.

"Let's get on with this." Sitting forward, I drag the laptop along the bar, open it, and check what Travis was looking at.

She double takes, looking at the screen that pops up. "Google? Seriously? You're *Googling* how to enter the dark web?"

Travis and I exchange a look.

"Fuck's sake," she says like we're idiots. Lauren moves Travis out the way, taking off her bag and sitting on the stool. "We need to unscramble the random sequence that's generated the URL you're looking for."

My lips part but I have nothing. Instead I look at Travis, feeling inadequate. "Drink?" I ask him, clearly not needed.

"Coke," Lauren answers, and both Travis and I look at her. She doesn't look up.

"Coming right up." My tone is nothing short of mocking. Normally the prospect or one of the girls would be behind the bar, but none of them are here right now. So I get up, pour her a Coke and stay behind the bar, watching as she taps the keys.

We stay like this for a while, then she slaps the bar top. "Fuck." She really does need to stop that.

"What?" Travis asks.

She cracks her knuckles like she's got a lot of work ahead of her. "I've accessed the deep web, but I need a few more tools to get to the dark web. If I could have some help, maybe this could get done quicker?" Her eyes jump to mine over the top of the screen.

"Not going to happen." I keep a straight face.

"Then don't blame me if it takes longer."

I can't argue with her. She's right, but I can't be worrying about Lauren and Legs. "What do you need?"

She blows her cheeks. "I need to install a reliable VPN."

"A VP what?"

She eye rolls me, looking closer at the screen. "Do you want to get caught?"

I look at her, my face expressionless.

"Then a virtual private network is what you'll need before I can get on to the network you want to see."

Travis is just as confused as me when I look to him. "Right."

"Looks like you might need the boy," he says reluctantly.

My body slumps. Fuck it. "Go fetch him."

Travis walks away yelling Legs' name.

"You know we're just friends, right?"

I lift my head, my body instantly turning to ice. I know I'm going to have to get used to this, but I don't want to have to admit to her that I *will* kill him if he's touched her. Kid's almost sixteen. Legs is nineteen. I'm not cool about it. At all. "I need some fresh air."

I'm panicking like a chump. Walking out. Shutting down the fear. Fear of what though? Giving advice to a teenager? I'm in no position to be giving advice on life. I need to just step back, take a minute and quieten down the building panic rising inside me.

"Wait," Lauren yells, making me stop.

I hesitate, but turn, facing her.

She looks around the clubhouse checking that those who are here, are still upstairs. "I've never even had sex. I'm a virgin," she whisper shouts.

Fucking hell. A heavy weight drops in my stomach. That was a low blow to my self-esteem. What the hell do I say? How do I play this? Clearly I take too long deciding.

"I don't see him like—"

I'm saved when Travis appears, bickering with Legs. They go on and on before I've simply had enough. I shake my head then quick march myself back to the laptop. "Get over here." Heart rate out of this world, I turn the screen. A distraction. I have no fucking clue what I'm looking at, and it's clear they all know as much. "Can you or can you not access the fucking website we need?"

I stare hard at Legs who slowly looks at Lauren. "Yeah. No problem," he says confidently.

"I don't even want to know *how* you got her into this—"

"—Hey!" Lauren stamps closer. "What makes you think *he* got me into this?"

I look between them. "*You* got *him* into this? How? Why?" My eyeballs are about to pop from my skull.

"I know her brother." Legs casually sits on the stool nearest the bar, wiping his dirty hands on his jeans. "Jay called, asked for a place to crash for him and his sis. I let them stay at mine."

Still frowning, I look at Lauren.

"Yeah," she replies, angry with me.

"What about when Jay went missing? What happened then?"

The look Legs gives me brings him closer to getting throat punched. "What do you think? I wasn't about to kick her out. I promised him I'd keep an eye out for her."

"What?" Lauren hits his arm, making him look to her. "You knew he was planning on leaving?"

Legs gives himself away, his posture suddenly stiffening. He better not look at me for backup. "He told me not to tell you, wanted to keep you out of this."

"Out of what?" She squares up to him.

"Your uncle!" he shouts looking concerned. "Jay wasn't sure if your uncle would come looking for you, or if he'd wait until you resurfaced. He knew I was prospecting. Jay figured you'd be better off with me around than him."

"Why would he think that?"

Legs puts a hand on her arm but must feel my eyes penetrating his skin. He whips it off, stammering as he continues. "Your uncle's not about to storm in *here* and demand you go with him. But with time, it's inevitable he'd want you both back with him. With you closer to the Rippers, he'll look for Jay first."

Lauren shakes her head, looking sad. "So, Jay's never showing himself. Not unless my uncle..."

Not unless the cunt dies. I stand straighter, spying everyone reading my thoughts.

Lauren sighs. "Will you do it?" I see a stray tear run down her cheek. A plea for me to help bring her brother home to her. I will, but we're absolutely not having this conversation.

"Can you take over?" I nod towards the laptop, looking at Legs.

He bends, taps a few keys then nods. Good.

"Travis, make sure he gets in. We have until tomorrow." That's it. That's all we fucking have. I move, ushering Lauren away from the laptop. "Come on."

"But I can help."

I give her a smile. "You've done enough, kid."

Pulling out a chair for her, she takes a seat. "But, what do I do now?" she asks.

I drop my arse to the chair opposite her, raking a hand through my hair. "How about, you don't worry about any of this stuff, and tell me what you thought about the house. We didn't get to talk much after I left you."

With a wipe of her eyes, Lauren smiles, genuinely. "I loved it. You and Mads will be so happy there."

I brush a few crumbs to the floor, then lean my elbows on the table, waiting for her to look at me. "Will you?"

She draws back, startled, her eyes bright like jewels. "What?" she questions.

I smile at her reaction. "You heard, kid."

"I... are you for real? You would have me live with you?" Her voice cracks.

I can't help the tightening of my face. It's an automatic reaction to hearing her think so little of herself. "I'd *want* you to live with us, yes. But for Mads' sake, you'd have to stop the swearing."

She laughs a little, sniffing. "Like a real family." When she looks up to me, there's a zing that punches between us. A moment like the crashing of waves. I see her sense her belonging. See her realise she really does have people who care for her.

Then click.

I sink in my chair.

A mirror, that's what I realise I'm looking at. Seeing my own goddamn self looking back at me. Except this reflection won't break. There's no shattering this hardened image. There are no physical similarities nor shared interests, except for our love of bikes. I'm talking about the deeper sense of connection piercing my skin because the kid sat opposite me is more like me than anyone I know. She knows of loss. Knows of pain. Knows how to survive.

We're the same.

"A real family, kid. You think you're ready for that?"

She smiles, staring fixedly, searching my expression. "If you are," she holds out her fist, face beaming, "I am too." And fucking hell if I don't feel my nose crinkle and my throat burn.

Validation. Understanding. Acceptance. It all comes crashing into me, bulldozing the walls I built around me in order to survive.

I hold out my fist, returning the gesture. Grateful.

CHAPTER FORTY-ONE

DEAN

My emotions are running wild like the heavy steps beneath me. My lungs burn. My muscles scream at me to slow down. But I can't. Today marks the start of the end. The eve of the beginning. Today is the day I send a kid into hell. A hell I brought our way. I don't want to; I'd rather feed myself to the wolves—we all would. But we can't, and I can't do this on my own. I fought for far too long on my own and got nowhere.

Now, I have a family. I'll allow my demons to fuel me to the finish line, then I need to stop fighting them. I've remained a victim to their emotion for far too long. I need to leave them where they are. Behind me.

Last night, I saw in Lauren's eyes the promise of hope. The promise of a family. I have to be that for her. Have to be the one to give her hope. Redemption only comes if I succeed though. This plan of ours can't go wrong. There will be no freedom if it does. No future. No light.

Thinking of Mads, I push harder, ignoring the feeling of nausea that starts to rise. I won't let my head beat me. Not today. There's too much to be done.

My feet hit the ground faster, freeing my mind until I'm back at home.

Once out the shower, I give Mads a call, noticing the time as the phone starts to ring. It's seven. No way she's up yet. I smile around the rim of my mug as it goes to answer phone.

"Hey, beautiful." I walk to the kitchen. "Just calling to say I hope seeing your dad went okay." I pull out a chair, sitting down. "We're almost there, babe. The life I promised you... I'm nearly fucking done. Then you get all of me. Every scar, every truth, you'll know all of it, I promise you. Call me if you get a chance."

When I hang up, I stare around the room, twirling my phone in my hand. My memories overshadow any good left in this house. My life before Mads wasn't a rollercoaster or a journey... more like a prison. Caged. My choices weren't always my own, but deep down I craved an impossible freedom I didn't know how to find.

A quiet streak of contentment suddenly flows through me, making me smile. In the end, once I'd stopped looking, it found me. My road to freedom; it followed me one night, argued with me, kissed me and trusted me. There were finally eyes that saw me. Loving arms that held me. I'll never be able to repay her for that, but loving her back the way she loves me? Like she said, that's the easiest thing I can do.

I swipe open my phone, knowing exactly where to start.

I arrive at the clubhouse later that evening, still not having heard from Mads. We sit down at the table and run through the plan one final time. There's some time to kill once we're done, so I make my way downstairs, lighting a smoke as I go.

My phone rings, and I pull it out. "Hello."

"What time's he getting there?" Vincent hits me with his question.

"One hour."

"Right. My men are in place. Sonny's drafted in the extra charter you asked for."

"We don't want a blood bath, but if it goes that way..."

"We're ready."

I pinch my lips. All day I've tried to think of a way to make today happen that didn't involve a nineteen-year-old acting as bait. I got nothing.

"And once it's done. You'll honour our agreement?" he asks.

I sneer under my breath but what choice do I have. "Yes," I grate.

"You don't sound too sure."

Closing my eyes, I rub my forehead with my other hand. Calm. "You have my word." Club voted in favour; he'll get what he wants. Power.

Behind the bar, Red pours me a whiskey, sliding it closer. She nods as I accept it, then looks up as the main door opens.

"I've got to go." I hang up on Vincent, then stand. "Didn't think you were getting here yet?"

"Yeah, well, change of plan." Jack doesn't once look at me as he talks, stepping closer.

I turn to Red, waiting for her to—

"Hi." Her face shines.

After a beat I cough, making her look at me. She shakes herself out of her daydream, then flusters pouring another whiskey.

Jack steps beside me, and we both watch her hand shake as she pours. When she's done, she hands it to him.

"Thanks, darlin'." The atmosphere suddenly feels heavy. "Jack." The twat holds out his hand for her to take. I stare, my eyes widening. What the fuck is happening?

"Red," she says nervously, her cheeks blushing.

"Like the hair." His eyes flicker to her head.

I've seen enough. "Need you to run out, make sure we've got enough beer and supplies in." I open my wallet slapping some cash on the bar for Red.

She scoops it up, raises a small smile, then walks away.

"What the fuck was that?" I ask once me and Jack are alone.

Jack pauses, his glass close to his mouth. "What?" He shrugs.

"Biggest day for all of us and you come here, to do what? Hit on a woman?"

"I'm not hitting."

I let out a breath. "Can we just get this over with? Then you can look to get your end away elsewhere."

He frowns then swallows his drink in one. "You spoke to Travis yet?"

He must see the tension I feel at his question. "No. After today, I'll tell him."

"What about you? What will you do once it's done?"

He semi laughs. "I'm not done until I get my man."

Silence. "We will."

He slowly looks up at me. "*I* will."

Everything inside me sinks. Jack will spend the rest of his life searching for this one man if we don't find him within the next twenty-four hours. Will he expect me to join him? Would I? *Could* I? No. When I think about that notion, anger crawls up my back.

Don't let your head win. Don't let your head win. Not today.

Jack slaps my shoulder.

Making his way down the stairs, we spot Legs with a few others. He sees me, hesitates, then checks his step before he starts moving again. Fuck, he looks nervous. He pulls at the edges of his leather like a child who knows they're in trouble. I bury my thoughts until he reaches me, and we standoff, staring, neither one of us sure where to start. He slowly slips his leather off his back, folding it and placing it on the bar. Final. Deathly silent. "Guess I'll be off then." He drops his head.

Everything in me wants to explode, lay into him for being so fucking stupid. Instead, I stand straight, grab his shirt and pull him closer. "Not once will you be on your own. We'll be watching every fucking second." I pat his back as he grabs me tighter.

"I'm not scared."

"Never said you were."

He stands back.

"Here." Jack reaches in his pocket. "We've got six hours until Rippers are due to move the shipment. Means once you're auctioned," the words make me feel sick, "they're likely to move you for transport straight away."

"How long does the Rohypnol last?"

Jack attaches a small device to the front of Legs' shirt near one of the buttons. "Twelve hours," Jack tells him. "Once you've had it you'll be out like a light."

Legs slowly looks up. "Then it's over to you."

Fucking hell. "What is that?" I ask.

Jack finishes what he's doing. "Nano tracker. Has GPS. It's linked to my phone. It will send what you see back to me. If anything should go wrong—" Jack cuts himself off.

"You'll know where to find me," Legs says for him instead.

"That isn't going to happen."

A silence descends, making my skin itch. No way I'm letting anything happen to this kid or any of the people we're going to see on screen. No fucking way.

Legs turns, scratching a hand through his hair. After a few steps he looks back to us. "If Jay doesn't come back, you will look after Lauren, won't you? I promised him I'd look after her."

Suppressing the urge to growl at his insinuation that he isn't coming back, I nod, unable to communicate any actual fucking words.

He smiles half-heartedly, then he's gone.

"He's a strong kid," Jack says.

"No. He's just a kid. Trying to patch into this fucking club. I want him on screen right now."

Jack nods and pulls out his phone, bringing up Legs. If I

could have dropped him off, I would. If we could be camping out at the airfield, we would. Instead like morons, we have to let this play out to avoid raising any suspicion. We can't risk Costa taking off. We can't risk those people being killed for their silence. We have to let it run its course. Play our part. I hate it. Hate every fucking second of it.

As planned, we're soon sat around the table, various laptops and phones open. The atmosphere is heavy with tension. Travis fills my glass, but there's no more after this. We need clear heads, clarity for when we need to leave.

"He there yet?" Mop asks as he walks in, looking between us.

"He's there," Jack replies tapping on his screen.

We watched Legs make his way to the airfield, seeing no signs of being rumbled when he walked in. He was met by Costa's men, patted down, then ushered into a makeshift room on his own. It tears my insides apart seeing his vulnerability. The only good thing at this point is that the GPS tracker hasn't been found.

Blowing out my cheeks, I rub my eyes, seeing my phone dash across the table.

Mads: I'm so sorry it's taken me this long to reply, been crazy here. I think Bex's entire family is coming tomorrow. I miss you. Hope you're still breathing x

Me: On my final breath. You're not leaving me again. I don't like it

I have no right to say that to her. But it's the truth.

Mads: Same to you. Promise me x

Me: You have my word x

Mads: Love you, VP x

I smile to myself, my heart picking up pace at her words and her fierceness.

Me: Love you, my fucking sunshine. Always

Before I put my phone away, Lauren messages letting me know she's checked on Lynn. I thank her and say goodnight, dropping my phone back on the table.

"Here we go." I look up at Travis who points at the screen from where he stands.

"Who is it?" I ask leaning closer.

"A woman," Jack tells me.

I let out a small sigh of relief before my body goes stiff.

The woman sits on a chair, a camera thrust in her face, the bright light shining, forcing her to keep her eyes half closed.

I clench my fists, outraged we can't go get her right now.

Fear rests on her face as she looks at the people stood just out of shot. Her eyes flicker between whoever's there. Then one figure steps forward, his face covered. He stalks to the woman, his hands covered by black gloves. He wears a black top and black trousers. Hidden. He treats her with no respect, tilting her chin as though she's a piece of meat. Fucker's showing her off.

Jack checks his phone, still seeing Legs sat in his room, then he angles the laptop towards him, tapping the keys with force. He hits enter, angling the screen back for us all to see. "I got the passkey for the chatroom. Now we can see what the bidders are saying."

I recoil, as does Travis. "Anything been said?" Travis hisses from his place by the door, leaning against the wall.

Jack's temple twitches, his frustration evident. "One bidder's in the chat." He huffs in disbelief. "They just bid three thousand dollars."

I look at Travis, dreading my next question. "For?"

Looking at the screen, the man forces the woman to her feet. He removes her shirt, ripping it down the front, revealing her bra. She closes her eyes, unable to look at her body as she's showcased.

Watching her chest rise and fall as she takes laboured breaths; I start visualising the different ways this prick will pay. A bullet to the back of the head? Too fast. Slicing his throat? That could work. Or maybe what would serve him better, would be to cut every organ out of *his* body and lay them out before him? Take our time. Make him watch.

Jack snaps me out of my depraved trance. "Make sure you kill the feed when you get in there. First fuckin' job."

I nod, not forgetting.

There's a flash on the screen. "Two more bidders," he informs, "make that three, now four,"

"What the fuck?" Travis steps forward, his big hands resting on the table as he watches.

"Bid's at ten grand."

"What fucking for?" Travis demands to know.

"One of the bids is in French, I can't fuckin' read it."

The woman's turned, her round behind slapped, then faced back towards the screen. The man cups her breasts but it isn't sexual. He's showing, for the sake of the camera, how big they are.

"Jesus Christ." Another bid pops up confirming my suspicion. I shut my eyes, dropping my head, hearing each man in turn read the screen. They curse to no one in particular, then the room turns deadly silent. The inhumanity of it sucks any faith I had left clean out of my system.

"Her reproductive organ?" Captain asks unsure he's read that right. Even with his eyes, he has.

"Her womb." My thumbs rest against my forehead as I lock my hands, my face tightening.

"Can you even survive that?" The Joker asks.

No one answers because of course, we don't fucking know. The sad reality of this whole operation is that I don't think the buyer nor the seller give any fucks as to whether the woman survives or not.

"Will she go to a hospital at least?"

Jack looks at me hesitantly, knowing I'm asking him. I hear him sigh. "Depends on the highest bidder, I guess." He lifts his shoulders, holding out a hand to the laptop. "Surgery of this proportion? She has to."

"Then what?" I ask.

He scratches at his head. "Then... then with the money she receives, she lives her life."

Womb-less. No family. If she survives, where will she go? Will there be people waiting for her? My mind spirals, whirling with frustration and apprehension. I check my watch, lower my hand, then check it again.

I feel Travis' eyes on me, silently telling me to calm the fuck down. "Dean," he says, when I obviously don't.

All eyes swing to me. It's only then I realise my fists are white knuckling, the pain absolutely nothing in comparison to what this woman will face.

With a heavy heart, we sit through six more live bids. I can't say I watch them all because I don't. Can't. Sending my glass through the opposite wall, I can't watch a poor boy no older than eight, stand there whilst monsters bid for his eyes.

His *fucking* eyes. And the most tragic element to his being there? Clearly his father following after him, knowing he's signed them both up. Wherever he's looking to get them, for shelter or for safety, he considers *this* worth the risk?

White hot rage burns me to my core trying to wrap my head around it. I stand, unable to momentarily quieten the shouting voices behind my skull.

Breathe. Breathe. Breathe.

"Fuck," Jack whispers.

I turn, knowing by his tone that Legs has come on to the screen. I move around to see, but refuse to sit. God knows how many more we have to sit through before we can move. I've just about got a grip on my ability to stay put, but I'm itching, clawing at the exit, ready to pounce.

I bite my tongue tasting the copper tang when I see him being made to stand. We know what's coming before it even happens. His shirt is discarded, our feed to the GPS on him, momentarily lost.

Jack keeps his phone open, but the screen is blank. "Ten bidders already in the feed."

Fuck.

"Do we know what for yet?" Len asks, standing furthest away from the screen.

Answering our question, one bid for fifty thousand pounds is placed. For his lung.

I just about swallow the putrid taste of bile before another bid for his liver comes in. "More than one?" My voice shakes as I point out the obvious. No one that we have watched to this point has had more than one organ bid for. It's always been one. "Why are they bidding on more?"

Legs is turned like the woman, his arms raised out to the side.

The man wearing black must have an earpiece. He muses, nodding, clearly being told how to *show* what the bidders want to see.

He's spun around again, and when the bright light hits his eyes, there's nothing. Legs doesn't react. Not even a wince or a blink. He's withdrawn himself. Cut off his emotion to be able to endure this.

Seeing his detachment, a cold sweat prickles at my brow and the back of my neck. My blood turns to ice as fear and confusion manifest in my head like an infection, slowly multiplying and spreading through my veins.

My sanity is plagued by panic. My vision blurs as a thick fog descends before me.

"Deano," Jack says worried, but I don't hear him.

My feet carry me as far away from the screen as they can. I hear someone follow me, but I don't stop until I've made it to the bar. I grip the wood, my fingers curling painfully into it.

"Deano." I can't look up at Jack as I battle to contain the attack. He waits.

Silence presses my ears. The ticking of my watch the only thing I can hear. It's isolating, caging me in darkness. *Tick. Tock. Tick. Tock.* It goes on and on and on, mimicking the rhythm of the first time this happened.

Breathe, you fucking idiot. Now is not the time. Breathe, breathe, breathe. I suck in strangled breaths as the room rocks around me. I'm going to pass out if I don't get a hold of myself.

A hand's placed on my shoulder, a showing that he's still here. Still with me.

My next breath reaches my lungs a little easier, and I feel the oxygen start to steady the galloping rate of my heart. Shakily, I open my eyes, seeing my feet. A deceptive calm leaves me hollowed.

More feet pound the floorboards, edging closer. "Dean?"

I wearily stand, looking up to Travis.

His face casts a shadow over the slight relief I feel. "We have a fucking problem."

CHAPTER FORTY-TWO

DEAN

"What do you mean they're collecting him separately?"

"Exactly what I said, brother. The bids are coming in fast. Now at one hundred thousand." We file into the room. "One said they'd collect within the next two hours—that they didn't want to wait."

"What they bidding for?" I ask stammering.

"Lung, liver. Some cunt even bid for his fucking intestine."

This can't be happening. I edge closer, my feet like heavy blocks of lead. "No way he could survive with all of those missing," I say out loud, making the mood of the room shift.

Beats and Captain stand, and I catch Mop check his weapons. They know we have to move.

"Fetch our order," I tell them.

Jack shifts on his feet, looking between all of us. "What are you doing?" The slow draw of my eyes to his says everything I need to as Mop and Beats leave the room. "Deano, no." He looks at Travis, then back to me. "You'd risk all those people for one man?"

I feel my brothers move. Like a pack of wolves they stand behind me, ready to fight. "That one man is *family*."

Jack's face tightens. Charged. "*I'm* your family," he grinds.

I tilt my head. "You know as well as anyone in this room, the patch goes beyond blood."

Jack pushes past The Joker towards me. "We've come too far to let them get away now. *You've* got too much riding on this as well."

I clench my teeth, unable to miss Travis looking at me out the corner of his eye. "Who said anything about letting them get away? Everything runs as planned, but I will not risk someone turning up early to collect the kid."

Jack's temple twitches. "Fuck," he whispers, running a hand through his hair. I can hear his thoughts as he wrestles with himself. He's not ignorant. He knows we won't leave a man behind. He just wants *his* man. His man that we now know is close.

Mop enters the room with Beats, grabbing my attention. They each carry two duffel bags, loaded with guns. The bang of them on the table crashes down with a thud.

I move to them, unzipping one, grabbing what I can before my men do the same.

Jack drops his head. "We get close but stay out of sight."

I load a handgun, then slip it inside my cut. "Agreed. We only move if we see them taking Legs. You'll have to wear his cut to blend in." The sound of guns being loaded filters around the room. "Are your men already in place?" Jack nods at my question. "Better let them know this is happening. If it goes south, they need to be ready to move."

Jack pulls his phone from his pocket.

"Cap', stay here, keep a watch of the screens. You're our eyes," I tell him.

He looks at me stone faced. "That a fucking joke, boy?"

I smile like a deranged man. "No, but it was a good one." Slipping another handgun in the back of my jeans, I pat his shoulder. "You call me if anything changes. I'll cut the feed as soon as we get there, then you bring the truck as planned. The swap needs to be fast."

He moves the laptop on the table, turning it where he can see.

"Beats, load the bags into Jack's truck," I order.

We move taking what we can from the bags, and run to our bikes. I start my engine, nodding over my shoulder to Jack who'll follow in his truck. He won't keep up, but he knows where to go.

Pulling back on the throttle, I don't stop pushing us until mile after mile passes. With every second that ticks by, every thought that drops into my head is torture. I know how to handle what we're about to do. I know how to shut down everything in order to get things done. I've proven that time and time again.

But what I don't know how to handle, and clearly I've a lot to fucking work on, is the self-doubting torrent that consumes me in these moments when I face fear. Fear of what I've done. Fear of what's to come. At least I see it now. And that in itself is something I never knew I was capable of.

It's a vicious circle; living in a world you no longer want, but reaching for a life you never thought you deserved. Can I do it? Can I make it over the line?

I twist the throttle.

I've come this fucking far. I'm not stopping now.

Cutting the engines a quarter of a mile away from the airfield, Jack's tracker shows Legs is still inside. "We wait here," I say to my men, grateful nobody came to collect him before we got here. I pull out my phone and call Captain, my blood boiling but my head kept in check. "Where we at?" I ask when he answers.

"They're on to the next bid."

"Okay. Keep watch. Let me know once they've had the final one."

He hangs up, and we wait, time seemingly taking forever to pass. But we're here. Ready.

Captain messages forty minutes later to confirm the bidding has finished and that he's left the clubhouse. We got lucky; no one arrived in the time we waited. It's only as we approach the two-hour mark do we mount our bikes, making our way towards the hangar at the same time as a handful of Saviours arrive.

No one will suspect we were here camping out.

We pull up and dock our bikes, then we're greeted by a man in a suit. "Travis," he says, not bothering to shake his hand. My heart does a double beat when the hangar door is then slid open, six large crates lined up in a row, staring back at me.

Another vehicle arrives, the low whir of its engine purring behind us. I look at Travis as two men dressed in suits step out of the car. These must be the men here for Legs. One nods his head as he buttons up his suit jacket, walking past us.

Fucking scum.

They enter the building through a side door.

I watch Travis move with the others towards the crates. He gives me a knowing look, and I hang back signalling at Jack to follow me. We snake our way along the outside of the hangar, stopping at the other exit. We wait for five minutes before the door swings open.

The men in suits walk out with Legs under their arms.

The sight of him being carried like a fucking object sends fury to hit me like meeting a train head on. I clench my fists, grinding my teeth.

One man pulls out his phone, the light from the screen narrowing his vision.

I seize the opportunity and creep up behind him. Taking no chances, I pull back his head, swiping my knife across his Adams apple with precision.

He gargles, choking on his blood as he sinks, dropping Legs to the ground.

Before the other man can withdraw his weapon, Jack steps forwards, mirroring the murder, his furrowed eyes hitting mine as the man drops to the floor. I can tell he hasn't done that before. But the expression on his face is hollowed. Unfazed by what he's just done.

We share a moment, then the corner of his mouth lifts.

I raise a brow pulling out my phone. I call Travis. He doesn't answer, but the crack of a gun firing suggests he got the message. "Take him to your truck!" I urge Jack, watching as he dips and lifts Legs over his shoulder effortlessly.

I pull out my weapon, opening the door, and make my way inside. I move through the hangar, treading lightly, finding it empty apart from the makeshift rooms. Flicking back one of the curtains, I find where they filmed the bidding. I pull out my knife and cut the wires attached to the camera on a stand.

Most men in here presumably moved towards the crates once the gunfire started. It's empty, no signs of life as I continue to work my way through, finding only mattresses on the floor, clothes and empty food packets. These people really haven't been here long, but clearly long enough to leave a dank smell in the air.

There's a distant yell to my left, and I swing my head, my blood pressure spiking. More gunfire. *Shit*. Then it's quiet.

"Dean?" a voice then shouts.

I let out a breath and move my feet, running towards the crates. Three of them are loaded on the lorry. All of Costa's men are dead, their bodies sprawled across the floor. Mangled. "Everyone whole?" I call.

Travis rubs at his chest. "We're whole." He turns to Beats. "Get them out of there. You two," he points at Len and The Joker, "you work on those."

Beats and Riggs move quickly, stepping onto the lorry, lifting the lids off the crates.

Len and The Joker do the same with the three still yet to be moved.

"There's a couple of mattresses back there, get them first," I instruct, prompting them to move.

"Legs alright?" Travis asks as we start towards Jack's truck.

We approach seeing Jack trying to wake him. "Kid's out cold," he tells us.

Legs doesn't move or stir as I push past Jack, shaking him to wake up, checking for myself.

"Don't believe me?"

"Fuck you." I need to make sure he's okay.

Legs is breathing but has clearly been drugged, his pupils pinned to black dots. I feel guilty seeing him so out of it, but we knew this might happen.

"Uh, guys." The three of us turn to Beats. "You need to come see this."

We leave Legs laid on the back seat of the truck, then Travis leads the way to the crates.

Beats lifts a woman's arm, turning it to us in his hold. A small bruise covered with a sterile strip lays between her elbow and armpit. "What is it?" he asks.

I pick up the man's arm next to her, rolling back his sleeve, seeing the same.

"They all have them," Travis says, as Len and The Joker appear dragging a few mattresses.

"And the boy?" I look to Beats who confirms, nodding his head slowly.

"Trackers. Has to be." Jack huffs pulling out his phone. "Insurance for both parties. My guess is the buyer and seller have eyes on their movements. Legs told us they had tags—like serial numbers. This must be it."

"Will they see when we stop?"

Jack holds his phone against the lady's arm. "Shit."

"What?" I take a step closer.

"Thought I might be able to scramble the signal, but it's no good. We'll have to take them out..."

Fuck. Thinking on the spot, I grab my knife, moving to the biggest guy here. I lift his arm, then gently slit his skin across the bruise. A small slither of blood trickles from the incision. Squeezing, I feel a small tracker; like the ones Legs had to go on the crates, except this is smaller. "Jesus." The device pops out. I turn it in the palm of my hand. "We have to move them, get them on the road. We'll take the devices out whilst they're still asleep."

Jack steps forward. "Deano, wait." One hand rests on my shoulder as he takes the device from my palm, inspecting it closely. He sighs, but I sense his worry. "We have to assume these detect life."

My face drops. My stomach bottoming out. "Fuck."

"Meaning?" Travis asks, his voice quiet.

Meaning we're fucked. "Not only will they know we've stopped, when we do, we can't swap the crates with the hay bales like planned."

Irritation and fear line Travis' face as his body shakes. He snarls, turning on the spot. Thinking. I don't interrupt him. "Get all of them on the lorry, like planned."

The mattresses are dragged on the lorry, and like machines my men take care, quickly moving the people and carefully placing them in the back.

"What you thinking?" I ask him, moving towards everyone to help.

We both bend picking up a crate, and carry it to the lorry. We slide it onto the back, wiping our hands as we move to the next. "I'm thinking my uncle's going to fucking hate me." My face scrunches as we pick up our pace, grabbing the next. "Just call Vincent and tell him we're on our way. We've already been here too long."

CHAPTER FORTY-THREE

MADISON

I peer over at Jess sound asleep in her bed. She snores heavily, the low rumble of her nose and steady rise and fall of her chest, makes me smile. Do I sound like that? I let out a small laugh, rubbing my eyes after only managing a few hours sleep.

Today is the baby shower, and I'm awake at the ridiculous hour of 2am. Christ, it's going to be a long day. Everything's set. Every surface decorated to within an inch of its life. Bex's place looks fit for a queen.

I'm not at all secretly uneasy with the fact I have nothing like this organised.

I turn, rolling to my side, throwing back the covers. The chilly morning air sweeps across my toes as I tap them against the carpet in search of my slippers.

Cup of tea. That's what I need.

Slipping my feet in the warmth of the fleece material, I grab my phone and Dean's hoodie I packed, then make my way downstairs. Growing slower or not, this hoodie used to swamp me, now it's tight around my bump. I slip my hands in the front pocket, shimmying it down.

In the kitchen, I fill the kettle and grab a mug, waiting for it to boil. *The life I promised you, it starts tomorrow.* Dean's words have been swimming in my head since I listened to his message.

I've been so busy with seeing my dad and helping Bex, I haven't managed to speak to him. I texted but… it's just made me feel nervous.

I think back to being alone when he was gone. Endless hours spent staring at my phone wishing he'd call. The sleepless nights. The pretending everything was fine. I can't do that again. My heart pounds against my ribs as heat rushes to the surface of my skin. The growing fear elevates like a scream, amplified by the rising noise from the boiling kettle. As soon as it clicks off, I take a steadying breath, walking to the fridge for the milk.

I wipe my head, closing the fridge, jumping back when I see Bex stood in the doorway. "Jesus!"

She smiles, scraping her long, glossy hair back, tying it in a messy bun on top of her head. "Sorry. Couldn't sleep." She walks into the kitchen.

I exhale dramatically. "Didn't have to frighten me like that."

She laughs again.

"Want one?" I hold up the milk.

"Please." Bex pulls out a chair at her dining table and takes a seat. Her legs are parted wide, and she slumps looking exhausted. "I know why I can't sleep but what's keeping you up?" she asks.

I put the tea bags in the mugs and fill them with water. I want to tell her how my sleeping habits have changed. That without Dean there I never manage more than a few hours. Last time we talked about him though, things were left in a way they never have been with her. Tense. Awkward.

Bex will always see right by me. She's fiercely protective and does not care who she's up against. But she's almost always right. And last time she spoke the truth, I didn't want to hear it.

"Baby was kicking. Couldn't get comfy." My lie seems to be accepted as I pour in the milk, stirring the mugs.

"Dean alright?"

Maybe not. I turn to face her, and she gives me a smile, one side of her face lifting smugly.

With an exasperated breath, I grab both mugs, then place them on the table, taking a seat opposite her. "I need to apologise."

She rolls her eyes. "Don't be a twat. I'm your best friend. I can read you like a book."

I lift a brow, then take a sip of my tea. The warm brew makes me instantly relax. "Then you already know."

With a smile, she leans forward with a delayed pull of her body. "You're worried about him?"

I'm never not worried about him or what he does. I've got better at living with it, but he and I both know it's not the life we want. A small smile stretches as hot tears prickle my eyes. "I must be a small book."

Bex giggles, picking up her mug. "I never meant to upset you when we spoke. I'm sorry." She shakes her head from side to side. "Just looking out for you."

"I know." I let my head drop. "I was just so happy he was home." I didn't care how or why. And I still don't know *how* or *why.* But Bex is right. "I know how crazy it is."

"I know you do. You're not stupid."

I look to her.

"I'd be more worried if you were so blinded by love, you couldn't see the wood through the trees."

My face contorts. I wipe under my eyes with one hand as the other grips the mug a little harder. "Before we left, I told him I'd give him the space to finish whatever he needs to get done. Then he said he was getting out."

Her eyebrows lift. "You believe him?"

I suck in some air. "I believe he *wants* to get out," I sigh. He came home determined enough.

Bex's face drops. "You're not so sure?"

"I'm sure he'll do anything to get what he wants."

Her round eyes dance between mine. "Which is?"

I try to swallow the burning lump lodged in my throat. "To be free," I sob, unable to contain the sadness anymore.

Bex rushes to me as fast as she can, wrapping her arm around my shoulders.

I let it all out. Every silly tear. Every pent-up piece of emotion I've kept in check since we arrived down here. It all comes rushing out of me in uncontrollable waves.

"Hey," Bex says. She rubs the side of my arm, resting her chin on my head.

"Shit." I wipe the tracks of tears lining my cheeks. "I'm sorry."

"Don't be." She moves back to her chair, taking my hand in hers on the table. "You'll get your freedom. Both of you."

"How can you be so sure?"

With a smile, Bex looks at our hands. Both of hers are now wrapped around mine. "Do you remember how you used to overthink every situation? How you'd obsess and worry about things out of your control. Or things that are just downright ridiculous?"

I roll my eyes on a slight embarrassed laugh. "Yes," I say, knowing I've gotten better.

"Well, sometimes life throws shit things at you. Not because you deserve them. Not because it's trying to test you. Simply because it knows you deserve so much more. It makes you strive for more." I smile. "Since you two have been together, you're once again the woman I've known my entire life. He's your more." Trying to control the wobble of my bottom lip, I can barely see her through the mist clouding my vision. "You *were* made for each other. That's how I know."

I let out a snotty laugh as my nose runs uncontrollably. "Get me a tissue."

Bex laughs, grabbing a box of Kleenex off the windowsill.

We both turn our heads hearing footsteps approaching.

"What did I miss?" Jess' hair is dishevelled, one side more knotted than the other.

"Nothing. Just two emotional women crying at two o'clock in the morning."

"Great," Jess says rubbing her eyes, moving to fill up the kettle, her feet dragging across the floor. "I came here for a break, you know. Even Axl doesn't wake me at this god-awful hour." She drags a hand down her face, catching her bottom lip against her palm. "Urgh," she grumbles, dribbling, "and we have to deal with your moody aunt today."

"Yep." Bex's face is smug as she drops the tissues on the table. "And my cousin Elle."

"The one who swears she can forecast the weather by how hard her nipples get?" I ask.

Jess freezes, one eye half open, looking between us. "Don't expect me to be nice to them. Not now."

Bex and I laugh as Jess makes her cup of tea, then joins us at the table.

"So, sleeping beauty, do we need any last-minute bits before the shower?"

Jess waggles a finger, her eyes still not fully opened. "No. Got it all after we left Dad's."

"You always this cheery when you wake up? I thought you'd be a pro at early mornings."

Jess lowers her mug. "Early mornings, yes. Middle of the night, not so much. Plus, Axl hasn't woke in the night for six months now. Even when he does, Max sees to him."

Bex purses her lips. "That's sweet," she says.

Jess smiles, clearly missing him, even with their rough patch. She runs her hands through her hair. "I think being away from everyday routines has made me feel more tired. Made me realise how much we both do. I might go message him actually, see if he's still awake." She stands, tucking in her chair, her eyes now fully open. "You two going to be okay?"

Bex and I exchange a look. "We're good," I tell her.

"Okay. Night. I'll see you in the... well, I'll see you *after* eight am."

I laugh. "Night."

"Goodnight," Bex says at the same time. "You want another brew?" she asks once Jess' feet pad up the stairs.

"I might do the same." I pull out my phone knowing there is every chance Dean will also be awake at this hour. I sigh though when I hold it up and the screen remains blank.

"You messaging Dean?" Bex asks. She stands picking up the mugs and places them by the sink.

I hold up my phone. "Battery's dead. I'll call him in the morning."

"Okay, love. Try and get some rest."

"I will." I walk to her, holding out my arms. "Hugging another pregnant woman is hard." I laugh as our bellies get in our way, making it awkward.

"You're not much of a hugger anyway."

"Should we stop?"

"I'm going to," she says pulling back.

"Love you," I tell her with a smile.

"Love you. See you in the morning."

I turn and make my way upstairs, leaving Bex to turn off the lights before she follows me up.

Jess is already snoring again in her bed. Half a mug of unfinished tea sits on the side. I plug in my phone, pull back the covers, and slip myself under the duvet. I close my eyes, smiling, finally feeling sleep take its hold.

That's until Jess' phone starts ringing from the bedside table. It buzzes on the wood, and I roll my eyes pushing back the covers to silence it. Clicking the button on the side, it's only then

I check to see who's calling.

"Dean?"

CHAPTER FORTY-FOUR

DEAN

"I knew you'd burn me, boy. I said, didn't I?"

"It's not like we have a fucking choice." I slip a smoke between my lips, quickly lighting it. I don't have time but my body's tense. I need the calm. "I thought you wanted nothing to do with this, so why are you here?" I put my lighter back in my pocket.

Travis' uncle shoots his death stare on me. "It's my fucking livelihood you're shitting all over right now."

"Dean!" Travis shouts, urging us to pick up the pace.

Mick glances his way, but Travis has already turned, having placed the last of the crates near the pen.

I grunt shifting the iron gate we walk past, open.

Stood at the back of the lorry now parked at the farm, nomads and the other Saviours are waiting. They *were* waiting to simply receive these crates, swap the contents, then be back on the road. Now we're up against fucking trackers that can potentially track a heartbeat.

We have no choice but to do this. It's genius, really.

"Ready?" I ask Travis.

His dark eyes travel to mine threateningly. "Why's it got to be me?"

"It was your idea."

His uncle lifts both palms to the heavens, then slaps them down against his thighs in disbelief.

I look up to Travis. His eyes narrow. *Shit.* He might actually kill me after today. If I survive it. My nerves are going to kill me if this doesn't. My hands are trembling. I'm one step closer to the light.

"Just hurry up," Vincent says shaking his head. He's on edge like the rest of us. "We've got twenty minutes. That was all I could buy us."

"What'd you say to them?"

"Told them Bills' bike broke down on the way to us. We had to stop and get him. They bought it, but we haven't got long. They're expecting us at one-thirty. We need to be on the road, stat."

The pigs start to squeal, turning all of our heads. They know something's wrong. Their collective noise sends a horrific shudder down my spine.

"Here," Mop says stepping forward. He holds out his hands full of trackers, his skin stained red.

"Right," I say. I look down, the tip of my knife about to cut the thick, hairy skin.

"What the fuck do you think you're doing?" Mick asks grumpily.

The knife shakes in my hand. "What does it look like?" His forehead rolls in confusion. "Trackers need to go *in* them."

His face turns bleak. "So, you think you're just going to make a hole in their rubber skin and slip it in?"

I look at Travis then back to him.

"Did you forget how we do things?" he aims at Travis with a snarl.

Travis doesn't retaliate, but his jaw is ticking ten to the dozen.

Twenty people including a child are now safe in the barn to

our left, their trackers removed, courtesy of Mop and the others all working fast. I can't say I'd given a huge amount of thought as to how we were going to pull this next part off, but Travis apparently should have, given his upbringing.

"You need to use the gun," his uncle says. He huffs, walking to his bag. Pulling out a yellow device, he clicks it open, then picks up one of the trackers. "Should fit," he says to himself. He slips the tracker in the end, pinches the skin on the back of the pig between its shoulder blades, then pulls the trigger. There's a sharp click. "Done." He slaps the pig's rump as it moves to the pen I opened. "How many more do you need?"

"Two per crate? Eleven more."

He laughs. It's fake. "I want two-grand per pig if they don't make it."

Two fucking grand? I look at him. He knows I really don't have time for this. "Fine," I spit. Cheeky fuck, extorting us. I guess I did promise I wouldn't burn him. He's just insuring himself. Makes sense.

We proceed to put the trackers in the pigs, working against the clock. I'm sweating as our production line works effectively. "How long we got left?" I ask Vincent, wiping my head with the back of my hand.

"Down to ten minutes."

"Fuck."

"They eating it yet?"

The Joker nods. "Oh yeah. They're eating," he shouts. "Greedy fucks."

The pig feed laced with the sleeping sedative has all but gone. I see the first pig go down with a thud. "Okay, let's move them into the crates."

I hear Skitz grimace as another pig goes down, and he and Beats lift it into the crate. "This better fucking work."

I grab the feet of another pig as Jack grabs the front. We

make light work of lifting it into our crate.

"Fucking show-offs," Skitz grumbles.

"Two minutes!" Vincent shouts.

We all move quicker, loading up the last crate with the last pig just in time.

I make my way to Mick, holding out my hand.

He stares at it before gingerly lifting his hand to mine. He pulls me into an embrace and slaps my back. "You've got a couple of hours before them pigs start waking up. Okay?"

I nod.

"Be safe."

I pull back and attempt a smile. The loud bang of the back of the lorry shutting, rings in my ears. "Some of my men will stay here. You know who to call if you need anything."

He nods.

Patting his arm, I then turn, heading towards Travis. We mount our bikes. Beats is driving the lorry, Billy and Skitz riding up front with him.

Jack comes over as I adjust my top button. He gestures towards it, and I grab my helmet off the bars. "Stay out of sight. Only move once my men are out of there."

"I'll wait for your signal," he says. Jack walks to his truck, running a hand through his hair.

I scan everyone as they start to move, taking this all in.

This has to work.

CHAPTER FORTY-FIVE

NOT SO UNKNOWN

Fuckin' Christ, that was unreal. How we scraped through that little shit storm is beyond me. The pigs though? That was a nice touch on Travis' behalf.

Driving as fast as I can, I'm desperate to get the man responsible for killing Mum. He may be wanted for multiple crimes, but there's no way he's getting away this time. He's mine. ASIS said I could do what I want with him, and I swear on my mother's grave, he's going to feel every bit of rage that has fuckin' driven me to this moment.

Closure. Peace. Revenge.

It's almost mine.

The satnav shows I'm twenty minutes away from the docks. Deano should be arriving there now. Making me double take, one of the phones on the front seat next to me starts ringing. I pick it up, momentarily peering at the screen. I don't recognise the name, but when the other phones start simultaneously lighting up, I pull the truck over with a screech.

Can't be a coincidence that the dead men we took them off are all suddenly receiving calls.

Trusting my gut, I call one of my guys running surveillance. The call doesn't connect. I frown checking the screen, then try again. No answer.

Shit.

Quickly finding his contact, I call Sean. "Something's fuckin' wrong," I blurt when he answers. "Surveillance aren't answering, and the phones I took off Costa's men are blowing up."

"Let me check surveillance." I hear him tap buttons. "Shit. We've lost comms."

I slap the wheel. "What about these phones?"

"Where are you now?"

I take a breath. "Still twenty minutes away from the docks."

I hear Sean tapping more keys in the background. "Head there as planned; we've got to assume they're on to us. I'll send my team to the farm."

"Fuck. Okay. I'll call the Rippers, let them know to start getting those people out of there. Keep me updated."

I make my call and floor it to the docks, having to park a mile away to avoid being spotted. Grabbing what I need from the truck, I quickly open the live feed to Dean. It shows him walking, the camera picking up men carrying crates to the boat. I sigh a breath of relief, then turn, running in the direction of my men.

I need to be quick. Need to be with my team ready to move once we get the signal.

Approaching where my men are a few minutes later, the sense of something out of place is immediate. The air surrounding me is heavy. I steady my breathing, treading lightly, watching my footing as I make my way closer.

My men should be here. Where the fuck are they?

I crouch near the small monitor set up. There's blood spattered on the screen, and my guy's weapon left on the ground. An ambush. This was hurried.

I pick up one of their earpieces, crumpled on the floor. *Please fuckin' work.* The sound of Dean talking comes through. I open up my feed to him. He's on his knees. *Shit.*

I go to stand as the sound of snapping bark comes from

behind. I duck. But not quick enough. A heavy boot ricochets off the side of my head, forcing me to spin, my head knocking against the cold, hard ground. Brain rattling, I drag my eyes to the man lifting his foot to strike me again.

If I don't move now, Deano will be in danger. The man I need to kill will get away.

Forcing my heavy body to roll, I avoid his heel, reaching for my gun at the same time. I fight the black darkness descending in front of me, aiming my gun at the man stood over me.

His gun is already trained at my head.

Closure. Peace. Revenge.

It was almost mine.

CHAPTER FORTY-SIX

DEAN

We pull up at the drop off just over an hour after leaving the farm. I lead the lorry into the dimly lit car park near the dock. No doubt Costa has this place locked down. We're out of sight, but there's a small lane running adjacent to the tree line sheltering us. It's the only way in and out of here by land.

With Travis by my side, we start towards the armed men stood by the boat. There's ten of them that I can count. Vincent follows close behind with Billy and his VP, whilst the rest of my men stay by the bikes. "Were they this armed last time?" I whisper, my lips hardly moving.

"No," Travis replies, doing the same.

We come to a stop. My heart races, and I take a subtle, steadying breath.

"Gentlemen." Costa looks between us, his hands in his trouser pockets. He signals to the men stood behind him, and they walk to us, disarming all of us of the weapons we're carrying, including my knife.

"What is this?" Travis asks him.

Costa's eyes are grey. His face creased with lines of annoyance. We made him wait. He's suspicious. Only natural given the contents of the crates.

Three men walk from behind us carrying heavy bags. Presumably, they're the rest of the weapons my men were carrying.

"Getting shot. A breakdown." He peers over my shoulder. Is he checking if Billy's on his bike? "Maybe next time we try to avoid any hiccups." One of his brows lifts.

Travis folds his arms. "Hiccups or not, your shipment always gets here," he says bullishly.

The corner of Costa's mouth twitches, and I swallow. Hard. "That's why I put you on point." He takes his hand from his pocket, clicking his fingers. "Ignore me taking weapons. It's just a precaution."

Another man steps closer. I don't instantly recognise him. He looks up, his eyes fixating on mine as he talks to Costa. He reminds me of the officer from the custody station a couple of months ago. You'd think he knew me the way he stares.

Before I can get a better look, he turns his head as he speaks, his mouth dipped to Costa's ear so only he can hear what's being said.

Taking a sharp breath, I watch him walk away, making a call. Travis said they didn't check the crates last time; they counted them and that was that. So, when men start walking forward, I step aside letting them past, my eyes flicking to the man who walked away, before I follow.

"Who's that?" I ask Travis hushed, nodding in the man's direction.

I beg my eyes not to look for a hidden Jack and his team as Travis discreetly looks over his shoulder. "Costa's right-hand. Guy's a cunt."

I look back quickly when an unexpected shuffle comes from the back of the lorry. I reach for my smokes, busying myself. *No. Oh fuck no.* I dart my frantic eyes to Travis, wondering if he heard it. He doesn't react. Maybe he didn't. Beats and Billy on the other hand, their eyes are wide. Being the two stood closest to the lorry, they're definitely thinking along the same lines as me. If those pigs wake up anytime soon, this place will be a blood bath.

Another rustle.

This time, I see the slight widening of Travis' eyes as comprehension dawns. The lights lighting up the dock aren't too bright, but they're enough for him to read my expression.

One of Costa's men moves to unlock the back of the lorry. It clanks open, and he pulls himself up. "One, two, three, four, five, six," he says out loud. He then signals to Costa, giving him a thumbs up.

Even I can smell the hum of pigs. Or maybe that's just on me? Costa's men don't seem to react as they offload the crates, systematically carrying them towards the boat.

With every crate that gets moved, a small weight lifts from my shoulders. I can feel myself moving beyond the fear.

"Can you smell shit?" The man who asked lifts his arm, sniffing his pits as he slams the door to the lorry closed.

I turn away from him so as not to draw any more attention, then step closer to Costa.

He holds his phone to his ear, turning to face me. He glances to Vincent stood alongside us, then to the tree line.

Fuck.

"Yeah. Understood." He ends the call slipping his phone in his suit jacket. "Next shipment will be in two weeks."

Me and Travis look to one another. "That's sooner than planned," I reply sceptically.

Costa rubs his chin with his palm. "What can I say. Business is booming."

I glower at him. "I bet."

Anger starts to surface when I think of the little boy now back at the farm. Of those less fortunate in this, *business*. Like the girl washed up along the shore, and the many more they've found just like her.

"Problem?" Costa holds his questioning gaze on mine.

Only that I plan on you being dead in about two minutes. I undo my top button, giving Jack my signal. "Two weeks is fine."

Making my blood turn to ice, loud banging suddenly kicks from inside the last crate about to board the boat. The men drop it to the ground with a thud. The pig clearly destined on getting us all fucking killed, wakes up even quicker.

More banging.

One of Costa's men double takes. The way he's taking slow steps toward the boat, his head tilted to one side, he's clearly wondering whether he's going mad.

I look over Costa's shoulder, seeing him attempt to look inside the crate.

"Uh, boss," he says.

Costa turns his attention to his man.

Shit.

Like being taken to slaughter, a deathly squeal from one of the pigs then wails through the gap between us, and the man closest steps back. I don't react, but the noise makes me fight the rising unease rushing to the surface.

Costa has a look of confusion on his face. He turns his head when another unquestionable scream rips through the air. Then his enraged gaze is back on me. Lifting his hand he then snaps his fingers, and Travis and I find ourselves staring down the barrels of two guns.

Motherfucker.

I hear my men move behind me, the sound of them stepping closer halting when I raise my hand.

"Did I just hear a fucking *pig*?" Costa asks, confusion etched across his face as he looks between the two of us.

The heavy beat of my heart thrums in my ears, but I hear footsteps approaching behind me. "Pigs?" Vincent says indifferently.

Costa frowns, and my stomach drops. "Plural?"

Vincent, the fucking idiot, realises his mistake. "I didn't hear anything," he says dismissively, trying to cover his tracks.

Come on, come on. Now's the fucking time to show yourself, Jack. Where the fuck are you?

Costa's eyes narrow with pin prick precision. "You're going to fucking lie to me? Twice."

"What are you—"

"—Don't play fucking dumb with me," Costa snaps, cutting Vincent off. Costa rips his gun from the inside of his jacket, pointing it at Vincent. "Explain to me why my men at the hangar aren't answering their phones."

Vincent takes a breath, his face now hardened. "I don't know —"

Costa fires his gun in the air, making everyone flinch. He points the gun back at Vincent. "Last chance you fucking idiot. Why are my men who *you* collected from, not answering their phones?" Costa's face is deadly. We all see it. He knows.

"Signal was—"

Jamming the handle of the gun into Vincent's face, Costa smiles as a thick stream of blood pisses from Vincent's nose.

He staggers back, trying to catch himself. "Alright," he says holding up one hand. I look at him as he stands straight. The way his face tightens before he looks back at Costa has me weighted down with an evil dread.

My stomach knots. My head swims. Panic rises.

"Rippers killed them," Billy shouts from behind us.

Vincent's head snaps towards him in shock.

Shit. What the fuck's he playing at? I don't risk looking back. Is this fucking happening? I hear a low growl from Travis. My own anger matches his as I bite back the need to throw myself at Billy and gut him with my bare hands. I should have known better than to trust he would play along.

Costa laughs and it's callous. It makes my body turn numb. "On your knees," he spits at us.

I sneer as I drop to my knees, briefly looking over my shoulder at the men behind me. The two Sodom Saviours stand clear on one side, whilst my men are held at gunpoint.

I've seen this before; felt the end nearing itself in a way I hadn't foreseen. The men meant to be storming in should have been here by now. Something's definitely wrong. This should be over.

As if reading my mind, Costa steps closer to me. "I can see you wondering where the *other* men are. Let me guess, they should have arrived *before* the pigs started waking."

On cue one squeals, and he turns firing three rounds at the wooden crate. Silence. And I'm down two-grand. "You wannabe gangsters fail to realise that men like me are used to working with scum like you. *I* disappear, hundreds of people lose billions. *You* disappear, the world simply doesn't have enough fucks to give. That's how insignificant you are in all of this." I'm completely unarmed as Costa stalks in front of me. "Care to know when you fucked up?"

I can't bite my tongue any longer. "No, but I'm sure you're desperate to tell us anyway."

A smile, one that screams he can't wait to kill me, pulls across his face. "We had cameras at the hangar. Saw Rippers MC go in all guns blazing." He waves his gun between me and Travis. "Nice job cutting the wire by the way, but you were too late. And the trackers we use for situations *just like this*, they led to an interesting location. You know," he laughs sarcastically, throwing his head back, "the pigs actually make fucking sense now. Ten out of ten for effort."

Jackknifing, my insides contort, the pain unbearable. There's no fucking way of knowing whether he's serious about finding the farm. But if he has? And the majority of us are here bar a handful of Rippers left behind... I royally fucked Travis' uncle. Why the fuck did I think we could pull this off?

If Jack's men don't stop them, he could already be dead. Those people we saved could have been picked up already.

Legs.... I curse under my breath as satisfaction swims in his eyes. He has me. "What was my second mistake?" I ask flatly, trying to buy time in case Jack *is* still coming. What if...

"The men you have situated out on the road?"

Fuck.

"All dead. For a surveillance team they definitely didn't see us coming."

It's then I let out my sigh, unable to restrain the excessive turmoil twisting in my head. Fear pulses through me, my mouth turning dry. We're dead. All of us. Because of me.

Costa checks how many bullets he has in his gun. "Anything you want to say before I singlehandedly wipe you all clean off the map?"

Catching my attention, Costa's right-hand man walks over with fury and malice in his face. His feet stomp the concrete, his fists balled down by his sides. Stood side on to Costa, he withdraws his weapon, clearly wanting to be the one to end us.

He holds up the gun, then sends a bullet right through Costa's skull.

CHAPTER FORTY-SEVEN

DEAN

I peer through one eye. The sound of the gun mixed with the splattering of brain against the ground, forces my jaw to the floor. Costa's right-hand man stands over his boss' corpse, looking down at the fragments of his skull now coating the gravel.

Scraping a hand through my hair, I watch as he bends his legs with his elbows resting on his knees, then scoops the tip of his finger through the remnants of the bloodied mass he once took orders from.

What. The. Fuck.

My stomach flips when he turns to face us, lifting his finger to his line of vision. He stands as he inspects the squelching matter in the dim night light, pressing his forefinger to his thumb repeatedly. The sound makes the glands in my throat, swell.

As if realising all eyes are on him, he quickly wipes his hand on the side of his trousers, making my jaw lower even more. "Tsk, tsk, tsk," he clicks his teeth, shaking his head. Deranged. "This was never *his* plan. I'm sick of him taking credit for *my* work." He points to Costa's body. "Liar."

He holds out his hand for Vincent, completely unperturbed when Vincent doesn't react; too confused, too in shock like the rest of us. "Well, come on." He smiles, pleased with himself as he drags Vincent by the elbow.

I see Billy and the other Saviour inch closer in my peripherals.

Like a ferris wheel, time moves slowly like a never-ending cycle before me. My mind can't work out what the fuck is happening. He killed Costa; the man leading this entire operation.

"Look. Do you like it?" The man turns his palm to the sky, waving it over Costa as Vincent looks down at me for help. I have no words. My eyes manage to find Travis, but that's it. "Well?" He nudges Vincent, urging him to speak.

"Who the fuck are you?" Vincent asks, his voice heavy with uncertainty.

The man mutters as though deep in conversation with himself, his head bobbing from side to side in sharp, quick-fire movements. Then he looks at me square on, his shoulders instantly dropping. I see it; like being released from a straitjacket, I see the moment things shift.

Snap. The deranged man is gone. He vanishes before my eyes with one blink.

Holding himself much steadier, he slowly draws his hand to his pocket, removes a pair of glasses, then places them on his face.

Fuck. I think it's him.

He runs a hand through his hair as though wiping away the last persona. "Who the fuck am I?" He grins. "I'm Cain. Maybe he remembers me?" he says confidently, gesturing towards me. I hear him take a steadying breath as he undoes his suit jacket, cocking his head ever so slightly to one shoulder, the movement unnerving.

I go to look at Travis. "There's no use looking at him. He wasn't there." He waves a finger, his voice calm, no longer jumpy.

My heart drops. "Where?" I question knowingly. I shift on my knees, keeping my voice calm, even though my insides are anything but.

The corner of his mouth raises. Licking his lips, he then lowers his chin. "Let's rewind time." He coughs, and when he speaks again, I'm gripped by white hot rage. "There were two of you in the woods," he says, his Australian accent no longer masked.

"You son of a bitch." I grit my teeth hearing Travis curse under his breath. This cunt's responsible for killing my aunt all those years ago. I don't know where Jack is or whether he's still watching, but I sure as hell know this bastard's dead. If not Jack, I'll be the one to make sure he meets his end.

"That's it," he chides, his voice cackling with a psychotic edge. He bends his legs, looking at me with disdain. "The memories come flooding back, don't they?"

A vortex of burning flames slash at my skin as my demons fight for their freedom. I close my eyes, still able to picture the scene before me. My aunt's body. Jack's cry. It rings so loudly in my head like a jolt of lightning throwing me back into the pits I fought so hard to escape from. I'd almost left this behind me. Almost accepted there was nothing more we could have done to save her. Once again, I'm clawing for the edge, desperately trying to hold on to my sanity.

"Shall I tell you how she screamed? How she begged for her life." He speaks slowly. Threateningly. Dark.

I'm on my feet, Travis shadowing my move. We barely make it a foot closer to him before we're both grabbed from behind, a gun pressed firmly to the back of our heads.

"No! No! No!" he shouts again, like a madman not getting his own way. "You don't move unless *I* fucking say you can." He swings his boot, winding me.

Pain courses through my ribs as I bend. The scatty,

delusional man is back. But so are my demons. "Her screams will be nothing compared to yours," I cough, my eyes gluing to his.

"Dean," Travis warns, as I slow my struggle with the man holding me. I'm going to goad this motherfucker until he snaps. If he's found the farm, found Jack and his men who were waiting, then what else is left to do but fight. We're not getting out of here, that much is clear. If this is it, we go down swinging.

The man laughs, sucking his teeth. "This part's my favourite." One of his eyes twitches. "Here." He holds out his gun to Vincent. "A gift to you. Pick one."

My eyes dart to Vincent's as Travis and I struggle. He doesn't move. He's just as fucked as we are, even if the clown to his left seems to favour him.

"Come on, come on." Cain grows impatient, uncurling Vincent's fingers and placing the gun in his hold. "Shoot one!" he shouts.

Like pinballs, Vincent's eyes ping left to right. Worried. Maybe he won't shoot one of us?

Cain sighs. "It's easy, watch." He snatches the gun back, lassoing it above his head. "Line 'em up."

There's a flurry of activity behind me. I fight against the man holding me. "No!" I push against him, no longer caring for the gun still pushed against my head. This prick's here to draw this out—put on a show. I won't be killed. Not yet.

My men are pulled to my line of vision, each one thrown to their knees. My heart constricts as though an icy hand has torn through my chest. It tightens its grip, indescribable fear radiating from within.

Beats. Mop. Riggs. Skitz. The Joker. All of them are here.

Cain strides forwards. He taps the gun in his hand to each one of their heads, starting with Beats. "I need you boys to know why this is happening." He moves slowly, sizing them up. With every step that he takes, my fear that he's going to kill them in cold blood, magnifies. "You see, I wanted to be one of you so badly. Well, not you, more like them." He swings his arm, pointing at Vincent. "I would have done near on anything to get in. Hell, I *did* do everything that was expected of me. And what did I get in return? Do you know?"

He pushes Mop's head back with the barrel, twisting his head with a demented glare. Mop doesn't give him a reaction. Not so much as a look. Cain huffs. "Or maybe you do?" He taps Skitz's head twice. Skitz similarly doesn't show any emotion to the loon stood over him.

"How about you?" He reaches the end of the line, then turns to look at me, flashing me an evil grin. I catch The Joker's eyes before the trigger is pulled.

BANG.

There's no fear there before his lifeless body then hits the deck. My men next to him drop their heads. The air is suddenly deathly silent as I stagger, my eyes wide as everything around me blurs.

I'm consumed. Overcome by hate and the desire to kill. I should have known I never stood a chance of leaving.

Taking confident strides, Cain walks to me. His face is daringly close to mine as my lips part; harsh, heavy breaths escaping my lungs. "I did what I was asked and they wouldn't patch me in... apparently I was too hot headed—made too many rash decisions. But I've shown them, haven't I?" I don't answer. "Haven't I!" he roars, spitting on my face.

Vincent moves forward, his hands up in surrender. "You have!"

The psycho in front of me looks to him, then back to me. He snarls as he smiles, a vicious twist in his lips as he sucks in a deep breath. "You think *I* need *your* approval? Ha!" He throws his head back releasing a manic laugh. "You're not worthy of *that* cut! Only pussies struggle to kill their enemies."

Walking around me, he leans in closer, whispering for only me to hear, his hand resting on my shoulder. "Want to know a secret?"

I move my head away from his.

"Weak men don't belong in our world. I did this for the Saviours. To show my loyalty to the club who rejected me. But I've changed my mind, they don't deserve it. You see, it's within chaos I find my peace." He points his gun at Vincent.

Vincent looks between me and Cain. None of this was part of our plan. He doesn't get time to speak, but he dips his chin as his eyes lock with mine. It's enough for me to know; to understand.

The gun fires, and I see a moment. A window of an opportunity as Vincent falls. Pushing back against the man holding me, I kick out, disarming Cain. He doesn't see my second kick that flies through the air, landing on his nose. The crunch vibrates up my leg, but I shake myself free, moving to grab his gun on the floor.

Another loud crack then sounds.

I crumple, my leg giving way. Adrenaline hides the pain in the back of my leg as it gets wetter, warm blood soaking through my jeans. *Fuck.* Trying to stand, I'm grabbed as I push myself up, refusing to back down. Every one of my men has a gun aimed at them. Those lined up in front of me and Travis behind me.

Swinging my head, a light flickers in the moonlight near the trees. It's gone as soon as I try to focus my gaze.

Billy steps forward, but he's unarmed like us. Nothing he can do even if he wanted to. At this point, it's me and Cain in the middle of a warped circle.

Another flash catches my eye, sending my heart racing. Is someone there? Jack? I sigh knowing it can't be. Costa said they'd found them. Jack wouldn't have let me down, and Costa wouldn't have let him live. He'd be here if he could.

Cain looks at his man behind me, deciding my wound is bad enough to not have to hold me.

Straightening, I put my weight on one leg, the other bleeding out, blood now flowing freely to my boot. As the adrenaline starts to subside, fresh pain stings. It rides its way through my bones trying to cripple me.

Wiping the blood from under his nose, the crazed man steps closer once again. "Do you want to know how I did it? The kill that set our hatred for each other in motion."

His breath hits my face he's that close. I try to phase him out, but I can't ignore how he licks his fingers clean of his own blood before he speaks again. "When she struggled, I held her down." The cunt smiles, remembering. "My grip was so tight around her throat, she purpled quicker than I had hoped for. Death was close, but I learned a lesson that day."

He spins on his heels waving a finger in the air as I see a movement in the shadows. "When killing someone," he begins, and I focus back on him, "you gain deeper satisfaction stealing their life if they're tiptoeing on the edge of consciousness. I could see the way her eyes bulged for days."

He hums closing his eyes as his words stroke my anger. I have no time to react though as he strikes his fist through my face.

I spin, hitting the ground, fearing I'm not walking away from this. This is it. My eyes lock with Travis'. He senses it too. We're surrounded. Unarmed. Dealing with a psycho. It's me this guy wants before anyone else. I'll hold on as long as I can. Whatever I can do; buy time, stall, I don't fucking know, but I'll do it.

Pushing myself up, I accept my fate along with another hit to my face. I spit blood, sniffing in through my now blocked nose. "What about Costa?" I point out, and again I see movement, a figure loitering in the shadows. "Vincent? You shot them both like a coward."

"They deserved it!" he fires back furiously. "This is *my* operation. These are *my* men. Costa was a good front, but—"

"Let me guess, you wanted the glory." Travis earns himself a whack on the back of his head as he joins in. He drops his palms flat to the ground. Dazed.

"*I* built this from ruin," Cain spits loudly, looking at his man behind me. I'm struck on the temple without warning. My hearing fades, my vision swimming before me. "*I* was the one who really started the war! It was *me* who should have risen to power! Not him or the men back home." I catch the last part of his speech as he jerks his head to Vincent's body.

Fuck, my eyes won't stop spiralling. I rest my hands on my knees to steady myself, knowing someone is close by, edging their way closer. "Shame they never patched you in," I say cooly. If I keep this nut job talking, maybe, just maybe, whoever is closing in will have enough time to take him out.

Like a prayer being answered, one of the armed men stood by the boat is dropped to the floor carefully. I can't see the man who took him out, but I know. I can fucking feel it.

Cain turns to me, his smile wide, no life behind his eyes. Blank. The soles of his shoes crunch against the ground. Standing in front of me, he slips his hands in his pockets no longer shouting and fired up. "Does it hurt to know you were only a few seconds too late?"

I stand straight but my face drops.

He steps closer, lifting his gaze to meet mine. "Does it make you feel responsible, knowing she was under my body when I squeezed the life from her."

I swing my head, crunching my skull to his nose. I fall, and he staggers as he laughs. He's enjoying this.

On my knees, my leg soaked in blood, Cain steps closer, pushing my head back, his blood dripping on my face. "Best part about killing that bitch?" His lips curl up. "When I thought I'd killed her too soon, I let go. She took a few moments to come around, but when she did, I liked the lifeless way she looked at me."

He stares through me, his words about my aunt burning every part of my body. I grit my teeth, my jaw aching from how hard I bite down.

"I did it again and again and again, taking her to the edge then bringing her back. Just when I thought I'd do it one more time, the idea came to me." He pulls out my knife they took off me, turning it in his hands, the tip spinning on the end of his finger.

Behind him, two more men drop, and the figure hunts closer. I ignore Cain stalking around me, keeping my eyes trained to the dark; willing them to find the person I want to see.

Cain laughs by my ear. "She watched me cutting through her throat. Even after I knew she'd gone, my hands kept going." My knife is held to my throat from behind, the pressure harsh, directly across my Adam's apple. "Her eyes stayed open the entire time I sliced through her bones. You should have seen her... she was so *fucking* beautiful." His breath stammers.

"I'm going to *fucking* kill you."

"You know what?" He jams the blade in from behind above my right hip, his other arm wrapped around my throat, holding me in place. "I just don't think you'll get the chance."

Searing pain blazes through me, ripping through every muscle and bone in my body. I grit my teeth again, biting through my tongue. Fucking hell, it's like nothing I've felt before.

My cry out has Travis shouting and cursing at the wind.

"Now you get to watch everything you built, every one of your men, die under my hands."

I have nowhere to go. No moves to make. Fixing my mind on Mads, my eyes fill as I realise I won't get the ending I want, then a smile creeps on my face when I think of my girls.

"*I* win," he says pulling the knife from my back.

I'm dizzy from the gripping pain, but manage to look up, seeing a commotion by the boat. The man I knew was coming raises a gun. "No," I cough.

Cain leans closer still unaware that help is here.

"You lose."

Jack's gun is fired, taking down the last man by the boat.

Travis jumps to his feet, shrugging off the man behind him, knocking his gun away. They fight, and guns are fired to my right.

No. I turn my gaze to my men. I can't make out who's who, my vision's beginning to blur. I need to get up whilst there's still a slither of hope that my brothers can get out of here. They're fighting back. I need to help them.

Raising my good leg, I haul myself to stand, the movement tearing the wound open on my back. It burns like a wildfire, the blinding pain disorientating as I drag my bad leg next to the other.

"Deano," I hear Jack shout.

The psycho behind me starts breathing heavy. He looks up and sees Jack, his eyes blackened, his stare soulless. A sinister smile then licks his face, and he turns demonic, snarling when Jack steps closer.

They stare at each other, oblivious to everyone. Jack checks his empty gun chamber, then throws it to the floor. Judging by his expression, he heard every word Cain spoke about Linda. He wipes his face with the back of his hand whilst Cain spins the knife in his.

"Watch closely," Cain whispers next to me. He unbuttons his jacket, the handle of a gun pokes out of the inner pocket.

Jack charges, but Cain doesn't move. He remains smiling, waiting for Jack to get close to him. *Fuck*.

Swinging his arms and legs, Jack drives himself towards us,

fury fuelling him. He doesn't know the animal next to me has a gun.

Lifting my hand, I yell at Jack to stop, falling to one side as I fight with my weakening body. He can't hear me. He gets closer, and my panic rises.

I see Cain reach into his suit jacket, seconds before Jack gets to him.

Adrenaline eclipses my thoughts. Like a slate being wiped clean, I throw myself at Jack, blocking the bullets that Cain fires.

"Nooooo!" Jack's voice pierces the air.

My eyes widen, staring at him, the pain in my leg and my back making way for the new one in my chest. I hiss, sucking in any air that I can as Cain runs away.

Jack catches me, and my body slumps, my head dropping to his chest. "Deano, no!" he yells frantically. "Travis!" He trembles as Travis helps catch me.

Lowering us to the ground, Travis grips my arms tightly. I try to hold on to him but it's no good, my body's shutting down.

"Take him," Jack orders, slipping his hand from underneath me. He then runs in the direction of his man.

In Travis' hold, my body's useless as he sits on his knees, propping me up against his large frame. "Dean, stay with me!"

My head rolls, and he looks down at me, terror in his eyes. It's the first time I've seen him look scared. "I'm… sorry."

His face tightens.

"I'm… getting… out," I finally tell him, my voice sore. It's not the way I wanted. But it's the way I knew I'd get. My life and the way I've lived deserve nothing more.

The pressure in my chest is almost unbearable. Travis looks down at me, his grip on my arm tightening. "No you're fucking not."

I raise a weak smile, taking a long blink as I try to breathe. The darkness coming for me feels oddly peaceful. I don't fear it as it tries to swallow me. My lower back's numb, my leg without feeling. Sucking in more air, I don't know how the rest of my men are, who's hurt or if we're even whole.

Travis scrambles through my pockets, pulling out my phone.

I tap my right pocket, making him look down.

Removing my wallet, he sees I can't move my hand to it. He breathes heavier, his fear rising. "What'd you need, brother?"

I close my eyes. "Note." My head swims but I have to finally know for sure.

He moves fast, opening it up, flicking his thumb through the contents until he sees it. He holds the piece of paper, unfolding it. "Fuck," he says, now understanding. His voice shakes as he puts the note in my hand, curling my fingers to hold it. Is the stubborn bastard finally emotional? "I can't wait to see you try to handle this," he says, light amusement in his tone.

My dying heart warms before a stabbing sensation tears straight down the middle. "You'll take..." I cough, my mouth filling with blood, "care... of them." My eyes flit to Billy. "*All,* of them. Lauren, Mollie... your... son."

He frowns, tears filling his eyes. "I won't need to because I'm not letting you leave. That little girl's going to need her daddy." Moving quickly, he takes out my phone and dials someone, holding it to his ear. "Shit," he says.

"Ma... ds?" I gargle, feeling the pressure in my lung increase.

"Yeah mate, I'll get her. Hold on. For fuck's sake, you hold on!" His fingers tap the screen, the light reflecting the look of panic on his face. "Mads!" he shouts when she answers.

I can't hear what he says as I let my head fall back, no longer able to hold it up. The distorted image of Jack slips into view. I don't know if it's real or if I'm seeing what I want to believe.

He's drilling the man who killed his mother's head into the ground. Over and over he slams it down, his hands dripping with blood, his face tight with anger. Unconsciousness almost has me, but I know Cain's already dead.

Jack heard every word. It's done.

Even with all my broken pieces, a calming peace washes over me. It ripples, numbing me from my head to my toes, dousing me in a fervent bliss. There's no pain anymore. All my fear has steadily slipped away.

My hand tightens around the paper in my grasp. For them—the last thing I can give Mads and my daughter—I finally admit I was enough.

I close my eyes.

Three things I would change. It's no longer me, myself and I.

I wasn't perfect.

But I *was* enough.

CHAPTER FORTY-EIGHT

MADISON

We've been on the road for three and a half hours. They're so quiet at this time in the morning, a false sense of calm has set around us. It's unnerving. Like the calm before the storm, I know the worst is yet to come.

My hands haven't stopped shaking. My tears haven't stopped falling. As soon as I answered Jess' phone, I knew by the rattle of Travis' voice that my worst fear was coming true. Dean was hurt. And for a man who's never shown me any signs of being scared, I knew Travis was terrified.

He wouldn't tell me the extent of Dean's injuries; he simply begged me to get to the hospital. *There wasn't much time.*

We grabbed our things and said goodbye, getting on the road mere minutes after taking the call. I'll speak to Bex properly once I know what's going on, but right now, under the pulsing beat of the lights lighting up the motorway, all I can see is the image of the man who *is* my world. Without him, I don't see how I make it through.

I send Lauren and Mollie a message as fresh tears spill over my lashes. The thought of not seeing him before... No. I shake my head. That isn't an option. He'll make it. He'll pull through whatever's happened. He has to.

"Drive faster," I tell Jess.

Already pushing 85mph, her foot hits the floor, and I'm sucked into my seat. He just has to wait. My promise to always run to him has never changed. I'm coming back to you, VP. Wait for me.

Jess brakes hard, parking the car directly outside of Accident and Emergency. My head bangs, my legs ache from sitting down for so long.

I swing open the car door, running toward the entrance as fast as I possibly can.

"Go steady," Jess scolds, but I ignore her, unable to think about anything other than getting inside to Dean.

The glass doors zip open. "Dean Carter?" I say to the desk before I'm even there. "He was brought in earlier." My voice cracks. My bottom lip wobbles uncontrollably. All I can think is that it took too long—we took too long getting here.

"You are?" The woman's eyes search mine.

"I'm his wife." I don't know why those words come out. But I know that's how I feel—it's what I want. "Where is he?"

She scrolls through her computer, looking intensely at the screen. Seconds feel like hours. The only sound I can hear is the drum of my heartbeat in my ears. "He's still in theatre."

I spin away from the desk.

"Hey! You can't—"

Ignoring the people in the waiting room, the lady behind the desk shouts at me as I push open the double doors through to the next set of rooms. I hear Jess apologise as I read the signs suspended above me, seeing 'theatre' up ahead.

Running as best I can, I make my way to the end of the corridor, taking a right past endless bays, some with curtains drawn, some open. I feel eyes on me as I keep going, my feet slipping on the polished floor. I fling open another set of doors leading to another waiting room. Where is he?

A nurse doing her rounds shouts at me to stop.

"Madison!" I hear Jess from behind.

I keep going, feeling the pull of my heart as I round the final corner. I'm so close to him. I can feel him. Can feel my soul being pulled to its other half. Putting one foot in front of the other, I make my way through the doors, stumbling when I see Travis and some of the guys waiting. They don't talk. None of them are looking at one another. Their heads are lowered, their bodies bloodied and bruised.

What happened?

Travis looks up, and I know I'll never forget the look on his face. His gunmetal eyes are empty. Sunken in and bloodshot, the spark they usually carry has gone.

"Travis?"

He stands, and the guys look at him. They follow his gaze, and I look at them all in turn. Beats and Mop exchange a look of uncertainty.

The door opens behind me, and I hear Jess speaking to someone. Then it's quiet. My eyes fill when no one speaks, the deathly silence, utterly crushing. "Where is he?"

Jess places a hand on my shoulder. "Madison," she starts, but my gaze is trained on Travis.

He rubs his beard, his eyes flicking towards a door to my right. Rubbing the back of his neck, the door then opens. I see men and women in scrubs moving around.

A nurse makes her way to Travis as I beeline for the door, causing everyone to jump to their feet. I don't need to hear what she's going to say. I need to see Dean.

I let my feet carry me to one of the theatre rooms. Filled with machines, the sterile smell of the room floods my nose as my eyes land on the bed in the centre of the room.

Men and women in scrubs swarm Dean's body. I know it's him although he's almost unrecognisable. Covered in blood, his eyes are taped shut. He's laid on his side as they probe and prod at his back.

"What are you doing in here? This is for patients only," a nurse tells me, although I pay her no notice.

He looks so helpless. Fragile. "Dean," I sob, choking on my words.

"Miss, please, you need to leave."

Heavy hands land on my shoulders as my heart starts to pick up speed, matching the beeps of the monitor by the side of the bed. The nurse moves as Travis takes hold of me, pulling me into his arms. "Mads, come on."

"Keep her out of here," the nurse tells him over the sound of my uncontrollable sobs.

"Yeah, I got it," he snaps back, his annoyance rising.

Tears stinging like acid, the gap being forced between us rips through me. It leaves nothing but devastation and sadness in its wake as Travis sits me down next to him. All I want to do is go back in there. I need to let Dean know I'm here.

He can't be alone.

It's not fair. *None* of this is fair.

I try to stand but Travis puts me back in my place. "Sit down."

"I need to do something," I sob.

He brings me into his side like the last time we sat like this, wondering when Dean was going to come home. "We have to wait, Mads." His arm around me tightens.

Dropping my head, I stare at my hands, twisting them as if that will somehow help hold back my inner turmoil.

Jess comes to sit the other side of me, taking one of my hands in hers. We don't speak. Sadness and despair simply roam the waiting room. I let go of the breath I was holding, releasing a fresh wave of tears.

I can't lose him. He has to come back to me.

I don't know how long we waited. None of us left until the nurse came out to talk to us. We haven't seen him yet; we only know the list of injuries the nurse trailed off. One stab wound to the right hip. One gunshot wound to his left calf and two bullets in his lung.

Her words had cut like daggers through all of us. Of course, the guys knew what he came in with—they were the ones to bring him here, but I haven't had the strength to ask what happened. I know Travis isn't going to tell me. So, I stay mute, saving my energy for the man who needs it most.

And I wait, no longer prepared to plead to know what caused him to be so badly hurt. I know what caused this; men fighting men. But for what? Some bullshit honour? Some lifelong grudge they haven't allowed themselves to get over? I know I still don't fully understand how someone could hurt another like they do, maybe I never will. But I am sure my child will not be raised in this world.

Seeing Dean covered in blood on that hospital bed... there's no place for children there. There's no room for peace when evil as vile as that lurks at every bend. I know Dean wanted out, but I had no idea how he planned on doing it. He kept telling me he was almost there, that he was almost done. He couldn't have meant like *this*. He couldn't have meant that *he* was almost out without taking me and our baby with him.

It went wrong. Whatever he thought he had to do, he clearly didn't achieve it. Otherwise, why else would he be fighting for his life the way he is? There's no room to envision the possibility of him not coming home. Looking around at those of us still here, do I really want to live amongst this without him? If he... if he doesn't wake up, what is there here for me?

I bite down on the pain, looking up when the door to the theatre room opens. I stand, seeing the same nurse from earlier approaching. I don't need to say anything as she studies my face. "We're moving him to a room on the ICU. You should be able to see him soon."

"Thank you," I say on a lost breath. My throat burns from crying.

As she walks away, Jess—who refused to leave, stands next to me. "I'm going to grab us some coffee. I'll be right back."

"I'll help." Travis pushes to his feet, stretching his back. He's exhausted, and judging by the blood all over him, he was the one who carried Dean in.

He steps past me, but I place my hand on his arm, stopping him. When he turns, I slowly curl into him, a silent thank you and show of love that I'm glad he's okay.

He wraps his arms around me. "He's going to be okay," he says into my hair, before he lets me go and walks with Jess.

Moments after they're gone, the theatre doors open, and a rush of cold air kisses my cheeks.

Mop quickly moves to my side as Dean is wheeled out. It takes every piece of strength I possess to stay up right. If it wasn't for Mop's hand on me, I wouldn't manage it.

Dean isn't awake. His body's still covered in blood and destruction. It's bleak, a grim slap to the face that he's not out of the woods yet.

"Do you want to come now?" Another nurse holds out her hand for me to follow.

I look up at Mop, giving him a nod as I go. Following the rolling bed, I hold my breath until he's pushed into a private room. Looking through the small glass window, the machines come to life and start beeping.

The nurse sees that he's covered with enough blankets, and I wait as various wires are plugged into different tubes coming out of him. He's so pale.

"Mrs Carter?"

I turn to look at the doctor stood holding a clipboard.

"Has a nurse spoken with you yet?"

I shake my head, looking back at Dean.

"Your husband," my heart sinks, "suffered a punctured lung caused by the bullets to the chest. He was lucky in the sense they didn't hit any major blood vessels or arteries, but he's currently unable to breathe by himself."

My throat clogs. Wrapping my arms around me, I manage to look to the doctor. "Will he make it?"

The doctor quickly scratches his head, his eyes sunken in. "Surgery was difficult. There was shrapnel in the lung damaging part of the oesophagus, but we were able to remove most of the larger parts."

"Most?"

"He may require further surgery. It was too risky to continue at the time." The doctor drops his head. "He lost a lot of blood. He's had a blood transfusion and been given IV fluids. He's also been given some antibiotics. The tube we placed to drain the blood and fluid in his lung has helped, but the machine you can hear beeping is breathing for him."

My tears fall but I don't wipe them away.

"I know how scary things must look, Mrs Carter. Rest assured he's in the best place he can be. If he manages to start breathing for himself and is stable enough, we'll be able to carry out more surgery."

If he manages. All I can do is nod. Understanding.

Placing a hand on my arm, the doctor tries to smile. "Make sure you get some rest."

I smile as best I can before he leaves.

Gathering strength, I step into the room with cautious feet, my legs shaking. His back is torn up, the stitches stretching from the top of his shoulder to the middle of his spine. Above his hip, an incision is swollen and angry. I struggle to breathe looking at him this way. It's agony. He's been in surgery for hours. His body needs to heal.

"Let me get you a chair." The nurse sees me stood still, sensing my hesitation. She moves and pulls a chair to the side of the bed, facing the side Dean's laying on.

I thank her and slowly drop to the seat. "How long can I stay with him?"

I don't miss the sudden way her eyes turn down as she sighs. "As long as you can."

Because he doesn't have long? I turn ice cold, fear that I'm going to lose him setting in.

The nurse moves to a noticeboard near the door. "He's allowed two visitors up here. I'll put your name down, and who else should I add?"

Two visitors. That's it? I remember only seeing Jack the bare minimum when he was in hospital before he... "Travis Johnson," I tell her before I look back to Dean.

Marked with bruises and cuts, his face looks so beaten up. His chest rises and falls as the machine works, breathing for him. I don't care how bad my heart hurts, what he's gone through must have been a thousand times worse. I suck in a breath, my head falling, the tears unstoppable. I don't look up as the nurse checks us before she leaves.

The door clicks shut, and I bite my top lip, catching the salty wetness from my tears. Taking his hand in mine, I hold him tight, pushing my damp lips to his knuckles. They're covered in dried blood, but I don't care. I breathe him in, keeping myself as close as I can.

I stay like this, my head lowered to his hand until I can feel my lack of sleep catching up with me. I blink a heavy blink, pushing myself up. "I love you," I tell him, aware he might not be able to hear me. I know he won't say it back, but I stare at him for the longest of moments, willing him to.

"Please stay with me, Dean." A ragged sob escapes me, leaving me feeling drained. "I don't know how I'm supposed to do this without you." Sniffing, I wipe under my chin, catching my tears. "You can't leave me. I won't say a goodbye."

I tilt my head to the ceiling, sending up a silent prayer. "You go now," I choke out, "you take my heart with you. You take my soul, my mind, my happiness... you take it all, because it belongs to you." My lungs scream, my throat burns. "I don't want to have to remember you for longer than I knew you. Do you hear me? I spent too long living a life not knowing who I was or how to find what I truly needed. Then you came along and made me yours with one touch. You had me from that first moment I looked into your eyes. Then you showed me who I am. You showed me what it is to feel alive. We're in this together, VP. So, wherever you are, you don't stop fighting until you come back to me. You can't give me a life then take that away from me. I won't let you."

CHAPTER FORTY-NINE

DEAN

There's a smell of disinfectant, harsh and intense. It burns the hairs in my nose; makes my weighted eyes start to water. My eyelids feel heavy. No way I can move them. A bright white light mixed with orange streaks across my vision, glowing from the other side of my lids. It does it again, and my brain comes around a little.

Where am I?

My chest strains as I try to breathe. My throat's dry. With each inhale I take, there's a tightening in my lungs. It burns like an electrical current, constricting and releasing as my chest rises and falls. *Fuck.* I try to move my hands, try to lift my feet but my cold, heavy limbs don't budge. Adrenaline starts to pump through my veins as panic rises. A tingling buzz slowly starts waking my dormant body.

A machine beeps.

Someone talks.

"It's been five days, Mads. You need to get some rest." It's like I'm listening under water. My ears strain to hear a man talking. Five days? Is that how long I've been gone? "He isn't going anywhere."

Then I hear it. "Well neither am I." The most beautiful sound that calms my racing heart. She's here. But how? I saw the dark creep over me. Saw my end.

She can't be *here*.

Their voices drown out, getting deeper and deeper. Feeling as though I'm freefalling, panic that I won't find her again sinks its teeth in. I try to hold on but it's no use. My head turns light, my breathing constricts, and I slip, leaving her.

The next time I wake, my nostrils burn again. I hear the familiar, steady beeps to my left. This is where I found her last time. She was here. I'm back!

Squeezing my fingers, I meet resistance as I try to lift my hand.

"Dean," I hear her say.

The beeps quicken, and I know I've found her. My girl.

Desperately trying to open my eyes, they still refuse to budge. I try, fuck do I try. I need to see her. Need to set my eyes on my sunshine.

There's a shuffle of feet, and a door opens. Unlike last time I was briefly here, I'm more aware of the sounds around me. Gentle fingers then stroke my hand, and I try to squeeze the one in mine. "Can he hear me?"

Yeah babe. I hear you.

"It's hard to say," someone else says.

How would they know what I can and can't do?

"You said last week you thought the surgery might set him back?"

"The antibiotics are working. The surgery was a success. All the fragments of the bullets were removed successfully. A small piece of bone was lodged in his oesophagus, but surgeons removed it avoiding any major damage or blood loss."

"So, he's over the worst?"

"I'd say we're almost there. Once he wakes up we'll be able to assess the extent of aftercare he'll need. For now, keep talking to him. He's responding well to you."

I am awake. I'm here. *Babe, I'm right here!* Short, sharp breaths send shooting pains to slice through my lungs.

The door closes, and a silence drops in the room.

My eyes dance behind my lids. It's only when I feel soft lips press to my head do I feel the fire in my lungs start to subside.

"I've got to keep talking to you."

Yes, keep doing that.

"You'll be sick of me soon. It's all I've done." Her voice is soft. It's like music to my ears. I'd never grow sick of her. She moves to sit on the side of the bed next to me. It dips as she lowers to it. "You need a shave." She kisses me, and inwardly I smile. "I'm going to go home later. I don't want to leave you, but it appears you had everything we chose in the shop, delivered to the house." She laughs knowing I'd do anything to make her happy. "I don't even know how or when you did that."

Before all of this, I wanted to make sure she had everything at the house ready.

"I have an appointment, and Travis is probably right. I should go, try to sleep properly." I hear her let loose her breath with a sigh. "Lynn sends her love. And Mum and everyone else. Hopefully, if you wake up soon, you'll be able to see some more people. For now, I'm keeping them away. I don't want to overwhelm you."

There's a long moment of silence. Jesus Christ. Move you idiot, move.

She lifts off the bed, once again kissing me. I can smell her sweet smell. It's intoxicating. "The safest place I have ever known is in your arms, Dean. I need you to wake up and let me back in."

An avalanche. That's the only way to describe the emotions that barrel their way over me. They smother me, leaving me once again unable to breathe.

No. Not again.

Don't take me away.

I won't go.

Let me stay!

Straining against the weak muscle, I slowly lift the lid of one eye. I've been gone longer than I wanted. I can't make out anything around me. It closes, and I try again. Lifting it higher this time, the silhouette of a woman comes into view. I squint my eyes to make her out better. Judging by the fuller belly, I'd say that's my girl.

My lips part, the skin so dry I feel it cracking. Movement on my left lets me know she's not alone in here. I close my lips as a man steps closer to her.

"Do you not think you should be taking it a bit easier? The midwife said you shouldn't be putting yourself or the baby through unnecessary stress."

Travis.

Mads laughs. "Unnecessary stress? Travis, my whole life has been unnecessary stress. I'll be fine, they're just minor pains."

Oh, my girl is tired judging by her tone.

"You're tired."

"No shit," we say and think in unison. I smile and prise my eyes open to look at them. Mads is standing, her hands on her hips.

"Come on." Travis moves her to the seat in the corner of the room, making her sit. Neither of them have seen me coming to. "Talk to me."

"About?"

"About what's stressing you."

She rolls her eyes. "Seriously?"

"Hey, I talked to you about Mollie."

Mads huffs a small laugh as Travis sits in another chair. "Me asking you how things went and you grunting at me in response, is not you talking to me." She pauses, shifting her position. "How did it go anyway? Did she tell you the truth?"

Travis sighs. "It went as I expected, Mads. Look, once I know Dean's alright, I can think about that properly. For now, just tell me what's got you all worked up."

She looks at him. "How about the fact my little boy or girl will be here soon, and everyone keeps calling me Mrs Carter when the one person who needs to know I said yes when he proposed, has been asleep for almost two weeks."

She takes a heavy intake of air and so do I. She doesn't know we're having a girl? She didn't look? And she said *yes*?

"You said yes?" Travis asks sounding shocked.

"*Yes* I said yes."

Travis smiles. "When did he ask you the last time?"

She cradles her bump. I can't remember the last time I asked her to be my wife. "When he came home drunk."

What?

Travis turns, and I quickly close my eyes. Listening. "And he doesn't know? Fuck, he's going to hate that."

No, it just means I'm going to ask her again.

"Well, I'm sure he'll ask me again," Mads says.

That's my girl.

She shuffles from the chair, and I hear her walking towards me. Her breath hits my face when she kisses my lips.

I can't help but smile.

She freezes, and I slowly open my eyes. They way she looks at me, it's the best thing I've ever seen. Her brown eyes are full of relief and happiness.

Her lips part as she tries to breathe. "You... came back."

I swallow. "You said yes." My voice is croaky.

Between her tears, she smiles again, dropping her head to rest against mine. "I did."

"I want to hear you say it," I whisper, forcing one of her tears to drop to my cheek.

I hear Travis stand.

"Then ask me," she says sobbing, but still very much smiling.

"Marry me, Madison Reed."

A racked sob escapes her as she sags, her body deflating into me. "Yes."

I slowly lift my arms to wrap around her back. And I hold her. Fuck the pain. That isn't going anywhere. And neither am I.

"That's it, Mr Carter. You're free to leave."

I look at Mads, giving her a wink as the nurse signs my papers. With five weeks left until the baby's due, she's looking fuller and carrying lower.

"Don't forget this." Travis wheels the chair forward.

He can get fucked. "I'm walking out of here," I tell him seriously. With a push, I stand off the bed, my legs like jelly. It's been a long time since I used them properly. I'll give them a minute.

"Please try to remember everything we spoke about," the nurse says. "Use the chair when you can. Avoid driving initially, and no more smoking." She turns to me, notes in hand.

I briefly look at Mads, seeing her raise a brow. Smoking, easy. Driving, sure. Using the chair, maybe. But… "Can I ride?"

The nurse looks at my leather cut on the bed. "Anything involving extreme effort, sports or physical contact needs to be avoided. At least until you see your doctor and they give you the all clear. Your lung is still healing, Mr Carter."

I feel Travis' gaze sinking into me. "Right."

I look down at my feet as Mads steps closer. She rubs her hand up and down my arm. "Thank you," she says to the nurse.

The nurse smiles, and Travis opens the door for her as she leaves. He then walks to the side of the bed, grabbing the wheelchair. He taps the seat with a grin. "Hop in."

The prick. "Fuck off."

Mads' hold on my arm tightens. "Don't be stubborn," she soothes.

"I just want to get home." I want my bed. No machines or hospital food. Mads pushed up against me.

"I know." She moves to the end of the bed, putting the last of my things into my bag.

"Did you get it?" I mouth to Travis, looking at Mads as she folds a t-shirt.

He nods, handing me what he grabbed from my place.

The door then knocks before it opens. My eyes double take when I see the man stood before us.

Silence.

Travis is watching me, but my eyes are on Mads.

"Hi," Jack says.

Mads' hands pause mid-fold, instantly recognising the voice coming from behind her. With her back towards my visitor, she looks up at me through her lashes, wide eyed and confused when I don't speak.

Placing the t-shirt in my bag, she slowly turns, her gasp audible when she sees Jack for the first time since she thought he was dead. It's a shock, and I know how I reacted the first time, too. I was angry. Guarded. Shit, I even punched him.

Using my hands on the bed—fully expecting Mads to kick off with one, if not all of us, I hold myself up then turn, my feet still not used to standing. "Mads," I begin, but I really don't know where to start. I don't even know if she fully knows what happened yet.

Some parts are sketchy for me, but seeing Jack now, I can see him finishing it. He killed the man who had killed his mum. I remember he was a man possessed. "Jack," I start, shuffling my feet. Fuck, it's good to see him. We've spoken on the phone, but this is different.

"Sorry, I tried to come by sooner."

I nod my head back, and he steps into the room. Mads is still unmoving. Jack looks to her. His eyes narrow, like he doesn't know what to say.

"How is this possible?" Mads asks no one in particular.

I manage to make my way to her, but she double takes, seeing my struggle. She sympathises with my pathetic inability to stand properly. "You should be sat down." She's right. I feel dizzy. Even after the physio I've had, this will take some getting used to.

Travis moves to help me. Jack too. They loop my arms over their shoulders. "Get him in the chair," Travis says with a smile.

They sit me down and I can't deny it's a relief.

Jack turns slowly, his hands going into his back pockets. "Mads, I—"

He gets cut off as she walks to him, wrapping her arms around his broad back.

He doesn't move at first, but I see his body relax. Eventually he hugs her back, resting his chin on her head.

"I'm so glad you're okay," she whispers.

"Me too," Jack replies. "Sure feels good to see you."

Mads sniffs and pulls away. "It was you who kept trying to come see him?" She takes one last look over him, then looks between Travis and me.

Jack nods his head. "My name wasn't on the list. Nurse wouldn't let me in."

She smiles a little sorrowfully, her eyes dropping, her hand going to her hip as she arches her back. "If I'd known..."

"We should have told you," I say gently.

The way she looks at me, I can tell she agrees. As if sensing there's business we need to catch up on, she smiles and turns to leave. "I'll meet you down by the car."

"Mads, wait."

She turns.

"Stay," I tell her.

Her expression changes, her dark eyes dancing between all of us. She's not sure. Considering I've kept most things from her for the past—however long, I'm not surprised.

"Dean?" Jack says, uncertain she needs to hear this.

I sigh. "No more secrets."

With a breath, Mads waddles closer to me as Jack begins. "They all pulled through."

"And the boy? Him and his dad have somewhere to stay?" Travis asks, his arms crossed.

Travis and Jack caught me up a couple of days ago once they knew I was allowed to go home. Costa assumed he'd got all of Jack's men. Little did he know, Jack was one step ahead. He had the phones of the men we left at the hangar. Once he knew Costa was trying to get a hold of them, Jack's men moved in on the farm in case Costa's men showed. Which they did. Jack's men got them all. And all of the people we saved from the crates were fine coming around, except the little lad.

"The boy's fine. Set them up in temporary housing. It'll do for now."

"Boy?"

Mads' hand in mine tightens, and Jack rubs the back of his neck. "There were people who needed help, Mads. We got them," he says.

She stares at me, hard, before looking at Jack. "And the people who did it?"

Jack looks Mads straight in the eye. "We got 'em all."

Mads stands a little straighter.

After Jack's men had secured the farm, the team running surveillance at the dock were found when Costa's men checked the perimeter. None of them made it. That's why Jack was delayed getting to us.

"Is it over?" Mads asks, her voice shaky, holding back tears.

I look at Travis. "Once we bury The Joker, it's over," he replies.

"What about the Saviours?"

He huffs. "They lost Vincent and Billy."

Mads didn't know already?

Her eyes widen. "Lauren's uncle?"

Travis put a bullet in between his eyes before they got me out of there. "He's gone, Mads," I tell her.

She tries to read between the lines assessing all of us. "What does that mean?" Her tears fall.

I grip the chair, pushing myself to stand. I'm weak, but I soon find my strength. Taking her head in my hands, I wipe away a tear with my thumb. "It means Lauren's safe. It means her brother can come home now."

"Dean." She cries, and I pull her into me.

Before long, the four of us are making our way down the hospital corridor. It feels good to be leaving, even if I'm being pushed like a geriatric. I said I'd walk out of here, but Travis can take me to the door. I'll humour him.

Mads walks beside me, her pace slow.

"You okay, babe?" I ask.

I notice her cheeks have flushed. "I'm fine. Pleased we're finally leaving." She waddles side to side as we walk. "It'll be nice to get some proper rest." With that she yawns. "Excuse me," she apologises, her hand going to her hip.

"Did you get any sleep without me?" I don't know why I ask because I know the answer.

"Some," she lies. She's hanging on here. She lets out a breath. "So... Jack."

I drop my head, ashamed she didn't know sooner. "I was going to tell you. I just didn't know how."

"I'm just glad he's back. *And* that I'm not losing my mind."

I give her a slight grin. I felt bad for letting her believe she was going crazy.

Mads raises a small smile. "What about Lauren? Where will she go now her uncle's... gone?"

Travis stops as we round a bend, seeing the exit.

I stand, taking Mads' hand in mine.

Travis keeps wheeling the now empty chair as I tell her, "Mollie drew up some papers before all this shit went down." She looks lost as we walk slowly side by side. "They're guardianship papers, Mads."

She stops. Frozen. "What?"

Turning, I look at her properly, finding her eyes swimming.

With no living parent or carer, I applied to become Lauren's guardian. "She's sixteen now. She can live with us if she wants."

Mads' jaw drops. It's like she's in a trance. Tears overflow, and I see a tremble in her bottom lip.

"Babe."

Mads covers her face with both hands.

I step forwards, enveloping her in my arms, letting her sob. She's wanted nothing but peace for Lauren. And now she'll get it. They both will. When she pulls her head back, I can't help but push my lips to hers.

"You're the most beautiful man I know."

I give her my cheeky grin. "Anything for my girl."

On a laugh, I hook my arm over her shoulders, turning us back towards the exit. "Come on, let's get you home. I have plans for you."

She nudges me playfully. "Oh no you don't. Nurse said no physical contact. You're under strict orders."

My face drops. The thought of not touching her as soon as I get her home is unbearable. Bullets in my lung or not, I'll get my way. "We're not married yet; don't nag me."

"I don't have a ring yet; listen." No, she doesn't. But she will as soon as I get her home. "Shit," she grimaces, taking a hesitant step forward.

"What is it?" I ask. I pull her into me as her body goes rigid.

Mads wipes her brow, and I notice she's sweating. "I don't feel so good."

I hold my hand to her head. "You're burning up. Travis, the chair."

He swings it towards us.

"What's going on?" Jack asks, his keys already in his hand, ready to drive us home.

"I'm fine," Mads starts, but her body folds on a loud cry. "Shit. Dean!"

I scoop her, trying to help her to the wheelchair.

She takes one step before crying out again.

"Breathe, Mads. Tell me what's happening?"

She starts drawing air in through her nose, releasing it from her mouth. Her grip on my arm is excruciating. She gives another ear shattering cry. "The baby… I think it's coming."

CHAPTER FIFTY

DEAN

"Don't push, Madison. Try to take nice deep breaths for me."

This midwife has a death wish. The way Mads growls at her leaves me a little surprised.

On her knees, arms crossed on the back of the raised hospital bed, Mads' head is dropped to the pillow. She's not moved for the past hour, but is contracting nicely. Whatever that means.

"It's too early," she cries in agony.

I stand by her head, slowly stroking the damp hair off her face.

She rolls her head to me, eyes closed, face scrunched. "It hurts."

Her broken cry has my heart bleeding. Natural or not, I don't like seeing her in pain. My breathing quickens, the flaring pain in my chest pulling tight. "Is there anything you can give her?" I ask the midwife, who's currently three fingers deep in my girl.

She sits behind Mads; one hand holding a heart rate monitor whilst her head's dipped to see what's going on. "Let me get you some gas and air." Taking off her gloves, the midwife grabs what she needs.

Mads moans, long and drawn out with another contraction. She's crying, her tears in full flow down the sides of her face. Her glistening eyes meet mine. "Is the baby going to be okay?" She sobs as she asks, rolling her lips as her tears coat them. "It's too soon."

The midwife comes into Mads' view attaching the gas canister to the side of the bed. She places a reassuring hand on Mads. "The baby's heart rate is just dipping slightly with each contraction. The doctor will be in any moment to check you over and we'll go from there. You're doing a great job. For now, try not to push. Take this." She hands Mads the nozzle. "As soon as you feel your next contraction, start sucking. Breathe in and out through your—"

Mads grabs the nozzle, shoving it past her lips. She sucks in and out causing the machine to churn. Her eyes roll into her head, then, rather amusingly, her eyebrows lift to the sky.

Oh, she's high. "Feel better?" I ask, seeing her find relief.

Barely opening one eye, still sucking on the gas and air, she gives me a thumbs up. A fucking thumbs up.

I laugh, looking at the midwife. "Well that worked."

The midwife smiles, checking the monitor.

The door gently creaks opens, and we're greeted by the doctor. He introduces himself, then walks straight to the midwife, pulling down his glasses from his head.

I try my best to listen as they talk, flitting my gaze to Mads. She's as high as a kite, sucking down the magic air as if there's no tomorrow.

"VP?" Her eyes don't open.

"Yeah, beautiful?" I press my lips to her head.

She lifts one hand, slapping the side of my face harder than she means to. "I'll walk in your darkness for the rest of my life."

Her statement kisses my ears. Fuck, this woman.

She takes two-fully-working-lung fulls of gas and air.

I leave another kiss on her head. Grateful. So fucking grateful. "And I'll stand in your light, no longer fearing my darkness."

The doctor turns as Mads appears to drift away, high. Will she remember any of this? "We're going to need to examine the baby's position, Madison." Mads doesn't reply. "We need you to turn for us."

With some protest and a lot of effort, Mads—unknowingly, turns to lay flat on her back. The heart rate monitor is placed on her bump, and we all look at the screen, bar Mads. I don't know what I'm looking at, but the slowing of the line definitely coincides with the more noise Mads makes. It happens a few more times before the doctor conducts an internal examination.

Can't say seeing another man touching my girl doesn't make my hackles rise, but it's essential. "I'm going to go ahead and make the call for a section."

My heart rate suddenly runs wild.

"Madison?" He pauses before he continues when she simply nods. "We're going to take you to theatre. Baby's getting distressed, I think it's best we get little one out now."

Mads nods but she isn't with it.

The doctor turns to the nurse. "Baby's heart rate's too low for an epidural. Call the anaesthetist."

The midwife nods, taking her orders.

I don't know what's happening, but the doctor stands. "This way, Mr Carter."

I follow the doctor as two porters come in to wheel Mads out. Everything happens so quickly, I'm not entirely sure what's happening.

Taken into a side room, Mads is pushed past me, and I watch her go, my nerves fried. "Will she be okay?" I ask the nurse before she walks away.

"She'll be fine. One of us will come and get you once the baby's delivered."

I won't get to be there? I feel the usual worry, but oddly, the normal tightening of my chest doesn't come. Fear doesn't rise. Panic doesn't slip through the gap. Instead, I feel like my life is waiting for me.

I sit, waiting, knowing that soon the little girl in my dreams will be in my arms. My future—my life, truly begins the minute she enters this world. She'll never know fear, or hate… not in the way that I do. She'll never want for anything. I'm going to give her the entire world. Every star in the sky, I'll make it hers.

There's a subtle knock on the door a while later. "Congratulations, Mr Carter," one of the nurses says stepping into the room.

"The baby? She's here?" I ask, my heart suddenly racing as I stand.

The nurse smiles and nods.

I follow her down the corridor as another nurse wheels out a small glass cot from the theatre room. My tears make me unable to see the tiny baby wrapped up inside. I step closer. The smile on my face hurts. The hole in my heart is suddenly filled.

My daughter is no bigger than my forearm. She has a mask over her face; the nurse giving her oxygen. "Is she okay?" Fuck, my voice wobbles.

A full head of dark hair just like her mum, my little girl cries louder with each breath she's helped to take. "We're going to take her to NICU, but she's doing great." The nurse has her wrapped in blankets to keep her warm.

"Can I hold her?"

"As soon as she's stable, you'll be able to." She turns, releasing the brakes on the trolley. "Do you want to follow us?"

I look back at the theatre room, wanting to see Mads.

The nurse reads my mind. "Madison's fine," the midwife reassures me. "They'll stitch her up and bring her to the ward as soon as the anaesthetic's worn off."

My emotional eyes look back down at our daughter. I can

only just see her face. She's fucking beautiful. I nod because all words fail me. Walking behind the nurses, I smile knowing she got all her looks from Mads, feeling like the luckiest man on this planet.

CHAPTER FIFTY-ONE

MADISON

Peeling open my eyes, I come to with Dean holding my hand in his. Less than twenty-four hours ago, it was him lying on the bed with me by his side.

His smile stretches wide when I look to him. "Hey, beautiful." Dean stands, pressing his soft lips to mine.

His smell washes over me, and I remember where I am. "The baby?" I ask, taking a long blink as my mind wakes up. My throat hurts, and my heart accelerates like a rushing wind. "Is the baby okay?"

With steady hands, he strokes the side of my face, cupping my chin. He kisses me again. "*She's* dreamy."

He said she. "She?" A torrent of warm tears cascade over my lashes. My heart swells a million sizes. Judging by the glimmer in Dean's eyes, I know she's okay, wherever she is. "We have a little girl?" I shake out, laughing because he knew. From day one, he knew.

"We do. She's so small, but she's… everything."

I close my eyes, thanking God she's okay. "Can I see her?"

"Nurse said once you came round we could go. What do you remember?"

I think back. Last thing I remember is the excruciating pain. "I was on the hospital bed."

Dean nods. "Her heart rate was slowing. They took no chances considering she's a little early. They delivered by c-section. You had to have anaesthetic."

I sob. I'm so happy and thankful, yet my heart feels suddenly weak. I missed the birth of our daughter.

"I made sure she was okay, but I haven't held her yet. She's in an incubator receiving oxygen. She's totally fine though, babe. You did it."

Dean's words ease some of the worry and the helpless feeling within. "Can we go now?"

He smiles. "I'll get the nurse."

Once allowed, Dean wheels me steadily to the NICU ward. "Are you okay?" I ask him, because he should also be taking it easy.

His lips press to the top of my head. "My chest hurts. Not because of the holes." He kisses my hair again. "My heart's too full."

I wipe the corner of my eye, sweeping away my tear.

Dean pushes me through the door and onto the ward. There's incubation cot after incubation cot, each with large monitors and machines around them. All of the babies have parents sat around them. Except the last one. "You ready?"

I nod but I can't speak past the dry lump clogging my throat. My baby is ten feet away from me. Colliding with the inside of my ribs, my heart drums. Thank God I'm sat down, my body's paralysed with happiness.

My hand lifts to my mouth when I see her. My baby girl. She's got a nappy almost the size of her back on. There's a small tube coming out from her nose, and her feet are covered in pink socks too big for her toes. She wriggles, nuzzling the side of the encasing blankets raised high either side of her.

I don't tear my love-struck gaze from her as a nurse steps closer to us. "She's stable enough to hold. Would you like to?"

My misty eyes are busy admiring the full head of hair my

daughter's grown. I nod, and Dean moves to sit in the seat beside the cot.

Carefully, the nurse lifts her—tubes and all, and I tighten the dressing gown Jess packed and dropped off for me. Bracing my arms, she's placed in them. I sob happily, kissing her wrinkly face.

"We need a name," Dean says dotingly, his green eyes watching us closely.

I smile, letting my tears dampen my face. With Dean away for such a long chunk of time, we haven't had this conversation properly. "I like your mum's name."

Dean purses his lips, a faint shimmer in his eyes. "She'd love that."

Another tear slips free down my face. "What about a middle name?"

Coming closer to us, Dean wraps his strong arms around us both. I'm filled with overwhelming love as he kisses the side of my head, then rests his chin on my shoulder. "I know," he says softly. Confidently.

I turn my head to look at him, checking his gaze.

His eyes fall to the baby in my arms. "Grace, Rocco Carter."

He looks at me for approval, and I lift my chin, my head dropping back.

His right hand strokes the side of my face before running into the back of my hair. The name he's chosen is perfect. "Rocco means rest," he says, dusting a thumb over my cheek.

Looking deep into his soul, I can tell he's given this some thought. This isn't spur of the moment. "My saving Grace is going to be just that. You and her," he looks down, "you are all I've ever needed. With you, I want to rest. Free from fear, I want to live for you. You dived in to save me from drowning, and I will spend every minute of the rest of my life showing you how grateful I am that you fell over that night."

I laugh, my nose streaming, my eyes soaked. "It was Beats

who knocked me down."

Dean laughs too, his hand gripping my shoulder. "Well, I'll buy him a beer when we get back."

With that, my smile fades a fraction.

Getting back will look different when he leaves. That was the hardest part of him being asleep for so long. I wanted to scream at Travis that Dean was getting out every time he spoke about having his president back. I still don't know how he's going to make that possible. Dean's made it clear leaving the club isn't a decision that comes lightly, nor is it met with open arms. I've never seen a member leave. "Have you told them yet?"

He sits on his heels, his arm still around me sat in the wheelchair. He looks at Grace, then back to me. Searching my features, he says, "Whatever they decide, I'll have to go with it."

"Meaning?" I ask.

He takes a second, looking at Grace. "Meaning, Ronnie and Rocco made some now old-fashioned rules for getting out. The club will take a vote."

Grace makes a noise, and we both look down to her, her little chest rises and falls, fast.

"There is nothing you need to worry about. I mean it. My biggest hurdle is Travis."

I lean my head to him. "He loves you. He knows what you need." I can see in his eyes he hopes I'm right.

"Speaking of *need.*" Dean reaches into his cut, taking something out of the inner pocket. "This belongs to you." He opens the box. A gold ring holding a red ruby lined with twelve small diamonds shines brightly.

"Dean." My eyes water, flicking between him and the ring. It's beautiful.

Taking it out, he reaches for my hand.

I uncurl my fingers from around Grace, still holding her.

"Do you like it?"

"It's... I love it."

Pushing it all the way on, he holds my hand, dusting his thumb over my knuckles. "I've wanted to do that for a long time."

I let out a small laugh between my tears.

I don't count how many minutes we sit in silence, simply marvelling at our future. Dean holds Grace, his chest bare, the skin-to-skin contact recommended by the nurse. Grace is blissfully unaware of the light she's brought into his life. I vowed to make sure he never loses himself again. I can see by the way he watches her; he's never going to forget now. Because our little girl deserves the best of him, the side I saw from the first day I met him. He was never a bad man. Just lost in his darkness.

Together, we gave each other a second chance. Not to do better, just to do it differently. He taught me love still exists after I thought it was gone. I taught him to never let how he feels make him forget his worth.

We saved each other.

A little under three weeks later, we manage to make it home. Grace was born weighing 4lbs and is now a healthier 5lbs 2oz. We no longer have to tube feed her after she took so well to breastfeeding. Boy does that girl like my boobs.

Dry, cracked nipples are definitely not sexy, and they have never been so sore, but you will not hear me complaining. To be able to bring Grace home with no infections or complications, knowing she can breathe well on her own, has been an absolute miracle.

Unlike her father who has moaned everyday about being unable to ride, she's been a dream. "Let's go," he says, grabbing my car keys off the side with a huff. He only has few more weeks before he's allowed to ride again.

He picks Grace up in her car seat, and I take one last look back. "Are we crazy?"

He walks to my side, draping his free hand over my

shoulder. "When has anything we've been through not been a little crazy?"

I smile. "You grew up here. This house literally holds all of your memories."

His lips press against my neck. "Look at our baby girl."

I turn into him, resting my head against his chest, one arm around his front, one around his back as we both look down at Grace.

"We have a million new memories to make," he says. Calm. Peaceful. "I don't want to waste a second more."

When he wasn't at the hospital, I knew he was busying himself with the house he bought for us. Adamant my name go on the mortgage, I only agreed if he'd let me pay towards it. My job provides a steady income, and once he gets today out of the way, Dean will continue the painting and decorating business. That's the plan, anyway.

We both know how huge today is.

CHAPTER FIFTY-TWO

DEAN

The door to the clubhouse swings open, all heads turn to me and Mads. Over the past three weeks I've worked myself more than I should. I know it. She knows it. Do I give a shit? No. Getting our new house ready was a priority. Not only that, but we buried The Joker. There was no time for rest, not until it was all done. Now that we're nearly there, all I can see are my girls in our home.

My family.

I still smile from ear to ear when I think or say that. Not even a year after meeting Mads, and I'm stood here carrying my daughter with my fiancé under my arm. All. Mine.

There isn't anything I wouldn't do for them.

We step towards the bar as everyone either smiles, cries or hugs us. There's no denying the men and women here are also our family.

I'm patted on the back, and I look around seeing Travis. "Looks good on you, mate," he says, dipping his bulky frame for our embrace.

My chest expands wide. Fuck, this is going to be hard.

Telling him I'm getting out could go one of two ways. He'll either accept it, or he won't. If the tables were reversed, I wouldn't want to be here anymore. Not without him. Although business is looking brighter for the club, new deals will have to be made to secure its future. He'll have decisions to make without me here. He can handle it. But will he want to?

Letting him go, he looks down at Grace. "Got Mads' genes I see."

Dick. But he's right.

"Your folks would be proud, mate," he says softly, still looking at her.

A small smile raises, pride warming me. Travis is right; they would be proud. And Linda. Rocco too.

Ronnie won't like me leaving, but there's nothing he can do. The club is his life. We strengthened the Rippers back here in the UK, and for that, he's happy. I tell him I no longer want to front the club he built, he'll see it as dishonour, perhaps I'll even be a letdown to him. He thinks he lost one son. The thought of his other boy walking away from the life might finally send him over the edge.

But he's blood. I'll have to start with that when I call him.

"Mollie coming?" Mads asks, taking Grace from her seat and holding her. I know she's desperate to see her.

Lauren searches through the baby bag, grabbing a bottle of milk and handing it to Mads.

"Later," Travis says without looking up, his eyes still locked on Grace.

Mads looks past him at me.

I widen my eyes. We didn't realise they'd had recent contact.

"Before both of you get weird, it isn't what you think. I called her with an update on Mads. I still need more time, before..." his voice trails off.

I see Jack walk in. "We understand, brother," I reassure him, patting his back.

"But—"

Moving to Mads, I snake a hand around her waist, pulling

her into me as I rest my arse on a stool. Her body stiffens. I know she only wants what's best for them both. It isn't our place though. They need to sort that shit out themselves.

"Do you want to hold her?" Mads asks him, her body relaxing.

He looks at me. "Probably break her."

"You won't," Mads says.

My hand stays on her hip as she moves forward, placing Grace in Travis' arms. Grace is swamped by him. "See," Mads coos. She steps back into me, turning her head back to face me. Is she softening him up before I sit down with him?

I dip my mouth to hers, her smell suddenly making my jeans tight. We haven't had sex since Grace was born. Mads has been healing and so have I. It hasn't stopped me wanting her every hour of the day though. The love I have for the woman looking up at me is immeasurable.

Jack coughs. "Sorry to interrupt."

I look up, then extend a hand, leaning forward as he hugs me.

He turns to Travis, his eyes widening as he looks at Grace. "She's a little ripper, mate."

Travis looks up to Jack, and the pair exchange a weird look.

I can't help but laugh. *Idiots*. Sure am going to miss them, especially if the club deserts me and Jack leaves. But they're the rules.

"What will you do now?" I ask Jack.

He signals to Talia behind the bar, pointing at the bottle of Jim Beam. "Another glass, darlin'."

"Sure, honey," she says. The glass is placed next to our still empty ones.

Jack scratches his head. "Fuck knows. I'm going to have to go home, see the old man. Not quite sure how to explain it all to him."

Where would he even begin?

"Will you keep working?" Travis asks, and I notice how he makes sure Grace's feet are covered under her blanket. He's a natural.

"Like to. I'd also like to stay, see what lays ahead for me here, you know?"

Travis dips his chin, and I spot Red walking to a table. She bends, and I look at Jack. He's watching her, staring fixedly as she wipes the table down.

"Dude?"

Mads cottons on, following his gaze. "You should go talk to her."

"What?" I say, shocked Mads would entertain it.

She looks at Red. "I think she'd appreciate someone actually getting to know her."

As opposed to just fucking her?

"She's made some changes. Trying out something new for herself."

Jack looks intrigued.

"She didn't want to join a threesome when I last asked. I'd say that's new." Travis shrugs his shoulders with a joking look, moments before Red walks past.

"Hi," Red practically sings at the sight of Jack.

His eyes don't leave her as she walks to the kitchen.

"Come on." I gently slap Mads' arse. "I don't want to watch this disaster unfold." I stand, and Travis passes Grace back to Mads. We're here to wet the baby's head before we move to our new home, but there's one last piece of business to see to first.

Bending down, I press my lips to my baby girl's head, then I get a piece of the woman I'm going to marry. "This is it," I say against her lips.

"Almost there, VP."

I kiss her again. They let me walk away, and I can go back to being just that.

Upstairs, all the men sit around the table. Jack stands at the back of the room. We discuss day to day dealings; check fees, all the usual things I seem to have missed lately, then all eyes are on me. "Tell me about Sonny, what did he say?" I breathe, pouring myself another drink from the bottle we brought up.

Travis pushes his glass closer, then takes a sip.

Mop leans forward, his fingers steepled together in front of him. "We haven't got to worry about Sodom Saviours no more. The Saviour who made it out of there—Vincent's VP, he filled them in on how it went down. They're still going to take the offer we made to Vincent. They'd rather run guns than none at all. They just won't be running guns near us. Scottish pipelines and routes further south have been locked down. None of them impact the Rippers here."

That's good news.

With everything else going on, I had wondered whether they would want some sort of payback for Vincent's death. He was their leader, regardless of what we thought of each other. "They finally see we're better off not killing each other," I muse, bringing my glass to my lips.

"Old habits are hard to kick though," Skitz adds playing devil's advocate.

I take a breath, then look at Jack. "You'll let Ronnie know? Think maybe he can finally calm things over in Oz?"

Jack takes a sip from his glass, still leaning against the wall. "I think if I go back, fill him in on all of this, he'll see it was worth it."

Jack finished what he needed to do. Killing the man who killed Linda finally put an end to his turmoil. He won't be the same after what went down—none of us will. But for the first time ever, it won't be for the worse.

Everyone will be better off.

"Anything else?" I take another sip of my drink, enjoying the way it relaxes me. I need it for the way my body's tensing, knowing what I'm about to drop on all of them.

Most men stay in the club until the day they die. What I want is unheard of. I'm in good standing... at least I was until Costa came along. Maybe they'll see it differently now.

Skitz pipes up. "The Joker's family will be looked after. There's already a fundraiser in his name. Riggs was going to make sure everyone came."

"Yep," Riggs says, acknowledging. "I've put in all the calls. We're good."

"Good," I tell him.

The Joker didn't deserve to die the way he did. It fucking turns my stomach, knowing I wasn't in any position to make sure my men got out of there okay. But Travis did. And Jack.

Jack's men ensured all of Costa's men and Cain were never found. Criminals of their stature, they'll be missed, but who the fuck's going to go searching for them? No one. That's who. They wouldn't want to risk outing themselves.

"When you were inside, I made a decision for the club and called a supplier I know."

My head snaps to Travis.

"Thought you were getting back into farming," Mop jokes.

Travis looks at him deadpan, his middle finger held up at Mop. "Think it might be good for us." He looks back at me. "The gear's good quality. It's low risk. We can take a vote."

I nod my head slowly. Contemplating. "There's another vote you need to take first." I spin the tumbler on the table around in my fingers.

Silence drops, shattering my ears. Their gazes all land on me. It feels like the first time I sat in here with them as their president, not that long ago. Some legacy. Some impression to leave on them.

"We'll take this one first," Travis says.

I frown. "I'm being serious."

"So am I," he quips. "Whatever you want to say, we take *my* vote first."

What the fuck? "Travis—"

"—Vote's to check out new business," he looks squarely at me, his eyes black and round, "without you at the table."

My stomach drops. I hold his gaze, not wanting to look guilty. Grinding my teeth, I don't know why I feel so riled. This is what I want. "You want me to leave the room?"

He smiles. "No, brother. We took another vote."

Mop stands, pushing out his chair.

"Without me?" My hands start shaking, my fists curling. I look at Mop. His face is flat. Hard lined. This is what I knew was coming. They don't want me anywhere near the club. They have to kick me out. Take everything I have related to Rippers MC. Cut off my ink. Banish and beat me.

"You were busy," Travis says.

Yeah, busy looking after my family.

Jack steps forward. His shoulders tense. Can he sense this turning sour? I didn't think it would. But fuck, it just might judging by how Travis' forehead wrinkles.

"What are you saying?"

Mop walks beside me, clearly backing whatever decision's been made here. They have no choice but to do what comes next.

My body tightens.

"I'm saying that, when I thought you weren't coming home, I started getting in the head space that I might actually have to take over this club. I found safe business, stable enough to keep the club on its feet. Then you came back."

I watch as some bow their heads. The mood around the table, shifting.

"I was so fucking relieved you were back, but it's obvious,

mate." He turns his frame toward me.

"What is?"

Rubbing a hand down his face, Travis continues. "Another life's waiting for you."

My eyes shoot to his.

"We can find business that won't bring heat to us." His face softens. "But we voted you out."

I balk, looking around at them all.

Their heads slowly lift.

"You *voted* me *out*?" No pleading needed? No forcing them to listen to why I need to go? "Why?"

Travis shrugs. "We know how rough you've had it."

"But the club..."

Mop rests his hand on my shoulder. "You're our family, Prez."

"We look out for family, don't we?" Skitz adds.

I look around all of them, my hands shaking for a new reason. I sit forwards, linking my hands, pushing my thumbs into the bridge of my nose. My heart's going like the clappers. "When did you vote?"

Travis leans back in his chair. "When you sacrificed everything for us, knowing what you really needed was the two people downstairs. You deserve to live the life you want, mate, not the one expected of you."

Is this happening? "But the rules?" I'm unable to look at them.

"Fuck the rules," Beats says, and it's then I peer over my hands. "Rules are made to broken."

None of us have ever questioned the rules for leaving because none of us have ever had reason to leave. The club's been a lifeline for most of the men in here. It became my life when there was nothing else going for me. Now I have. "What are you saying?" I look at Travis.

The dick's smiling at me. "This isn't the eighties. No one's going to shoot for wanting out. Ink out your tattoos but keep your cut. Keep your bike. Most importantly, keep in touch, and don't ever fucking forget we're your family. You've given everything for this club. It's about time it gave back to you."

I hold it in, but the dry, harsh lump in my throat stops me from speaking. Mop slaps my back. Then they get out of their seats, and suddenly I'm swamped by them, a loud raucous ringing out.

Fuckers.

They took a vote to give me the life I want. Is it what I deserve? I can't honestly say either way. But will I take it? Absolutely.

After I've hugged every one of them, I pull out my knife, then slip my leather off my back. The missing weight is freeing, but it also marks the end. I lay it on the table. Everyone's silent, their gazes watching as I take off the President flash. My heart pulls, but dutifully, I hand it to the man now holding the reins, along with the gavel. "You need these."

Travis nods. "I won't let you down."

"Couldn't if you tried."

He holds out his hand for me to take. I slap mine into his, and he embraces me, patting my back. This might be the end of one part of our lives, but it's not like we'll never see each other again.

"You know, we still have a decorating business to keep running."

Travis laughs, stepping back. He keeps one hand on my shoulder. "It's your turn to handle the business now. I got this." He nods to the guys behind him.

Yeah, he does.

We make our way downstairs almost half an hour later. Between the sea of people, I spot my girl anxiously watching as the guys file past me, stood on the last step. She checks their expressions, her eyes finally finding mine. I see worry in her eyes as she spots the empty space on my cut where the flash was.

She's holding Grace, various wives and girlfriends all stood around her, cooing over the baby. But she's not looking at them. She's watching me, waiting for me to tell her we can now live the life we've dreamed of.

I take the last step, slowly making my way to my girls. The women around her move, and I come to a stop, towering over her. I kiss Grace's head, then I stand, taking Mads' face in my hands.

"Are you okay?" she asks unsure.

I smile, licking my lips before I push them to hers. I feel her tremble as I rest my forehead against the top of her head, looking down at her.

She blinks, her eyes filling with tears.

"You get all of me now, babe." Her breath hitches. Relieved. "My good, my bad, it's all yours."

"Mine?" she asks on a whisper, the smile she's giving me, glorious.

Curling my fingers, I tilt her head back so she's looking up at me. My sunshine. "Yours."

EPILOGUE ONE

MADISON

One year later

"You are my sunshine, my only sunshine, you make me happy when skies are grey, you'll never know dear, how much I love you..."

The broadest of smiles stretches across my face. Has there ever been a sweeter sound? I stretch my arms above my head hearing Dean's feet pad across the landing.

"There she is," he says softly.

Grace is snuggled deep into his chest as he walks into our room. The light from the large bay window bounces off his skin, waking up all my senses. He's wearing only boxers, his hair's roughed up. My fiancé is devilishly handsome.

"Morning, baby." I hold out my arms for Grace.

She swings down to me, and I take her letting her snuggle in close. I kiss her head as Dean places a cup of tea on the side. "What time is it?" I ask him laying back down.

Grace sips her milk from her bottle, her eyes dreamily half open. Her long brown curls are fanned across the sheets. She's beautiful.

"Almost seven."

"You better get going then." I yawn, stroking Grace's hair.

Dean rounds the bed, climbing in behind me. Leaning on his

elbow, he props himself up, his body moulding to mine. "Not yet." Soft lips kiss my shoulder, his hand traces the curve of my hip.

"If you're here when the girls arrive, they'll kill us for breaking the rules."

"Let them try," he says, dotting kisses up to my neck. "Grace will go back to sleep, then I'm making you my whore once last time before I make you my wife."

I arch my back, pushing myself against him.

"Mrs Carter." His fingers grip my skin harder.

"It's Miss Reed, actually. I still have six hours until I'm yours."

"We both know that's bullshit. You've always been mine."

I look over my shoulder at him. "Always," I whisper.

He kisses me, his tongue roaming with mine. The doorbell then rings, making Dean groan. "That can't be them."

"I did say."

"For fuck's sake." He pushes off the bed, jumping on one leg as he pulls at his boxers. I laugh as he dips, chucking on some joggers. "What could you need doing that means they have to come here this early?"

I fluff the pillow under my head, and Grace sits up. I twirl a strand of her hair in between my fingers. "My hair. Makeup. They need to help me get in my dress." I don't care about my hair and makeup if truth be told. All I care about is getting down the aisle to the man of my dreams. The man who changed everything for me. The man who's now finally free, no longer filled with hate and self-doubt.

Dean straightens, his dazzling green eyes meeting mine. "Babe, you could walk down that aisle right now, and still be the most beautiful woman in the room."

My cheeks flush.

"And as for the dress, I'm only going to be ripping it off you once you say I do."

I laugh. "You can't rip it. I want to hand it down to Grace when she gets married." I lean forward, kissing the back of her head.

He frowns. "She's one, and never getting married."

Lifting a brow, I smile. "Never?"

"Not whilst I'm alive, no." He steps closer, his hand resting on the bed as he leans over, brushing Grace's hair back, then kisses her head. "You'll be Daddy's little girl forever."

I smile, pretty sure I'd collapse with happiness if I wasn't already laid down.

The doorbell rings again and again. "Daddy's going to go mad."

"*Daddy* should go let them in then."

He smirks at me calling him daddy, and I roll my eyes as I move to sit up.

Grace holds out her arms for Dean.

"You coming with me, baby?"

She nods her head, holding her bottle between her teeth as it swings.

"Let Mummy enjoy the last few moments of peace she's going to get for the next few days."

I slump back down, feeling tired, knowing I've never felt this happy. I smile also knowing there's more to come.

I hear Jess and Bex scold Dean for taking so long to answer the door, then they make their way up to me. The bedroom door swings open. I brace myself as they both jump on the bed. "Happy wedding day!" they sing together.

Bex's daughter, Poppy, climbs up onto the bed, and Grace follows, having been carried up by Jess.

Lauren walks into our room, her eyes barely open, her feet heavy on the floor. She just woke up, having spent the evening with her brother.

Jay came back once he heard of their uncle's death. It didn't take long for Lauren to forgive him for leaving, and I'm pleased, because it appears the time away did them both some good. Lauren's focusing on college and finding work. As for Jay, he started apprenticing for Dean five months ago.

"Morning sleepy head."

She climbs in the bed. The more the merrier. "Morning," she yawns.

I give her a hug.

Grace climbs into her arms, and Lauren holds her. They really have become the closest. Grace adores her, and well, Lauren's great with her, doing everything Grace demands.

"Don't suppose I can get changed before I have to leave?"

Rolling over, I look to Dean. He stands holding the frame of the door with one hand, a bunch of red roses in the other. I feel needy looking at him stood the way he is.

"Don't worry, we're leaving," Bex says. She holds her hands out for Poppy. "You have five minutes."

Dean's eyebrows raise as Poppy waddles out, following Grace and Jess.

Bex walks to Dean, and he drops his hand as she passes. She stops, looking him square in the eye, then she looks to me. "Five minutes," she holds up her finger, "I mean it. We have a lot of work to do."

Everyone leaves the room leaving just me and Dean.

He closes the door before he walks to the side of the bed.

I push up to my knees, biting my lip. Taking the roses, I lift them to my nose, taking in their sweet smell.

His hands then slide under my thighs, and he lifts me until my legs wrap around his waist.

I let out a laugh. "We don't have time for this," I say against his lips.

He lays me flat on the bed, crawling his body over mine. "I'll be quick." He holds my hands above my head, pinning me down.

His mouth finds my neck, and it takes every bit of strength I have not to give myself over to him. He smells so good, I could lose myself.

"Dean," I moan, managing to push him back a bit with another laugh. "You'll have to wait."

"I don't want to," he moans, leaving another kiss on my neck below my ear.

"Four minutes," Bex shouts from the hall.

Dean silences my laugh, his tongue invading my mouth.

I squeeze my legs. She really is going to make sure we stick to her schedule. "She will come in here," I pant when he pulls away.

"I'll give her a good show." His lips drop to my mine once more.

"You're being bad."

"You love it."

"Three minutes." Dean groans as Bex shouts.

He drops his head into my neck. "Get me on our honeymoon." One week in Greece, the ocean, sand and sun. Bliss. Dean climbs back, holding out a hand for me. He pulls me to stand. Holding my head in his hands, he studies me, his green eyes cruising across my face. "I'll meet you at the altar, beautiful."

I stand on tiptoes, wrapping my arms around his neck.

"Time's up!" Bex swings open the door, one hand across her eyes. "Put her down and step away." She blindly reaches for me, finding my arm and grabbing me. She pulls me back, playfully dragging me away as Dean simultaneously hands back my roses.

I smile, holding them in front of me. "I wouldn't miss it for the world."

"There." Jess places the last pin in my hair. She steps back, admiring her handy work, her eyes swimming.

I lift my hand, looking at my reflection.

"You look beautiful," Bex says.

I smile shyly. Jess really has done a good job. My hair's tied in a low bun at the base of my neck.

Dad steps forward. "You really do. I'm proud of you."

I struggle to hold back my tears at his words. "Car's outside." Lauren appears at the doorway, Grace securely in her arms. She spots my tear-filled eyes. "Want me to tell him to wait?"

"No, no, I'm fine."

Dad holds out his arm.

I smile, dabbing my eye, looping my arm through his. "Let's go."

We pull up outside the church, arriving in the car Dean bought for us. It's bigger than the Fiesta, I'll give him that.

Legs jumps down from the driver's seat, coming around and opening the door for me.

"Thank you," I tell him.

He closes the door. "You're welcome, Mads."

I look down at his new patch. He more than deserved becoming a full member. Leaning forward, I place a kiss on his cheek.

Lauren steps closer with Jess and Bex, Grace walking by her side.

Legs then escorts them past the ample amount of Harleys lined up. It's a sea of black. I honestly can't count the number of bikers here. Even the doors to the church can't close for the men and women stood in the doorway.

It warms my heart.

Dean's been out for a year but the club has remained close. Able to ride, able to carry on working with Travis, Dean found freedom without carrying the weight of the world on his shoulders. He's finally free from his demons. Finally able to see the people around him who love and adore him. None more so than our daughter.

His true happiness comes from her. The life we made.

The life we deserve.

EPILOGUE TWO

DEAN

"She's here." Travis returns his head to face forward. My heart hammers yet I finally feel calm. The music starts, and I rub my hands together in front of me, holding them down. This is it.

The door to the church is already open but I hear everyone gasp. I chance a look, seeing Jess walking down the aisle first. She looks stunning wearing a champagne bridesmaid dress. She waves at Axl sat with Max, closely followed by Bex who looks equally incredible, holding Grace's hand. Grace understandably looks frightened. The men watching her would be fucking terrifying to a one-year-old.

Bex looks up to me when Grace stops walking.

Unable to watch my baby girl looking so scared, I walk down the aisle to her.

She sees me coming then opens her arms for me.

I dip and pick her up, and her little arms wrap around my neck, finding the safety and comfort she needs. I feel my emotions catch in my throat, but the feeling is fucking euphoric —knowing I'm the hero of this little girl.

Bex loops her arm through mine. "You're going to cry when you see her," she whispers, as we walk steadily to the front of the church.

My nose wrinkles, already feeling it. “Is she okay?” Dumb question. I know she’s finally ready to be my wife.

“Better than that.”

I look down at Bex, trying to pass Grace back to her once we’re stopped.

“She’s madly in love with you.”

I smile, then bend down and kiss her cheek.

“Keep Grace with you. It’ll make Mads happy having you both here.” A lump starts to burn in my throat. Bex is right. She rubs Grace’s back then moves to stand next to Jess.

I move back to Travis and Jack.

“Wow,” Jack says, his jaw hitting the floor looking over my shoulder. “Quick, give him a tissue,” he says to Travis, making him grin. The gasps and coos tell me my girl is in the church. That and Jack’s mouth is still open.

“You’re dribbling,” I quickly point out. “Maybe you need the tissues,” I say with a frown.

The dick grins before his eyes widen. My girl is taking everyone’s breath away, and I haven’t looked at her yet.

Grace leans towards Mads behind me, seeing her mummy.

It’s then I turn, taking a deep breath. It’s not enough. *Fuck.* All oxygen leaves my body at the sight of the angel making her way toward me.

She smiles at a few people, her gaze dropping to the floor, embarrassed all eyes are on her. When she looks up, I find it too much. She shines so brightly, I swipe at my eyes, blinking the tears back. It’s no fucking good.

Jack nudges me from behind. He can keep his tissues. I want the woman spending the rest of her life with me to see what she does to me.

Uncle Ronnie whistles as Mads passes him, sending the church into uproar.

Things may have calmed down for him back home, but he

sure knows how to rouse people up. I'm also pretty sure half of these men haven't set foot in a church before, because it shows. They clap and whistle, cheering out loud. The sound bounces off the walls, echoing all around us.

Our eyes never leave each other's as Mads takes the final steps to my side.

Her dad lets her go, moving to sit beside her mum.

Breaking the rules, I step to Mads, pulling her body flush with mine. Where it belongs. My lips brush against hers, and her breath hitches like it always does. I grin. "My fucking sunshine."

"My VP," she whispers back, before pressing her lips fully to mine.

More claps. More whistles. More cheering. I'm no longer a member, but the people inside this church will always be my family. They'll always want what's best for me. For us. They finally settle while we say our vows, stood hand in hand, our daughter in my arm.

The day she told me she was pregnant was the happiest day of my life. This is definitely the second. My cheeks ache from smiling so much. I don't think it could get any better than this.

Later at the reception—if I can even call it that, we gather at the local pub where we live. Not following all the usual traditions, there's no sit-down tables and speeches. What we have is our family, *all* of them, here. Naturally, the place is teaming.

I haven't seen Mads for the past hour. I'm feeling withdrawals. I spot Jainey and Michael playing with Grace, keeping her entertained. "Have you seen Mads?" I ask them.

Neither of them look up when they tell me they haven't, too engrossed in my daughter, who's really bloody cute, still in her little dress.

Smiling, I turn spotting the guys huddled near the bar. Jay's with them.

Beats holds out his hand.

I take it. "You seen Mads?" I ask him.

Legs turns, smiling at me like the cat that got the cream. I don't miss him wink at Jay.

"What?" I ask, looking between them.

"Nothing," he says, then turns sipping his beer.

I look at Jay flatly. "You told them, didn't you?"

The guys choke on their beers in unison.

He may have patched in and took a giant one for the team, but still, the way Legs laughs has me rolling my eyes.

My recent fall down a ladder resulted in an unwanted trip to hospital for something minor. "It's not that funny."

"It really is. Watching you get carted off to hospital for a broken toe was fucking hilarious," Jay laughs.

"How long do they think your recovery will take?" Beats asks with a snort into his pint.

They all laugh again.

My eyes narrow. "Fuck you guys." I turn walking away with a huff, leaving them to break out in another round of laughter at my expense. Fucking Jay. I'm deducting his pay next week.

Passing Bex, I see Jess and a few of the girls from Mads' work dancing in the small space made for a dance floor. Mads isn't with them. To my surprise, Red is. She looks happy.

It still blows my mind he's with Red, but Jack seems to have found what he wants. The pair seem pretty serious having spent a lot of time together this past year. There was even talk of them finding a place of their own. I might not get it, but if it means he stays, I'll support whatever decision he makes.

Undoing the top button of my shirt, I step out the front of the pub finding Travis and Mollie in an embrace.

They hear me. Both their heads swing to look at me.

Mollie smiles then kisses Travis' cheek before he lets her go. She walks towards me, gently placing her hand on my arm as she walks by.

"I don't think I'll ever get used to seeing you two *not* trying to kill each other," I say as I turn to look at him.

Travis grins as he lights a smoke. "She's still the only woman I would enjoy killing."

My eyes widen a fraction. "What you doing out here?"

He holds out the packet of smokes, offering me one. "Thinking."

I shake my head. Travis isn't one for heartache and feelings. "About?"

"The usual. Club shit. Life."

"Anything I can help with?"

He sighs, rubbing his face. "No, brother. Not this time."

So, it's club shit. He knows if he asks, I'll help in some way. So he won't.

"Everything good with your boy?"

He inhales from his smoke, throwing his head back. Finding out he had a son changed a lot of things for Travis. "Apart from the fact he's still holding a lot of grudges? Yeah, perfect."

"Kid just needs time, he'll come around."

Travis frowns. "It's been a year, Dean. He's had plenty of time. Mollie's done everything she can. Kid wants the dad who raised him, you know? Not me."

"It's a big change for him." I step closer. "You still got that number I gave you?"

He turns. "I'm not fucking calling your therapist." He lifts his chin. "Anyway, shouldn't you two be leaving soon?" Travis throws his smoke to the ground.

I look at my watch with a slight smile. I don't want to aggravate him any further. "I need to find her first."

Travis starts walking towards the entrance of the pub. "Knowing Mads, she probably found the quietest place away from everyone."

Shit. Why didn't I think of that? My feet are moving without thought. I walk through the pub, passing everyone still having a good time, coming to a halt when I see her.

Out in the garden, Mads stands looking up to the stars. I take off my jacket, placing it over her shoulders before I wrap my arms around her waist. "You okay, beautiful?"

She leans her head back against my chest. "Better than okay."

I kiss her head. "Why aren't you inside?"

"Needed some air."

I notice her glass of champagne is still untouched. "You sure?"

Mads turns in my arms, sliding her arms around me. "I'm sure."

Pushing her body against mine, she closes her eyes, worn out by the day.

Wondering Why by The Red Clay Strays plays from inside, the slow beat loud enough for us to follow. I start moving my feet, gently making her sway. "Our song."

She smiles up at me, her eyes twinkling in the white of the garden lights.

I can't help myself. Angling her chin with my thumb, I lower, seizing the opportunity of it being just the two of us. Slowly, my tongue dances with hers as her body gently rocks against mine. In the dim light, I don't see her tear, I taste it as it hits my lip. My hand slides to the side of her face, my fingers in the back of her hair. "Mads?"

She leans forward. "I'm fine." She nuzzles her face against me. After a few moments, she starts sniffing my shirt. "Did you smoke?" Standing to her tiptoes, she presses her nose to my neck, her hand using my hair as an anchor.

My dick twitches.

"You did. Didn't you?"

Fuck me. "I didn't, I swear." I protest my innocence, only serving to make myself look more guilty. I haven't smoked for months. Damn her super strength smell. Last time she was like this she was... My eyes dart to hers.

She's smiling, her eyes now soaked.

"Babe?" I don't think my heart can withstand the drilling rate at which it beats. I'm sweating. A pathetic mess of man stood before her. "Are you? Are we?" Why is my voice so high?

Mads chokes out a sob, her smile still wide. "We are."

I hone in, taking my girl in my arms and lifting her. "Are you fucking serious?" I let her body slide down my front until her arms are resting on my shoulders.

"You're going to be a dad. Again," she laughs, her hands either side of my face.

The ability to breathe has gone. My throat burns, my eyes fill, just like hers. It's overwhelming. Emotional. Absorbing.

Blinding.

Mads showed me what love looks like. What it feels to *be* loved and to have something worth living for. She became the part of me I'll always need. The part of me that shines the brightest.

Love was our first thing, and she will forever be my always.

This is our life now.

I wouldn't have it any other way.

AFTERWORD

Thank you for reading Come Back to Me. Your continued support means the absolute world. A special thank you to Cat. Without your help, ideas, support and hand holding until the early hours, none of this would be possible.

Travis and Mollie's story will be coming soon, in the final instalment of The Rippers MC series.

To find out more, you can visit:

www.authoremilycatlow.com
Facebook: Author Emily Catlow
Instagram: @catlow_books
TikTok: @catlow_books

Made in the USA
Las Vegas, NV
13 March 2024